BENEDICT SPARKEL

and the

BUCKET LIST

Denis Bright

The characters and events portrayed in this book are fictitious. Any similarity to real persons, living or dead, is coincidental and not intended by the author.

Cover design by: Christopher Venning

ISBN: 9780645040708

DEDICATION

TO MY WIFE VICKI

AND DAUGHTERS MARAYA AND JILLIAN

Vengeance is in my heart, death in my hand

Blood and revenge are hammering in my head

William Shakespeare

1

My New Abode

There was no chance of salvation from above. On the home front, the co-ordinates I'd dropped into were an uninspiring blend of tar, cement, acrid industrial smells, sneers, veneer and wary acknowledgements, with sudden outbursts of vulgarity thrown in for good measure.

No wonder Dunkley lived here.

Too far inland to be affected by the coastal breezes, the suburb was experiencing above-average temperatures for this time of year, a harbinger of what was to come. The place would sizzle come January when the real heat arrived. My balcony roof was constructed of thin plastic. It did the job, but it would melt away like a tub of margarine once the sun got serious.

Some houses had front lawns, but most were in a sorry state. Trees were few and far between. The ones I could see from my balcony sagged badly, having been massacred by local council hacks to keep them from interfering with the poles and wires.

The vibe on the street was never pleasant. Hotted-up cars roared by, burning rubber. Shoes hung from electrical wires, signalling that the local drug dealer was no more than a stone's throw away. Youths on skateboards and scooters crawled along the footpath. Occasionally, dodgy-looking locals – high on ice, at a guess – meandered past, creating a sense of menace.

My presence at this location was no accident. After I'd been notified of an early release, finding somewhere near Dunkley had been my number one priority. I'd started incessantly checking real-estate sites from the prison library computer, and it had been a stroke of luck that a suitable place came up so close to Dunkley's. With the help of my diligent parole officer, I paid the deposit.

The opportunity had ignited a spark of life in my usually dour demeanour. Witnessing my pleasure on finding the place, the real-estate agent must have thought I was crazy. It wasn't cheap, though nothing was in Sydney. But the rental was perfect. Across the road and just twenty metres along. In the Goldilocks Zone, you could say – not too far away, but not too near. During the day the road was busy. It may well have been a turbulent river, such was the lack of interaction between those living on opposite sides.

From a distance my townhouse looked like a cardboard doll's house put together in a hurry. The garage door was covered with graffiti – mostly black, but with splashes of colour; nothing classy, just scribble that could have been done by an irate three-year-old. Despite the tacky exterior, the place was secure – locks and bars on the windows were obligatory in this neck of the woods. The garage that gave me internal access to the house had a roller door and a remote control, important factors in choosing the place. My white Nissan had tinted windows, which made me hard to see. Even so, it was prudent that I avoid driving in or out as much as possible. Certainly during daylight hours.

My plan wasn't perfect. In my favour was the fact that Dominic Bruno was hardly a stand-out character in the Wild West. But there was always the worry of running into Dunkley.

If he recognised me, I'd pretend it was an unfortunate coincidence and tell him some cock-and-bull story. Or would I lose my nerve and flee the scene, like a fearful tearaway character in a Disney cartoon?

If I did have to flee in a hurry, there wasn't much I couldn't live without – just my computer (incriminating in the wrong hands), a change of clothes, my pet snake Cerberus, and my Brett Whiteley print (a birthday present from Lydia, my ex-lover). The cheap furniture and kitchen appliances I owned were not worth worrying about.

My townhouse was spacious, impossible for me to fill. Like a palace after having been confined to a cell for near on eight months. Downstairs there was a kitchen, dining and lounge room. The backyard was small. I rarely went out there because it wasn't private.

There were two bedrooms, both upstairs. The main bedroom had a balcony. It was perfect for observation. My first task on arrival had been to construct a thick hessian barrier around the perimeter of the balcony and install a surveillance camera, hidden between two bamboo pot plants. The balcony offered panoramic views, but the camera was mostly pointed in one direction: right at Dunkley's house.

The camera was fitted with a zoom and a high-definition image function. It was linked by Bluetooth to my computer and phone. It had been advertised as high tech – the kind used by scientists to observe and study wildlife. That made it perfect for my needs because Dunkley could definitely be classified as wildlife – an endangered species on the brink of extinction, if I had any say in it. I'd also purchased a fancy listening device. It was battery-operated, came with headphones and supposedly had a range of three hundred feet.

Returning to the townhouse after being out on an errand, I'd race to the computer in anticipation, as excited as a reality TV junkie. Munching on a snack with my eyes glued to the screen, I'd watch a replay of what had occurred at Dunkley's house. Gradually I became familiar with the neighbourhood and his routine.

An elderly couple lived in the adjoining townhouse. A few days after moving in I introduced myself, but from then on I'd purposely kept our interactions brief – just a cursory hello or a comment about the weather. *Be friendly, but don't encourage* was my motto. I did feel for them. Such a bleak prospect, to have to live out your senior years in such a run-down and unsafe part of the city.

Swinging the camera on the balcony away from Dunkley's and in the opposite direction, I could see as far as the park and corner shops. The park was often inhabited by baby-faced drug dealers wearing baseball caps and oversized pants, and riding bikes that were too small for them. Some young women ran with the pack. At a guess, they were either girlfriends or sisters tagging along. The males were full of bravado, constantly clowning around and showing off. The older ones had cars. The smart ones would find a road out of this place.

One day, late in the afternoon, there had been a larger than usual number of people mingling in the park. It appeared to be business as usual, until suddenly there'd been a cacophony of noise, atonal and allegro. This was followed by an outburst of insults and threats, culminating in an almighty bang, followed by complete silence.

It took me a while to realise what had occurred. Someone had copped a bullet in the guts from what sounded like a .22 pistol. My camera caught it all from the get-go, right up to the gunman's getaway in a Holden Commodore. The wounded man was left writhing in pain on the ground. The ambos must have been nearby because they took only a few minutes to arrive and, by that time, except for the victim, the park was deserted. The police arrived a short time later.

Talk about audacity. Two of the aspiring gangsters who'd been involved in the incident rode back to the scene on their bikes, acting like the inquisitive innocents they were not. I watched them chatting with the cops, pretending they didn't know anything about what had gone down. They soon lost interest, clamped on their headphones and took off, seemingly unperturbed by what had occurred.

After editing the footage of the shooting, I stopped by an internet café in Bankstown and uploaded it to YouTube. I titled it 'A Shot in the Park'.

Some kind of drug deal gone wrong. That was how one media outlet reported it. The victim remained in a critical condition but was alive. Perhaps it had been a warning. The culprit with the gun would have to have been blind to miss from that distance.

My response was to raise the balustrade, making it impossible for anybody bar Spider-Man to enter my place via the balcony. It meant I could nod off in relative peace. I found it hard to sleep. Mostly I just took short naps on the sofa downstairs. If I did go upstairs, I'd use the second bedroom. The main bedroom with the balcony was already inhabited. A naturalist's delight, it was furnished with logs, branches and luxuriant plants in large pots, creating a miniature forest of verdant green. The room was home to a variety of insects and bugs. At first this might sound bizarre.

But the establishment of this biome was not a reaction to the starkness of the suburb I'd found myself in, nor did it mean I was a closet greenie. The setting was created as a home for my pet snake, Cerberus – quite a unique character himself.

Lydia might barely tolerate me now, but it wasn't always like that. When the two of us had fled to the bush in our teenage years to escape the wrath of our parents and the hungry media, we'd encountered Cerberus – a carpet snake, then just a baby, sunning himself in a clearing near where we'd set up camp. What a bizarre sight! At first we thought we'd encountered two snakes, but soon realised it was one snake with two heads. We hadn't had any idea that was even possible. It was my idea to keep him, in the hope that it would help cement the bond between Lydia and me.

Lydia had taken care of Cerberus during my stint inside, but it hadn't been an ideal situation. Her housemate had been terrified of him, and Cerberus had to be kept in a cage, much to my ire. It would have unsettled him. Ironic, really. Both of us in cages. While his premises now were not as alluring as a sunny spot in the bush, they provided some freedom, a place where a two-headed snake could be fed a rat or two and feast on insects in relative safety.

In the early days after my release, making plans, watching Dunkley and editing the footage kept me occupied during the day. But when darkness fell, memories of the big man's carnal assaults were a terrifying constant. Unable to sleep, unable to weep, I lay awake in the depths of melancholy. Nobody deserved to have been left to the mercy of a depraved soul like Dunkley.

2

Lydia

It was a cold, rainy day in June, just a week after my sixteenth birthday, when my ordinary life underwent a fantastic transformation. My old man wed Lydia's mother and the four of us moved into a house together in Randwick. Lydia's mother went out of her way to create her version of the happy family. A bit too happy, as things turned out, for her liking. While our parents gallivanted about town, Lydia and I were left to our own devices.

Up until then I'd been raised by my father. He was a selfish man with a restless spirit. A surveyor by profession, he dragged me all over the country. My social network had consisted of short-term school friends and gamers I met online. There'd been girls I was attracted to at school, but nobody like Lydia. She was stunning to look at – high cheekbones, hypnotic blue eyes and classic long blonde hair. At first I was in awe of her, but it wasn't long before I became comfortable in her company. She'd grown up in northern New South Wales and had an easygoing, amiable nature.

Lydia was useless at most practical tasks. An only child and with a father as the sole parent, I was used to fending for myself. I could operate a sewing machine and Lydia would get me to do alterations to her clothing. I'd jump at the chance to impress her by cooking up her favourite dishes. She loved spinach pie and pancakes.

One day Lydia came home from school upset. This was unusual for her. She'd had an altercation with a teacher over something or other. I was able to console her, making light of the matter. A comforting cuddle became a passionate kiss. That was the day something changed between us. For the first time in my life, I was incredibly happy.

We managed to keep this newfound propinquity a secret for two months or so. Then the inevitable – Lydia's mother came home from work early one day and walked in on us. On most matters, Lydia's mother was a broad-minded, tolerant woman. But not on the matter of her daughter's chastity.

She went ballistic, issuing an ultimatum – either I went, or she and Lydia did. What surprised me was the ease with which my father made that decision. He moved at warp speed, finding me a bedsitter nearby within twenty-four hours. It was bye-bye, Dom. I was dumped by my own father at sixteen.

But it wasn't all bad. After I'd gotten over the hurt, I began to appreciate the independence. And my father paid the rent – something he continued to do until I finished school. As so often happens in those types of situations, by trying to force Lydia and me apart, our parents only drove us closer together.

To Lydia I became the forbidden fruit, and she would sneak around to my place at every opportunity. We had to be careful because Lydia's movements were closely monitored by her mother. Before venturing out together, Lydia and I would disguise our appearances. I even installed a camera at the entrance to my flat so we'd have prior warning if Lydia's mother or my father made an unexpected visit.

As it turned out, this gave us a false sense of security. One day, Lydia's mother – my old man must have given her a key – snuck in through the back entrance and caught us in the act. We had been too preoccupied to notice. All hell broke loose. Lydia's mother threatened to go to the police. Lydia and I ran off together and camped out in the National Park.

We were reported as missing persons and our photos were plastered all over the place. Eventually, some camper recognised one of us and informed the authorities. But it was a newspaper reporter who found us first. We became infamous as 'The Incestuals' – the teenage brother-and-sister lovers.

'But she's not my sister,' I'd say.

He protests too much.

Fabricating details to turn the bland into something newsworthy was nothing new. The fact that we had similar skin colouring gave the story verisimilitude.

Lydia and I had no idea how the media worked. Neither did our parents. The more denials, the more interest. The more we tried to explain, the more muddied the waters became. We attracted all sorts of trolls and freaks with opinions. We were reviled by preachers from their pulpits. Lydia was packed off to boarding school and we didn't see each other for a couple of years.

When Lydia finished high school, our parents decided to move to Port Douglas, a place Lydia's mother had always wanted to live. Lydia was expected to move north with them, but she was being offered modelling work and insisted on remaining in Sydney. Her mother organised for her to stay with a family friend.

With our parents out of the way, Lydia and I picked up where we'd left off. We found a place of our own as soon as we could afford it. When our parents found out, they disowned us. Their rejection hurt Lydia more than me.

After completing a work experience stint at FGI, an international investment company in the city, I was offered a job. I was thrilled to be earning decent money. Adrian Bozanski was my boss. As the new kid on the block, it was wise for me to attend staff functions, even though they were not my cup of tea.

The first two functions I attended were predictable and eminently forgettable. The third would have been the same if I'd followed the golden rule – never bring a partner to a staff function. Particularly if the partner is as gorgeous as Lydia.

On this particular Friday night, Lydia had just flown back from Brisbane. It was just before the Christmas break. I'd thought she'd be worn out and crash for the night, but Lydia was in no mood to stay home and insisted on coming. I tried to talk her out of it, telling her that nobody else would be bringing their partners and that it would be really boring. Furthermore, I warned, Bozanski would be all over her like a rash. She wasn't deterred.

As it turned out, it wasn't Adrian Bozanski that I had to worry about.

It was always on the cards that at some stage, Lydia would want more than what I had to offer. But that she would be seduced before my very eyes, at a staff function and by such a despicable person! It drove me to despair.

3

Subterfuge

The moonlight glistened on the water and the stars sparkled like diamonds in the night sky. The surreal, romantic setting on the candlelit balcony made the memory of what followed even worse. Lydia was her usual loquacious self, the cynosure of all eyes, swimming in the attention, impressing my work colleagues with her warm, friendly manner. Most attentive of all was a woman Bozanski had invited along, Sabrina.

Bozanski introduced her as an old family friend. Impeccably dressed, dripping with bling from ear to ear, Sabrina managed to position herself directly across from Lydia at the dining table. I'd met Sabrina once before. She had been full of her own importance and not at all friendly. But then, I was at the bottom of the pecking order at FGI.

Sabrina was the head teacher of English at a Sydney high school. Not just any school, but a prestigious school that catered to foreign diplomats and high-fliers. When Sabrina dropped a few names (well-known political figures), Lydia began to lose interest, but the moment Sabrina claimed to know people in the television industry, Lydia's face lit up. (Come in spinner – talk about knowing what buttons to press.) I became increasingly jealous as I watched Sabrina draw Lydia in. And there were more strings to Sabrina's bow. She was a published author of erotic fiction.

I should have bitten my tongue, but at that stage my blood was boiling.

'Erotic fiction. You write trashy stuff like *Fifty Shades of Grey*?' I quipped.

Someone laughed. Most didn't. Sabrina threw me a death stare before citing a review that praised her writing as being 'powerful and brave'. The way she used the quote gave me the impression she'd got plenty of mileage from it.

Then Lydia turned on me.

'*Fifty Shades of Grey* was a bestseller, Dom. I wouldn't mind half the royalties from that book.'

From that point on, I was powerless. For the rest of the night I was a mere bystander as the two talked and joked like long-time pals. Thankfully there was no physical intimacy. Still, my insides were churning up as I tried to maintain a calm exterior. More than once I attempted – without success – to drag Lydia home early.

After that night, Lydia and Sabrina kept in contact. Sabrina dropped in once or twice while I was home. I tried to be cordial, but I disliked being in her vicinity. Her bonding with Lydia was excruciating, painful to observe.

Early the next year, Bozanski began pressuring me to hold a barbeque. According to him my place was perfect, as it was central and easy for everyone to get to. When I mentioned it to Lydia, she offered to help with the catering. So a date for 'the do', as Bozanski referred to it, was set.

To me, it would always be the do that led to my undoing.

Unbeknown to me, on that lazy Sunday afternoon while I was busy outside cooking up a feast on the barbeque, Sabrina was inside my home office, cooking up trouble for me. It was not an accident that she came across files and was able to recall names that would be used by the FGI solicitor to crucify me. It was due to the information she provided that I, Dominic Bruno, was hauled off by detectives, interviewed and charged with misappropriating funds.

In court, Sabrina claimed to have stumbled across FGI files after inadvertently opening the door to my office, thinking it was the second toilet. I just sat there like a stunned mullet, dumbfounded by the magnitude of her deceitfulness, aghast at her explanation as to why she had passed on the information to Mr Dochmar, the Chairman of FGI.

'I was praising Mr Bruno for being such a conscientious employee,' she said. 'It was meant as a compliment, Your Honour. Not everyone is prepared to work on the weekend. Of course, I had no idea that removing files from the FGI premises was forbidden.'

Although it was common practice at FGI, the regulations said otherwise – employees were not allowed to take files from the premises.

The real clincher came when Sabrina claimed to have remembered one of the names, A. A. Santos. It was one of the false accounts through which money had been embezzled. My solicitor shot back with what I thought was a great question.

'How could Sabrina remember that name a month later when she claimed to have only got a glimpse of the file?'

'Sabrina's memory was exemplary,' claimed the FGI barrister.

The smart thing to do would have been to deny the files were on my premises and let them try to prove it. But Dumb Dom had admitted at the first police interview to having the files at home and was left without a leg to stand on.

My excuse sounded lame. 'It was obvious to me that something was not right. I had the file at home because figures needed to be checked.'

The FGI barrister pounced. 'You do admit to knowing something was wrong?'

They had me on toast. Telling the truth made me sound dishonest.

'Despite knowing something was wrong, you never thought to tell someone higher up at FGI? Why didn't you tell your boss, Mr Bozanski?'

'I didn't know there was anything illegal going on. I just thought it was a mistake.'

'A mistake for FGI to trust you, Mr Bruno, that's what I would say. By not reporting the irregularities, you have been derelict in your duty. Surely you can see that?'

That was checkmate. The solicitor from FGI had been given plenty to work with and there was no other obvious suspect. Dom Bruno was branded a knowledgeable man who was too smart for his own good – a clever Dick. Sentenced to six years. My career was finished.

At the time, it felt as though my life was over. But the rollercoaster ride had only just began.

What a performance Sabrina put on outside the courthouse after she'd testified! Hands held together in the universal position for prayer and forgiveness.

'I couldn't live with myself, Lydia, if I didn't tell the truth in court. So sorry, so very sorry.'

I had to then suffer the indignation of watching Lydia and Sabrina engage in a heartfelt consolation hug. Lydia had always been a sucker for emotional displays from those she liked. My raging gaze of anger bore into Sabrina and I must have caught her third eye because she looked up and our eyes met for a split second before she quickly turned away.

But it begged the question – Why did Sabrina have it in for me? It was clear I exercised no control over Lydia. Why did Sabrina come forward and give evidence in court against me? Not because of one lousy insult after a few drinks. Perhaps I was just unaware of my own insignificance.

Was she simply a jealous and devious opportunist who wanted me out of the way so she had Lydia all to herself? Or did Bozanski have something on her? Was she on his payroll?

I had few friends after the charges were laid. I'd been fooled by Bozanski. I didn't suspect him because he was out of the office at the time of the illegal transfers, and apart from the American, Wayne, who did security work for FGI on occasion, Bozanski was the only person willing to make a positive statement to the court with regard to my character.

Of course, Bozanski's sidekick Rodney Chaffer – my former colleague – would have done the dirty work, and undoubtedly did.

4

Prison

At times in the cell I had nearly gone under, ensnared in his inescapable grasp – in a situation so dire you either die inside or burn with anger.

For six months I endured Dunkley's abuse. It was a living hell, the most hideous version of Groundhog Day imaginable. Throw me into a bear pit, anything but the big man's sweaty body – the groping and panting, his grisly beard scratching my fingers probing my body like rusty nails. Add to that the amalgam of olfactory delights – his shitty dog breath, the adrenaline stench and the sickly cheap cologne.

Letting the prison authorities know that I was sharing my cell with a sexual predator resulted in fuck-all being done about it. They called it an 'unsubstantiated allegation'. My complaint caused extra work for staff, and as often happens in those types of situations, the person complaining becomes the problem. Besides, what were my chances when a senior warden was involved?

But don't worry, Mr Superintendent, Mr Bruno won't be making an official complaint. There were other methods of ensuring justice was done.

A fellow prisoner had told me that an understaffed prison had been the reason Dunkley and I had been tossed in together in the first place. While that was possibly true – the place was seriously overcrowded at the time – there was something more sinister at play. The story on the ground was that Dunkley was a crooked ex-warden who'd been caught running a drug ring inside the gaol. Not a surprise to me. It made sense. Certain guards went easy on him. Of course, you could never trust half of what you heard inside. But it did explain Dunkley's relationship with his partner in crime, Cyril Turner, the man I dubbed The Warden.

The prison chaplain displayed some sympathy for my situation. His visits did come with the implied condition that he was given the opportunity to spin his spiel.

It took a great deal of willpower on my part not to goad him. Sometimes the bitterness was so overwhelming I couldn't help myself. I'd been permitted to attend art classes, so I decided to do a drawing for him.

A sooty, ethereal aura surrounded the central figure, who was praying before a statue of the Lord. A man nearby was reading a proclamation – *This is a community announcement. If you are considering praying or begging for JUSTICE, please be aware that the Father, Son and Holy Ghost are all out to lunch.*

The chaplain was a polite man and he did give the picture a proper viewing. He said I had talent, but the work was rather cynical.

I wasn't sure who I could trust. The chaplain was on friendly terms with Turner, The Warden, which made me wary, but in the end I decided to risk it, using a drawing to make him aware of my dire situation.

During his next visit, when the opportunity arose, I pulled out the drawing from under my mattress.

'I'd like to know what you think of my latest artwork. It's more challenging than the one I showed you last time.'

In the drawing, a rough-looking man in prisoner's garb was in the process of shoving a crumpled-up piece of paper down another prisoner's throat. On the right side of the page, a gelid-eyed man in a warden's uniform was watching on. The speech bubble said *At least this time you're not getting it up the arse.*

The chaplain didn't say much after that. When he left I ripped the drawing into shreds. Heaven help me if Dunkley ever set eyes on it.

The next day the chaplain made a surprise visit. He didn't stay long. He knew about the headaches I'd been experiencing, and he advised me to make a complaint to the warden on duty that afternoon, exaggerating the severity of the pain.

I did as he advised, putting on quite a show, and was sent to the prison doctor. The doctor performed a series of tests. Having had no choice but to trust the man, I revealed details of my ordeal at the hands of Dunkley, only to feel violated all over again by his reaction, an apathetic nod of the head. *Par for the course in this place, buddy,* his body language seemed to imply.

Nevertheless, putting my trust in the chaplain seemed to pay off. Liberation from Dunkley came a short time later when authorities moved me to a holding cell in another part of the prison. I was told that I would be placed with another prisoner the next day. Although I was greatly relieved to be away from Dunkley, I still felt on edge, not knowing what to expect next. I still faced four years minimum inside, even with parole.

My new cellmate turned out to be a revelation. Congenial and capable, Tran was a computer geek, and the two of us soon became friends. We had technical skills that complemented each other's, but more than that, he was entertaining to be around – and as it turned out, he became someone I could trust. He showed me some tricks on the prison computer, and his knowledge became invaluable as I planned my revenge.

But just when things were looking up, I got another kick in the guts. The test results came back.

The diagnosis – a malignant tumour on the brain.

It was like being hit by a bus. I felt shattered. The doctor's disgusting attitude added to my woe. I'll never forget his rude and impersonal manner. He'd even made a joke. 'I've got good and bad news.' Just like that – good and bad news.

The good news was that the diagnosis gave me grounds for an early release. Astoundingly, the bastard doctor had tried to contact me after I was released from prison. As if! If I ever set eyes on that prick again, I'd do him in on the spot with his own scalpel.

One of the wardens, who mostly worked nights and often patrolled the area, was a big, bloated, hairy bloke with protruding teeth and a grey moustache. Bucky, the inmates called him. He was also nosy, priding himself on knowing what the inmates were up to. One day he stuck his head over my shoulder, reading with interest what I'd written in bold type on my iPad. A real sarcastic bastard – before he'd even uttered a word, it was clear he planned to ridicule me.

'Your list… It's called the Fuck It! List, right?'

'Yep,' I replied. 'Just like in the movie, "The Bucket List". Things to do before I die. Only, this is the Fuck It! List, and it comes with a twist. My list is a list of betrayers. Those I intend to get even with. Those on whom I intend to take my revenge.'

Bucky stared at me like I'd gone stark raving mad.

Then he began laughing hysterically, spraying spit all over my face. 'You are one mad fucker,' he said.

I caught his gaze before speaking, my tone cold and calculating.

'We all need to do things before we die. Settle the account. Take out a *bastard or two.*'

His laughter turned to something akin to apprehension. I could almost see his mind ticking over – *Is this species venomous or harmless?*

In a world where snakes are plentiful, it is sometimes difficult to tell.

5

The Local

Not long after my arrival in my new neighbourhood, I'd sought out a pub about five kilometres from my new home. Across the road from an industrial estate, it was within walking distance of the railway station and did a roaring trade. To an outsider, the Imperial Hotel appeared to be your ubiquitous suburban establishment, old-style tiled walls on the outside and a bland interior. There was a large public bar with a walkway through to the mandatory TAB. Adjacent to the bar was a carpeted lounge area furnished with a run-down pool table and dartboard that looked to be rarely used.

No matter where you sat, there was no reprieve from the barrage of screens and sounds that tugged at you from every direction: races, football, cooking shows and Keno. The intermittent jingles emanating from the poker machines ran interference from an oblong-shaped space accessible from both bars.

In prison I'd learnt of the Imperial's notorious reputation. One of the inmates called it Diagon Alley and told me it was a place where honourable criminals could acquire, at a reasonable price, the tools required to apply their trade. When I'd asked Tran if he knew of the place, he said it was a zoo, full of drunks and conmen. But Tran was a non-drinker and hanging around pubs was certainly not his thing. It wasn't really mine either, but if you wanted to achieve anything in life, you had to be connected to a hub. A den of inequity it may be, but the Imperial was undeniably a hub.

Ironically, it was Dunkley who had first mentioned the pub to me. But there was little danger of seeing him there. He'd been blacklisted. Most of Dunkley's boasts were intended to impress or frighten, or both. He'd told me he'd beaten up a gang of men who had picked on his mate. The Heroic Adventures of Dunkers, as I called his stories, were all scripted with Dunkley as the hero. Another prisoner had told me the real story, or at least another version, and that one was rather different. After having too much to drink and doing his dough on the poker machines, Dunkers had king-hit a man who had disagreed with him.

On my first visits to the Imperial I decided to heed the advice of the famous American philosopher, Groucho Marx – *The secret of life is honesty and fair-dealing. If you can fake that, you've got it made.* My plan was to find a way in, to make friends and gain people's trust, and to do it reasonably quickly.

The hotel manager was an affable hard nut. Built like a brick wall, he appeared pretty calm and businesslike, but it was clear from the get-go he wasn't a person to cross. The message was – *Welcome, patrons, drink and enjoy, but behave. Trouble will not be tolerated.*

Although the vibe was mostly relaxed and non-threatening, there were a number of shady characters who strolled through the place late in the day. Nothing illegal was visible to the naked eye, but it had the hallmarks. I wondered if the manager got a cut. Perhaps he paid people off or was in cahoots with someone who mattered, because from what I saw, the cops never came near the place.

Depending on the day of the week, the mood shifted from an anodyne sleepiness to high-spirited party mode. It was not a young person's pub – most regulars were over thirty. The exception was Saturday afternoons, when a local band played and the place rocked.

My favourite table was set back a few metres from the walkway that led through to the TAB. From that position, it was possible to see and be seen. I wore the uniform of the common man – nondescript jeans, T-shirt and denim jacket. When in Rome…!

With me on all occasions was the horse-racing form guide from the daily paper. I'd have felt naked without it. It gave me a sense of purpose and a reason for being at the pub. I studied it often. Hopefully I projected the persona of the knock-about punter, part of the horse-loving fraternity.

I'd give a friendly nod and smile to whoever looked my way, and sometimes say 'Gidday' if I thought it was appropriate. My rule was to respond pleasantly, regardless of whether I was snubbed or growled at. Some of the patrons wouldn't talk to a stranger like me in a month of Sundays. They didn't trust newcomers.

I'd often put on a bet in the TAB section. While waiting in line at the window, I'd make a laconic comment about track conditions or the attractive odds on a particular horse to whoever was nearby. Gradually, some of the regular punters began to acknowledge me.

One night, after I'd ordered my drink, the manager came over and introduced himself. I took the opportunity to try to impress him with a firm handshake.

'Do you live local?' he asked.

I told him I'd just moved into the area, skipping a beat before adding,

'Walters Road. Been there just a few weeks.'

'Walters Road!' he replied, shaking his head. 'You might be needin' something a bit stronger than beer, mate.'

'Better give us a scotch chaser, then,' I replied, adding that I was only joking.

A man sitting nearby sniggered as the manager set off to get back to the bar and serve the next customer. Some of the other patrons had witnessed the exchange, and their blank faces left me wondering how much headway I was really making in my attempt to fit in with the locals.

A minute or so later, the barman brought a glass of scotch to my table. 'On the house, mate. Cheers.'

That did give me some hope.

Later that week I was presented with another opportunity to ingratiate myself. The Western Sydney Wanderers had qualified for the finals, and after hours of watching replays of football games and studying the history of the club and its players, I took the opportunity to display my loyalty to the clan.

Enthusiasm is something a sports atheist finds hard to fake, but it was surprisingly enjoyable being part of a group with the same passion, chanting and behaving with heightened emotions. I was as teary-eyed and upset as the rest when we lost to Sydney FC in the dying stages. Those who share tears of sorrow shall be forever united. Or not.

It wasn't until my third week, during my eighth visit to the pub, that the breakthrough came. I was on my second drink when one of the men I had spoken to at the TAB invited me to his table. Hallelujah.

He introduced himself as The Case. His friend he introduced as Bubba.

Shaking hands, I felt a quiver of excitement. I'd seen the two together often. Both were around forty. The Case was a hefty, strong-looking man with a dark complexion. Bubba was shorter, with a wiry build. He had brown hair, blue eyes, a chipper manner and a baby face – thus his nickname.

Without being prompted, I told them I'd moved to the area from the Eastern Suburbs after breaking up with my girlfriend, and that it had been too expensive to get another place in that part of the city. They listened to what I said but didn't pry or ask questions. Case told me he lugged boxes at the fruit markets most mornings.

My rule was to keep my conversation within the confines of the vernacular. *Don't appear to be a know-all and don't appear to be stupid. Get the balance right between intelligence and ignorance. Worth engaging with but not seen as a threat.* What I also had to remember was that some of the patrons would be, if not friends, then at least acquaintances of Dunkley. Of course, I wasn't trying to get a wooden horse into Troy. After my prison stint I had come to feel like one of their ilk. But from the stories I'd heard inside, I would never be in the same league as some of the criminals who frequented the Imperial.

After a while, Case and Bubba carried on as if I wasn't there. They indulged in dry, witty banter, and it was hard to get a word in edgeways. While they were polite to me, they paid out on each other endlessly, like two squabbling siblings. It was all done in good humour, however. I wondered whether Case had invited me to their table so they had an audience. Occasionally they would make comments about current affairs and politics, although I must admit to being a poor judge as to how astute or otherwise their opinions were, as I no longer had any interest in all that hullabaloo.

31

Bubba was a horse fanatic. He attended country meetings and was a regular at the yearling sales. He knew people in the industry all around the state. As a kid he'd hoped to be a jockey but grew too big. Case joked that in a previous life Bubba had been a racehorse. Bubba was famous for his insider tips, apparently from a jockey friend who rode trackwork at Flemington. Although the horses were often favourites, or started at short odds, they invariably won.

Bubba told a story about being chased by a brown snake near Blackheath in the Blue Mountains while having a pee in the bush. I hadn't laughed so much in ages. Case matched it with a tale where he was cast as the hero, fighting off a pack of wild dogs on a property west of Taree. After that they proceeded to tell jokes, including a couple I hadn't heard before. Then Bubba turned to me.

'You got one, Dom?'

From the way they looked at me, I knew I had to come up with something. I could never remember jokes. Racking my brain, I recalled one Lydia had told me.

'Okay,' I said. 'Here we go... A blonde woman goes into the hairdresser. She is wearing a set of headphones. Before having her hair cut, she makes the hairdresser swear not to remove her headphones under any circumstances. The blonde lady nods off and the hairdresser, unable to get access to all the woman's hair because of the headphones, becomes frustrated. The hairdresser thinks, *What harm could it possibly do? She won't even know.* She removes the headphones. The blonde lady slumps to the floor. The distraught hairdresser realises the blonde woman has stopped breathing. She attempts to revive the woman using CPR but is unable to do so. The blonde is, in fact, stone-cold dead. The hairdresser is perplexed – why had the headphones been so important? She puts them on. There is no music, just the same message repeated over and over – breathe in… breathe out… breathe in… breathe out.'

They laughed, probably out of politeness, because my delivery was rather wooden.

There was an attractive girl who worked behind the bar. She often started late in the afternoon and worked until closing. My visits often coincided with her shifts. I became mesmerised by her elfin face: the sensual lips and the cute upturned nose. Her name was Tracy, and after a while – probably because of my association with Bubba and Case – she began acknowledging my presence. Everybody liked her, it seemed. Case would pay out on her and she'd give it back in spades. She was a beauty amongst beasts. Sometimes she'd wear an old school jersey with her name and her old school, Darwin High, on the back.

Buoyed by the jovial company of Bubba and Case, when Tracy came to collect our empty glasses from the table, I called her Cyclone Tracy – a nod to the rapid rate with which she moved around the place. Everybody within earshot laughed, and from her reaction, it seemed as though she too approved of the nickname, so I continued to use it.

Around that time, I was in an internet café, curious to know how people had reacted to my YouTube upload, 'A Shot in the Park'. I was pleased to see that the footage had attracted a lot of interest. From the comments, it appeared as though many people assumed it had been staged (imagine the logistics of actually staging a scene like that). One comment in particular had my interest. Alongside a caricature of a man asleep on stage, a caption read – *Excellent money to be paid for brave work like this. If interested contact Mr Twinkel.*

Mr Twinkel! What a peculiar name. The site was easy enough to find. The homepage contained the same caricature asleep on stage, with a universe of stars flickering in the background. In the corner of the screen was an image of Van Gogh's 'The Starry Night'.

The site was popular, but the content was not what the name suggested. It was what could best be described as soft porn. There was also an international dating section.

Why was this Mr Twinkel interested in me? Perhaps he was branching out – horizontal integration.

To sign in, a name and password was required. A clothing brochure that somebody had left behind sat on the computer desk before me. I scanned the document. One of the words, *sparkle*, caught my eye. It was in a similar vein to Twinkel. Another word, *Benedict* (a clothing brand), seemed to sit well with *sparkle*. Swapping the last two letters, I signed on as Benedict Sparkel.

The moment I did so, a spotlight came on, illuminating the caricature. The man began yawning and stretching out. He got to his feet. Dressed in tight white jeans and a colourful shirt, both laced with diamonds, he had long red hair and wore a glistening gold chain around his neck. He adopted a dancer's poise and proceeded to perform a folk dance which, at a guess, was Germanic in origin. As he danced, comments about his performance were posted.

A real showman, this one.

Mr Twinkel is both alluring and eye-catching.

Must be a gym junkie.

When Mr Twinkel finished his dance, he bowed and spoke in an assured manner.

'Mr Twinkel, at your service.'

His eyes were mesmerising. I experienced an eerie feeling as he stared back at me from the screen. *I'm intrigued*, I typed. *But I don't see what your service can provide for the likes of me.*

On the screen, a video began to play. It took me a moment to recognise what I was watching. It was the footage I'd uploaded on YouTube, 'A Shot in the Park', but the visuals had been enhanced. Music – at a guess, a Dr Dre remix – accompanied the visuals. I was astonished at the quality. The amateur footage I'd taken from my balcony had been turned into a professional production.

Very impressive, I typed. A document appeared on the screen.

Contract on offer

1. All future uploads – minimum one per month – to be sent to Mr Twinkel

2. Mr Twinkel takes thirty percent of revenue generated

I typed, *What is thirty percent of zilch?*

Mr Twinkel laughed, a warm, human laugh that exposed his teeth, which were perfect apart from a crooked upper incisor. Then he became serious.

'If you accept this offer, as a display of good faith you will be forwarded an advance of ten thousand dollars.'

Dollar signs flicked before my eyes. Ten thousand. It wasn't as though I was flush with funds. What did I have to lose? One upload a month was hardly demanding. I could cut the connection to Mr Twinkel at any time, and my Benedict Sparkel alias would keep my real identity secret.

After I accepted the offer, Mr Twinkel did a short celebratory shuffle before he spoke.

'Can you send Mr Twinkel some information about yourself – aspirations, inspirations, inclinations? An account number will be

required so funds can be transferred.'

Here we go, I thought, *just another con artist.* I sent Mr Twinkel a curt message: *Account details – no way. You must think I'm crazy.*

Mr Twinkel replied almost immediately – *Provide post office box number if you prefer cash.*

His reply caught me by surprise. I searched the internet for more information on Mr Twinkel, but other than the website, there was zilch. Three other companies with similar names caught my attention. Twinkel of an Eye, a multimedia company based in Spain; Twinkle Systems, an Indian wholesale provider of routers, motherboards keyboards and other computer accessories; and Twinkl Educational Publishing, an international online publishing house based in Sheffield, England, that produced children's learning resources. I thought about Twinkel of an Eye. Like Mr Twinkel, it had the 'l' and 'e' of twinkle interchanged. It claimed as its clients, several major corporations. It was a private company, and I couldn't find out anything more about it. Being in the multimedia business, it would have been capable of pulling off the production job on my upload, 'A Shot in the Park'. The two Twinkels may have been linked, but I had no reason to believe Mr Twinkel was not a successful stand-alone entity; there was plenty of money to be made from online dating and pornography. In any case, it made little difference to my decision. I decided that if I was careful, nothing I posted could be traced back to Dom Bruno. Besides, if the reaction to 'A Shot in the Park' was any indication, the pundits would assume my postings were staged anyway.

From the relative safety of the internet café, I told Mr Twinkel about the Fuck It! List, making up the names and altering some of the details. I must admit, it gave me a thrill, relating my plans for revenge to someone

– even if that someone was just an animated character on a screen.

Afterwards, my lofty Fuck It! List ambitions seemed that much more plausible. When nothing happened for a couple of days, I decided it must have been some trick to obtain information. What a surprise it was when, two days later, an envelope containing ten thousand dollars in cash was delivered to the postbox I'd nominated. The sender information simply said 'Mr Twinkel'. There was no postal address.

6

Fear and Loathing

Dunkley drove a prime mover, which he parked outside his house overnight. I checked the legality of this with the council. As I'd suspected, the length and size of his vehicle – six-by-four bogie axle – meant that parking such a colossus in a residential area was forbidden. And forbidden for good reasons – the space they take, the decibels they reach when the engine starts. You can imagine the sound of that almighty engine growling to life as Dunkley headed off at five in the morning.

After I followed him a few times, a pattern began to emerge. His pick-up point was a warehouse about ten kilometres away from his home, where he hitched up a loaded trailer of hardware goods. From there he drove out onto the M4. Most days he returned late in the afternoon. Sometimes he was away overnight. One day I tailed him along the expressway to the foothills of the Blue Mountains. Dunkley had one or two days off a week – Sunday, or Saturday and Sunday.

On this particular Sunday, I was watching Dunkley carry out his household chores. It was noticeable how quickly he had lost his prison-honed physique. Shirtless and in thongs, his newly developed gut was a work in progress, sagging from the front of his stubbies, with the crack of his arse invariably smiling at all and sundry from the rear.

After mowing the array of weeds that masqueraded as a lawn, he wasted fuel as his Victa blower blasted away a leaf of two that had blown onto his driveway from a lone tree twenty metres from his house. The fact that the debris would blow back onto his driveway the moment the wind changed direction seemed lost on the man.

Problem solved, Dunkley proceeded to undertake another crucial chore, hosing the cement. Watching the water hit the surface, I wanted to scream – *cement doesn't grow, you idiot. Don't you know there's a water shortage?*

Afterwards, Dunkley sat on the front verandah with a beer in hand, admiring his handiwork. A dreary dullness seemed to have set in over the neighbourhood, when a passing Holden ute tooted its horn, did a U-turn and pulled up behind Dunkley's truck. A man who was frighteningly familiar climbed out of the driver's side. Cyril Turner, The Warden.

My reaction was to pull back from the screen, even though it was impossible for him or Dunkley to see me. My breathing quickened and my heart began pounding. Dunkley got him a beer and The Warden stayed for a couple of hours, chatting, drinking and sharing a joke with his mate. The Warden's dodgy smile was as unforgettable as those cruel, icy eyes. Even though I was well out of sight and in the safety of my house, seeing both men together sent waves of fear rushing through my body.

Later that night, while I was making assessments and passing motions at the executive meeting being held inside my head, I was affected by a strange listlessness. For a moment it was as though I'd never escaped that prison cell – the angst, the filthy, sour smell, the indignity of being forced to do what I did. The Warden and Dunkley still had a hold over me. My body began to shake and a cold sweat enveloped me.

Perhaps the Fuck It! List was a joke and I didn't have the courage. What had I actually done since being released from prison? Visited the pub where Dunkley used to drink, hoping like hell he didn't turn up. Watched the recordings from my balcony like some pathetic voyeur. I felt like a fake and the townhouse felt like a tomb. I was suffocating. I had to get out.

Out on the road, I drove aimlessly around. I couldn't rid myself of the negative thoughts. Maybe the tumour was progressing faster than expected? That prison doctor could have been telling me anything.

Desperate for company, I thought of Lydia. There was nobody else. I turned onto Parramatta Road and joined the queue of slow-moving traffic crawling into the city.

Approaching her Surry Hills home with my head still in a spin, I pulled up behind another car and was waiting to turn into Lydia's street when her white Mazda passed me, travelling in the opposite direction. After making a U-turn, I accelerated in pursuit.

As Lydia passed through Darlinghurst, it hit me. If she kept going in that direction she would end up at Sabrina's place.

There were other possibilities. Her friend Jillian lived over that way. Perhaps she was visiting her. Instinctively, I feared the worst, and pangs of jealousy raged through me. Then I hit a red light and the Mazda was gone. Sabrina's unit was situated on the water's edge at Elizabeth Bay, so I continued in that direction.

When I arrived there wasn't any sign of Lydia's car. Sabrina lived on the first floor. The lights were on, but the curtains were drawn. It was impossible to see inside. The building had an underground parking station, so I began walking over to see if it was possible to gain access.

I was just about to cross the road when I stopped in my tracks. Video cameras lurked like raptors at all entry points to the apartment. Returning to my car, I was stymied. The thought of Lydia staying overnight cut like a razor through my thoughts. I had to find out.

A crazy idea came into my head.

Using a burner phone, I dialled Sabrina's number and waited until she picked up. I rang Lydia with a second phone and put it to my left ear. I spoke slowly to Sabrina, using a high-pitched voice and purporting to be canvassing for organ donations, while my ears focused on the background noise. Sabrina mumbled something about the consent for such a matter being on her licence. Just hearing her pompous voice made me angry.

'No, no. Not that type of organ. I'm from the church. We need a new organ for the choir.'

My joke sounded lame and gave me little joy.

'Who the fuck is this?' she roared. 'Is that you, Paul?'

As Sabrina hurled invective into my right ear, Lydia picked up. Ever so faintly in my left ear, I could hear Sabrina's tirade.

After hanging up, I felt ill to the core. I waited outside the flat all night. At around seven the next morning, Lydia drove out of the underground parking lot. Hungry and overtired, my rage reached Richter-scale magnitudes as I followed Lydia back to her house at Surry Hills.

I waited for twenty minutes or so to gather my thoughts before going up to her house and knocking on the front door. Lydia welcomed me inside, making a pot of tea while we indulged in small talk about computers and internet speeds. Just being with her in the kitchen brought back memories of a happier time. But there was an undercurrent stirring and knowing she had spent the night at Sabrina's meant I couldn't hold my tongue.

'Do you see much of Sabrina?'

Lydia didn't reply, just gave me a quizzical look. I tried to be logical and not overplay my hand, but there were things she should know. I repeated my solicitor's damning assessment of Sabrina's claim that she had a great mind for detail and could recall the name on the file she'd seen in my home office.

'She's not like that, Dom.'

'Not to you. Have you ever wondered why she was in my office?'

'She explained that in court.'

I was going over old ground but couldn't help myself. I couldn't believe Lydia wasn't awake to Sabrina's antics.

'And just happened to recall the name on the file. What a lot of bullshit that was!'

'You don't know her, Dom. She's got an amazing memory. And I saw her agonising over it all. In the end she thought it best to just tell the truth.'

'Do you still see her?' I asked again, wondering whether she would tell me the truth.

'She's opened doors for me, Dom, introduced me to people in the entertainment industry.'

'So that's it. You think she might be your ticket into television or whatever. I'm telling you, Lydia, don't trust the woman.'

My words made little impact so, driven by despair, I upped the ante. I gave her a snarly gaze.

'Sabrina is a nasty, calculating bitch. You're in a relationship with her, aren't you? Biased because you're fucking her.'

That was childish of me, but not ridiculous. Lydia had been in a relationship with another girl when she was at boarding school. But my comment had really pissed her off. She gave me the line about her life being none of my business, then asked me to leave. I managed to reel in my anger and leave without causing further trouble.

By the time I got home I was in a depressed state. I was angry at Lydia and my hate for Sabrina knew no bounds. But I was also feeling stupid for the inept way I'd handled the situation. My head was throbbing with pain. The thought of the cancer taking over my body and mind filled me with dread.

Still, one thing was certain. It was time to get on Sabrina's case. The Dunkley, Bozo and Co. Show could wait. There was a need to feed the bitterness that shrouded me, and it had only intensified last night.

7

Spyworks

Tran had once obtained Sabrina's IP address and accessed her school account from the prison computer. Whether security at the school had improved or my skills were inept was uncertain, but my attempts to crack her account proved unsuccessful.

At one stage I'd considered breaking into Sabrina's harbourside abode. But as I'd discovered, security was tight. Even entering the foyer was fraught with danger. Being unskilled at break-ins, my chances of pulling it off were in the realm of farce. Besides, she might not even have a home computer.

Sabrina worked at Saint Teresa. From studying the website, I knew that the teachers at Sabrina's school had computers with USB drives. I'd been able to obtain an auto-hacking device from the internet. If the device did its job, I would be able to gain access to Sabrina's details from a remote computer.

There were doubts in the back of my mind. Would this prove to be an act of stupidity? What if I got caught? Maybe it would turn out to be a complete waste of time. Tran's advice would be to wait until he was released. I was in no mood to wait. Ever since the idea of following Sabrina came into my head, I'd felt energised. This Sherlock Holmes caper had heightened my senses and made me feel alive.

Commuters swarmed around Strathfield Railway Station like bees to a hive. Some had arrived at their destination, while others were on their way into the city for work. There were a lot of glum faces mixed with the occasional spark of excitement from groups of school students.

Sabrina was going in a different direction to most. She took long strides and crossed the road without waiting for the lights to change. When she diverted into a cake shop, I took the opportunity to get in front of her.

She came out a short time later, carrying an extra bag. Sabrina had changed little since my pre-prison days – maybe she'd put on a little weight, but the woman was still annoyingly attractive. Of average height, she had a voluptuous body with prominent breasts. Men turned noticeably as she passed. But her sharp facial features and over-active eyes told me what I already knew; she was one nasty piece of work.

Sabrina had been inside my house, got drunk on my grog, smoked illegal substances in my kitchen, but never once had she responded to one of my comments in a positive way or even sniggered at one of my witty asides. Maybe my jokes weren't all that funny, but even Bozanski chuckled at times. Still, I wouldn't want to be accused of doing someone in just because they didn't like my jokes.

Anger rose in me as I thought about how conniving and calculating she had been in setting me up. At times in prison, thoughts of Sabrina and her outright cunning had me in a state of rage. When I read a comment on somebody's Facebook page that she and Lydia had attended a weekend retreat together, it made my blood boil. Again, the thought of her and Lydia experiencing any type of intimacy – let alone as lovers – drove me to distraction. I couldn't shake it.

At that stage of the game, just how my acts of revenge would play out and how they would affect me was unclear. When I'd seen Lydia leaving Sabrina's apartment that morning, I'd felt like murdering Sabrina, but the truth was, I really didn't know whether I could physically harm a woman. Not that she didn't deserve it. A profiler would classify her as a psychopath. And that's not a word I'd use lightly.

Preparing for the occasion had been all-consuming. Totally uninspiring yet perfectly appropriate for the occasion: a grey wig, black trousers, a blue shirt, a dour brown-and-white tie, with thick spectacles to hide the eyes. My plain woollen sports coat, with a tiny spy camera attached to a buttonhole, helped me achieve the 'mature teacher' look.

Applying the base and pencil to create wrinkles on my face was time-consuming, but it was vital I looked the part. Adding to the charade was a briefcase and a walking stick with the obligatory limp. The walking stick unfortunately couldn't fire a bullet like in a Bond movie, but it was solid, a useful weapon if things turned nasty. Given the choice, I was always going to flee rather than fight.

I hid behind a neatly trimmed row of murraya bush. The sense of adventure was absorbing as I furtively observed Sabrina walking through the park. I wanted to be there when she arrived at the school gates, so I rushed ahead. Once I was away from the hustle and bustle of the station, the mood of the suburb changed considerably. I walked down a wide tree-lined street in which there were several grand old homes sitting on massive parcels of land. Some of the properties had stunning manicured gardens. Getting closer to the school, I spotted an increasing number of students in their blue-and-white uniforms.

The Saint Teresa website had provided a goldmine of information. It was surprising just how much was revealed. There were six departments and over eighty teachers at the school. Routines had changed little since my own school days. After homing in on a series of photos, I'd forged a green lanyard, the insignia required for a casual teacher; it had been a choice between being a guest, a casual or a temp.

The office lady, a Mrs Bower, booked the casuals. She would know who was supposed to be replacing whom. So would the deputy principal, Mr Baldwin, from what I could work out. He was a fearsome-looking man. The other danger, apart from Sabrina herself, was the head science teacher. If the staff photo was any indication, she would be vigilant and notice anything odd in a flash. The science staffroom was down the corridor from Sabrina's.

I approached the school with caution. At least at this high school they didn't have surveillance cameras – not yet. There were cars dropping off students, while others seemingly materialised out of thin air. Now and then a bus would arrive. Students would pour out, then momentarily pause to gain their bearings before moving towards the school gates as though being sucked into a vortex. It was an impressive sight; the collective sense of purpose as the students and teachers passed through the narrow entrance and headed off to their various destinations.

Walking on past the school gates, I halted, ostensibly crouching low to tie my shoelace – but my real objective was to observe Sabrina's progress. I needed to be certain which staffroom she was in. As an English teacher, one would expect it to be the English staffroom, but I needed verification.

I watched on as Sabrina entered the school grounds. Occasionally her head would turn to acknowledge a greeting from a student. Sabrina would be a dominating figure as a teacher. For a young student being reprimanded, she would be impossible to argue with. Was she like that with Lydia?

In years past, a school of such religious persuasion would have crucified a female teacher for having a female lover. It would have been met with instant dismissal and excommunication from the church. I wondered how much opinion had shifted. Was the Lord more tolerant these days?

The map I was using had been downloaded from the school's website. I'd viewed the layout on Google Earth, but still needed to do a quick check to ensure the distances and positioning of buildings and gates were accurate. It took only a matter of seconds to do so, but when I looked up, I'd lost sight of Sabrina.

There was only a short time until the bell. For my plan to work, I needed to be inside the school and out of sight by then. A man passed in front of me and said hello. The face was familiar. From what I could recall from the school magazine, I think he was the PE teacher who coached the senior basketball team. I followed him in through the gates of Saint Teresa and was soon one of many in the throng.

I adopted a fatigued disposition, as though I might barely survive the day. That's what it was like for casual teachers in my day. Nobody showed concern or interest in my presence. It was the start of the day and most teachers I passed were preoccupied and in a hurry. Occasionally, one would view my badge and acknowledge my presence with a nod.

Still unable to find Sabrina, I was increasingly on edge with the fear of accidentally running into her. Beads of sweat appeared on my brow. Where had she gone? Would she recognise me in disguise, limping along with my walking stick? I started towards B Block, which was about twenty metres away. The English staffroom was on the first floor.

All of a sudden, Sabrina was coming towards me. She had been in the library. Mercifully, under a statue of Saint Teresa, she was interrupted by a student. But it forced me to change direction, and I found myself heading towards the main administration building. Those were shark-infested waters; the deputy principal's office was there.

Once again, I pretended to be tying up my shoelaces. Chancing a glance in Sabrina's direction, I realised with horror that she and the student were walking towards me. Lucky I was such a dreary-looking specimen, because just when I thought the game was up, Sabrina parted company with the student and darted off without a glance at the grey-headed man crouched nearby. She walked across the playground and into B Block. I could see her silhouette through the opalescent glass windows as she reached the top of the stairwell.

Nearly nine o'clock, and all was well.

On the street outside the school, the cars dropping off students had begun to thin out. The latecomers were still arriving. The bell would sound in less than a minute. I made my way swiftly across the yard to the lower-level toilet, which was at the base of the stairwell in B Block. It was unoccupied, so I stepped inside, locked the door and checked myself in the mirror as I waited.

The bell began to ring. It was followed by the bustling noise of students as they made their way to their roll-call classes. According to the timetable, this would last six minutes.

I made two calls from my hideaway. First I rang 000 and told the operator I could see smoke billowing from a school building. Giving a false name, I claimed to be a neighbour who lived across the road at number twenty-six.

Next, I rang the school and informed the front office there was a fire in D Block.

Later, they might be able to trace the call back to the school by locating the base cell tower and adjacent towers. By then I'd be long gone.

As I waited for the school to react, I thought back to my original plan. I'd considered making a small smoke bomb from potassium nitrate, sugar and water, and waxed paper. That was before I found out that the fire brigade responded to all emergency calls, even if they suspected it was a false alarm.

Time seemed to stand still. Finally, the bell began to sound. Peeking out from my hideaway, I could see students and teachers emerging from the buildings in an orderly fashion and making their way to the school oval, where rolls would be checked. Someone, probably a head teacher, would be returning for a final check of each block. That was when I would be vulnerable.

In the distance I heard the wail of a siren. The fire brigade was reliable, and the sound of them approaching was my signal to act. Sights set on Sabrina's staffroom, I emerged from my hideaway and climbed the stairs. I sighted Sabrina and another teacher up the end of the corridor, chivvying students out of the building. They had their hands full.

I was caught by surprise when two female students came quickly up the stairs and stopped at the top. They viewed me with disinterest. Nobody important. One said to the other, 'Do we stay in the room or go to the playground?'

'Who knows? It's probably just another drill. Go to the oval, I think.'

I needed them gone or they would attract attention.

'Down to the oval now,' I said sternly, pointing to the stairwell.

They obeyed. I felt a strange sense of power. Maybe I'd missed my calling.

I approached the English staffroom and paused near the entrance. Hearing no sign of life, I opened the door to step inside and got the shock of my life. A teacher coming from the room nearly bowled me over.

'Sorry,' he said, but when he didn't recognise my face, his expression changed. Was he questioning my presence? I must have appeared flustered. *Don't come undone now,* my inner voice hissed.

I said, 'I need to contact the front office – I've just received news that my mother has been taken to hospital.'

He looked at my lanyard. 'Oh, that's terrible. You'll need to tell Mr Baldwin, the deputy. He might still be in his office. The number's near the phone inside. I've got a roll to mark.'

The man took a few steps, then paused. I tightened my grip on the walking stick.

'Don't forget to pull the door shut. Hope your mother's okay.'

With that, he was gone.

Sabrina's desk was easy enough to find. It was tidy and had a big swivel seat. A small white statue of Buddha stood in the lower corner. A picture of Saint Mary hung above her desk. Was she having a bet each way? There were carrot and celery sticks on her desk in a plastic bag. But what brought my eyes to life was the laptop computer sitting open near a bundle of papers.

I hit the space bar and it sprung to life. It was still logged on to the school website, open at a page containing the Year Ten students' reports.

On the screen was the photo of a stunning-looking student with high cheekbones and deep-blue eyes. Her name was Charlotte. I read the report before me.

Some of my own school grades had been dreadful at times, but Charlotte made me look like a genius. All Ds and Es. One C, in drama. Sabrina had made some inane comment about due diligence and the need to complete the required classwork, as well as undertaking a program of systematic revision of key points before examinations. Yeah, right! Most students would need an interpreter to understand that.

I took the USB from my pocket. I had just inserted it into the slot when the knob on the staffroom door began to turn.

I grabbed my briefcase and scrambled for cover. There was a small alcove with a chair, table and telephone. A portable whiteboard blocked it off from the rest of the staffroom. I sat there, facing the wall with the phone in my hand, as though listening to someone on the other end. I dared not make a sound. Seconds later, the door opened and there were people in the room. From the hushed tones, it soon became apparent that they were not teachers, but students. What were they doing? Were they stealing from the staff? In the schools I'd attended it was a major offence for students to enter a staffroom without a teacher.

From what I could make out there were two of them, both boys. They were up to no good, laughing and carrying on, but I had no idea just what they were doing. If I came out from my hiding place, it would have given them the shock of their lives – but they would have been able to describe me, and that might have come back to haunt me.

One of the boys said, 'Hey, Jase, check this out.'

That was when I remembered I'd left Sabrina's computer open.

All of a sudden the school bell stopped abruptly, leaving an eerie stillness. It must have frightened the two boys, because they left the room soon after. I went back over to the computer and had just taken the USB from the drive when the dreaded pitter-patter of oncoming footsteps had me ducking for cover again.

Somebody else entered the room. What a shock I got when I peeked through the partition.

It was Sabrina.

At least this time I'd closed the computer before heading for the alcove. Again, I picked up the phone and pretended I was listening to somebody on the other end. Would she check the alcove or assume it was empty?

Seconds later, I was panic-stricken as my worst fears were realised.

'Hello,' said Sabrina.

I didn't dare turn around. Conflicting thoughts raced through my mind. Should I just make a run for it? Even if Sabrina did recognise me, I might be saved because she may well not want to admit to knowing me. Why had I put myself in such a ridiculous predicament? *Don't panic,* I told myself. *You can get out of this.*

Then she spoke again. 'Is that you, Sandra?'

Why was she calling me Sandra?

Then I realised she was in conversation with somebody on her mobile. I breathed a sigh of relief. Still, I knew I wasn't out of the woods by a long shot. With time ticking away, I was cornered.

'No, that's alright,' Sabrina said. 'Wednesday will be fine.'

As the conversation continued, she gradually moved away from where I was sitting. Then I heard the sound of the door closing and the lock engaging, followed by rapid-fire click of heels echoing on the walkway as Sabrina made her way down the corridor.

With my nerves on edge, I waited a minute or so before cautiously taking a peek outside. There was nobody about, so I left the room and descended the stairwell. Through the window I saw a fireman chatting to the principal. According to the evacuation plan, everybody else should have been down at the oval. They would have worked out it was a false alarm and, with any luck, assumed it was a recalcitrant student, or an ex-student with a grudge. Maybe the two boys who had been in the staffroom would cop the blame.

Reaching the bottom of the stairs, I was relieved not to have encountered anyone. I walked around to the back of the building, hugging the fence line so I would not be easily seen from the road. The side entrance was supposed to remain unlocked until nine-thirty. Still, it was reassuring to find the gate open and not a person in sight. What a different story it might have been if the gate had been locked early and I'd been forced to backtrack to the main entrance.

Just when everything seemed to be going smoothly, things took a turn for the worse.

I was about to leave the school grounds when my presence was noticed by the eagle eye of the deputy principal. It gave me a real fright. Although I didn't think he would be able to see through my disguise from that distance, I had no desire to test my hypothesis. *Stay calm,* I said to myself as I continued at a normal walking pace. Once I was out of his line of vision, I took off like my life depended on it, only slowing when I spotted a woman up ahead weeding her garden. I slowed my pace, hunched my back and waved as I hobbled past.

The next five minutes were crucial. Would somebody come after me in a car? Had the deputy rung the police? The thought of a police car appearing on the scene had me worried.

I approached the park I'd walked through earlier. It seemed like aeons since I'd watched Sabrina from behind the murraya bush. I made my way to the public toilets, where I could safely change out of my disguise.

Stepping inside the cubicle, I felt like a trapped animal. I hastily took off the wig and clothes and placed them in my briefcase. I put on a T-shirt, old jeans and a baseball cap, before using a towel and make-up remover to erase the wrinkles from my face.

I came out from the toilets and surveyed the surrounds before making my way at a leisurely pace to the bus stop across the road. A smile of relief bloomed on my face when a bus came chugging along the street a short time later. Who said buses didn't run on time?

Thirty minutes later, I was sitting in a café near Burwood Plaza, sipping a flat white and munching on a sandwich. Once the pressure was off, I was on a high. The experience had been a blast. I felt alive, like a character in my own movie.

After censoring the footage I'd recorded, I dropped by an internet café and sent it to Mr Twinkel. The spy camera I'd used had done the required job. There was no shortage of material, though most of it was rather droll. It would be interesting to see what Mr Twinkel did with it.

When I got home, I logged on to the computer. There was a post from Mr Twinkel.

Mr Twinkel dances onto the stage and steps up to the microphone.

'Introducing Benedict Sparkel and the Fuck It! List.'

The limelight finds a faceless man dressed in a suit running down a track, looking over his shoulder as though trying to escape someone or something.

Five shadowy figures appear above the faceless man. They hover above him for a short time before transforming into fearsome assassins. They attack the faceless man. He is eventually picked up and flung through the air. He lands in a paddock, where he is savaged by baying hounds. The Grim Reaper can be seen on a distant hill. Wallowing in offal, bleeding, his clothes torn to shreds, the faceless man struggles to his feet.

Applause. A voice from afar calls out.

'Hey man, tell 'em the one about the night long ago in Africa, when the

butterfly flapped its wings.'

The faceless man gathers himself.

'It's all just a case of cause and effect, my son.'

Someone offers encouragement. 'Come on, man. You can do it.'

In the distance, dark storm clouds are gathering. The faceless man's body begins to glow.

An encouraging voice calls out, 'I think he's up for it now.'

Another yells, 'Give it to 'em, mate. Go on. You show 'em.'

The faceless man's voice becomes full of fire and brimstone and the storm clouds intensify.

'If you were not long for this world and had been shafted and cast adrift, would you bide your time crying woe-is-me and wait until the Grim Reaper comes knocking, or would you muster the courage and act? Settle a personal vendetta or two before departing this earth?'

He pauses, seemingly too overwhelmed to continue. The audience sighs.

But then the faceless man grows in size, transforming into something fearless and menacing.

'To those who have treated me abysmally – you won't be needing some soothsayer to predict YOUR future. Did you really think that life would just roll along, verdant fields and daisies, la de da? Well, it doesn't work like that.'

The ground shakes and people scream in fear as they try to escape the impending catastrophe. The faceless man's words reverberate like thunder.

'THERE WILL BE AFTERSHOCKS.'

Later that night, the elation I'd experienced visiting Sabrina's school had worn off. It was replaced by a feeling of stupidity. The deputy had definitely seen me. What if that English teacher who nearly bowled me over mentioned me to Sabrina? And then there were the two girls, plus the neighbour I'd passed. Would Sabrina find out that her computer had been compromised?

I'd taken risks that could jeopardise everything. Tran would have undoubtedly been able to achieve the same result without going near the school. The joke was that although I could access Sabrina's school account, I was too scared to do so, lest I reveal my identity or leave a trail.

8

Tran

I awoke early the next day in a better frame of mind. Tran's impending release was a bright light on the horizon. And there was the ten thousand dollars Mr Twinkel had paid me.

Later that day, while waiting for Tran in the prison carpark, I reflected on the argument with Lydia. In the back of my mind was the sad realisation that Lydia would never need or want me ever again. Even at my best, I was a lump of lead around any woman's neck. Let alone a woman with Lydia's options.

I sat there, reminiscing about my time inside with Tran. It could be a lonely place, prison, and you couldn't trust anyone, but after a while, after Tran and I got to know each other better, our personalities did gel. We discovered a propinquity in that cell that was rare for a lone traveller like me.

For someone with my life experiences, Tran's worldly perspective and computer skills were impressive. He lived with the peace of mind of a thousand religions. He had eyes that smiled emeralds and carried himself with an unflinching calmness. He was about twenty-five and looked sixteen. His size and gentle manner belied an inner resilience. Rumour had it that he was connected to a triad. If it was true, he didn't say a thing to me about it, although he did have the contacts that enabled him to launder money.

Sentenced to five years for hijacking the Social Security network, his real crime was that he had embarrassed a government that bragged about its cybersecurity capabilities. Tran had not made a cent from his crime. He had redirected money to randomly selected pensioners and was dubbed a modern-day Robin Hood by one reporter.

Like me, Tran also had a sad sack of stories. He was dobbed in by the jealous suitor of his ex-girlfriend. A family matter, as he described it. His father was Australian and his mother Vietnamese. They had met in Vietnam just before the end of the American War. His mother and most of his family still lived there, in a village thirty kilometres out of Ho Chi Minh, not far from the Mekong River.

'Computer Whiz', I'd dubbed him, after he found his way into the prison administration system from the library computer. Singing 'Go, Tran, go' to the tune of 'Johnny B. Goode', I'd encouraged him on his forays into the aether. I listened intently when he spoke about the ins and outs of hijacking accounts, concealing identities and moving money by piggybacking off other servers.

Tran seemed genuinely interested in my personal story. He was also intrigued by the mechanics of what had occurred at FGI and wanted to know all about the security and operational systems they used. When he heard the figure of thirty million, he whistled.

'I might be able to trace it,' he said, and I loved Tran from that moment on.

It was risky trying too much from the library computer, but in the dim grey penumbra of the prison cell, Tran and I discussed the possibility of tracing the money Bozanski had embezzled, fantasising and scheming from our bunks, whispering into the early hours.

Tran, like me, knew that nobody would be clambering to hire him once he got out. With his hacking ability and my knowledge of the software used in business systems, we made a formidable duo. That Tran became an integral part of my planning was not surprising. Let's face it – I didn't have a great number of hackers to choose from. Without help, I had zero chance of finding out what had happened at FGI.

Business is business was one of Tran's favourite sayings; it was separate from other aspects of a relationship. We agreed on a fifty-fifty split if we were successful in our endeavours.

An hour later than scheduled, Tran walked out of the prison gates. When he got into the car, I threw him a bag containing a thousand dollars. After checking the contents, he looked at me with amazement.

I said, 'A down payment.'

I drove Tran to a small bedsitter at Crows Nest, which was within walking distance of the Sydney Harbour Bridge. It was on a busy street just off the Pacific Highway. The area had a pleasant vibe, so different to where I was living. When I asked him how he could afford the bond and rent in such a well-heeled part of the city, he said a rich uncle had organised it for him.

I told Tran about hacking into Sabrina's account, without mentioning my visit to the school. The truth would have made me appear amateurish. Maybe he'd have refused to work with me, which would have been disastrous.

We went to a coffee shop that had a room full of computer booths out the back, a short distance from his place. Tran logged on to Sabrina's account and was impressed by what I'd managed to do. From his reaction, it appeared he didn't know I'd had to access her computer directly.

Tran's serious disposition transformed into one of excitement. He had found Sabrina's bank account numbers and password in a file labelled 'Bank Details'. We joked about how lax her security was. It meant we wouldn't have to wait until she next logged on to her bank accounts to find out her password. Watching over Tran's shoulder, I relived the raw thrill of the visit to Sabrina's school, the gut-wrenching moment when I was nearly cornered.

Then came the moment that, to some extent, validated my risky venture. Tran discovered Sabrina had ten grand in savings and an overdraft limit of fifty. With Tran's magic fingers, I also got the answer to a puzzling question that had been running constantly through my mind since my conviction. What was in it for the haughty, independent Sabrina?

The answer was money. There had been three deposits of ten grand, each made into an account she rarely used. The first deposit had occurred a week after the barbeque and the last just after I was sent to prison. Tran couldn't link the transfer to Bozanski, but who else would it have been?

After logging off, Tran said the next time we logged on to Sabrina's bank accounts, he wanted to be in a position to act. The best course of action was to raid her accounts in one go, after which we wouldn't go near them again.

'So we can't be traced,' I said.

He smiled. 'To minimise the risk of being traced. Nothing's untraceable.'

Tran said he knew a banker, a friend of the family, who could be relied upon. We would need to pay him, of course. It would cost us about six grand, which to me sounded like a good deal. The man would set up a proxy company into which the funds would be transferred. Also, which apparently was not always the case, this bloke wouldn't insist on being paid upfront.

Later, I logged on to the Mr Twinkel site. He'd posted his interpretation of the footage I'd given him. He'd labelled it 'Alarm Bells'. And after watching it, alarm bells were sounding for me.

I'd changed the colour of the school uniforms, but he'd gone further – altering the style of the blazers, making them more fashionable. I'd blanked out the faces so they could not be identified. He superimposed caricatures that were Disney-like in design, yet original in that they weren't a copy of any particular Disney character. He gave each person a fancy Halloween-style hat. It gave the visuals an edge that had been absent in the footage I'd sent him.

He'd cut the material severely, turning it into a six-minute segment. He'd added music and sound effects and even an ending. The clip finished with a crowd of people chasing after a man who was running down the street.

It wasn't until I'd watched the video for a second time that I noticed something that sent my head into a spin. The initials Twinkel had superimposed on the school blazer were 'SL'.

Sabrina's surname was Lorenzo. What were the chances, I wondered, of it being a coincidence? How could Twinkel have known it was Sabrina I'd been tailing? Did he pick it up from when I was in the staffroom? I reviewed the footage I'd sent him but couldn't see where he could have gotten the information.

I asked him about it. He replied, '*That, my friend, is the Benedict Sparkel slogan. Surreptitious. Lethal.*'

I was unsure what to make of that explanation. Call it my mistake, or an incredible coincidence! But I could cut the tie with Twinkel anytime.

That was my advantage.

9

The Professor

Most afternoons, Bubba and Case could be seen sitting at the same table, sipping beer, yapping with cheer to all and sundry, placing bets, or sorting something on the phone. They seemed to have their fingers in a few pies. Case didn't just work at the markets, I discovered – he operated a legitimate business importing coffee, tea and nuts.

Case could sometimes be seen in conversation with a woman. She was in her early thirties, at a guess, and she never stayed longer than ten minutes. With a trim, toned physique, she could have passed for a personal trainer. Maybe she was.

Although they barely knew me, Bubba and Case displayed an avuncular affection, and that made me feel part of the clan. Tough nuts and villains both, they were amusing when they tried to out-boast each other, be it about sporting feats or their purported success (tongue-in-cheek) with women. They were surprisingly trusting, but then, a person like me posed no threat. Dom Bruno appeared to be a safe bet. If they got up to half of what they claimed, they deserved to be locked up and the key thrown away. But of course, their stories were delivered with a degree of poetic licence. Sometimes the banter was like a performance, an act honed over years of knowing each other.

At the Imperial they began calling me The Professor after it became known – due to me bragging about it to Tracy – that I'd lectured at Sydney University. That was quite an exaggeration, but not a complete untruth. The 'lecture' consisted of three one-hour tutorials for a group of aspiring business students. Part of a move to get people from the industry into universities.

Speaking to the group of students, I was the starry-eyed neophyte, talking myself up as a man on the way up at FGI. Just thinking about it makes me ill. How I'd love to do *that* talk again! It would be far more interesting than the claptrap delivered back then. We could discuss skimming money from accounts, sending funds offshore, insider trading, or how to set colleagues up.

Dumb Dom was always just a short step behind, mocking me from my past.

Bubba and Case refused to accept my explanation that speaking at a university once or twice does not make one a professor.

The Imperial felt like a haven from the outside world. Of course, it *was* a pub, and despite the relatively calm vibe, there were some incidents. They were contained and swiftly dealt with. The first occurred when two men, neither of them regulars, appeared to have had a few too many drinks. Their behaviour became increasingly loud and obnoxious and attracted the ire of the patrons nearby, then one of the two pulled out a cigarette, lit up and began puffing away. The barman pointed to the 'Smoke-free Zone' sign. When the fella fobbed him off with a stroke of the hand, the response was immediate. Within seconds the bartender and two other regulars pounced, snatching the cigarette from the man's mouth and frogmarching the offender off the premises. His friend wisely followed.

The second incident had something to do with a fracas that had occurred near the cinema complex. A tough-looking, heavily tattooed dude in his early twenties came strolling into the public bar. He stood over an older bald-headed man and began hurling insults.

The barman, who was in the process of serving customers, went on with what he was doing as he spoke. 'Leave it, Frankie. Don't go bringing your arguments into my pub.'

Frankie turned to the barman. 'It's not your business, squire.'

The barman stepped out from behind the bar, towering over the man, as fierce as a Highland warrior.

'You're not welcome in my pub. Get out! Now.'

The place had gone eerily quiet while Frankie considered the situation. Watching the drama unfold, a lump formed in my throat. For a moment it looked as though things might explode. The violent fug of adrenaline reminded me of my time inside.

In the end, Frankie backed down. On his way out he pointed at the baldheaded man and mumbled a few harsh-sounding words. A thinly veiled threat or the promise of revenge – I didn't hear it all, but the baldheaded man laughed it off.

Somebody suggested Frankie might return with his gang, but the barman scoffed. 'That won't happen. They're a bunch of cream puffs.'

Another man commented that if we were in America, Frankie was the type who would return with an automatic and wipe us all out. People laughed at that.

As relaxing as it might have been down at the local, I reminded myself often of the prudence of being guarded. There must have been some conjecture about my circumstances – appearing on the scene from out of the blue. My association with Bubba and Case gave me a degree of safety, but one wouldn't want to get on the wrong side of these people.

Exactly what activities patrons were involved in was not clear. You would never see people handing over money or receiving goods, but if you paid attention, you got clues as to who the wheelers and dealers were.

Case was friendly with a fella, Mario, who sometimes sat near us. On one particular occasion, a news item on television caught Mario's attention. He asked the barman to turn up the volume. There had been another massacre in America, at a rock concert. Many people had been killed and hundreds injured. There was a female politician advocating for stricter licensing of gun ownership. In reply, a representative of the National Rifle Association appeared on the screen. He claimed it was the person, not the gun.

'Did you know that gun sales in America increase after every mass shooting?' said Karl, Mario's mate.

Mario made a quip about massacres being good for business. This had everybody laughing.

'You can't blame people for wanting to protect themselves,' he said.

I took the opportunity to suck up to him. 'You're not wrong there, Mario.'

From what I'd observed, Mario dropped into the pub most afternoons. I'd seen people approach him. After that day I had Mario pencilled in as someone who might be able to get me a weapon. I didn't feel comfortable approaching him or anyone else at that stage. The big items could wait. First I needed to build some trust, to display a willingness to break the law.

I'd arrived at the pub late one afternoon. Bubba was standing near the screen, watching the last race at Caulfield. Case was deliberating over some matter at a table not far from where we usually sat.

Then Bubba was shouting, 'Go! Go, you good thing!' He threw his form guide in the air. 'Got the trifecta,' he yelled, sauntering over to the bar and bragging to the barman.

I could see their drinks were nearly empty, so I went to the bar and ordered three schooners. As well as the beers, I bought a large packet of cashew nuts and a packet of chips. Opening up both, I placed them in the middle of the table where we usually sat. A short time later Case came over and sat down, thanking me for the beer.

'Bubba got the trifecta again. Can you believe it?' I said, sounding like an insider, part of the cabal.

'It's uncanny, how he can pick 'em. Cheers,' said Case, lifting his glass and sipping his beer.

After we'd been chatting for a while, there was a pause in the conversation.

I said, 'Can I buy some weed off you, Case? Six grams or so.'

'You'll have to see Hassan when he comes in, mate.'

His response was a touch unsettling. It was common knowledge that Case dealt weed. I wasn't that stupid. Had I overstepped the mark? Maybe he had run out. Perhaps they had rules for who could sell inside the pub. Maybe I wasn't as well connected as I'd thought – didn't even have the pull to buy a lousy bit of weed.

It did, however, work out in the end. When Hassan arrived, Case spoke to him on my behalf. Hassan was an unusual, almost comical character. He had a tanned body, bleached blond hair and a surfer's build. Wearing designer jeans and a Barcelona football jersey, he was probably in his mid-thirties. He reminded me of a surfer dude I'd scored coke from for our FGI office parties – a bit overcooked. He spoke with a hint of a British accent.

'Ah... You the new dude moved in down the road?'

'Yep,' I said. 'Love it there. People have been really friendly.'

He gave me a disbelieving, raised-eyebrow response.

'Even gave me a "welcome to the neighbourhood" present.'

'You serious?!'

'Yeah, a gift from *Better Homes and Gardens*. A piece of bushrock came in through the window. Delivery bloke must have had poor eyesight or didn't realise it was shut.'

'Funny bugger, eh?' he said, with a larrikin smile and turn of the head.

When a couple came in and stood within earshot, he changed the topic, and we yapped on about European football until they moved on.

'How much you after?'

Wanting to make it worth his while, I decided to increase my order. 'Can you get me a quarter?'

He told me a figure that sounded about right, so I nodded my agreeance.

He said, 'Meet me on the corner of Cowper, across from the RSL Club, in half an hour. And stay in your car.'

A short time later I left the hotel and drove to the RSL Club. It was only five minutes away. Hassan came over to my car as soon as I pulled up. I hadn't seen him, but he must have been waiting nearby. He hopped into the passenger side and gave me a friendly hug. As he withdrew, he placed a paper bag under my seat. He patted my shoulder.

'Commercial in confidence.'

'Of course,' I replied in a sincere tone, reaching for the envelope I'd put in my top pocket.

Panic set in. The money had vanished.

'Lost something?' Hassan said, deadpan.

He waited a beat before holding up a bunch of notes and the envelope that had contained my money. Then he burst out laughing. He brushed my knee playfully and laughed.

'Correct weight.'

'Amazing,' I said, marvelling at his artifice, the way this Dickensian pickpocket had been able to lift the dosh from my pocket without me knowing.

After I thanked him for the weed, we began talking about the weekend races, but his attention was soon elsewhere. Perhaps his lift had arrived. Hassan put a finger up to his lips, shot me a cheeky grin, opened the door and was gone, disappearing just ahead of a group of boisterous schoolchildren.

I must confess to having a clandestine motive in purchasing the weed. Besides creating the impression that the newcomer could be trusted and was a bona fide member of the fraternity, I'd thought it also might prove useful in coaxing Cyclone Tracy back to my place.

Her despondence had been noticeable lately. Bubba said something about splitting from her boyfriend. I knew Tracy liked a drink and a smoke. I'd overheard enough of her conversations to know that. And she had no money for extras because she had to pay the full rent since the boyfriend moved out. She'd said as much to Bubba.

My interactions with Tracy had been brief, just a quick hello in passing. Lately I'd positioned my chair in such a way that it was possible to sight her with a slight turn of the head when she was behind the bar. Her short black dress – part of the uniform – revealed a body of splendid, youthful roundness that drew lustful eyes, including mine. She used little make-up and wore her hair tied back.

At times she would encounter customers who would pester her, but she was an expert at fobbing them off, usually with a joke and without drama. If she ever did encounter a difficult situation, all she would have to do was click her fingers and half the pub would come running to her aid.

Returning home, I'd flicked through the balcony camera footage, feeling unusually anxious, fearing Dunkley and Turner might appear together again, laughing and carrying on. I decided to test the marijuana, something I'd never done alone before.

After finishing the joint – it reeked and had me coughing violently – the strength of the weed soon became apparent. It was a different strain from the stuff I'd experienced in prison. I wondered whether it had been mixed with some other drug. It made me feel dizzy and paranoid. Then I remembered what was wrong. I'd neglected to mix it with tobacco.

My imagination ran wild. My body became the setting for an offbeat movie where benign cells (superheroes) fought the destructive abnormal cancer cells (villains) that were trying to take over. I began reflecting on the situation I found myself in. There were so few people with whom I was connected. Even my friendships at the pub were based on self-interest. Maybe my relationships with other people had always been shallow – mere ripples compared to other people's waves. With the exception of Lydia. But that relationship was past tense.

That night, the thought of being sent back to prison frightened me. Losing myself in a miasma of paranoia, my anxiety was somewhat appeased by concluding that apart from the illegal visit to Sabrina's school, I'd not done anything seriously wrong. My mind became a universe of strange, questioning thoughts. Was I no longer capable of feeling empathy for other humans? Had the cancer altered the way my brain worked? Or was it something else entirely? A cerebral transformation that began when I was betrayed by my colleagues and was seasoned by Dunkley's abuse?

I thought back to a party I had attended in my teenage years. I'd met a friend's grandmother who was suffering from Alzheimer's disease. The frayed connections in her brain meant that she had lost her inhibitions. The grey-headed woman swore and made salacious comments to all and sundry. Her daughter was beside herself, apologising furiously.

Apparently, throughout her life, the woman had been a real conservative prude, nothing like her changed self. Her licentious behaviour was something she herself would have once deemed cheap and inappropriate. Had she lost her moral compass, or just her inhibitions? I had no idea. But what I did know was that I was in the process of losing both.

I began thinking ahead to what needed to be done. My disguise had been adequate for the visit to Sabrina's school, but it hadn't been seriously tested. There was more that could be done on that front. Thanks to The American – Wayne, the security guy who worked for FGI – I had reason to be confident on that front. One Friday night at the pub, he had a group of us intrigued with his stories about changing one's appearance. Wayne had said some people were more suited to disguising themselves than others. It had a lot to do with physicality. He'd used me as an example. I didn't possess a big nose or ears, or piercing eyes that would be hard to hide. My average build was useful as well. It could be easily altered.

The next morning I woke up in a positive mood. I visited a theatre costume shop in Bankstown and bought some more items, including a brown wig, fake beard and fake moustache, all in colours as close to my natural skin and hair tones as I could get. To give myself the option of adding bulk, I purchased a false stomach and shoulder padding. Some combinations made me look like an anachronism from another time, but it wasn't hard to create versions of myself that even Lydia would struggle to recognise.

Using YouTube clips, I practised an Irish accent. Just a few sentences were all I'd need. Accents, due to the proliferation of communication, were becoming less distinct. Could the average person identify my fake accent in this globalised world? It was not as though I was trying to be an Irishman in Ireland.

My fear of Dunkley had to be dealt with, and it motivated me to do what I did next.

I was dressed in a wig, fedora (camera attached) and moustache. The false stomach had the buttons on my green sports coat stretched to the limit. My walking stick completed the disguise.

I decided to first test my disguise on my ageing neighbours, the Shapiros. When I knocked on the door, Mr Shapiro answered. Using the fake Irish accent, I introduced myself as Donal, a friend of Dom's. I asked whether he knew when Dom would be home. Mr Shapiro said he had no idea, which was welcome news. I left after wishing him a high-spirited 'Top of the morning to you.'

Pleased that the exchange had gone off without a hitch, I felt my confidence grow. Waiting until late in the day when Dunkley was lazing in his front yard, having a beer, I cautiously drove out of the townhouse and parked around the corner.

With the walking stick held firmly in my grasp, I crossed the road and approached Dunkley. Watching him like a hawk in case I had to flee, I gave him a second or two to check out the man standing before him, and then spoke.

'Sorry to bother you, sir, but you don't happen to know a Mr Clancy, who I believe lives around these parts?'

Dunkley gave me the ignorant reply I was expecting. 'No fucking idea, mate. Never heard of him.'

'Well, thanks for your help, mister,' I replied politely, before waddling off like a duck.

That was as close to Dunkley as I ever wanted to be without a serious weapon. Being able to fool the man, to look into the face of that evil predator and keep my nerve, gave me a raw, emotive thrill. Seeing him up close made me determined to push ahead with my Fuck It! List agenda. My days might be numbered, but before the cancer takes me I'll get even with the bastard, I promised myself.

10

What Were You Thinking?

I had been about to feed Cerberus when a taxi came to a halt outside Dunkley's house. What a surprise it was to see a woman emerge from the vehicle with a young boy in tow. The taxi driver unloaded two large suitcases and drove off. The woman and boy stood there, staring at Dunkley's house, until the big man himself came lumbering out to greet them a short time later. Staring at the two with his crooked smile, he took a bag in each hand – what a gentleman he was – before shuffling off and intimating to the woman that they should follow.

The woman was well-dressed, slim and attractive, her long, jet-black hair lustrous in the afternoon sun. She possessed an ageless face that was typical of many Asian women. Was she eighteen or thirty-something? The child was about four or five and of fairer complexion, but with the woman's high cheekbones. Of course, the first thought that occurred to me was that at least the kid looked nothing like Dunkley. His refined features were a species away from Dunkley's pig's-arse face.

Ten minutes later, Dunkley, the woman and the boy appeared out the front of the house. Dunkley, beer in hand, sat there gawking at the woman (where was her drink?). I put on the headphones. The listening device I was using had sufficient range to pick up the conversation, but the passing traffic meant I only heard snippets. I did learn that the woman's name was Suzi. The boy's name was Dylan. He was her son. Dylan didn't venture far from his mother's side.

What was Suzi's situation? There seemed to be more going on than just a lady on a holiday renting a room. Had Dunkley purchased an Asian wife? Maybe Suzi was from a place where a single mum with a kid was doomed to poverty and public disgrace. But this woman had no idea what she and her son were in for. If she knew Dunkley like I did, she'd know that sooner or later, his true nature would come to the fore and his base instincts would run rampant.

As the night unfolded, the situation became more palatable. The blinds were pulled up in the second bedroom. This was one of the few places where the living area faced my balcony and where it was possible to get a glimpse inside Dunkley's house. Zooming in with the camera, I was pleased to see two single beds with a suitcase on each.

From what I'd managed to observe that first night, Dunkley made no attempt to make a move on Suzi. But there was no getting around the fact that *the woman and kid were in danger*. My dilemma was whether to ignore the situation or attempt to save them from a date with the devil incarnate.

The next day Dunkley drove off to work early, and Suzi did her tai chi routine in the backyard. The boy must have been still asleep. Suzi had just gone back inside when I received the news I'd been waiting for.

Tran was ready to move on Sabrina's bank account.

My job was to ensure Sabrina was following her usual routine. Our plans would have to be postponed if she was out of town. The bank would be more than suspicious if Sabrina used her bankcard in Melbourne one minute and then did a massive transfer in Sydney the next.

Driving across to the Eastern Suburbs, I could barely keep the green-eyed monster at bay. How I'd react if Lydia had again stayed the night was uncertain. Before I knew of Sabrina's treacherous behaviour in setting me up, it used to annoy me that she would never accept me into her precious circle, yet for Bozanski she would click her heels and go to the ends of the earth to impress.

The first time Bozanski had lured Sabrina onto his yacht, he was proud as punch the next day, parading around the place like the fisherman who had landed the big one. If only Sabrina could have heard the all-conquering sybarite entertaining the cloying Chaffer and whoever else wanted to listen. Was it a one-off? Not according to Bozanski. I wondered whether Sabrina had slept with him since Lydia appeared on the scene.

After waiting for half an hour, I was pleased to see Sabrina come out of her unit alone. Maybe Lydia was beginning to tire of her. Probably just wishful thinking. Sabrina appeared dressed for work, but it was prudent to follow her to the train station before giving Tran the all-clear.

With her marble-like complexion and flashy navy-blue outfit, Sabrina was the epitome of fashion as she strode along the pavement. She caught me by surprise when she stopped at the Café De Beaumont and sat down at an outside table, where an older grey-headed woman was already seated. I noticed that Sabrina was wearing a silver necklace bearing a large cross. The Queen of the Western Buddhas was masquerading as Saint Sabrina! But who was I to point the finger? When I was inside, I often attended the weekly service at the prison chapel. Not to forget my pathetic attempts pleading for intervention from the big boss up in the sky, during those long nights trapped in the cell with Dunkley.

Tran had a friend he called Miss Saigon – there was a joke connected with the name the two shared. From listening to them communicate over the phone, I got the impression they'd known each other for some time. Tran had managed to alter Sabrina's contact details and hack the answers to her security questions. He directed the mandatory phone call from the bank to Miss Saigon, who pretended she was Sabrina. Taking fifty grand from her main account and thirty grand from the other, Tran pulled off the raid in one fell swoop from a busy internet café on the north side of the harbour. Miss Saigon was paid two thousand dollars for her part in the swindle.

Tran said it would take a few days to turn the funds into cash. During that time we would not contact each other. When it was all cool, he would send me a text and we would meet up. My orders were to erase everything from my home computer concerning Sabrina's account and have nothing further to do with her.

I went onto my computer to do as Tran had asked. When I clicked on the link, it went through to Sabrina's school account. Before me were Sabrina's reports, with the same stunning face that I'd seen on her school computer staring back at me.

I discovered what the two boys who had come into the English staffroom had been laughing about. They had added their own comments to the girl's report.

Charlotte is a real spunk. She's hot and I'd love to hook up with her. My mate Rollo reckons she's as dumb as. Be lucky to spell her own name proparly.

Either the boys were lousy at spelling or they had a good sense of humour. They did know Charlotte's capabilities. Surely Rollo wasn't one of their actual names. Most probably it was the name of another student they didn't like.

Clicking on Charlotte's file, I found more information. It was clear she was often rude to her teachers and had even been suspended for insolent behaviour. From another comment, it seemed Charlotte had been responsible for harassing a fellow student to the extent that the girl had left the school. Charlotte's father, a Doctor Longworth, had written a derogatory letter to the principal recently, claiming Charlotte's teachers were inept and couldn't control the class. According to Daddy, Charlotte's education was suffering because of this. He had even threatened to take his complaint to the minister.

Seeing that the class reports were all signed and labelled 'Ready to send', I couldn't help myself. I erased all the previous comments and replaced them with my own. I must admit to getting a bit carried away. I had to add an extra page to the report.

Charlotte's reworked comments read; *Charlotte is a wilful young lady with limited ability. Put simply, you cannot make a silk purse out of a sow's ear. Teachers may be part of a circus, but we are not magicians, and with Charlotte it would take some magic. In a nutshell, Charlotte possesses stunning looks but not the smarts. This can happen with genetics – the wrong sperm wins the race.*

Below average is okay. Some people in my own department are below average. It might help to think of it like this: if we didn't have below average, we couldn't have above average. Charlotte may be below average, but she allows others to shine. Charlotte is an important cog in the wheel (some might say Charlotte clogs the wheel).

With regard to her vocational prospects, here I can be most positive. Charlotte's body is an asset that should not be undervalued. Unfortunately, due to the number of dance schools all over town these days, strippers are a dime a dozen. Best prospects are at the high end of the escort service industry.

May I suggest a week or two of work experience to find out whether Charlotte is suited to the vocation? Charlotte can pick up the appropriate forms from Mr Bolton, the careers teacher. After her initial training – I'm willing to help with that – a permanent position with a prestigious agency is not out of the question.

So, hang on in there, Charlotte. There is more to life than hitting the books and being a nerd.

You'll have to run this by Charlotte's science teacher Mrs Barnes first, but Charlotte might also try kissing frogs down at the swamp. She may not find her prince, but the activity will count towards her (yet to be submitted) Environmental Science assignment.

Finally, Charlotte, don't despair. Your time in the sun will come. Speaking personally, it wasn't until I had a full-on lesbian relationship and fucked around a bit that I found my true self.

I pressed send and then erased all of Sabrina's data from my computer.

11

Desire

I'd just driven into the car park. In the grey crepuscular light, I saw Cyclone Tracy arriving for work at the back of the Imperial. She moved speedily with a sprightly young woman's gait, her chestnut-coloured hair dancing tantalisingly around her shoulders. What a stroke of luck to have seen free-flowing Tracy before she had tied back her hair in a bun for work

It was the fourth Sunday of the month, the last night of her work cycle, after which she'd be rostered off for two days. It was usual for me to leave at least a small tip. Tonight my generosity knew no bounds. As did the need to impress. I became fascinated by Tracy's mannerisms, charmed by her light-brown eyes that sparkled like jewels whenever she engaged in banter.

Tracy missed her favourite show, *Masters of the Cuisine*, when she worked her usual shift. I'd heard her tell that to Bubba's mate, Tosh. I'd familiarised myself with the content of the cooking show and awaited the opportunity to approach Tracy when she was alone at the bar. While she was pouring my drinks, I mentioned *Masters of the Cuisine* and she took the bait. Soon we were discussing the merits of the various contestants and the upcoming challenge. Then I sprung it on her – emboldened by the three beers I'd consumed, I invited her to my place to watch the show.

'I'll cook,' I said, 'and we can have a few bongs, if you like.'

I waited in hope, but there was no response from Tracy. Had my attempt to sound cool made me seem like an idiot? Another customer had come to the bar and Tracy moved on to serve him. As I slowly picked up my drinks, my worry was that as well as making a fool of myself, I'd pissed her off.

In for a penny, in for a pound, I decided. While she was pouring a beer and within earshot I said, 'Hey, and Tracy, you can meet my flatmates, Cerb and Erus.'

She gave me a strange look. 'Who in the hell are Cerb and Erus?'

'My two-headed snake, Cerberus.'

Tracy threw me a dirty look. 'Are you taking the mickey?'

'Seriously. I'm not joking.'

'What…? You have a pet snake?'

'Yes, I do.'

'With two heads?!'

I nodded. An amused expression appeared on her face. At least she hadn't been offended.

Later that evening, while I was on my way back from the toilet, Tracy came up to me.

'Just TV and a smoke?'

'Of course!' I replied, absolutely delighted. 'If you want, I can pick you up.'

'No, no,' she said. 'I'll find my own way.'

I discreetly slipped her a beer coaster with my address. When Tracy looked at it, she raised her eyebrows.

'What's up?' I asked. 'The area's not that bad. Is it?'

'No, no, it's not that. I know someone who lives over that way, that's all.'

Tracy had said five o'clock. When the clock struck five-twenty and she hadn't arrived, I thought she'd reassessed the situation and decided not to come. But just moments later Tracy appeared on the monitor, jumping out of a Honda Accord. I ushered her in, unable to hide my pleasure at having her inside my home.

When I asked her if she had been dropped off by a friend, Tracy said she'd used Uber. She made a comment about how bare the place was as she walked through to the living room. I offered her a drink.

'You don't have any vodka, do you?'

'Sorry, I don't. I've only got beer and wine. But just hang on a second. I've got an idea.'

I picked up my phone and searched for a local business that delivered alcohol.

'What vodka do you like, Tracy? What's your favourite?' I asked as I waited for somebody to pick up.

'Smirnoff,' she replied, with a quizzical turn of the head.

The lady who took the order said it would be delivered within the hour. I gave out my details and thanked her, saying I'd tip the delivery driver a dollar for every minute they arrived early.

Tracy cottoned on. 'You are actually paying someone to drop it off.'

'Yep.'

'I'll walk down the street and get it if you like. Save you the money.'

I'd pulled the same stunt to impress Lydia when she was having doubts. That time it had been a spectacular Hunter Valley red she'd raved about.

It hadn't worked then, and clearly wasn't working now. The feeling I got from Tracy was that she thought I was an idiot for wasting money. She would have to work a lot of hours to earn what I'd just spent.

'It's good for the economy's health. To keep the money circulating,' I offered as justification.

Tracy's eyes did a sweep of the room, landing on the bong and the bowl on the coffee table.

'Go for it,' I said.

She sat down and polished off a cone or two, then took off her shoes and tucked her feet up snugly on the sofa. Tracy became talkative after the smoke, telling me funny stories about some of the people who drank at the Imperial. Then she put me on the spot, wanting to know how I happened to have a coaster with my address on it to give her when I invited her over. Was I that certain she would say yes?

I replied that it was a matter of being prepared. 'In case you said yes.'

'You don't go around giving them out to every woman you meet?'

'No, no, of course not.'

The alcohol arrived twenty minutes later, and when I tipped the young fella forty dollars, Tracy shook her head in disbelief.

After we'd had another drink, Tracy wanted to see Cerberus, so we went upstairs. When she saw the habitat I'd created, she was impressed. Her eyes darted around the room like Alice in Wonderland as she stared open-mouthed at the array of plants and insects. I had been worried that she might find it a bit odd. But she was intrigued and not in the least afraid of Cerberus, who was curled around a branch about a metre from the ground.

'The snake sure looks freaky. Why do you call him Cerberus?'

Naming it Cerberus had been Lydia's idea. I had wanted to name it

Ronnie-and-Reggie, after the Kray twins, a pair of infamous English criminals.

'Cerberus is the multi-headed guard dog in Greek mythology.'

'But it's not a dog.'

'Aren't you the clever one?'

'Please don't make fun of me.' She froze momentarily. An unpleasant memory, perhaps.

'Sorry.'

Tracy continued with the conversation as though my offensive comment hadn't been made. 'You've got beetles, grasshoppers – even frogs!'

I resisted the temptation to make a lame joke about her having a biology degree. 'Yeah, I want Cerberus to have as normal a life as possible.'

'Are you being funny? A normal life. For a snake with two heads! Can I hold him?'

Most people wouldn't go near the snake. After getting Tracy to sit still, I placed Cerberus on her knee. He crawled over her legs and across to me, eventually settling on my shoulders. While sitting there, I noticed a gap in the corner where the jungle met the floor. Cerberus must have tried to get through. It was a potential escape route that would have to be fixed. For the moment, I jammed a block of wood into the space. He wouldn't go far, but he'd terrify the neighbours.

Eventually Tracy's curiosity was sated. We returned downstairs.

'You like vegetable curry and yoghurt?' I asked.

'Is that what I could smell?'

'Yep. I'll just have to warm up the rice.'

'Smells delish! Need some help?'

I said, 'Your night to relax.'

She enjoyed the meal and was generous in her praise. She wanted to know how I'd made it. I named the main spices that were in the vegetable korma but didn't tell her they'd come as a paste in a jar.

Once, I'd cooked up a similar curry for Lydia's bunch of Western Buddhas. Sabrina let everyone know I hadn't mixed the spices from scratch. She even named the brand of curry paste I'd used. One of the women, whose name I can't recall, asked how far each of the ingredients had travelled from the farm to the plate. That type of analysis was trendy in the city at the time. My reply didn't endear me to the woman or get any laughs, but it made me feel good. I told her I had no idea, but that next time I'd ask the vegetables and maybe get them to sign some kind of indemnity to show they had no objection to being used in the dish.

Chilled-out Tracy was a different person to the efficient work-mode Tracy, who raced around the place like the proverbial blue-arsed fly when on duty at the pub. Different, though still really likeable.

Tracy commented on the number of screens and computer equipment in the house. I told her that sometimes I did work for a detective agency, tracking down cybercriminals.

'What do you do when you find them?'

'Sometimes I tail them,' I replied.

'Like a spy.'

'No. I'm not a spy. Look at me. Do I look like the James Bond type?'

She paused for a second. 'It's hard to know when you're bullshitting.'

We talked about the Imperial again. I praised her ability to work so efficiently while at the same time chatting to the patrons. She said she enjoyed the social aspect of the job. But the pay was lousy. One of her teachers from school had told her she had the potential to achieve academically – that she was capable of attending university. She looked at me, wanting my opinion.

'I'm sure you are. It's obvious just from being around you that you're smart.'

She told me stories about the good old days, as she called them – before she was forced to get her own place and fend for herself. Her parents had split and her mother ended up with a new partner. She didn't get on with her stepfather and decided to move out.

When, in a moment of reciprocated honesty, I told her about doing time, she didn't seem surprised. Knowing how news travelled down the pub, perhaps she already knew. I gave her the short version and she digested the information without comment.

We decided to watch the cooking show, *Masters of the Cuisine*. Soon we were laughing and paying out on the contenders like we were old mates. I was grateful to get the opportunity to show off.

'I can't believe Christina and Zoe,' I said. 'Aren't they both real bitches, the way they treat each other? Imagine saying that about your family on television. It's amazing what people will do for attention these days.'

I poured more drinks and Tracy had another bong.

If she keeps it up, I thought, *she'll finish off my supply before the night's end.* I began calling her Trace, and she didn't seem to mind.

Pushing my luck, I told her she had a gorgeous body – it wasn't a lie. When she didn't respond I felt like a deviant. She was nineteen, seven years younger than me.

'Sorry, I shouldn't have said that.'

'No... It's okay,' she said, blushing a little, and I realised I'd got it wrong. Tracy wasn't used to being praised. She stared at me intensely, as though weighing up the pros and cons of the situation. Then she surprised me by asking the strangest question.

'Would you jump in the water to save me if I was drowning?'

'How deep is it?'

'Fucking deep. Just answer.'

'Of course I would,' I replied, wondering whether she'd noticed my slightly uncertain tone.

'What if there was a shark circling?'

'What type of shark?'

'You can't see it clearly enough to tell.'

'Tracy, who knows for certain how I might react in that situation? But I would definitely attempt to save you. How big was the shark again?'

'Seriously, Dom.'

'Trace, the thought of you being in distress unsettles me. I couldn't live with myself if I didn't jump in.'

Her facial expression hadn't changed much throughout the dialogue. She got to her feet and moved closer to where I was seated, brushing up against my knee. My initial reaction was to sit more upright on the lounge.

She spoke in a solemn tone, as though trying to keep a painful experience at bay. 'This is just a one-off, okay?'

'A one-off,' I replied, slow to grasp what she meant.

She leant forward and kissed me on the lips briefly before pulling away.

'Have you got any music?' Tracy asked.

'Music. Sure… What do you like?'

Tracy named some artists and bands, most of whom I'd never heard of. We settled on Radiohead.

Tracy had come prepared. She had a packet of condoms, which she pulled from her bag and wanted me to use. They were peculiar. A type that I would not think to purchase. They had a roughened exterior that she must have found particularly pleasurable.

It had been well over a year since I'd slept with a woman, and that had been Lydia. Unlike Lydia, Tracy didn't talk during lovemaking. And she closed her eyes, something Lydia never did. Perhaps she was trying to imagine she was with somebody else.

We sat around chatting afterwards. She was comfortable with her body – nudity didn't bother her in the slightest.

'Do you like my tattoo?'

She had an amazing tattoo. An orange-and-green fern that began under her right breast and twisted and turned, meandering down and around her hip, eventually coming to an end on her left thigh.

'It's so beautifully done,' I said. 'A real work of art. It suits you.'

She made a matter-of-fact comment about the feminine shape of my thighs before asking whether I'd been with other partners lately. The topic didn't last long. I later thought about why she'd asked such a question, and realised she probably wanted to know whether there was a risk of picking up a sexually transmitted disease.

We dressed and had a cup of tea. Tracy asked me about the Whiteley print hanging near the wardrobe that Lydia had given me. I told her she would have made an excellent model for an artist, and I meant it. She was chuffed.

'You're kidding me. You really think so?'

'Sure, look at you. Young, sensual, alluring.'

'I lucked out in the breasts department,' she said.

'Small but sexy,' I said.

It was getting late. I told her she could stay for the night, but she wanted to go home. Too pissed to drive, I offered to pay for a taxi. Initially she refused, but in the end she took a fifty.

While we were waiting for the taxi, Tracy asked me about university. Due to my previous boasts, she thought I had some pull.

'Perhaps you know people there who might be able to help me get a job?'

She had no idea of my isolation and disassociation. I thought of Tran and wondered whether he could access and manipulate the university records and create a job for her on the payroll. He probably could, but he was already taking enough risks. Still, there was no point in disappointing Tracy.

'Sure... I'll do what I can.'

I questioned whether Tracy would have slept with my pre-prison self, who had arms like spaghetti. Then I imagined the unimaginable. In the afterglow of the night with Tracy, I wondered if this could be the end of my obsession with Lydia.

Later that night, after Tracy had left, the ghouls of the past visited me again. Dunkley and Turner, memories jabbing like darts in the dark. Soon it was intense – the acrid smells, the shower block. In a split second I was back there.

Dunkley was supposed to be at the gym, pumping iron. I was aware of the need to hurry. But as soon as I turned on the tap, warning signs appeared – the shower block was suddenly empty, as vacant as a nuclear test site.

He pounced from nowhere and soon had me on the ground, face down. Spit shooting out of his mouth like semen, the hormonal stench fused with the shower cleanser. Then Turner appeared.

'Hold him,' he said, and Dunkley gave me the look – *move and I'll smash you.*

At least Turner used a condom. Perhaps he thought I was diseased.

Sweating and distraught as I was from the flashback of horrid thoughts, part of me was still emboldened from the sex with Tracy. Something snapped inside me. What if the cancer took me early and Dunkley got off scot-free? Unable to think clearly, breaking all my own rules, I picked up a knife from the kitchen and, with it concealed in my back pocket, walked out of my townhouse – without a disguise. I crossed the road and marched towards Dunkley's place.

Reaching his front gate, I stood there glaring at his house for a few seconds before coming to my senses. As I returned home, part of me felt like a hero for having the courage to do what I did. But there was also a sense of foolhardiness – I'd lost control and engaged in such a stupid, impetuous act. There was no point in attaining revenge if it landed me back in prison.

Still shaken, I drank what was left of the vodka. As the alcohol kicked in, my thoughts turned to the cancer and what little time I had left. If only I could meet Lydia for the first time now, I wouldn't argue with her or put her down in a condescending way by poking fun at her beliefs. Lydia's concoction of beliefs was as good as any on offer from the traditional or the smorgasbord of new age offshoots.

Earlier, I'd wondered whether my obsession with Lydia was at an end. But at that moment it was stronger than ever. Somnolent, but with my mind racing, it was impossible to sleep.

I logged on to the Mr Twinkel site.

Mr Twinkel is dressed in a lab coat. There is a drawing of two mice and two men. The title reads 'Of Mice and Men'. One man and one mouse are labelled 'aggressive' (brain highlighted in red) while the other man and mouse are labelled 'meek' (brain highlighted in pink).

Mr Twinkel points to the drawings.

'The question is – did he reach a tipping point, or was he always destined for the tip? Was it simply a bad seed? Now, I'm no frigging Siggy Freud, but were the signs always there? Did it start at school, when he punched out another student or pushed them down the stairs on the way to class? The thrill of getting even. Did the sadistic trait surface even earlier – squashing ants in the backyard with a tennis ball at age seven? Had he been impersonating a meek mouse, keeping a lid on the atavistic urge, biding time until the opportunity arose for the sly gutter rat to emerge?

'Well, at this point it's all conjecture, because this bloke is all talk and no action. Promising start and all that, but the question is, will this Benedict Sparkel turn out to be a dud?'

That Twinkel was goading, pushing, trying to get me to act was annoying, but something else had my attention. Two of the scenarios he'd mentioned were true. I'd been in fights at school. My father and I had moved often when I was an adolescent, and as the new kid on the block I had to stand up for myself or be stood on.

Of course, a boy getting into a fight at school and feeling elated after winning was not unusual. But I'd also killed ants with a tennis ball in the backyard as a kid. And how could Twinkel possibly know that?

Maybe I'd told Lydia. I couldn't remember ever telling Tran. It wasn't the sort of thing I'd ever talked about with Chaffer. Again, though, Twinkel was probably guessing, because he was wrong on number three – I'd never pushed a fellow student down a stairwell.

12

Old Mates

Bozanski came to visit me once while I was in prison. Desolate and with my life in tatters, in a comatose state and incapable of thinking about anything other than my dire situation, at the time it was humbling to get a visit from anyone, let alone Bozanski, my esteemed ex-boss. Of course, that was before Bozanski's role in setting me up became apparent.

'Dom, you poor bastard. I can only imagine how bad you must feel.'

That should have been enough to set the alarm bells ringing. Because if you knew Bozo, you knew he didn't give a toss about how anyone felt. He might thank you. He might praise you. But he never gave a fuck about you.

I was facing the possibility of around six years behind bars. And what did Bozo want to talk about? He wanted to discuss prison security and the cell locking mechanisms. Dumb Dom even attempted to satisfy his curiosity. Can you believe it?

Back then I'd suspected it was somebody from senior management who'd set me up. With Bozanski out of the office, it was the logical explanation. When Bozanski visited me in prison I'd asked him about this. He'd slammed the reputation of Josh Harding, an FGI director, insinuating the man was under investigation. Of course, no charges were forthcoming. Another Bozanski cock-and-bull manipulation, fabricated to muddy the waters and keep himself well out of the picture. He went on to make some inane prediction about an upcoming football match of which I had no knowledge or interest, before tapping his fingers on the table, performing his version of Morse code to signal that the visit was coming to an end.

'We'll have a cold one when you get out, Dom,' he said, calling for the warden.

I can still recall my insipid reply.

'Yeah, sure, Adrian. I'd like that.'

How that visit later riled me! When the truth became apparent, his fake empathy and attempt to shift the blame intensified my hate for the man. His cheery disposition and talk of having a drink when I was released had exacerbated the dread that shrouded me at the time. Of course Bozo had been feeling pleased with himself. And relieved. Relieved that I still had no idea. They were the Dark Ages, stuck with Dunkley, fighting the demons.

After my release, I tried to get through to Bozanski on several occasions. He was always too busy. Eventually he picked up after I lied to his secretary, pretending to be a client. I told him there was a tax matter that I'd like to discuss with him in private. I suggested a bar we used to frequent. He suggested the Archibald Fountain in Hyde Park. The alcoholic arse wouldn't even have a drink with me.

On my way to meet Bozanski, the hubs of the city were humming. Some people were motoring, others cycling, most perambulating. The mood was vibrant. And why not?! It was Friday, and the end of the working week was nigh – the city was switching to party mode.

'Well, I'm walking along, singing a song, bye-bye Bozo…' The silly tune wouldn't leave my head. People kept away from me as though I might be unstable.

Walking up the large sandstone steps that led into the park, through the manicured gardens and massive fig trees and past the statues of famous inland explorers, I came across a starry-eyed couple having lunch on the grass. Lovers, unaware of my prying eyes, their desire and passion palpable.

We were once like them, Lydia and me – lovers sharing lovers' special moments. We would meet not far from here, under a fig tree. Was it still there, or had it also died a merciless death, rotting at the roots? I didn't want to know.

We would sit and chat, mostly small talk, laughing occasionally over some silly matter as we drank hot coffee and shared a sandwich or a falafel wrap. People passing by would sneak a look at Romeo and Juliet. Men would be envious – *how lucky is he?* I would smile, proud as punch.

Bozanski's eagle eye spotted me first. It probably said something about my state of mind, but with his conservative outfit and brooding demeanour, he looked more like a KGB assassin than a business executive.

What a treat it was, to be greeted by that award-winning smile – even if it was an abridged version. Out came the hand, which was noticeably larger than mine, then the prolonged rugby footballer's handshake, a display of his strength and manhood. I resisted the urge to rip his thumb away with my other hand. Eventually I escaped his grasp, my fingers and ego somewhat crushed. Round one to Bozo.

I could smell alcohol on his breath. He'd had a nip or two of something. Dutch courage, or perhaps his usual intake with lunch. We engaged in polite conversation for a while, but it didn't take long for Bozanski's banter to get to me.

'Hey, Dom. I heard you're living out the Western Suburbs these days.'

From his derogatory tone, it was clearly meant as a put-down. Then it occurred to me that he knew where I lived.

'Yeah, well, there are opportunities out that way. In the city, for me, fucking zilch. And it's all I could afford… after what happened.'

'Aww, come on, Dom.'

I could barely contain my bitterness. 'It drained me financially. Left me penniless.'

He made some positive comment about my appearance and proceeded to rave on about his latest fishing escapades in the waters around Cairns. With all I'd been through, did the fucker think I cared about where he went for his holidays? When I failed to respond with enthusiasm – he was not used to his charm being ineffective – he attempted to move things along.

'What did you want to ask me – something about tax, you said?'

'Yeah, I need my tax certificates for the past two years. Can you fix that up?'

'Is that all? Olivia could've done that. I'll get her onto it. Still the same email address?'

'No. I'll send my new one through. Thought it best to make a fresh start after prison.'

My sarcastic tone was lost on Bozo. I told him I was extremely disappointed that my old buddy Chaffer wouldn't see me. Bozanski made a cutting remark about Chaffer's ability to do his job, before fobbing me off with the excuse that they were all under the pump at present. 'It's high time I got back myself,' he said.

It was time to up the ante.

'Any more news on Josh Harding?'

He became apprehensive. 'What are you talking about, Dom?'

'Remember when you visited me in prison? You told me you suspected Josh Harding had set me up. You said he was being investigated.'

'Now, that's not exactly what I said.'

Again he was playing me for a fool. Steaming with anger, my courage grew.

'I think I know who set me up.'

His gaze was steadfast, mine brazen.

'Who?'

'Who? I'll give you a clue. Rhymes with "boo"... *YOU, you fucking arsehole.*'

The hint of a nervous smile appeared before it transformed into a harsh firming of the upper lip.

'You are fucking kidding me, right?' He shaped his hand like a pistol. 'You repeat that again, with or without a witness, and I'll see to it that you get locked up for good. You hear what I'm saying, Bruno?'

What I did next was totally unplanned. I glanced over his shoulder and smiled, as though somebody was there. He reacted as I'd hoped, turning to see what had my attention. I stepped forward, crouched low and drove him with my shoulder, using enough force so he lost his balance and stumbled into the fountain.

'An old schoolyard trick, Bozanski. Never turn your back on the class clown.'

'You bastard,' he yelled, looking around to see if anyone had witnessed the incident.

Bozo slipped on the algae as he tried to regain his footing. What a sight he was, knee-deep in water, the bronze figures of Greek mythology seemingly mocking him from behind.

'The bloke's pissed,' I announced in a loud voice, laughing at him from a safe distance.

'I'll get you for this,' called Bozanski.

People were watching on with amusement – *is this street theatre?* Somebody clapped as Bozo stepped from the fountain, drenched, nostrils flared and fuming.

'Oh no,' I called. 'His London tweeds are sopping wet and his Italian shoes are covered in slime.'

He braced himself, as though he were about to give chase.

'Come on,' I teased, goading him, realising that if he did chase me he would look even more ridiculous.

Unable to contain my laughter, I took off like the wind. It was a trivial act, and some might say cowardly, but I knew he would be infuriated for days. And a blow had been struck. Seeing and hearing the arrogant Bozanski in person fuelled my appetite for revenge. Furthermore, I had recorded it all with a pinhole camera that was attached to my baseball cap. He might not have said anything incriminating but watching a drenched Bozanski scrambling to find his footing in the fountain would provide hours of enjoyment.

In prison I'd thought up a plan to steal his DNA and prints and place them at the scene of a serious crime. In the real world, my chances of pulling off something that elaborate were nil.

My day was far from finished. After having lunch at a restaurant near Hyde Park, I made my way along Elizabeth Street to a café from where I could see everybody who came in and out of the FGI building.

Where had Bozanski gone after the bath in the fountain? Definitely not back to the office. He wouldn't have wanted to explain why he was in such a dishevelled state.

What if he came into the café? He could be an intuitive bastard. In my present mood, I'd hit him up for that drink he'd promised when he visited me inside. Bozanski would be irate, but he wouldn't risk a confrontation in public. And being Friday, he wouldn't be putting in a full day. Neither would Chaffer. And Chaffer was the one I wanted to see next.

After spending an hour sitting studying the form for next Saturday's races, I saw the pimple-faced bastard Chaffer emerge from the building. With him was Wayne, the American whose advice on disguise had helped me recently. Wayne was one of few decent people I'd met at FGI. Again, I thought of the fact that out of all my colleagues, he was the only person who would give me a positive reference after I'd been charged with embezzlement. But what was he doing with Chaffer? Chaffer did need protection, but only I knew that. I just hoped Wayne wasn't going for a drink with him, because that would make my task difficult. When Wayne hopped into the passenger seat of a limo that pulled into a no-parking zone and the car drove off, my fears were allayed.

I followed Chaffer along Phillip Street towards the harbour.

He made his way to Carney's. The bar was a popular after-work destination. Chaffer was a habitual man, and this was usual for a Friday. He would most likely stay for an hour or two before making his way to the ferry terminal. He owned a two-bedroom unit near Manly Beach. Of course, Chaffer would be hoping a miracle would happen and he would pick up. A quickie in a hotel room nearby to hail the end of the working week. As far as I knew, this had never happened, but there was always the possibility that one day some susceptible young woman might create history and fall for Chaffer's droll rubbish.

Chaffer was not the type to impress at first sight – or second, for that matter. In fact, he was best left unsighted. But somebody tolerated him because he did have a wife. A woman few people had met – I'd not set eyes on her. Chaffer had never brought her along to FGI functions (smarter than me in that regard), and I'd never been to his place.

Camouflaged by trees and greenery, I watched Chaffer from the shadows of the high-rises. I was sitting in the small square opposite Carney's. Horns blasted intermittently. The grinding gears of buses could be heard as they navigated the steep descent to Circular Quay. As the buses slowed at the bottom of the hill, they were swarmed upon by office workers, determined to get a seat for the slow crawl out of the city. In my hand was the obligatory tabloid paper, which could be perused to kill time or used to hide behind.

Chaffer bought a schooner of beer and stood at a bench near the bar, where a group of men and women had congregated. It was noticeable just how much younger the women were in comparison to the men. Chaffer's line of conversation was easy enough to imagine. Some form of boasting about how important his job was at FGI – he was well versed in the art of Bozo bullshit. After the self-aggrandisement, he would pay the lady a sincere compliment. Of course, throughout his charade, he would give the impression he was single.

The bar became more crowded, so I moved in closer to the action. There I found a nifty hideaway behind the ornamental beer kegs.

Thereafter followed a series of events that nearly spoilt my plans.

Chaffer stepped outside with a mate to have a cigarette – another step or two and he would have walked straight into me. The two began discussing tactics. They decided they were going after the wrong girls, and that was why they were getting nowhere. They should have been targeting the bank mob sitting near the pokies. Chaffer told his mate he knew one of the bank girls. It made me laugh. *Have a listen to yourselves,* I wanted to shout. They sounded like high school students attending their first dance.

Then came the shock of my life.

'Dom,' called a voice from behind.

It was a woman's voice. Had I been spotted by someone from FGI? She repeated my name. If I turned to face her, Chaffer might see me.

I chanced a glance and was greeted by a smiling, inquisitive face. Her kind, wistful eyes were captivating. But who was this woman? She didn't belong with this crowd. In a red hat and long, loose-fitting dress, her attire was in stark contrast to the short skirts, tight tops and extensive make-up of the office brigade. Attached to her lapel was an anti-coal-mining badge. She needed to be warned. You could get strung up in this part of town, wearing a badge like that.

'You don't recognise me. It's Matilda. Lydia's friend.'

Talk about persistent. Head down, my face still half hidden by the newspaper, I pretended I knew who she was. 'Oh, of course. Matilda.'

The woman was partly amused but becoming increasingly pissed off. What an idiot I must have appeared to be. She was about to leave, so I chanced a glance in Chaffer's direction. He was making his way back inside.

I apologised profusely, inviting the woman to sit down. I told her the truth – there had been someone standing nearby I just had to avoid. Then I remembered who Matilda was. She and Lydia had been close friends at high school.

When I asked her what she was doing in town, Matilda said she worked as an environmental scientist and was on her way to the train station after meeting with some state government agency. She asked about Lydia. This gave me the opportunity to prattle on, thus avoiding having to talk about my own pathetic situation. She would probably have known about my court case. It had been given wide coverage by the major news outlets. Chances were that that was why she recognised me.

Before she left, I asked if we could exchange details. She agreed – my earlier peculiar behaviour mustn't have fazed her. Perhaps she wanted to reconnect with Lydia.

Returning my attention to the bar, I spotted Chaffer in conversation with a young, attractive, curlyheaded lady. The stars must have been aligned because the woman seemed to be reacting positively. She would no doubt tire of his monologue but after my close encounter, it was time to hurry things along.

I snuck into the bar and ordered a beer for Chaffer and a white wine for his companion. I paid the leggy barmaid handsomely to deliver my message, which was scribbled on a cardboard coaster.

I looked on from outside as the drinks and accompanying message were delivered. At first Chaffer smiled and held up his glass to somebody across the other side of the room, thinking the drinks had come from him. Then he read the note.

What a pretty young belle, Chaffer. Don't forget to tell your lovely wife.

His head went up like a periscope, searching near and far for the author. The trick worked – it wasn't long before he left the hotel and was on the move.

It was easy enough for me to remain unsighted, to blend in with the commuters as they streamed towards the ferry terminals, returning to their seaside havens. The pitter-patter of high-heeled shoes hammered the pavement as someone made a desperate last-minute dash.

After Chaffer had gone through into the holding bay, I pulled out my Opal card and followed. The ferry was due in eight minutes, leaving plenty of time for me to speak my mind. The cost of the trip was cheap, really, for ensuring a captive audience.

To catch him off guard, the encounter needed to seem completely accidental. Walking past him, I hesitated before backtracking.

'Chaffer... Hey there, old buddy! Fancy seeing you.'

It took him a moment to recognise me, and when he did, he didn't look at all pleased. I gave him a disarming hug and he had no idea how to respond.

'Thought you had moved,' he said, an anxious quiver betraying his uneasiness.

'Been having a drink with an old friend from FGI. Remember Hassan?'

He pulled back, his stance rigid. Hassan had worked in accounts. He'd left FGI just after I'd been arrested. We both knew he had been used as a scapegoat and put through the ringer by Bozanski.

'Oh really, Hassan!' he replied. 'He's moved across to Boone and Isaacs.'

'Moved across? More like pushed out, wouldn't you say?'

Chaffer was steadfast. 'He left us on amicable terms.'

I was struck by his use of that magic word, *us* – further proof of what a loyal Bozanski-ite he had become.

'Yeah, well, he's doing well at Boone and Isaacs. There might be a job there for me,' I said confidently.

He laughed fleetingly, before pulling back. Everybody knew Dominic Bruno was unemployable in finance.

What I said next would come back to haunt me.

'You think that's funny, Chaffer? Well, here's something even funnier. Hassan knows my signature was falsified, and get this... He has documents that will prove it wasn't me who swindled funds from FGI.'

Chaffer bit his lower lip. 'Not all that shit again, Bruno.'

'Chaffer, you can't fool me. What did they pay you for your part in it all?'

'Back off, Bruno.'

'Here's the deal. I want twenty grand by next week. Call it my cut. A small share of the booty, considering what I went through and the millions Bozanski scammed.'

He gazed back at me gamely. 'You're trying to bribe me, is that it?'

'Compensation, that's all I want.'

'I haven't got any money, just a fucking massive mortgage like everyone else.'

My finger wagged, almost touching his nose. 'Draw on your mortgage, ask your mum, I don't care. You've got one week.'

People were beginning to watch, so I stepped back and smiled. Chaffer wanted the last word.

'Come near me again and I'll call the police. I'm warning you, Bruno.'

'One week,' I said, before making my way back through the turnstiles.

From Chaffer's reaction, it was unlikely he would seriously consider my demand for reparation. It was interesting to note that he was still smoking. I remembered something he had once told me; there was a quiet spot near the back of the ferry where, according to Chaffer, one could have a quiet puff without being disturbed. He probably sneaked in one or two on the ride across the harbour, particularly on Fridays after a few drinks.

Just the place for a future meeting.

Would he tell anyone about my demands? It was doubtful he'd tell the police, as that would mean disclosing why I was harassing him. If he told anyone it would be Bozanski. But Bozanski, as Chaffer knew, didn't like being presented with problems. Chances were he'd brush off our encounter as an unfortunate coincidence and hope that was the last time he ever saw me.

Near the fast-food shops at the quay, there were a large number of paralysed cockroaches struggling in their death throes in a pile of litter and dirt. The pest control people must have just sprayed. It made me think of a conversation I'd had with Sabrina and her coterie of friends. They'd been talking about reincarnation and coming back as an animal in the next life.

One of the women, Christina – the same person who had, on a previous occasion, enquired as to how far the ingredients in my curry had travelled to reach my kitchen – imagined herself as a bird. Lydia was out of the room, and I'd made a comment about preferring the Islamic afterlife over Buddhism.

'Give me the vestal virgin option any day.'

Sabrina jumped down my throat, saying I'd be reincarnated as a cockroach. It had been light banter up until that point. I retorted that it wouldn't be all that bad if I scored a location with water views and plenty of rubbish to feed on.

'You won't have water views. You'll be reincarnated as a cockroach in some filthy slum,' said Sabrina.

That got a laugh from her friends, encouraging Sabrina to continue.

'I can picture you, sprayed with insecticide, suffering a painful death.'

At this stage, Sabrina's friend with the sullen face, whose name always eluded me, found her social conscience, claiming that rich areas also used pesticides – probably even more so than slums.

Sabrina's invective had unsettled me, but I did my best not to let it show. I turned towards the woman who had made the comment. I knew she was an academic, so I asked whether she had thought of doing a doctorate on the subject. Sabrina glared at me like I was an idiot.

I said, 'I can see the title now – *Buddhism and the Social Strata of the Urban Cockroach.* You could compare the life of the elite cockroach to that of your slum-dwelling roach.'

Some of the women found the comment amusing, but the battle lines had been drawn. Lydia reappeared and the sparring ceased. The mood, as well as the topic of conversation, changed.

I scored it a one-all draw.

13

Dismal Ambience

My phone rang. It was Lydia. After our last conversation, it caught me by surprise. I began to talk and she abruptly interrupted.

'Can you just shut up and listen?'

Hassan's partner had phoned. Apparently he was too shaken to talk. Two men wearing masks had forced their way into Hassan's apartment. They wanted all his files from his FGI days and asked if he'd had contact with Dominic Bruno. He told them he didn't have FGI files, nor had he been in contact with me. Not satisfied with his reply, they beat him up and took his computer – left him with two broken ribs and terrified out of his wits. He fibbed at the hospital, saying he had fallen from a ladder, heeding the warning from the two thugs, who told him they would return and finish him off if he spoke a word to anyone.

Hassan was a gentle and sincere man. He knew nothing. How stupid of me to use his name as leverage against Chaffer. It made my stomach turn. This was my fault, and a bad omen. As immoral as I might be, I disliked decent people being harmed. It was hard to tell where one's loyalty started and ended in the Venn diagram of life, but I was touched by the fact that Hassan wanted to warn me.

'Fucking Bozanski. He's behind this.'

'You don't know that.'

'Come on, Lydia, who else could it be? You don't have to be a genius to figure out it's all to do with the cover-up at FGI. Chaffer was involved in it all as well.'

'If that was the case, Dom, they'd all be under arrest.'

It really irked me that Lydia would believe Bozanski and Sabrina over me.

'Bozo has contacts and he uses people. Like he's done with me and Sabrina.'

'How dare you try to bring Sabrina into it!'

I couldn't resist the urge to goad her. 'I saw Sabrina the other day.'

'What! Why would you be seeing Sabrina?'

'No, no, not like that. She was in a café with someone and I was walking past.'

'What are you up to? Are you the one who's been harassing her?'

'What...? Sabrina's been harassed? Poor thing. Will you pass on my condolences?'

'That's enough, Dom.'

With that, she was gone.

After Lydia's news regarding Hassan, I became more concerned about self-preservation. And I needed a weapon sooner rather than later. The likely scenario was that Chaffer had told Bozanski about our encounter. Bozanski had dealt with the problem by setting his thugs on Hassan. Would he do the same with me, or was my reputation so trashed that Dom Bruno wasn't worth bothering with?

The answer to that question was soon to become apparent.

I'd been amusing myself, laughing heartily as I watched in slow motion the footage of Bozanski falling into the fountain at Hyde Park, when there was a loud knock on the front door. I checked the security camera. Peering into the lens were two heftily built men. At first I just watched them shuffling around impatiently, hoping they would go away. Then one of them walked over to the lounge room window and attempted to peer inside.

It didn't take a genius to work out they were Bozanski's thugs. The same two who had attacked poor Hassan, no doubt. They weren't wearing ski masks, but they did have a leather sports bag with them.

A myriad of thoughts raced through my head. Was the elderly couple home next door? They might see the men and ring the police. Although these two, with their solid builds and neat suits, could likely pass *themselves* off as the police.

My doors were solid and the locks first-class. The screen door was locked. They wouldn't be able to gain entry through the window easily. It was a matter of how far the two were prepared to go. If they decided to bash down the door with an axe, chances were nobody would bat an eyelid. You'd have to gelignite the block to get any attention around this neighbourhood.

I thought about grabbing Cerberus, racing downstairs and driving away – but what if they came after me? They would easily chase me down. And if they didn't give chase, they might break in, get hold of my computer and realise I had surveillance equipment.

Stand firm, I told myself. *Act like a resistance fighter confronted by the enemy.*

An idea came into my head. But it would mean being bold. With my phone in one hand and Cerberus resting on my shoulders, I made my way warily down the stairs.

As I opened the front door, the smaller of the two, the one who had been over at the window, spoke first. 'That's the fucker.'

'Open up,' said the other one, yanking at the screen door.

They both saw the snake at the same time. The smaller man jumped back, while the other fella didn't move.

'We just want to talk,' he said.

I said, 'Talk about what?'

The smaller man continued to eye Cerberus warily.

'He won't bite,' I said. 'But I've got two brown snakes inside who aren't as friendly.'

These two were standover men. They were used to having the upper hand. From the way they eyed each other, they were unsure of just what to do next. I took the opportunity to get on the front foot.

'If you don't leave immediately, I'll call the police. While I'm waiting for the cops, I'll upload your pretty faces I've recorded on my security camera onto Facebook. See who recognises you.'

I stared at them with all the intensity I could muster. Four or five seconds passed before the taller man signalled to his mate and they turned and began walking away. He was speaking on his phone to somebody, probably Bozo, as they got into their car. A short time later they drove away.

What would they do next? Would they be put off that easily? From the way the smaller man had reacted to Cerberus, he would be having second thoughts about breaking into my house. It did make me realise just what a vulnerable position I was in. What would get me first, the brain tumour or Bozo's thugs?

Later that night, still on edge after the visit from the two men, I received positive news. It was a text message from Tran – *Cerberus*. It meant that he wanted to see me, hopefully to give me my share of the money we'd swindled from Sabrina's account.

The next day we met at a busy café in the city. When Tran was late, I began to wonder whether the plan had gone off smoothly. Seeing his smiling face changed that. He told me the good news.

'Does this man Tran know how to make it happen or what?' I said, sounding uncool, but in genuine awe of his abilities.

When I asked him what he would do with his share of the money, he explained his situation. His was a nobler mission than mine. He had two sisters living in Vietnam. Beautiful women, from the pictures I'd seen. The money would help provide for their education. His mother also required expensive medication. His dad had died from injuries suffered during the war with America.

We had to pay out six thousand to the banker and two thousand to Tran's friend, Miss Saigon, leaving us with thirty-six thousand each – not a bad haul. I had the money and could move forward with my plans.

After the visit from Bozo's boys, the need to obtain a gun was paramount. And a gun would be required for my Fuck It! List endeavours. But what it came down to was whether anyone at the Imperial was prepared to sell one to me.

What I also needed was a reliable vehicle. One I could sleep in. Searching online, I found one van in particular that fulfilled the requirements, from a Ford dealer in the south-west of the city. It was advertised for just under fourteen thousand. The white Toyota Hiace High Top had air conditioning, tinted windscreens and a fridge, microwave, sink and water tank. It had relatively low kilometres and, according to the dealer, was in excellent mechanical condition.

The van was described as being a 'must to inspect', but I'd be taking the dealer's word on its condition. What I loved about the modern world was that it was possible to do a commercial deal without laying eyes on a soul – the dealer only cared that the money came through. I transferred fourteen grand with an accompanying message – *Keep the extra ten dollars; I'm a generous man.*

On the net I found a company called Quick Smart that provided a pick-up and delivery service. The instructions I gave were to pick up the vehicle from the dealer and deliver it at a designated parking station, not far from Ashfield RSL. The car keys were to be dropped into a postal box nearby. I'd wanted them put under the front tyre, but the girl on the phone deemed this against company policy.

I was there, waiting in the shadows, when the van was delivered, wearing the same disguise that had fooled Dunkley. The van was most impressive. The mattress needed to be changed – the scent of its previous occupants too odorous for my liking. It might also upset Cerberus.

I bought curtains for the windows and installed two cameras, one at the front and the other at the rear. I rented a garage in Ashfield, one of eight located under a large block of flats. Nobody took much notice of my presence in the brief time it took to open the roller door and reverse the van in.

When I got back to my car, I noticed in the mirror that the hairpiece had moved slightly. I had no idea how long it had been like that, but it was asking for trouble. Maybe in this part of the city people were used to idiots and just laughed quietly to themselves.

I drove home and immediately checked the video. There was no sign of a return visit from Bozo's thugs. Perhaps they'd asked for danger money after meeting Cerberus, or had believed my story about the brown snakes.

14

Neighbourly Love

From my observations of the goings-on at Dunkley's house, it seemed Suzi was feeling the pressure. She no longer did her tai chi in the yard. The blinds to Suzi and her boy's room were not opened very often, but one day I glimpsed her sitting on the bed. She appeared to be in a miserable state. By that stage Suzi would probably have realised the appalling situation she had placed herself and her boy in. That Dunkley would be insisting on sex and getting it was a given. I didn't have to imagine – I knew the acts he'd expect from her. Then one morning I spotted her with a black eye. God knows what other bruises he had inflicted.

Would he sexually abuse the boy? Who knew? He had barely left Suzi's side. She had the sense not to leave him alone with Dunkley. But she must have been getting jack of it, coping with Dunkley and caring for her boy.

If only there were a way of telling her that help was on the way. The cavalry was coming. But was she prepared to evacuate?

Familiar with Dunkley's routine, I could predict his movements with some degree of confidence. On Friday nights he would park his truck out the front of his house. His preferred parking spot was in close proximity to his neighbour's car. This was not just any old car. It was a vintage Mitsubishi Evo 3, the prized and proud possession of Stephen Murray.

From what I'd been able to gather talking to people at the Imperial, Stephen was the older of two brothers who lived with their mother in the house next to Dunkley. Stephen was a tempestuous character of about twenty-four or so. I'd witnessed him being a real arse. He would abuse his mother for no apparent reason. He was discourteous to the other residents in the street, and most people steered well clear of him.

There was little love lost between Stephen and Dunkley. On one occasion, Dunkley had reprimanded Stephen for revving his car too loudly. Stephen didn't stand up to him, but it must have pissed him off – what was the point of having an Evo 3 if you couldn't rev the shit out of it? It was hypocritical on Dunkley's part, considering the noise his truck made.

Brayden was the younger brother. A good-looking young man of around eighteen, he was the more self-assured and driven of the two, although he really didn't have much to beat. Each morning during the week, he was picked up outside his house at about 7 am by a man in a blue-and-white logistics van. He spent much of his time away from the house and was rarely seen on weekends.

The mum appeared to be about fifty. It's possible she was much younger. For a single mum, bringing up two boys in this locality wouldn't be easy. Brayden sometimes mowed the lawn and put out the garbage bins – chores that Stephen never did.

Since hatching my plan I'd been biding my time, waiting for the right weather conditions. Finally, the weatherman delivered an ideal forecast. Expected late in the afternoon, an intense low system was due to hit from the north-west. Flood warning alerts were issued for some areas and road conditions were expected to be hazardous. The gist of the message from emergency services was to stay indoors. The storm was expected to last most of the night.

As if conjured up by magic, at around six o'clock dark clouds began to form on the horizon, just as the Bureau of Meteorology had predicted. It took a while to build, but it wasn't long before the rain began to pelt down. There was a lull in proceedings around ten o'clock. Then, as though a malevolent giant had been suddenly awoken, an eerie howling could be heard against the backdrop of banging doors and rattling windows. Bursts of wind battered the suburb, sweeping waves of stormwater across the road. Visibility was very low. Only a fool or a villain would be on the streets on such a dismal night.

The Bureau had warned of falling branches. I didn't have to worry about that; you needed trees for that to happen. With the intervals between the lightning strikes and the peals of thunder shortening, I made my move, driving down the road and parking the car around the corner from Dunkley's.

My greying appearance blended perfectly with the bleak, dismal night. Dressed in a similar disguise to the one I'd used to visit Sabrina's school, I crept through the darkness. Concealed under my raincoat was a hammer, which I held firmly in my grasp. The absence of streetlights was helpful. Some houses still had their lights on, but as expected, most people had turned in for the night. There would always be the odd night owl and those suffering from insomnia, but I was confident Dunkley would be drunk and out like a light by now. Earlier that night he had been sitting on his verandah, drinking.

Approaching Dunkley's place, I could see the outline of his truck. It was parked just a metre away from the Evo 3, which was covered by a tarpaulin. I half expected to see Stephen standing in the shadows, guarding his precious Mitsubishi.

Untying the corner of the tarpaulin closest to Dunkley's truck, I calculated the correct place to whack each vehicle so the height and angle was realistic. With the storm howling like a banshee, I struck, giving each vehicle one almighty whack with the hammer. Scraping off flakes of paint from each vehicle, I swapped them around. The red paint from Dunkley's truck would be easy to spot on Stephen's white Mitsubishi. Tucking the hammer away, I quickly fled the scene.

It was calm the next morning, with just the odd stray cloud scudding across the sky. From first light I waited with anticipation, sipping coffee on my balcony, like an excited theatregoer waiting for the show to begin. The overnight low may have passed, but another storm was about to unleash its rancour.

First on the scene was Dunkley. Still looking hungover from the night before, he didn't even notice the damage. After collecting something from the cabin of his truck, he went back inside.

Stephen came out about twenty minutes later. When he noticed the tarpaulin was not fully covering the Evo, he probably thought the wind had blown it loose. Seconds later he was on his knees, gawking at the damage to his car with an expression of disbelief. Surely not – not the Evo 3! When the reality of the situation registered, he emitted a frightful screech.

'Mum! Mum! Have a look at this – the arse next door has backed his fucking truck into the Evo!'

It was fortunate I hadn't given it another few whacks, as he'd have collapsed from a heart attack on the spot.

Dunkley must have been drawn to Stephen's grief-stricken cry, or perhaps he saw the distraught boy hanging around near his truck. Either way, Act Two was soon underway.

Dunkley came out from his house and stood at his front gate with his arms folded. When Stephen saw him, he exploded.

'You've banged that fucking truck of yours into my car!'

Staring at the culprit, Stephen's anger was palpable. I zoomed in on the scene – the red paint from Dunkley's truck sparkled like specks of blood on the spotless white body of the Evo 3. An omen, perhaps.

Still without saying a word – I'd seen this passive-aggressive act before, and it was guaranteed to enrage the most placid of souls – Dunkley came out onto the street. He scrutinised the damage with the aloofness of a traffic cop.

Stephen couldn't contain his rage. 'See what you've done? The whole panel will have to be replaced.'

With twisted lips, Dunkley channelled his inner Clint Eastwood and begrudgingly spoke.

'Haven't done a thing, son.'

'You drove in after me! My car hasn't been moved.'

Although the blows had been of similar strength, there was more damage done to the car than the truck. As Stephen continued to make accusations, Dunkley looked up to the heavens – perhaps for inspiration.

After a moment of deliberation, he declared, 'Someone's had a go with a hammer or something.'

Dunkley's sagacity caught me by surprise. But Stephen was no fool.

'Yeah, and the paint from your truck was put on my car by the tooth fairy. You think I'm fucking stupid?'

Let's see you squeeze your way out of that one, Dunkers.

'I'd fucking know if I hit a car,' said Dunkley, rising to the occasion. 'And my truck would do more damage than that.'

Stephen's mother had appeared with a writing pad, and with Stephen's help, she began taking an inventory of the carnage.

'It'll need a new panel at least. And there's damage to the light casing. That will have to be replaced.'

Stephen took photos with his phone – indisputable evidence.

Dunkley continued to stay calm. If he kept it up, he'd be up for a Nobel Peace Prize. Was he on medication? Perhaps he'd been attending anger-management classes.

'You'll be paying for this,' mumbled Stephen.

Come on, Stephen, don't back down. Where was the young fella, Brayden? He wouldn't just fizzle out like a dud Tom Thumb.

'I'd say someone's having a lend of you, mate. Fuckin' with both of us,' said Dunkley.

'Are you kidding me, man? There's no other fucking car on the street.'

'You're not listening, son.'

Dunkley's cool arrogance was on display, his superior attitude. When Mum added her two bob's worth, I wanted to applaud.

'Anyway, what's your truck doing parked on the street?'

On this matter, Dunkley knew he didn't have a leg to stand on. He turned away and began walking back towards his house.

'I'll be passing on your rego number to my insurance company,' Stephen shouted at Dunkley.

Dunkley laughed. If Stephen thought informing Dunkley of the damage done or reporting the accident to the insurance company – it wasn't of sufficient magnitude to interest the police – was going to faze Dunkley, he was in for a surprise.

With regard to the truck being illegally parked, it was unlikely Mum or Stephen would report Dunkley to the authorities. Around here, dobbing was frowned upon – akin to singing 'God Save the Queen' in a Belfast pub.

Someone else would have to take that step.

Later that day, ringing from an unregistered mobile, I contacted the council, claiming to be a Lesley Murray, an uncle who was visiting. I told the duty officer that I wanted to report Dunkley for illegally parking his truck in a suburban area.

But when I disclosed the address, things began to go horribly wrong. The duty officer knew the family. He wanted to know how the two boys, Stephen and Brayden, were getting on.

Expect the unexpected – particularly when you are lying. I pretended we had a bad line and the call was dropping out to give myself time to gather my thoughts.

'Young Brayden works in the electrical trades now,' I said eventually. 'He nearly topped his year at TAFE last semester. A smart boy, that one!'

The man was so pleased to hear positive feedback that I couldn't help myself. Why stop with Brayden?

'So proud of the boys,' I said. 'Stephen recently won a citizenship award for his volunteer work at a nursing home.' That comment almost made me gag.

Getting down to the purpose of the call, the officer displayed concern as I relayed, in disturbed tones, how Mr Dunkley had nearly wiped out a kid on a bicycle when reversing his truck. To seal the deal, I climbed onto the moral high horse.

'Of course, I'm not one who would usually complain, but it's more than an illegal parking matter. It's a matter of child safety. What if Dunkley kills somebody with his truck?'

When the officer asked me to come in to sign the appropriate forms, my knowledge of council procedure proved useful. He accepted my excuse of limited mobility due to a hip replacement. I again stressed that it was imperative he do something about that damn truck soon. He assured me he would be on to it pronto, which, as I was to find out, did not mean immediately.

Watching the screen, hour after hour, wondering when somebody from the council would appear, I was at my obsessive worst. I eventually gave up and went about my business.

Four days after my call to the council, an inspector rocked up to the Murrays' residence late in the afternoon. The mother came to the door. It was unclear what was discussed, but she didn't invite the man in. Dunkley's truck was not there at the time, but I'd sent a number of attachments (digitally dated), establishing the fact that the truck had been illegally parked out the front of his house on many occasions.

The morning following the council inspector's visit, Dunkley came out of his house with guns blazing. He threw a wicked glance at the Murrays' residence before shouting a few cherished profanities. Stephen popped his head out from behind the door and Dunkley told him in no uncertain words what he thought of dobbers. He then strode towards his truck and mounted the cabin. Thrashing the motor angrily, he shouted something obscene from the window of his cab, and Stephen returned the salvo. From that point on, the roar of the engine made it impossible to hear. Dunkley hit the accelerator and headed off down the road like the devil possessed. *Not so passive now,* I thought.

Ten minutes later, a taxi arrived at Dunkley's place. Suzi and the boy came out the front and got in. They came back later that afternoon. What did Suzi make of it all – Dunkley's drinking, his uncouth and aggressive behaviour? Not to mention what he must have expected of her. Surely she must have wanted to flee.

As Stephen was to find out, Dunkley wasn't one to forgive or forget. That same evening, Dunkley's drinking buddy drove up in his ute. The two sat out the front, polishing off can after can of VB.

When Stephen and his mother returned home Dunkley was on his feet, screeching at the two before they'd even gotten out of the car. His voice was full of menace.

'Here comes the fucking dobbin' arsehole himself.'

You can't talk logic to a drunk, and Stephen should have known that. He tried to explain that he was not the one who dobbed. But Dunkley had a fixation and wasn't interested in what Stephen said.

'Dobber dog, dobber dog, dobber dog.'

Dunkley's mate thought that was real funny. Verse the same as the chorus; it was effective, if somewhat repetitive.

'Dobber dog, dobber dog, dobber dog.'

Dunkley was unrelenting. Stephen fought hard to keep his cool under the constant barrage. He tried and tried, but, but, but… in the end, he just couldn't hold back.

'You ran into me, you dickhead, and I didn't dob on you, okay?'

Stephen had bleated out the words nervously, and Dunkley seized the opportunity.

'Baaa!' he said. 'A dobber and a liar.'

Dunkley's mate was utterly hysterical. 'This is better than the movies,' he quipped.

'Stephen, Stephen,' called Mum.

'Stephen, Stephen,' repeated Dunkley, mimicking her.

Stephen baulked for a moment, and I thought he might jump the fence, but his mother screeched at him, corralling him through the front door. Neither was prepared to go that extra bit – not yet. Mum might have saved Stephen this time, but a storm was brewing.

After things had settled down for the night and I was left to the solitude that was my life, it became apparent that hearing Dunkley's voice and watching the sleazebag operate had affected me. Once again, my head was a sledgehammer of pain. I experienced flashbacks that left me debilitated and nauseous – the painful resurfacing of emotions that seemingly could not be erased or suppressed. How was it possible to still smell the odour of the man? Was it stored forever in my being?

I wondered how much the brain cancer had impacted on my emotional state. The latest Twinkel offering didn't help matters.

Mr Twinkel comes onto the stage dressed as a backwoodsman, swinging an axe. A few people in the audience clap.

'Presenting... "A Sheep in Wolf's Clothing".'

On the screen there is a lean and hungry wolf approaching a house in the forest.

The sign at the entrance to the house reads, This building is solid brick and wolf-proof. Constructed by Fuji and Garibaldi. Zappers have been installed at all entry points. And don't forget, a large tub of boiling water awaits any wolf foolish enough to try the conventional method – forget about the chimney.

The wolf stops when he sees the sign. After reading it, he pulls out his phone and talks to someone. He drops his head in disappointment, turns

on his haunches and, with his tail between his legs, makes his way slowly
back down the track.

'Pathetic,' someone in the audience calls.

'What sort of wolf are you?' yells another.

An irate voice screeches, 'I want me money back!'

The spotlight finds Mr Twinkel.

'A little disappointing, Benedict Sparkel,' he says.

The image fades.

Again, Twinkel was trying to hurry me along. I sent him an email.

I've kept to my side of the bargain – one posting a month. Furthermore,
although I do enjoy the wonderful animations, I will not be harried or
hurried by a character who only exists on the fucking screen.

He didn't reply.

It wasn't until I watched Twinkel's 'A Sheep in Wolf's Clothing' for a
second time, that it dawned on me – the builders of the wolf-proof house
were called Fuji and Garibaldi. Taking the 'F' from 'Fuji', and the first
and last letter from 'Garibaldi', you got 'FGI'.

Assuming it wasn't a coincidence, did it mean Twinkel knew my
identity? But why would Twinkel want me to know he knew? Was he just
showing off, or was he on a power trip?

15

Hidden Talents

The next day, after another night of restless sleep, I was left feeling exhausted and on edge. It was distressing, thinking of Dunkley and the power he still had over me. And although Twinkel's animation had annoyed me, there was truth in what he had said. I did need to move with more haste.

I'd been considering how to put the request for a weapon to Bubba and Case, and an excellent idea came into my head. There had recently been an article in a popular weekly magazine about financial fraud and the difficulties authorities faced tracing the money. The article not only mentioned my name and that I'd been released after a short prison stint but was rife with speculation about the missing millions. The media did love to rebirth a story and watch to see if it floated. The bastards even included a photo. It had been taken years prior and showed a skinny young man with greedy ambition. At least they hadn't gotten hold of my address. I'd been hoping they wouldn't do a follow-up article and praying that nobody from the Imperial had seen this one.

Then it occurred to me. The story could work to my advantage. Rather than trying to keep a lid on it, what if I did the opposite? What if everybody at the Imperial found out about the past deeds of Dominic Bruno and became aware of my perilous situation? If I played my cards right, it would provide me with an excellent reason for needing a weapon.

I left two copies of the magazine at the hotel, one in the men's toilet and the other near the betting slips at the TAB. Both were folded to display the relevant page. I then rang the hotel and put on a fake accent, pretending to be a reporter. The young barman was not willing to discuss his infamous patron on the phone, but from what I'd observed of this man's garrulous nature, the entire bar would soon know about the sins of Dominic Bruno.

Two beers and one hour later, Case told me he had read the story.

I pretended to be upset. My reply was terse. 'Let's keep it local, eh? Like, at the table level.'

'Dom, the bird has flown. Everybody knows.'

Some of the patrons who, until then, had barely acknowledged my existence, started saying hello. When I mentioned this to Case, he said there was some speculation as to whether I still had the missing millions. The rumour that had started during the court case and had been referred to in the magazine article was up and running again at the Imperial – Dominic Bruno had the loot stashed away. Knowing the reputation of some of the characters down the pub, that was not a good thing.

In for a penny, in for a pound. I told Bubba and Case that the information I possessed could blow the whistle on FGI. I went on to say that my brakes had been tampered with (untrue), and that someone had tried to break into my house.

'My enemies are powerful and dangerous people.'

'You might be needing a minder,' said Case.

'What would that cost?' I asked.

'Ten grand a week, for someone good.' He seemed to be well

acquainted with the subject.

'Use some of the missing millions,' joked Bubba.

'Not funny,' I replied.

I fantasised about hiring two or three mercenaries and forming my own mini-army. For the first time since coming to the Imperial, I felt like I belonged.

'I tell you what, though. I do need some form of protection. Can anybody here get me a gun?'

Bubba's eyes drifted towards Case, who said he'd see what he could do.

Tracy had been glancing in my direction, which I interpreted as meaning she wanted to talk. It had been a busy night and it wasn't until just before closing that she had time to spare. Tracy became unusually quiet, telling me she had an apology to make. She'd come across the magazine article and showed Bubba. She thought it was her fault that my past had been exposed.

'I couldn't hide the truth forever, Trace. People were bound to find out sooner or later.'

There was so much to like and admire about Tracy. Her unadulterated, unaffected nature. What I did next was equivalent to pulling out a bar of candy to entice a kid.

'Do you want to come over tonight? Have a smoke and watch Cerberus being fed?'

Once we were back at my place, I offered Tracy the bong. She had a few hits then wanted to go upstairs to feed Cerberus. She put him in his cage, and I got a rat from the pen and tossed it in.

'What the...!' exclaimed Tracy. 'It disappeared in a split second, like magic.'

'He's quick.'

The only evidence of the rat's existence was a bulge in the snake's throat.

'Quick? That was like lightning. Does one head get the rat more often than the other?'

It was a good question, and it surprised me that I hadn't thought about it.

'It comes out pretty even, I think. I'd say Cerb gets a tad more than Erus.'

'Let's see who got it this time, said Tracy, and I realised she'd recorded Cerberus eating the rat on her phone. We watched the replay of the rat being swallowed in slow motion.

'That one went to Cerb,' she said, enthralled. 'You'll have to watch out for that.'

Back downstairs, Tracy wanted me to watch a series I was unfamiliar with, *Orange is the New Black*.

Did she think I'd be interested in the show because I'd been to prison? Watching articulate women communicate was a far cry from my prison experience, but I did manage to block the memory of Dunkley and Turner for the duration of the episode, which was some feat.

When it finished, Tracy began to open up, talking in that honest way women do more naturally than men. She spoke about the problems of her previous relationships and how she seemed to attract men who became too attached. A couple of times it had turned violent, and her mother had blamed her for attracting the wrong type of men.

Was she on to me?

'What type would that be?'

'You know, Dom… The type who take you out a few times, do you a favour or two, and then think they own you.'

Finally, she got to the point.

'Don't think I'm not grateful. You've been really good to me. But I don't want a boyfriend. I just wanted you to know where you stand.'

'That's cool,' I replied. 'I wasn't expecting marriage. Not yet anyway.'

'Dom, be serious.'

Feigning humility was worth a try. 'You're an attractive girl and can do much better than a bloke like me.'

'Dom... It's not like that. You've got a lot going for you.'

It made me wonder what a serious relationship with Tracy would be like – she would not readily commit, but if she did, Tracy would stand by her man through thick and thin.

I thought that after our conversation it would be all over for the night, but Tracy surprised me by cuddling up close and becoming amorous. Eventually we went upstairs to my bedroom and had sex.

Afterwards we sat about, talking. We were both wearing large bath towels, and as I got to my feet to get dressed, she reached over and pulled the towel away. She began flicking me with the towel, and we were soon at it again. This time my body was not as willing. Not to be deterred, Tracy placed her hand on my hip, slipping it around and under. Her needs would not be denied. That was something Lydia had never done.

Lying there afterwards, exhausted, she allowed me to observe her nakedness, inviting comments on her figure. 'Do you think my hips are too broad?' She paraded about before me, so tantalising with her feline movements. She had no idea just how provocative her actions were.

'You look beautiful,' I said. A line from a Rodriguez song popped into my head. '*I wonder, how many times you've had sex and I wonder, do you know who'll be next, I wonder...*'

She laughed, probably at my singing.

We got dressed. Tracy wanted to see Cerberus again before she left. How could I not indulge her?

At the door to Cerberus's habitat, she hesitated. 'Why don't you use this room to sleep in? It's the main bedroom and has the balcony.'

'I need to be able to swap the pot plants around so they get some sun.'

'But you don't use your balcony. It would be great this time of year.'

After having dumped me earlier, Tracy was now rearranging my furniture. A closeness had developed between us, and at that moment I wanted to tell her the real reason the rooms were as they were, and what the balcony was used for. I wanted to show her the footage I'd recorded and see her reaction to the Benedict Sparkel site.

Only moments later I would be reminded of the foolishness of such impetuous thinking.

After visiting Cerberus, I decided to go back into my bedroom to close the window, as a breeze had sprung up and was rattling the venetian blinds. From where Tracy was standing at the top of the stairs, it was possible to see the tops of the houses across the road. She raised her arm and pointed in the direction of Dunkley's house.

'Brayden lives over there.'

'Who?' I replied – then it registered that she was referring to the younger of the two Murray brothers.

'Brayden... He used to be my boyfriend.'

What a jolt I got. And she said his name with such fond yearning.

I tried to sound calm. 'Your ex lives down there?'

'Yeah... He'd be so jealous if he knew I was up here with you.' She was amused at the prospect.

'He would?' I gulped, still grappling with the startling revelation and the fact that, moments earlier, Dumb Dom had only just resisted the impulse to show her the footage recorded from the balcony. Tracy then sent my head spinning again.

'Brayden is a chainsaw artist.'

'A chainsaw artist? Wow, good on him. That explains the loud buzzing sounds that have been keeping me awake at night.'

'You think he makes too much noise.'

'No, no, I'm not complaining. I get a real buzz out of it.'

'Dom... Not funny.' She whacked me across the shoulder.

Memories of an old horror movie, *The Texas Chainsaw Massacre*, filled my thoughts. I hoped that Brayden hadn't seen it and wanted to do a remake.

'He's going to the nationals this year,' Tracy continued.

'He's that good?' I replied, wondering how many of these maniacs with chainsaws were on the loose. Brayden and Stephen might not scare Dunkley, but they did scare me. If they had an inkling, they'd be after me like a cackle of wild hyenas.

Tracy showed me a small carving she carried in her purse. It was a piece of balsa wood that had been carved into the shape of a sensual female.

'He did that... with a chainsaw?'

'Not with a chainsaw, idiot,' she replied. 'He did that with a hacksaw.'

'So he's a true artist,' I said, trying to conjure up a gentler Brayden and exorcise the image of a jealous Brayden brandishing a chainsaw.

It was with a certain sadness that I kissed Tracy goodbye that night. Despite her many admirable traits and the fact that she was one of the few positives in my life, the decision had to be made. Tracy could not come near my house again. It was far too risky. My plans for evening up the score with Dunkley and Turner were at a critical stage.

It was important not to offend Tracy. Everybody loved her down at the Imperial, and if we did have a falling out, one didn't have to be a genius to work out where sympathies would lie. Lurking in the back of my mind was another selfish thought. From Tracy's descriptions of her home – small and dingy, but quiet – it was no palace. But it might make a great hideaway for a night or two in an emergency.

My thoughts drifted. I imagined Tracy as not just a lover, but a partner in crime, helping me achieve my dastardly deeds. But Tracy possessed a moral compass that would exclude the Fuck It! List creed. If I explained my thirst for revenge, she might not get enraged, and maybe she'd even understand – but she'd never live in the devilish swamp inhabited by the likes of me.

The next morning, two things happened that impacted my plans. First, after reviewing the action (or lack of it) at Dunkley's place, I zoomed in on a small Ford parked across the road. Of course, it could have belonged to somebody visiting, except the driver stayed in the car. It was unlikely to be Bozo's thugs, as they hunted in twos and had been driving a large car – probably so they could fit bodies in the boot.

After the car had been there for an hour, I peered out of the downstairs window. Immediately afterwards, the engine started and the car left. That did nothing to alleviate my fears. Was it related to all this recent talk of the missing millions from FGI? Had my actions down the Imperial brought on this additional threat? It was not too far-fetched to imagine some lunatic hunting me down. There would always be candidates for that gig – *give me the missing million! Tell us or you die.*

The other significant occurrence was the discovery of a yellow box covered with black and white dots in my bathroom. So obviously feminine, it soon became apparent that Tracy had inadvertently left her make-up kit behind. Opening the box, I tossed the contents about in my hands. Was what I had begun to think about possible?

My plan for getting even with Chaffer was becoming clearer. I'd been considering ageing my face and wearing a grey wig and beard. Although it was unlikely he would recognise me, approaching him dressed in that manner would make him wary. But what if I dressed as a woman? Knowing Chaffer, he would be caught off guard. Furthermore, it would increase my chances of throwing the authorities off the scent.

My mind drifted back to a 'change of sex' ball I'd gone to with Lydia at the University of Sydney. I had been apprehensive about dressing as a woman, and it was a reminder of the lengths I'd once gone to in order to please her. Dressing me up to the nines, Lydia had applied extensive make-up and schooled me in the techniques of walking and holding myself as a woman. She was so proud when her creation was chosen as one of the five most convincing impersonators amongst the hundred or so in the competition. Whether it was because of Lydia's presence or the alcohol, I'm not sure, but it was a hoot being paraded across the stage to the cheers and jeers of the crowd.

Tracy's kit was stacked with an assortment of items: mascara, cream, eyeliner, lipsticks, a brush, a bottle of make-up remover. Tracy's skin and hair colour were darker than mine, but not greatly so. The colours she had in her box might work for me. I tested the eyeliners, preferring the brown over the turquoise. Both the blush and crimson lipstick seemed to work. The problem was that despite my many attempts at applying the make-up, it looked messy. Sure, I wasn't entering the Miss Universe pageant, but it was important to look authentic. If this new disguise was going to work, it would take a lot of study and practice.

I researched the subject, reading articles and viewing countless YouTube clips. Then I went shopping to see first-hand what was available. I drove to Newtown, where I had often gone with Lydia. After finding a parking spot in a side street near the University of Sydney, I was soon strolling along King Street, gawking at the shops and the passing parade. There was a pub with a poster advertising live music seven nights a week, a couple of trendy bars, and a selection of inviting multicultural eateries. Lydia's friend Matilda lived somewhere nearby. I didn't have her address, but she'd said her house was in a street that ran off King Street.

Where I lived, the attire was more generic and blander, but around here variety ruled. With the number of freaks and oddballs out and about, a man trying on female attire would attract no more than a passing glance. Some women were thin, dripping in bling, others had tattoos with mighty biceps and prominent six-packs. There were men wearing make-up and women who looked as though they'd flatten you if you mentioned the word. From what I observed, the long-haired hippy look was making a comeback. With the high number of students living in the area, perhaps it never left.

I checked out a display rack out the front of a store, but there was nothing of interest. After passing the pub, I saw a dress in the window of a small boutique that seemed to be the right size and style.

I went into the shop. The young shop assistant had olive skin, long dark hair and a crucifix hanging from her neck. Italian heritage, perhaps. Working in cosmopolitan Newtown, she would be used to serving all genders, but something inside me couldn't admit the clothes were for me.

'Hi there, Gabrielle,' I said, reading her name tag. 'I'm interested in that cream-and-gold dress on display in the window. I'm looking for a present for a lady friend turning thirty next week. She's my size, so if it fits me, it should be fine for her.'

Gabrielle smiled politely, but I'd sounded idiotic.

'I bet you get that one all the time,' I said, trying to make amends. Better to be a friendly idiot than just an idiot.

Gabrielle laughed. She was probably thinking of nothing else but the sale.

Eventually I got into the swing of things, purchasing a charcoal-coloured number as well and adding a matching hat and two push-up bras to the order.

A visit to a nearby theatre costume shop soon had me enthralled, giving rise to endless possibilities. It took only a few seconds to paint on a distinguishable feature such as a scar or mole.

After buying a number of items, I was leaving the shop when a familiar face caught my attention. At first I wasn't sure, but when he turned his head there was no doubt.

Waiting at the pedestrian crossing nearby was Wayne, the American who did security work for FGI. He was in a dishevelled state, nothing like his usual dapper self. Hesitating and wondering whether I should say hello, I lost the chance when the lights changed and he was gone. I watched him disappear in the distance, wondering whether he was on a case. He did work in security, so perhaps he was undercover, although I'd never pictured him as a Gumtree detective.

I hurried home to try on my new clothes and test the items I'd bought from the costume shop. Remembering something Lydia had once said gave me encouragement. In an attempt to give me confidence on the night of the 'change of sex' ball, she'd told me I possessed shapely legs that many women would envy. But then came the backhander – my balls weren't difficult to hide. Thanks for that one, Lydia!

I shaved – fortunately I didn't have heavy growth – and applied the cosmetic base to my forehead, cheeks and nose, spreading it over the contours of my face as I had done with the ageing face disguise I had used previously. After hours of practice, I was still struggling to apply the crimson lipstick in a neat and even manner. The dark eyeliner was the right selection, but it took endless attempts to get it to look half decent. At that stage I could sympathise with women who refused to bother with make-up.

I tried on both garments and found the cream-and-gold dress seemed to work best with the cosmetics. There was no doubting that the clothes and make-up resulted in a drastically altered appearance. I'd avoided short, teasing numbers and anything else that put me in the category of a 'lascivious' woman. *Look attractive, but don't invite too much attention. Female and feminine, but not slutty.* It also became apparent that I would have to shave or wax my limbs.

I went online and ordered more items that would help with the transformation: two wigs, fake breasts, false eyelashes, beads, stockings and gloves – although my hands weren't big, they belonged to a male and had to be concealed. I saw a dress online that was similar to the blue-and-grey one I'd worn to the ball all those years ago. It was meant to be. It had worked then and should work now.

Studying YouTube clips of the female gait, I recalled Lydia's advice – it was vital to get the hip movement correct. I practised and practised the walk, recording and rerecording myself until it looked half decent.

16

The Sky Blinked

The sky blinked and I gave it a wink, feeling possessed of a delicious, wicked power. Into the pub I walked – notoriety amongst the notorious. Bubba and Case were sitting in their usual spot. Tracy hadn't started work yet. Case had arranged for me to meet a friend of his, Trevino, who could supply me with a weapon. I noticed that Case had with him a copy of the article about the missing millions. I was surprised it was still doing the rounds. I thought they'd have lost interest.

Apart from the presence of that unfamiliar vehicle outside my house, I was more than pleased with my newfound status following the revelations of my past. Still, these people weren't stupid. I thought it wise to display some displeasure on seeing the article, lest somebody work out that I was the one responsible for the story circulating. I pointed to the magazine on the table in front of Case and spoke in a raised voice.

'It's mostly bullshit. You'd think Dom Bruno was some super-clever dude, capable of all sorts of brilliant criminal deeds. Can't we just let it drop?'

Case was surprised by my reaction and seemed somewhat miffed. 'Hey, I wanted to show Trevino. So he knows why you need a gun. That he isn't selling to some crazy bastard.'

I apologised for being curt, telling him I'd been on edge.

Later, when Trevino arrived, Case went over and spoke with him. I'd not seen the man before. Short and plump, Trevino looked as though he'd been through the wars. He had a large scar across his cheek and just one arm. Case came back to our table five minutes later.

'All cool. He'll come over and have a chat shortly.'

Two beers later, Trevino came over. Case and Bubba got to their feet and said they were going to put on a bet, leaving the two of us to talk.

'Thanks for helping me out. I don't know what Case has told you, but...'

Before I could finish the sentence, Trevino raised his hand. 'Hey... I don't need to know your life story. You're not the first bloke to fuck up and do time trying to make a quid.'

He threw me a crooked smile – surely he didn't think I had the missing millions? – before continuing.

'What you need, mate, is a Taser, and maybe a small pistol that you can hide in your back pocket.'

I had no wish to be on the receiving end of his wrath, but that proposition was offensive. I channelled my inner Humphrey Bogart.

'The thing is, these people, they want me dead. I need a serious handgun that packs a punch, and shitloads of ammunition.'

He stared at me. 'Shitloads of ammunition,' he said, laughing out loud. 'What do you have planned, mate? You want to invade New Zealand?'

'This is serious, man. My life's under threat. Can you deliver?'

'I find it hard to imagine a fella like you needing shitloads of ammunition.'

I thought back to what Case had said earlier. Trevino probably just wanted to ensure he wasn't dealing with some lunatic who might carry out a mass shooting.

'I haven't used a handgun before. I'll need plenty of ammo so I can practise.'

'You'd be talking twenty grand for a serious handgun, one that's not easy to trace. Silencer and ammo included.'

Case had told me to bargain. But where to start?

'Ten thousand,' I said.

'You're a comedian.' He got up from his seat. 'Best say farewell.'

'Hold on,' I said.

After a bit of argy-bargy, we settled on fifteen.

'Can you also get me two sets of plates for a Toyota?'

'Yep, that's possible.'

'How much?'

'Three grand for ones that won't attract attention. You'll get them cheaper elsewhere, but they won't be safe.'

I accepted his price, telling him the make and model of the vehicle. Was I ripped off? I'd no idea, but I could afford it.

Afterwards I wondered just how safe dealing with Trevino was. He had been recommended by Case, but still, the dreaded thought of being caught and having to endure another prison cell worried me. But what was the alternative? Again the mantra – *Don't fizzle out like a dud firework. There's much to be done before the final sunset. Don't shirk it.* An hour later I handed over the cash.

Now that I'd ordered a gun, I began to consider what else might be required. What if I did manage to fulfil my Fuck It! List ambitions? I'd need to flee the country. For that, a fake passport would be required. I'd ask Tran about that. I'd begun to consider where I'd go. There'd be worse places to live out one's final days than in an opium den in the hills of South-East Asia.

Perhaps I was dreaming. Sitting in the pub with Bubba and Case I felt, if not as safe as a cardinal in Rome, at least as safe as a wolf in grandma's clothing. But the truth was that my situation was precarious, and with what I had planned, it would become more so by the day.

Events can unfold and opportunities present themselves in unexpected ways. Although it had worked to my advantage, I was still dirty on the media for insinuating I might have the missing millions. But soon I would be thanking them for giving me ammunition to use against Dunkley.

The story doing the rounds that week was about the number of drugged-out truckies on our roads. Listeners were divided on the issue. The trigger had been a dreadful accident down the South Coast where a truck had left the highway and ploughed into a house, killing two people, including a young child. The shock jocks were calling for more random drug testing.

There were a couple of Imperial regulars who sometimes sat nearby. They seemed to enjoy discussing politics and current news items. We mostly ignored them, but at times their conversations got heated and they were so vociferous it was impossible not to join in. They had been friendly to me since I'd been revealed as an ex-crim.

Hearing them mention Dunkley's name in the same conversation as that of the drugged-out truckies had my ears jumping out from my skull. I casually approached their table and pushed for more information under the premise of knowing Dunkley from prison. One of them disliked Dunkley intensely, and told me a story featuring his violent behaviour. It was a reminder of just what Dunkley might do to me if he discovered I was on his case – I'd be having an early funeral.

What my new friend then revealed made my day. Apparently Dunkley not only gobbled down uppers like Smarties, but he sold them to other drivers as well. I needed to get home pronto and review the footage I'd recorded.

Leaving the hotel earlier than planned, I trawled through the archives back at the house. After an hour I felt nothing but despondence. He had glazed and reddened eyes at times, but so what? He was a pisshead. It occurred to me that Dunkley might have stopped taking the pills, or that the fellow down at the Imperial might be exaggerating.

The hopelessness of the task was beginning to dawn on me when – *bingo!* Dunkley, having climbed into the cabin of his truck and scanned the surrounds, tilted his head back, took a swig from a bottle and tossed what appeared to be pills into his mouth. There before my eyes was Dunkley, a drugged-out truckie, the scourge of our roads, an insult to all we hold near and dear, a canker on society. I would soon be adding my weight to the campaign.

From the date on the screen, this had happened one week prior, on the morning of one of his overnighters. The next night, if he kept to his schedule, would be his night away. I didn't know if he was still on parole. Dunkley had been behaving like a muzzled dog lately, barely containing himself. If he did pop pills as regularly as the man at the Imperial claimed, what I planned to do would really stir things up.

Dunkley left the house early the next morning – the poor bastard had to catch a taxi – and went to Chullora to pick up his truck. I followed at a safe distance. From Chullora he drove to Bankstown, where he picked up his load before meandering through the backstreets and out onto the M4. If he followed his usual routine, he would be heading over the Blue

Mountains and out towards Bathurst.

I pulled over and rang 000. My voice quivered as I spoke. The lady on the other end told me to take deep breaths. She asked for my name address and phone number. Emitting a painful groan, I gave a fake name and address but the correct phone number, knowing the operator could check the caller's number. I would dispose of the phone later. Then I put on a real performance.

'It was so terrifying. This truckie ran me off the road, sideswiped a parked car, then abused me as he sped off hell for leather. Off his face he was, by the look of him. God knows what he was on.'

I told the lady where the incident had occurred – near the Wentworthville entrance – and the direction Dunkley was going, as well as the truck's numberplate. I agreed to make a full report at Bankstown Police Station pronto. The operator then caught me by surprise, asking whether I would be prepared to attend a tribunal if the driver challenged my story.

'Of course I will,' I replied adamantly. Again, I emphasised the seriousness. 'If this drug-crazed lunatic isn't taken off the road soon, he'll kill someone.'

Driving back out onto the expressway, I set off after Dunkley. I was hoping to see his truck by the side of the road with a police vehicle parked behind. But as the kilometres accumulated, my hopes dampened. I was beginning to wonder whether Dunkley had pulled over for fuel or taken a different route when the traffic in front of me began to slow.

Not a traffic jam, surely! Then I realised what was happening. Up ahead were police vehicles, plus the police bus – they were drug testing. A section of the road had been cordoned off. And what a pleasant sight awaited me.

There was Dunkley's truck, parked behind another semitrailer waiting to be tested.

Was it pure luck? It wouldn't have been possible to set up something so elaborate in the time that had elapsed since my phone call, though Dunkley's numberplate might have been sent through to the crew doing the testing. Maybe the testing had been a result of the attention given to the subject by the shock jocks.

I drove past Dunkley's truck, pulling over to the side of the road after fifty metres or so. My binoculars focused on the scene behind. Dunkley must have just been pulled over because he jumped from the cabin with papers in hand. The police officer abruptly directed him back to his truck. Still protesting, he climbed back into the cabin.

A couple of minutes later, the policeman approached Dunkley's truck and asked him to step down. From there I lost sight of what was happening. I assumed he was being asked to provide a tongue swab – as far as I knew, that was the procedure. At that moment I wondered whether he really did take drugs. Maybe what he'd tossed into his mouth was Panadol for his hangover, or mints for his disgusting breath.

Twenty minutes passed and he was still there. It filled me with hope. Was he being re-tested? About ten minutes later, sheer joy. Dunkley was driven away in a police car, presumably to face further testing at the police station.

I felt enormous pleasure watching him being carted off in the police vehicle. All that work was starting to pay off. The arsehole was in real trouble. I drove home in an ebullient mood to the tune of Pink Floyd's 'Another Brick in the Wall' – *We don't need no drugged-out truckies... Hey! Policeman! Get them off our roads.*

From the same man who'd told me about Dunkley's drug-taking, later that day I learnt that Dunkley had been charged with driving under the influence of a prohibited drug. His licence was suspended with a court case pending.

Twinkel's latest offering was a song. The style was surreal, futuristic.

Mr Twinkel appears as a puppeteer working the strings, performing his version of a Punch and Judy *show. At first all seems normal, with the puppets dancing together – but as the song progresses, Mr Twinkel swings the strings with increasing vigour.*

Eventually the puppets yell and scream as they bounce off each other and collide. Arms and legs begin coming loose and the puppets fall apart.

A song builds to a crescendo, a delayed effect applied to its vocals.

'It's your God-given right to a Sparkel way of life

To do unto others as they've done to you

Before you're off into the abyss, make a Fuck It! List

Get even with every bastard who gave you strife.'

17

Testing the Waters

It was a sunny Wednesday afternoon. I was waiting in a café across the road from the FGI offices. From where I was sitting I would be able to see Rodney Chaffer when he left work, which should be at five o'clock.

Talking to Chaffer would undoubtedly be a waste of time. I knew he wouldn't pay me a cent. He had sided with Bozanski and was an unlikely candidate for a conversion on the road to Damascus. But considering the seriousness of what I was going to do, it sat better with my conscience if I at least gave him the opportunity to make amends.

After my success with Dunkley, I had been on a high. But as usual, my mind would not allow that to be the case for long. There were too many dark shadows lurking just around the bend, waiting to pounce. Again, I was pondering my expiry date. Maybe it was time to visit a doctor and get a prognosis – to find out the rate at which my cancer was progressing. It was the logical thing to do. But then I began to talk myself out of it. I wasn't suffering from any obvious physical symptoms. And if I was honest, a large part of me was terrified – I didn't want to know or face the truth. Besides, I hated hospitals. I'd do nothing for the moment, I decided, see how I felt in a week or two. If I survived that long.

A short time later, Chaffer came out of the building. He made his way along Elizabeth Street, and I followed. I crossed the road and caught up with him.

When Chaffer realised it was me walking beside him he got a shock, but he didn't seem in the least bothered. Bozanski would have advised him on how to deal with me. Chaffer kept his cool and continued along the footpath as though I wasn't there, but then he suddenly stopped and turned to face me.

'What the fuck are you doing, Bruno?'

'Do you have the money?'

That cranky, *are you daft?* gape. 'Money?! Now listen. There's no fucking money. Bozanski wants to talk to you. He's not happy.'

'Oh no… Old Mate Bozo isn't happy. I'll have to tell him a joke or two to cheer him up.'

'You wouldn't call him that to his face.'

'I would now. And I'd call you a prick. You knew what was going on at FGI. And after we last spoke, you ratted to Bozanski. It's your fault Hassan got bashed. And I'll tell you something else, Chaffer – this is your last chance to fess up to your part in setting me up.'

He spoke loudly, happy for other pedestrians to hear. 'Or what, Bruno? Or what? Are you threatening me? That's what it's sounding like. I'm going. If you follow, I'll call the police.'

'Call the cops, Chaffer. Go on.'

'Oh, and by the way…' He held up his phone, a smug expression enveloping his face. 'I recorded everything you said this time. A little tip from Bozanski in case you pestered me again.'

I made a failed grab for his phone and he took off in his peculiar looping running style, one that was surprisingly effective.

Bozanski had his back. That was why he felt confident.

The next morning I was up early. I drove to Bankstown Central shopping centre. Most businesses had only just opened, so it was easy enough to find a parking spot within walking distance of the shops. Surveillance cameras were impossible to avoid. They made me nervous, and I had to remind myself that I was doing nothing illegal. It was not as though I was planning to blow up the joint.

I needed to find out whether my disguise was effective. I'd checked out the scene the previous day. The businesses I'd selected were ones where it was likely the same staff would be working when I returned for my second visit. It was imperative I was noticed on both occasions.

First stop was a newsagency, where I bought a packet of mints, engaging both members of staff in inane conversation about the weather.

Next I dropped into a small hairdressing salon and bought shampoo and conditioner, asking the hairdresser a string of questions about the effectiveness of the products.

My last destination was the pharmacy, where the chemist, a dark-skinned woman in white, was busy preparing a prescription. A middle-aged man with curly brown hair was placing items on a shelf near the front of the store. He hadn't been working when I was here before.

As I walked into the shop, the man stacking the shelves glanced up, begrudgingly. Was I supposed to apologise for disturbing him? The chemist acknowledged my presence, smiling briefly before returning to her task. I picked up a water filter and made my way to the counter.

The man eventually came over to the till.

'Just the water filter, thanks,' I said. 'What time do you close today?'

Looking irritated, he pointed to the sign with designated opening and closing hours behind the counter.

I paid in cash, and when I informed him that the parcel would be collected later in the day by a female friend, I received the Basil Fawlty response – the turn of the head and the peeved-off frown that told me I was pushing my luck. *That's okay, treat me like a dick* – at least I'd been noticed.

As I was leaving the shop I paused, delivering my parting words with enthusiasm. 'You won't miss my friend – she's quite the stunner.'

After leaving the shopping centre I drove home, where I showered and got to work.

Despite the practice, it took many frustrating attempts to get the base, lipstick and eyeliner right. In attempting to put on fake eyelashes, I smudged the eyeliner. I eventually discarded the eyelashes – they made me look like a female impersonator preparing for a performance. I decided to hide behind a pair of trendy, lightly tinted sunglasses.

The wig I'd chosen had a brown tint close to my natural colour. After clipping on a padded bra and attaching silver earrings, I put on a stylish light-blue V-neck blouse to match the cream-and-gold dress I'd purchased in Newtown. Then came the dark stockings, brown boots, colourful scarf and black leather gloves.

By the time I was ready to roll, I felt like I needed a strong drink. It was close to three hours before I was ready for the last item – the cream-coloured Panama hat with a small camera attached. Then I headed back to the shopping centre.

I parked the car and, with a leather handbag slung over my right shoulder, stepped out into the crowd, my head held high like a snake riding a fast-flowing river.

Once I was in motion, the dress felt too tight around the hips and thighs. Had I put on weight? Oh hell, the perils of being a woman. Maintaining a feminine stride was challenging in the elevated boots. At least there were no inquisitive stares from children nudging their parents, seeking an explanation. Nothing that saw me rushing back to the car in a panicky sweat.

I went back to the newsagency, where the woman who'd served me earlier was still on the till. I selected a packet of mints from the shelf at the front of the counter.

I said, 'Just the mints, thanks, ma'am.'

Relief – my voice hadn't cracked. Neither had the woman looked twice or given me a strange gawk.

Next stop was the hairdressing salon. *Pretend you have style and believe in your feminine side,* I told myself, mouthing the words to the Helen Reddy classic 'I Am Woman' as I walked. The pre-prison Dom would never have been willing to put himself in such a vulnerable situation.

Both hairdressers were busy. After a short wait, the same woman who had served me before came to the counter to accept payment for the hairbrush I'd taken from the rack.

'Thanks for that,' I said with a smile. 'Have a nice day.'

Again, my higher-than-usual voice held together, and the reaction from the hairdresser was not unusual – again, no gawk or anything that might indicate she'd seen my face before.

Gaining confidence, I began to observe the reactions of people waking past. Some ogled me in a way I'd never experienced. I passed two cops and they didn't put me under arrest. One of them actually smiled at me, and I smiled back before remembering – *don't encourage them, think like a woman.*

A few more lecherous glances had me feeling defenceless and exposed. *Channel your inner Kate Moss – sexy and you know it. This one's got attitude and doesn't take crap – you look good enough to get away with it.*

It was time to see how I performed in a more prolonged interaction.

Both the pharmacist and assistant were doing the same jobs as before, the chemist behind the counter and the man stacking shelves. But this time, when the man saw me, he kept on looking. He was over in a flash, nearly knocking over a stack of toilet rolls on the way. His response even caught the attention of the pharmacist, who seemed amused by his alacrity.

I reminded myself to use limited language and stick to phrases of one or two syllables – to find mellifluous flow and avoid comical screeching.

'Good morning, sir.'

'How can I help you, madam?' asked the shop assistant in a husky tone.

His voice had dropped an octave, while mine had risen by as much – that's tonal balance for you. His eyes sized me up in a way I hadn't experienced since visiting a gay bar years ago. The charm and enthusiasm that had been lacking earlier was certainly a revelation.

'My friend left a water filter for me to pick up,' I said. 'He was here earlier today?' The words came out smoothly, releasing some of the pent-up tension.

'Oh yes, of course,' he replied with a smile. As he pulled the package containing the filter from under the counter, he felt the need to fill me in on the quality of the Maxtra filtering technology.

Oh fuck up, I nearly replied, which would have been justified, considering his behaviour earlier.

What I actually said was, 'Are you paid to promote them?' The tone I'd used was definitely in the smart-arse category, but the man wasn't even insulted – he just made up some crap about being impressed by the product. Furthermore (lucky me), I'd be in the draw for The Big One if I left an email address.

I couldn't resist the temptation to go off-script.

'The Big One. Are you coming on to me?'

He began to laugh, thinking I had made a joke, but his laugher became stifled, changing into an embarrassed snort when he realised I wasn't joining in. I maintained an enraged glare as he turned scarlet.

'So sorry, madam, I didn't mean to offend you,' he mumbled.

Picking up the package, I gave him my version of an offended woman's grimace. 'You want to watch your manners, mister.'

I watched him from the corner of my eye as I left. The bloke couldn't keep his eyes off me. I swung my hips provocatively, enjoying the power. Wow, I must be something!

I began taking more notice of the type of person who gave me the once-over. Most of the ogling came from older men. Their gazes would wander aimlessly, then fix on me like a heat-seeking missile, some leering, others longing.

Men were more likely to peruse my face and body. Women checked my attire. As a man, most people, both male and female, would usually avoid prolonged eye contact with me, but dressed as a woman, I was less of a threat – people were more trusting of my female self.

It had been a peculiar experience and I was in high spirits afterwards. Although I was proud of myself for having successfully pulled off the ruse, there was no sensual elation in impersonating a woman. On that score, I was a fraud. It was all about fooling people. And I needed to be good at it. There was now just one thought on my mind – was the disguise good enough to fool Rodney Chaffer?

Moving with a new buoyancy, I went into a liquor shop and purchased a bottle of quality Highland whisky. This time I emitted a screechy 'Thank you, sir' that had me coughing, fobbing off my wonky voice as a cold.

I managed to get away with it, sure, but as I left the shopping centre, I reminded myself that even a small slip during my next endeavour could leave me in deep trouble.

was going to step outside and have his damn fag. We were almost at the heads, the part of the journey where the boat would be exposed to the open sea. Surely I hadn't caught him on the very night he decided to mend his wicked ways. Could another plan be conjured up? Calling it off was not something I wanted to contemplate.

Just as I was considering the possibility of having to follow him along the beachfront after the ferry docked, he got up from his seat and stood for a second before strolling out onto the outer deck.

Following my former colleague to the stern of the ferry, I watched on in the dwindling light as he pulled out a cigarette and lit up – quite a feat, considering it was so windy.

As I approached, he studied me. I had an unlit cigarette hanging from my mouth. I said, 'You wouldn't have a light?'

'Sure, no problemo,' he replied, fumbling in his pocket and producing a small green lighter.

I turned and crouched, lighting the cigarette in a small alcove as he watched on. After handing him back the lighter, I adopted a submissive posture. A glimmer of recognition crossed his face.

'You look familiar. Have we met before?'

You'll need a better line than that, Chaffer old buddy, I thought as I stood there watching the smooth operator at work.

'Dominique,' I said, proffering my hand. I took a puff on the cigarette, copying a sassy smoking style I'd seen in an old Western.

'I've seen you at the pub,' I said, with a coy, admiring shift of the head.

Chaffer looked chuffed – in with a chance, he thought. He raised his arm, wiggling a finger as he spoke. I'd seen Bozanski do that.

'Ah... the pub, of course,' he said, as though he remembered who I was.

Getting a whiff of the olfactory assortment that was Chaffer, witnessing the Mr Nice Guy routine of the two-faced man who'd betrayed me, I had more than enough motivation. He asked if I was feeling the cold. Barely able to contain the urge to strike out, I shook my head. *Next,* I thought, he'll be offering me his frigging coat.

The boat began to rock as we hit the heads. This was the opportunity I'd hoped for.

What I did next had been rehearsed over and over in my head a thousand times.

'Look,' I said, with childlike exuberance. 'Is that a dolphin?'

Chaffer automatically turned to where I was pointing, moving closer to the balustrade. After one quick check to ensure nobody was watching, using tackling skills instilled in me by my under-fourteen's rugby coach, I drove my shoulder into his body, hitting him side-on below the waist. I lifted with my improved upper body strength, and upwards Chaffer went, letting out a belated bellow – it would have been a hell of a shock – as I drove forward, pushed his body off me and dropped him over the balustrade.

On that Stygian night, the scene played in slow motion. For a second he clung to the rail. There was a stunned gape of what may have been recognition amid yelps of fear. Struggling against the momentum of the boat, he had no chance. It was impossible to hold on for long.

'Show us your stroke, old buddy,' I sneered, but before I'd finished the sentence, he'd lost his grip. He fell awkwardly, his head bouncing off the hull with a clunk. Whether the hit was hard enough for him to be rendered unconscious was impossible to tell. It was surprising just how fast the ferry was travelling. One moment I could see his arms and legs flailing, floundering before my eyes, then there was nothing but massive jelly blubbers bobbing atop the water in the diminishing light.

Jelly blubbers and Chaffer sharing the choppy, ashen sea. Conditions probably didn't suit his head-down swimming style, but hey, a champion would be versatile enough to pull through. For God's sake, the man bragged about his capability often enough! Sure, it wasn't his favourite distance, but you never know.

I gloated inwardly at my success, but moments later I was in panic mode. How long would his phone last in the salt water? Would some tech genius get the data? Probably! Why didn't I ask him if I could use his phone? He would have given it to me.

Then it struck me. Chaffer hadn't been wearing his coat when I tossed him over. Wild eyes peering about, I spotted it hanging from the life buoy in a dark corner. Inside the jacket was his phone.

The die had been cast, and the numbers were falling my way.

Placing the gear inside my bag, I cautiously walked back inside. Most of the passengers were occupied, some on devices, others reading. I made my way to the toilets. Inside the booth, I felt ill, and it wasn't sea sickness. Only then was the enormity of what I'd done registering. Had I killed him? My body was shaking, and my nerves were shot. Sweat began dripping down my face, playing havoc with the make-up.

Then the boat wasn't rocking anymore. We were no longer exposed to the open sea. At least we hadn't turned around to search for a man someone saw go overboard.

Flicking through Chaffer's phone, I found the conversation he had recorded two days prior, and in a matter of seconds it was erased. He hadn't sent it to anyone as far as I could tell, although chances were he had played it to Bozanski. In my favour was the fact that Bozanski wouldn't want my accusations broadcast to all and sundry.

There were messages from Bozanski, all social, nothing suspicious. Bozanski might be a bigmouth, but he was aware of the perils of saying too much on social media.

Only ten minutes remained of the journey, and I wiped myself down meticulously, touching up my make-up before sending a text message from Chaffer's phone.

I cannot believe you are threatening me. As I've told you, Adrian, I cannot continue to lie any more. I must tell the truth about the swindling of investors' funds at FGI.

I sent the text to Bozanski and, taking a punt, to an FGI director who may or may not have been corrupt. But just because someone wasn't a fan of Bozanski's didn't mean they were honest or had the integrity and courage to stick their own neck out. Who knew what he'd do with the information?

I should have dismantled and hidden the phone, but my inquisitive side got the better of me. I wanted to see if Bozanski responded. Would he suspect me once it became known that Chaffer was missing? Or would he think I didn't have the guts? If Chaffer survived, I would be ducking for cover. Arrows would be coming from all directions.

The ferry began to slow, which meant we were approaching the wharf. I waited until passengers were moving to leave the toilet. Disembarking from the vessel in the midst of the swarming commuters, I tried to ensure my face was eclipsed by taller passengers as we passed the CCTV cameras.

Out of the terminal and on the promenade, it was possible to breathe a little easier. I walked to the hire-car without incident and did a quick changeover, washing off the make-up as best I could. The drive home through backstreets to avoid major roads and motorways made the going slow.

Once I was home I felt on edge, half expecting a visit from the police or Bozanski – there were many ways events could unfold. I drank half a bottle of vodka and lay down on the sofa. 'Chaffer: The Movie' kept replaying inside my head like Groundhog Day.

There was no sign of the car that had been parked outside. The longer nothing happened, the more relaxed I became. Bozanski would be feverishly seeking Chaffer's whereabouts, wanting to know about the text message.

If Chaffer's body was found early, the CCTV from the quay and Manly would reveal that Chaffer got on but not off the ferry. Detectives might want to interview the other passengers. Did Chaffer realise it was me, or was that just my interpretation? If he survived the fall but drowned in the water, my wish was that in his last moments he knew it was Dom Bruno who had thrown him overboard.

Again, I imagined the scenario where Chaffer survived. He could have been lying unconscious in a hospital bed. Or maybe he was conscious and keeping quiet about the incident. He might not want to say too much to the authorities until he cleared it with Bozanski. Bozanski was likely to tell him to say it was an accident, and that he would take care of it.

Early the next morning I watched the news, but there was still nothing about the swimming sensation. In my head was an image of Chaffer ploughing through the water, stroke after stroke, swimming home.

Unable to rest, I decided there was no point in sitting around waiting, spending useless energy anticipating how it all might turn out. I was aware from Lydia's Facebook page that Sabrina's birthday party was on the following night. Knowing Sabrina and Lydia, it would be no small affair.

It was mainly jealousy – that and the desire to cause more mischief –

that drove me to do what I did next. Add to the mix a good dose of spite. Of course Lydia wouldn't let me near that soiree in a month of Sundays. Dom Bruno wouldn't even get past the front door. But what about Dominique?

19

An Unpleasant Surprise

It was a warm Sunday night. The outside light was on at Lydia's Surry Hills house. Her place was one of several large two-storey, semidetached terrace houses along the tree-lined street. It had been renovated to create a large, modern living space on the ground floor; perfect for partying. Lydia could do a brilliant dinner party – lucky Sabrina. And Sabrina had been most appreciative – cloyingly so in her online posts, thanking her dear friend for her support in what had been a very difficult period. *Difficult period?* She had no idea.

I was wearing the same make-up and cream-and-blue dress as I'd worn for the trial run at the Bankstown shops. I took a swig of whisky, checked the camera I'd attached to my hat and waited. People were arriving in ones and twos. The few parking spots available were filling up fast. I imagined myself in some parallel universe as the woman Lydia loved.

I'd once found parties appealing. Lydia had put on a soiree like this for one of my birthdays. Once she'd started to learn how to cook, nothing could stop her. I remember that birthday – the last one we shared – with wistful fondness. We were both in a buoyant mood after the guests left, and we fucked blissfully into the early hours, falling asleep in each other's arms. Back then Dom Bruno was a man with ambition and prospects.

I downed more of the whisky. *Be happy – nobody likes a morose whinger,* I told myself. *What's gone is gone. Something lost, something gained. Maybe!*

In the days before I was arrested, when Lydia was being seduced by the Western Buddha cabal, we fought often. I'd said they were a bunch of hypocritical Sunday believers. To them, spiritualism was just a hobby. There was more to being a Buddhist then a few weekend retreats and the annual ashram.

'Dom, they are trying to be better people,' Lydia had said.

'Trying to be better people? I'd hate to have known them before they started trying. All they care about is money and their investments.'

'Every sensible person plans for the future.'

'I thought Buddhists were supposed to live in the moment.'

'You're too bloody critical, Dom. And cynical. You deal with money all the time at FGI. You should join in the conversation. Offer some advice.'

How could I argue with that? Offer advice? No-one in that coven of witches wanted Dom to *offer advice.*

By that stage Lydia was through with me. Everybody knew. Nothing I did or said would work. My desperate declarations of love amounted to zilch.

At Lydia's house now, a lone voice sang inside, 'Happy birthday to you…'

There were cheers and shouts. False alarm – it was too early for the cake. Somebody else called out, 'Hey, birthday girl.'

Not drunk but certainly feeling the buzz, I got my chance to get inside when a vehicle drove up and five people, none of whom I knew, got out.

Following the group, I timed my stride to arrive at Lydia's door just after they'd rung the bell. In my arms were the bottle of grog and a box containing Sabrina's present with a birthday card attached.

The woman who opened the door was a friend of Sabrina's I'd met a couple of times before – a fellow Western Buddha. A rather vague woman, she would have no idea who had been invited.

'Hello, come on in.'

We all walked into the house together and I acted as though I was with them. The lady directly in front of me turned around once she realised someone was behind her. I said nothing, just smiled and, boomerang, she smiled back. I thought about how it would all have gone down had Lydia opened the door.

I made a beeline for the lounge room, catching a fleeting glimpse of Lydia taking something from the fridge as I did so.

There were probably forty people at the do. The sound of the Red Hot Chili Peppers filled the room. There was no sign of Bozanski. If he had been there, I would have had to rethink what I'd scheduled for the evening. There were some familiar faces, though, and I avoided direct eye contact. Nobody seemed concerned about my presence. At a glance there were more women than men, and hot competition from Lydia's modelling brigade.

The hallway was my bulwark, and on seeing a group of women who were in high spirits, I strode towards them. I manoeuvred my way into their circle and introduced myself with a southern American drawl.

'Angelina, as in Jolie.' I took a large swig of whisky, then proffered a limp hand. 'So pleased to meet y'all.'

The oldest of the four women shook my hand and introduced herself as Sylvia. The others ignored me, continuing their conversation amongst themselves. I was getting more confident, but it was wise to talk as little as possible.

'How do you know the birthday girl?' I asked.

Sylvia told me the two had done teacher training together. She went into a rave about the merits of being a teacher before asking me what I did for a living. I'd hoped to pass myself off as one of Lydia's model friends, but it seemed I hadn't made the grade. Damn it! My ego would just have to cope. Ignoring Sylvia's question, I raised the bottle and took a long swig, swaying on my feet as I swallowed. Sylvia eyed me with concern.

'Geez, love, you're hitting the grog a bit hard there.'

'You want some?' I asked, practically shoving the bottle down her throat.

She pushed the bottle away and backed off a bit, laughing but wary. *Who is this person? Is she insane?*

I searched the party and found Sabrina in the distance, perched upright like a meerkat, the high school teacher on a high stool, holding court. Her coterie of admirers included two women who seemed to nod a great deal, a gay couple, and an older grey-headed lady who was unsteady on her feet.

All of a sudden Sabrina was checking me out. I turned away immediately, afraid she'd recognise me. When I took another peek in her direction, she smiled. Perhaps I should make a play for her – that would set the cat amongst the pigeons.

I took another swig. It would be only be a matter of time before Lydia noticed the wolf in the henhouse. With her well-honed sensitivity, she could probably feel my presence already.

I said goodbye to Sylvia, who had returned to conversing with her friends, and meandered over to where Sabrina was seated. Sneaking up on her blind side with a beaming smile on my dial, I was in her face before she knew it.

Again, I spoke with a southern American twang. 'Happy birthday, dearest.'

She jumped – I'd scared her witless. I shoved the parcel onto her lap. The Queen of the Western Buddhas eyed the parcel and the person standing before her with equal curiosity.

I said, 'I'm Angelina. Like in Jolie.' When she didn't respond, I slapped her across the shoulders. 'You know, like the actress.'

'Of course I bloody know who Angelina Jolie is.'

I could tell she was trying to figure out who I was, so I answered before she could ask.

'I'm that crazy neighbour from across the road. I hope you like the present.'

My smile was exaggerated and ridiculous. Sabrina turned her head towards the kitchen, where Lydia was still in MasterChef mode, back to me, and then to the package.

'There's something moving inside,' said a woman standing near Sabrina.

'Then you better open it,' I said.

Sabrina's friends watched in anticipation. The grey-headed lady seemed to think I was hilarious. Sabrina didn't.

'What is it? I don't want a pet.'

'Is it a bird?' asked one of the men.

'No… It's not a bird,' I replied.

Sabrina's friends, some of whom were more sloshed than I'd realised, insisted that she open the package.

'Is it a battery-operated dildo?' asked one of the gay men. They all laughed like crazy at that.

'No, no. Nothing like that,' I said. 'Just something small. Nothing like the forty grand Adrian Bozanski gave Sabrina for services rendered.'

'What!' exclaimed Sabrina, mouth open and momentarily lost for words.

'Oh dear,' somebody said.

Ears pricked. Conversations nearby stopped.

Sabrina gazed at me with angry eyes. 'How dare you make such outrageous accusations! Who in the hell are you?'

The hostile frown on her brow worsened as she cast a worrying eye to see who had overheard what I'd said. Curious gapes were coming my way. It was time to leave. The wolves would soon be closing in.

Taking another swig from the bottle, I forced one last smile and said, 'Nature calls. I must be off to the bathroom.'

As I withdrew, I feared I'd bitten off more than I could chew. I bypassed the bathroom, my pace quickening when I glimpsed Lydia coming from the kitchen with a plate of food in each hand. The aroma of spinach and gruyere soufflé played tricks with my senses.

Blood pumping, high from the thrill, I made my way to the front door. When I realised nobody had followed me, I paused and waited. The music stopped. The party became ominously quiet.

'Who in the hell was that?' asked a woman with an amused lilt in her voice.

'Does anybody know her?' asked Sabrina, in a disparaging tone. The use of the word 'her' was gratifying to hear.

'What happened?' I heard Lydia ask.

Sabrina told Lydia the short version of what had occurred, leaving out the bit about Bozanski and the forty grand.

'She's probably from a delivery service or something?' said Lydia.

166

'What a weirdo,' said Sabrina, still sounding flustered. 'She said she was your neighbour.'

'My neighbour?' said Lydia questioningly.

'She's not in the bathroom,' I heard a man say. 'Must have taken off.'

'Open the parcel,' somebody insisted.

'Come on, Sabrina. See what's inside,' said another.

'Okay... okay!' Sabrina replied.

People began to talk again. I could hear voices approaching, so I quickly departed the scene. I'd just pulled the front door shut behind me when a piercing scream came from inside the house.

'A fucking rat! It's a *fucking rat*!'

The word *rat* was screeched at high volume amid screaming from the guests. The atonal symphony of the freaked-out partygoers waxed and waned before reaching a crescendo – the rat was on the move.

I heard the high-pitched squeal of chairs being dragged along the wooden floor amid further shrieking and shouting. People were moving to higher ground – it was primal, this rat business.

I'd just reached my car when Lydia and two men appeared at the top of the steps. I hid behind a tree and watched. After a cursory scan of the street, they went back inside. I doubted that Lydia had recognised my car from that distance in the dark. She hadn't seen me and my disguise was good, but the rat would make her suspicious.

As soon as I got home I hit the vodka. Again, maudlin thoughts haunted me. I could picture myself in a hospice bed, zonked out on medication, in my final mortal moments. Maybe Tran would drop by. But not Lydia. Lydia would be way too busy living her wonderful life. My thoughts returned to the party. Did Sabrina stay the night? It wasn't long before I was picturing the two in the same bed... imagining the things they did.

Find someone else, anyone but Lydia.

I couldn't sleep, so I edited the footage I'd taken at Sabrina's party and sent it to Mr Twinkel.

The next morning there was another unidentified vehicle – this one a panel van – parked nearby. After checking the footage, I realised it had also been there the previous night. Busy being Dom the jealous fool, I'd missed it. Bozanski's boys, or a new Dom watcher – some nut who thought I might lead him to the loot? At least nobody approached the house.

There was still nothing on Chaffer. But the storms clouds were surely gathering, as dark as Mordor. I could feel the barometer building. The truth was that this place was no longer safe. The poisoned spears would come from all directions and velocities. One didn't require the wisdom of Saul to know that.

It was imperative that I ensured I wasn't being followed when I left the house. After contacting Tran, I downloaded an app that allowed me to check the vista from the house camera using my mobile phone when I was out.

To distract myself I went online. Mr Twinkel had two new postings. He'd already edited the footage I'd sent from the party. That was quick! Again, his slick editing skills and tasteful musical accompaniment had done wonders.

'Cerberus at Mealtime' had been created from the footage Tracy took of Cerberus being fed. Cerberus looked twice his actual size.

The longer of the two was titled 'Smell a Rat', based on what I'd recorded at Sabrina's party. Twinkel had managed to superimpose the image of a rat so it appeared at the party in a number of locations much earlier in the night, well before Sabrina opened the package and it got loose.

As he had done before, at the end of the clip Twinkel thanked Benedict Sparkel for the contribution. But this time the acknowledgment was given more prominence. In the background was the Fuck It! List song.

Both productions had attracted international attention. I figured that should put me in Twinkel's good books and keep the bugger off my back for a while.

20

Wonder Woman

The destination was a park in Bondi. Since I'd run into Lydia's old schoolmate Matilda down near the quay, we had exchanged a few emails. Meeting up was my idea. I had to push off to somewhere else, and even if nothing eventuated from the rendezvous, at least it would stop me thinking about Chaffer.

Matilda and Lydia were close during their senior years at school. Matilda was one of the few people Lydia had confided in when we had camped out in the wild together (for me, two weeks of bliss) in the Royal National Park, after being exposed – fake news – as 'brother-and-sister lovers'. At Lydia's fancy school, it would have been a hot topic of conversation.

The place Matilda and I had decided to meet was at the east end of Cooper Park, a natural amphitheatre with massive sandstone walls. There was a sometimes-waterfall, and a pool at the bottom where ferns thrived in the cool shade of the eucalyptus trees. I'd been here before with Lydia. If I remembered the story correctly, Lydia and Matilda used to play tennis near here for school sport.

While sitting in the park waiting for Matilda, I read an article she had written slamming present governments for their lack of action over the Great Barrier Reef. Since we had agreed to meet up, I had read everything I could get my hands on about Matilda. For the reef, according to Matilda, the clock was approaching midnight. For Dom Bruno, the clock was also ticking fast – I'd be gone before the reef.

There was a series of photos posted on her Facebook page. One with her family, another playing hockey, and a particularly charming shot of Matilda in her late teens, barefoot and in hippy garb, wearing colourful beads and long earrings.

There were campaigns in the Antarctic, a photo with Bob Brown. *Who is the bloke with Doctor Matilda?* somebody had commented. My favourite was a serious Matilda dressed like Bindi Irwin's twin in khaki green, walking boots and backpack.

Matilda worked at Western Sydney University, lecturing in Environmental Science. Her articles were published in magazines and she was abused by shock jocks and quoted by politicians. I was out of my league, but in the back of my mind was a comment Lydia had once made, inferring Matilda had a soft spot for me. It gave me some hope.

Matilda was twenty minutes late. Or had she forgotten? Perhaps she was having second thoughts. A story Lydia had told about Matilda being dubbed 'Waltzing Matilda' due to her habit of strolling into roll class late came to mind.

It was only minutes later that she came into view, waving from afar. Strolling up to the bench where I was sitting, she stopped and stooped, pulling out a small plant that had sprung up on the edge of the path.

'Just a weed,' she said.

'And hello to you,' I replied.

She laughed. 'Sorry, Dom,' she said, giving me a cursory hug. 'Oh, and before I forget, thanks for the donation.'

'Thanks for the education. A donation is the least I can do,' I said, sounding like the proverbial try-hard. 'When I read your article I was dismayed. I can't believe those bastards want to put in a coal mine. The almighty dollar, eh!' My own hypocrisy and saccharine tone had me on the brink of gagging, but I didn't stop. 'If they really thought about the money, they'd worry about the billions that'll be lost to the tourist industry.'

'Have you turned into a greenie, or are you just trying to impress?' Matilda said.

Oh no – she was on to me.

'Both,' I replied. If I'd displayed my usual indifference to these matters, she might have been gone in seconds. Only a fool would have rolled up wearing their Clean Coal hat.

Again, I questioned why an attractive, high-achieving woman was bothering with the likes of me. Was it because of my friendship with Lydia? Had Lydia put her up to it? That was really overthinking the situation.

Matilda pointed to a bush loaded with purple berries. 'Hey, check these out.' She picked a few choice berries and put one in her mouth. 'As sweet as! Try one.'

I looked at her with apprehension.

She laughed. 'I wouldn't poison you.'

I did as she'd suggested. The berry oozed beautiful, rich flavour. I recalled eating them sometimes in my childhood.

'They might save you one day if you find yourself lost in the bush,' she said.

'I'd probably pick a deadly lookalike.'

As we walked along the path together, I wondered whether there was a lethal variety of berry I could use on Dunkley or Bozanski. That could be worth further investigation if I didn't get hold of a weapon soon. Still nothing from my friends down the Imperial.

Possessed of an eagle eye, now and then Matilda would stop to identify a plant or an insect that I wasn't aware was even there. Walking in the park with Matilda was akin to being on the set of a reality gardening show.

Daydreaming, I missed a question she had asked. She must have known her student was not up for the task, because her reproachful glare transmuted into disappointment. And believe me, I know that look. It's a look I've been on the receiving end of many times before. Still, she wasn't perfect – a bit nerdy, and with a tone to her voice that was droll and clinical at times.

Matilda asked me about a couple of her and Lydia's mutual friends, but I knew nothing about them. Her attention was diverted as we began to be bitten by mosquitoes. Like a knight in shining armour, I pulled a can of insect repellent from my bag – Dom to the rescue.

'Try some of this.'

'You must be fucking kidding. That stuff's toxic. Do you know, Dom, that without insects, there'd be no life on the planet?'

Despite her death stare, I wasn't going to cave in. 'I'm not trying to murder them, just keep them away. 'Cause I tell you something else, Matilda – without insect repellent, there'd be no Dom on the planet.'

She was slightly amused at that, so I muttered something about catching Ross River fever. She informed me that there were natural insect repellents available, and that the one she used was made from lemon and eucalyptus.

Our disagreement – my ignorance – didn't faze her. We began walking again and started to chat. She asked me about Lydia. I responded with a sheepish glance.

'I think Lydia has given me the flick. Can't blame her. Who wants to hang with a loser?'

She gazed back at me as though that didn't sound right. 'Nah, Lydia wouldn't be like that. Not with you.'

'Lydia's changed. She's become caught up with the wrong crowd. She doesn't like me telling her that they're a bunch of phonies. Since I've been out of prison, we've hardly seen each other.'

'You going to prison – that was ridiculous. It's not as if you were a threat to anyone.'

An experienced inmate told me that when people knew you have been to gaol, they would either hold it against you or respect you for enduring it. Whether Matilda thought I was guilty or not was uncertain. She probably did. I was traduced in court and found guilty as charged. As guilty as the mum who claimed a dingo took her baby.

'You don't look too bad, considering what you went through,' Matilda added.

If she only knew. Dunkley was always knocking, and he was back inside my head again. What would it take to erase those memories, to feel clean, to be free of him?

'Prison was fine,' I said. 'Plenty of time to read and reflect. Work things out. Made some friends. And as you can see, I've bulked up. *Me Tarzan.*' I braced my muscles. 'Another plus for prison life.'

The last sentence sounded flat, wooden, like a comedian on a bad night. Then I was crying.

'Hey, Dom.' She put her arm around my shoulder. 'It must have been terrible, being locked up in a cell.'

Sympathy was one thing, but nobody wanted to hang with a sad, morose fucker. To lighten the mood, I told her a story about an inmate who worked in the prison garden and painted the plants. It created a stunning effect. Monet, everybody called him. In the confines of the prison he had discovered the essence of an artist.

Then one day he began painting ladders on the walls. Stairways to heaven, he called them. The wardens took the paint off him. The poor old bugger was devastated. He had spent most of his life inside. His name was Kevin. The chant would go up, to the tune of 'Stairway to Heaven' – 'Give the paint back to Kevin'.

'Did he get the paint back?'

'Yes. The wardens couldn't stand the singing.'

'I've been locked up twice. Once for a week in South America,' said Matilda, out of the blue.

'Really?' That did surprise me. 'What for?'

'Chaining myself to a piece of mining machinery. Another time for trespassing in Queensland.'

Crazy stuff, I thought, but I did admire her tenacity. 'Wow, that's really standing up for your beliefs.'

'*Nihil sine dolore quaestus,*' she said.

'Are you swearing at me?'

'No pain, no gain.'

I winked to myself as I spoke, laying it on a bit thick. 'You know what, Matilda, despite losing trust in people, I am a stronger person for it. You learn a lot about yourself, being locked up, spending all that time alone with your thoughts.'

Matilda told me she would have to go, as there was an appointment she had to keep. Probably tiring of me – that was what I thought. Then she surprised me, asking if I was interested in meeting her later at a pub in Surry Hills.

'I'm meeting this American dude. He's recovering from post-traumatic stress. Poor Phil has been having a hard time of it.'

The reality of her words hit me like a jolt. I'd been close earlier when I'd hypothesised about her motives. Matilda wanted Down-On-His-Luck Dom to hang with Poor Phil. We could start a mutual pathetic society.

I was being added to the collection of damaged creatures she was trying to save.

Once I'd gotten over myself, though, I realised I'd received a lucky break. The way things were panning out, Matilda may well be the only friend I had.

I said, 'Thanks Matilda, I'd really like that.'

I meant it.

The meeting with Matilda and Phil didn't turn out to be at all dull. I met up with Matilda in the lounge and we went through to the public bar, which was loud and bustling with life. The clientele consisted mostly of students, dressed in T-shirts and blue jeans in the appropriate state of disrepair. There was a splattering of older men in scarves and odd hats, plus some transgender folk whom everybody seemed to know.

This trendy tribe was so different from the shady lot at the Imperial. I couldn't imagine Case or Bubba feeling at home here. How would Tracy fare? She'd attract attention because of her looks and personality. Would she keep up with the dry wit? Would she tolerate the political bullshit and displays of knowledge? She wouldn't take any shit from this lot. The manager from the Imperial would shake his head in despair at his plight, smile and be nice, put up the prices and make a buck, feeling confident he could provide security without needing a cricket bat.

We grabbed a table after a group left. One could be almost invisible in these circles – obscure in the vicinity of freaks. Certainly I'd be more interesting to this clientele as Dominica.

Matilda waved to a thickset man who had just arrived. His face lit up when he recognised her. He was genuinely thrilled to see her. Wielding a walking stick, which he lifted in acknowledgement, he walked towards us with alacrity, slightly favouring his right side. This was surely Phil, and he had the bearing of a wounded bear. His thick tan beard was clipped short. He had deep lines across his face and a small, sharp mouth. Although he bore the wounds of one who had suffered, he was a strong-looking man, albeit overweight.

The bear and Matilda hugged heartily, and I got the impression he could hug someone to death if he chose. Matilda introduced me as an old friend. Phil grabbed a chair from a nearby table and joined us. From his reaction on seeing me, I got the impression the American would rather have had Matilda to himself. Who could blame him for wanting that?

After a while he settled in and became more affable. He probably decided I didn't pose a threat. While Matilda was chatting to a group nearby, Phil told me his story. He hailed from Winslow Arizona, and without any encouragement from me, went about the task of describing the attributes of his home town in the patriotic way many Americans do. He smelt of wood and smoke, and when I commented on this he said he had spent the last few days out in the bush. Occasionally he would get to his feet and look about. He said he was expecting a friend, another American.

When the friend arrived, I received the shock of my life. I played it cool, but really my head went into a spin.

Phil's friend was Wayne – the Wayne I'd known from FGI. The same Wayne who had given me the positive court reference. Wayne, from his reaction, was as surprised as me. Phil couldn't believe we knew each other. Dapper and well-dressed, how different this Wayne looked from the man I'd seen recently, shuffling along King Street in Newtown.

The two Americans talked turkey – they had been in the US military together. Phil did most of the yapping, and boy, could he yap. Wayne hung back and listened. Matilda came back to the table and we got on to bands and music. As it turned out, Matilda possessed a collection of hundreds of independent Australian releases. Some bands I knew, a couple I'd seen at concerts. Most I'd never heard of.

When Phil went to the bar, Wayne pulled his chair close to where I was sitting. We talked for a minute or two about the people we both knew from FGI. At first Wayne didn't reveal much. I played my cards close to my chest. Then Wayne said something out of the blue.

'I know you got treated badly by FGI… definitely got a dud deal. I've no idea what really happened, but there was some funny stuff going on, and none of it was investigated properly.'

At that moment I was completely lost for words. It was like meeting another one of your species on a foreign planet. Phil came back and nothing more was said about FGI, but before we parted, Wayne agreed to meet up with me again.

Later that evening, I logged on to the Mr Twinkel site. He'd created a clip based on a drawing I'd sent. I'd called the woman Dominica.

Dominica comes on stage with heavy guitar music playing in the background. She begins to sing.

'Get a Fuck It! List

Seize control of your life

No use just getting pissed off

Feel irate

Use it mate.'

The tempo stays the same, but the music becomes sparse and more rhythmic. The face changes to that of Twinkel, and the voice takes on a disparaging tone.

'Tell me about Dominica, how would that woman fare?

From what they've been saying, she could make it anywhere

But will she hold strong when the real pressure's on

Or will she go to pieces like a cheap bloody thong?'

21

Wake Up Little Suzi

When I got home, Dunkley was out and Stephen was cleaning his Evo 3. Dunkley arrived home a short time later. He had been irate since losing his truck licence and he began berating Stephen for making too much noise the previous night – the Evo sure could roar.

'All legal,' replied Stephen, meekly.

'You do it again and I'll show you what's fucking legal, you dickhead.'

Dunkley's nostrils flared as something caught his eye. He ambled over to the Murrays' rubbish bins, which were out the front awaiting collection. After ensuring nobody but Stephen was watching, he kicked out with gusto at the red bin, sending the contents sprawling across the footpath. A tomato sauce bottle (rich and spicy) broke, and the mess took on the appearance of a crime scene.

'Keep your bins over your side, you fucking dobber,' Dunkley yelled.

Stephen stopped cleaning the Evo. He stood there, glaring at Dunkley, clearly unsure of what to do. After a few beats he mustered up the courage to speak.

'Pick it all up, you idiot.'

'Pick it up, you idiot,' said Dunkley, mimicking the kid's insipid nasal tone.

Anger boiled up within me as I witnessed Stephen's humiliation. Dunkley had often mocked me in a similar manner.

Stephen fought back. 'You still haven't paid for the damage to my car. You'll hear from the insurance company soon.'

Dunkley fired a gob of spit from his mouth. It landed at Stephen's feet.

'Stevie, come inside, son – now. He isn't worth it,' called Stephen's mother from the front door.

'Bloody Mum! Spoils all the fun,' said Dunkley.

Stephen gave Dunkley the two-fingered salute before going inside.

How long would Stephen control his temper? Not very long at all, as it turned out.

Later that night I heard somebody shouting out on the street. I hurried upstairs and out onto the balcony to see what was happening. Stephen was stumbling along the footpath, obviously drunk. A taxi was driving away. Standing directly outside Dunkley's place, Stephen upped the ante, cursing and yelling insults.

A man called from a house nearby, 'Just go home, you idiot.'

Stephen should have heeded the advice, but the constant harassment and the earlier incident must have affected him. Tonight he was full as a boot and without fear. It wasn't wise to step into the ring with Dunkley at any time, let alone in an inebriated state. Furthermore, neither Mum nor Brayden was home. There was nobody around to save him.

Stephen was loud and his repertoire eclectic. Dunkley didn't appear immediately, but he was bound to respond. He would have been near the end of his tether himself with the problems he was facing: suspension of licence, charged for driving under the influence of a drug, out of work.

From the manner in which Dunkley swaggered out of his house, it was clear he welcomed the challenge. Fronting Stephen with an ominous grin, he held out his chin, encouraging the kid to have a swing. And swing Stephen did. Dunkley even let the kid hit him a couple of times before mounting a response. Dunkley began jabbing with his left fist, landing multiple blows to Stephen's torso. Stephen's windmill style of fighting was inefficient and ineffective. His telegraphed punches were easily deflected by Dunkley, who continued to work away.

Dunkley's blows were surprisingly light and it seemed as though he was clowning about. At the time I thought he might have been concerned about the legal ramifications of his actions, but as I would later learn, there was something more sinister going on.

When Stephen did get lucky, landing a solid right, Dunkley merely smiled back at the kid as if to say, *is that the best you've got?* Stephen was soon out of puff. Dunkley then pummelled his opponent with a flurry of punches before grabbing him in a bear hug. With his powerful forearms, he flung Stephen to the ground. The kid went tumbling onto his backside, banging his head against the fence. Dunkley must have thought he'd done enough to win on points, because after he'd done a quick scan of the neighbourhood to see who was watching, he turned on his heel and headed back inside.

Stephen could barely get to his feet, but it didn't stop him hurling abuse and making more threats. As I focused on Stephen, I noticed something that had me puzzled. His shirt had been shredded. I was sure it hadn't been in that state prior to the fight.

It was then that I cottoned on to what Dunkley had done. Stephen was too drunk to notice the devious trick Dunkley had played on him, and too anaesthetised to feel the pain that would surely come.

There was an unfathomable moment when Stephen saw the blood, firstly on his T-shirt, and then cascading down his arms and legs. He began to yelp, an unnerving sound, like a dog caught in a rabbit trap. Zooming in close, I watched the replay in slow motion. Dunkley had concealed razor blades between the fingers of his left hand. The sharp end was protruding just enough to break the skin. It didn't cut deep into the flesh, but it did cause a substantial amount of bleeding.

What a vicious, calculating mind Dunkley had! His thuggish activism had me feeling sorry for the kid and a tad guilty. Watching Stephen limp inside, I wondered if he would report Dunkley. Around here, that was unlikely.

While I had been busy watching the fight, two emails had arrived. One from Tran – he was having difficulty hacking into Bozanski's files. The other contained news I'd been keenly anticipating. It was a notification from Case that said, *Goods from Trevino ready for collection.* Soon it would be all systems go.

Suzi and her boy Dylan had been at Dunkley's place less and less lately. Last night she had arrived by taxi, an hour after the fracas. Who would want to be with Dunkers at his best, let alone in his present state?

The morning after the fight, Dunkley went out early, leaving Suzi and the boy at home. Suzi must have known Dunkley wouldn't return for some time, because while Dylan was still asleep, she availed herself of the gentle morning sun. Clad in a brief bikini, she lay on a large Hawaiian beach towel near the clothesline, flicking through a magazine. Apart from my presence on the balcony, the yard was private.

All was quiet on the Western Front when a car drove past and stopped down near the park. I would recognise that Holden ute anywhere. Turner jumped out of the car and began to make his way towards Dunkley's house. He'd dropped by only once since I'd been watching the place, and that time he had parked out the front. So why had he parked down the end of the street? And why was he visiting while Dunkley wasn't home?

I needed to warn Suzi that a predator was on his way, but there was nothing I could do except observe. It was like being in a Hitchcock film. Turner made sure he wasn't seen before ducking around to the side gate. He unlatched the lock and entered the backyard.

What happened next showed the extent to which I'd misread the situation.

Rather than reacting with outrage (who would want this filthy pervert near them?), Suzi greeted him with a smile, getting to her feet and giving him a welcoming hug. Then a prolonged kiss – lovers' lips – with her boobs up against his body, leaving me flabbergasted. What the hell? Was she jumping ship to the only other boat in port? Talk about into the frying pan. What a poor, desperate soul. What about your boy?

Suzi returned to her sunbaking while Turner sat there ogling her body with his licentious gaze. A short time later he said something to Suzi before picking up a tube of sunscreen. He squeezed some of the contents onto his hand and began rubbing it over her back – what a helpful man! When his hands wandered down to Suzi's bum, she brushed them away slowly – far too slowly. The game of cat and mouse continued. *Benedict Sparkel, feast your eyes on this!* But why was she permitting Turner – at least twenty years her senior – to behave in this way? It was sickening, watching Suzi, so young and attractive, allowing her perfect body to be used by this withered, lecherous creep.

Turner's attention was suddenly diverted and he turned his head sharply towards the house. Suzi began making an effort to look respectable

– someone was coming. A weary-eyed Dylan appeared and Suzi greeted the boy with a loving smile. Maybe he could sense the precarious situation he was in because he looked worried. His sad little face said it all – *help*.

The boy began playing in the backyard with his remote-control truck. He didn't miss much, just Turner's grubby paws all over his mum's body. Half an hour later Turner left by the side gate, skulking out into the street and back towards the park like a thief in the night. Once he'd reached the safety of his car, he seemed pleased with himself. That smug expression on Turner's face – I knew it well.

Was Suzi actually playing Dunkley off against Turner? If so, she could end up being played herself. Knowing the two despicable men, I wouldn't put it past them to have some mates' agreement to share the poor woman. But that was unlikely. From the furtive way Turner had behaved, my guess was that Dunkley had no idea. He was being betrayed. Just because Dunkley shared the spoils in prison didn't mean he was willing to do the same on the outside. If he found out Turner had come on to Suzi behind his back, in his backyard, Dunkley would be livid.

I had an idea. But Suzi needed to be out of the picture. Her presence would only complicate matters.

I put together a sixty-second clip containing the choice moments I'd captured. I dressed in a blue uniform similar to that of a delivery man. Altering my appearance with a grey wig and beard, clipboard in hand, I presented myself at Dunkley's door. It felt peculiar being in the space he inhabited. Up close it was apparent the house needed painting. If the cards fell my way, Dunkley wouldn't be around to do that job.

I knocked. Suzi came to the door. After stating the address I said, 'Delivery for Suzi. No need to sign.'

'For me?' she said with surprise.

185

Like most delivery drivers, I was a man on a mission, departing quickly after delivering the package. It would take time to remove the sticky tape, open the package, read the note and get the gist. A minute at least. By then I was long gone.

I pictured Suzi reading the note.

Dunkley knows about your affair with his mate, Cyril. He is on his way home. Escape with the kid while you still have the chance. You are in serious trouble. Wake up, little Suzi. Dunkley and Cyril Turner are sexual predators. They are violent and dangerous. Don't allow your child or yourself to remain anywhere near them. Run, Suzi, run.

With the message was a USB containing the footage I'd recorded, plus a wad of fifty-dollar notes – five thousand dollars, to be exact. I wasn't rich, but due to the popularity of the Benedict Sparkel uploads, I wasn't short of cash either. Mr Twinkel had continued to be true to his word, leaving cash at the postal box I'd nominated.

Returning home, I watched Dunkley's place. How would Suzi react? Would she display some sense? She wouldn't be silly enough to ignore my message, surely. Then I began to wonder. Was I the idiot? What if Dunkley came back home at that moment? I began mouthing the word *idiot*, over and over.

Just minutes later I caught a glimpse through the bedroom window of a Corybantic Suzi, darting to and fro like a mosquito on speed. Soon after, she came out of the house with Dylan, carrying the same two suitcases she had arrived with. A taxi drove up and stopped at the door. The driver helped her load the luggage into the boot and they were gone.

Wow, I thought, *that's more like it.* But the thought that Suzi might take the taxi to Turner's place had me rushing into the garage. Catching up with the taxi, I followed it until it took the turnoff to the airport.

That night, Dunkley didn't come home.

The next day, as the time drew near for my rendezvous with Trevino, I felt uneasy. Wary of being tailed, I took a roundabout route to the industrial estate near Roselands that Trevino had nominated.

Trevino was in a relaxed mood when we meet, which had a calming effect on me. He heaped praise on the handgun – a Bersa Thunder 380 with silencer – as he loaded a full magazine (it would take eight rounds) and explained how the de-cocking lever worked. He said it was effective up to about ten metres.

I felt a thrill, like a four-year-old at Christmas, as he handed me the black handgun. The size was perfect. It fit snugly in my hand and would be easy to conceal.

Trevino passed me a backpack containing the ammunition, then gave me the two sets of numberplates for examination. Giving them a critical going-over before speaking, I sounded like the expert I was not.

'Excellent pieces of work, mate.'

Trevino thanked me for the compliment. He said it was gratifying to see that his work was appreciated, telling me he had a contact in a wrecking yard who selected plates that matched makes and models of vehicles that had been written off.

'A small-business success story in the globalised world,' I joked, adding, 'I won't pass a car with the same plates?'

'You don't go out around Dubbo much, do you?' he asked.

There was a moment's pause before we both laughed. I just hoped the joke wasn't on me.

Arriving home, I couldn't resist playing around with the weapon, loading and reloading, becoming familiar with the mechanical workings. Holding the gun did give me a sense of power – *in with a chance.*

My original plan was to dress as Turner (he was close to my height), shoot Dunkley and dump the weapon somewhere near Turner's house, where it would be easily found. The problem was that the police might want to interview all the neighbours living near the victim. Even if they didn't talk to me directly, my name could come up on the system as having done time, and some clever Dick might make the connection to Dunkley. It would also mean facing up to Dunkley head-on. That would take a lot of nerve, even with a gun.

But what if I did a switch? Shot Turner and set up Dunkley? He did have a motive and a history of violence – my recordings would establish that. There was also the possibility I wouldn't have to lift a finger. If Dunkley knew of the Turner's treachery, in his present frame of mind he might knock his old friend off and get life. I wouldn't put it past him.

Sending him the proof would tip him off. He'd know somebody had been spying on his house. The camera angle said it all. By my reckoning, he'd suspect one of three residences. The odds weren't good. But Dunkley was a one-task-at-a-time type of man. He'd probably be so angry at Turner and Suzi that it would occupy him for quite some time. It would be a while before he got around to trying to find the person who supplied the incriminating photos.

After checking the footage to make sure Dunkley hadn't come home while I was out, I dropped a package into his letterbox. It was labelled, *Cyril and Suzi – LUST.* The package was the same as the one Suzi had received. To whet his appetite, I'd tossed in an incriminating photo of the two – the one where Turner had his sleazy paw on Suzi's bum. I edited the footage to make it look as though the length of time his hand had been there was longer than it actually was. Bums and hands – you can do a lot with bums and hands. But if you're not careful, they'll get you into trouble.

In an attempt to put Dunkley off my scent, I included a pamphlet that highlighted the dangers posed by drones – 'Invaders of Privacy'. Whether he would fall for that was anybody's guess.

22

Exit Stage Left

I awoke in a lather of sweat with a splitting headache that a double dose of painkillers couldn't quell. Was the cancer on the march? It was a chilling thought. The need for something stronger had me pursuing the directory of local doctors' surgeries. The earliest appointment I could get was for the following week, which was somewhat optimistic bearing in mind what lay ahead.

There was still no news on Chaffer. For all I knew he was halfway to New Zealand. *Pull that one off, Chaffer old mate, and I'll believe you weren't just boasting about your swimming feats.* I felt no guilt – at least not for the moment. Who knows how those things can ebb and flow over time? For me, an old age of self-loathing was not going to happen.

A Mazda four-wheel drive drove up and parked outside the Murrays' house. A man, probably fifty or so, got out of the vehicle. He had a slim build and a dark complexion. The car was covered in red dust. On the back windscreen was a Shooters Party sticker. I hoped he had a weapon on him. He'd be needing one if he was thinking of taking on Dunkley.

Dunkley eventually came home. I was on edge, watching him take the package from his letterbox. He stood there for what seemed like years, examining the contents – he certainly didn't apply speed-reading skills to the information I had sent him on drones.

I zoomed in on him and watched as he opened the envelope containing the photo of Turner and Suzi. Dunkley stood there, seething.

An hour later Turner arrived. Dunkley came out to greet him. Dunkley didn't appear to be overly perturbed, but it was often difficult to tell with him. Turner waved as he got out of his car. Dunkley didn't wave back, just stood there, leaning on the front gate.

Turner approached, smiling, but Dunkley remained poker-faced as he handed Turner a photo. The Warden shook his head, dumbfounded for a moment, before he began apologising. He must have asked Dunkley how he got hold of the photo. Wrong question. Dunkley pushed the gate open, stepped out and smashed Turner with a solid right to the jaw. A barrage of quick punches followed, and Turner lay spread-eagled across the lawn.

Dunkley was never one to fight by Westminster rules. He laid the boot in, the last strike a nasty heel to the mouth. Dunkley towered over the man. I'd thought Turner was out cold, but he came to life and was soon scrambling towards the car on his hands and knees. Dunkley gave him one final kick to the guts for good measure, following it up with an intimidating salvo.

'This ain't finished. Not by a long shot.'

Blinds were moving, neighbours were watching. And all the birds were singing – couldn't have happened to a nicer bloke. Turner deserved all he got.

Dunkley turned on the stickybeaks with pure, powerful rage.

'Nothing to fucking see,' he yelled, to the one or two brave enough to linger.

Turner made it to his car and dragged himself to his feet. As he searched for his keys he glanced back at Dunkley, fearful he would cop more punishment. A shaken, bloody mess, he was slow to get the car started. Once he found the accelerator he fled like a bat out of hell.

Then, the worst of my fears – Dunkley crossed the road. The bastard was on my side of the street. He began checking the balconies and windows, scanning high and low. How many dwellings were perused by his evil eye was hard to know – he did have a long look at mine.

After he went back to his house, I began dismantling my equipment and packing it into the boot of the car. Bigger items like the fridge, bed and sofa would be left behind. Later, in the darkness of the night, I would flee. No more footage of Dunkley was required.

I'd just put a box of kitchen utensils onto the back seat of the car when, out of the blue, a taxi pulled to a stop outside my place. I stared in disbelief. It was Tracy.

Edgy and thrown off-kilter by her sudden appearance, I ushered her in quickly through the front door.

'Hi, Tracy – what the hell are you doing here?'

She wasn't put off by my uncivil welcome, but she wanted to know why I was acting so uptight. Her mood turned sullen when she realised everything was packed away.

'Are you moving out?'

I could hardly deny it.

'You were just going to leave. Without even saying goodbye.'

'Of course not. I was going to drop by the pub.'

'Where are you going?'

'I have a friend up north who can get me a job on a fishing boat.'

'What about your work for that detective agency?'

'My contract has expired.'

Three lies in ten seconds. That was impressive, even for me. How could I explain? Cowardice! That I feared Bozo's boys, Dunkley – not to mention her ex-boyfriend Brayden, who might decide to make a sculpture with his chainsaw, using me instead of a slab of wood. I was twice the man I used to be, but not half the man she thought I was.

In the end I told her dangerous people were after me – the real crooks who set me up and were worried they might be exposed. She became interested and wanted to know more. Again, I imagined her by my side. Maybe in some parallel universe, we were as infamous as Bonnie and Clyde.

I packed more gear into the boot of the car.

She said, 'You'll stay in touch?'

'Yes, of course I will. When things settle down. If I survive that long.'

'Don't talk like that. You'll be okay.'

Tracy became soulful, said she'd miss me. Perhaps she was the only person alive who would. Maybe Lydia, a bit. I'd miss Tracy's verve and spirit, her youthful sprightliness. But Tracy's attachment to me was based on her loneliness and my deceit.

We talked about the usual topics – people down the pub, Netflix and television shows. The longer we talked, the more we were drawn to each other. Her perfume had become familiar and enticing. Tracy told me about her times as a wild child. She had the devil in her and I loved her irrepressible nature. Half an hour later, we were lying together on the bed in the upstairs bedroom, making sweet, nothing-to-lose love.

Afterwards, with everything packed away, the sense of change was evident. We were both feeling it – neither of us said much, and when we did it was downbeat.

The night was quiet. Then, from nowhere, came the sound of angry voices. Tracy was on her feet and at the window, her attention drawn to the action down on the street, the shape of her nakedness stunning in the dull glow of the streetlight.

'That's Brayden,' she said.

So Brayden was in the mix tonight. Joining Tracy at the window, I stood there, watching.

Dunkley had his drinking buddy with him, the same man who had found Dunkley's ridiculing of Stephen so amusing. Brayden was fired up, no doubt angered by the damage Dunkley had inflicted on his brother. Dunkley was half-pissed – nothing unusual there. Brayden shaped up, and Dunkley gave his mate a wink – *this will only take a minute.*

And it was on. Just when I'd thought the war was over. The camera was packed away – somebody had forgotten to tell them filming had finished.

Dunkley blocked a straight left while harping away on a familiar theme. 'What fucking harm was my truck doing to you lot?'

'Where's my brother's money for the damage to his car, eh, Skunkley? You cheap arsehole.'

Skunkley – not only was Brayden a chainsaw artist, he was a poet as well.

They continued trading insults. Each time Brayden spoke he would punctuate his speech with a matching jab. Brayden ducked and weaved, while Dunkley stood his ground. Brayden had the longer reach and was quick, but he was fighting a few divisions above his weight. Dunkley, hefty and solid, had him by twenty kilos or so.

Stephen and the visitor came out from the house.

'Ah, look who's here, the fucking dobber himself,' said Dunkley, stepping it up a gear with Brayden.

'Save your shit for court,' Stephen scoffed.

'You're good with the lip, kid, but we all know you're a gutless wimp.'

Once Stephen made a move to help his brother, Dunkley's mate got to his feet, and was soon exchanging blows with Stephen.

Brayden managed to break through Dunkley's defence, throwing him off balance. He was making a better fist of it than his brother had, but with Dunkley it was like throwing stones at a tank. If the punches hurt Dunkley, he wasn't showing it.

Dunkley's mate began to get on top of Stephen. The Murrays' visitor joined the fray. Three against two – tactical advantage to the Murrays. It occurred to me that I'd missed a business opportunity. I could have sold tickets, or at least erected a hotdog stand.

Dunkley and his mate were crafty. They stayed close together, backing up against the fence so they couldn't be attacked from behind. Brayden hit Dunkley twice in the face in quick succession. It stung Dunkley, and blood began to flow. Tracy let out a cheer.

What Dunkley did next should have been anticipated because he had used the same tactic on Stephen. He advanced on Brayden like a grizzly bear, taking hits to the body and face, eventually grabbing hold of Brayden and lifting him off the ground like a rag doll. He squeezed Brayden's lean body tighter and tighter, and when he finally let go, Brayden flopped to the ground – *clunk* went his head on the cement.

The fighting stopped.

'Anyone else want to try?' asked Dunkley.

'That would be me,' said Stephen, unable to refuse the challenge.

Seriously, I thought. *Don't do it to yourself.*

With Brayden lying on the ground and Stephen sizing up Dunkley, Mrs Murray pulled up in a taxi. She hopped out quickly and was soon wielding a broom – she must have just bought it – swinging it wildly while yelling at Dunkley and Stephen to stop. Mum saves the day yet again – she deserved a Mother of the Year award.

I'd been recording it all as best I could with my phone, while regretting the fact that the camera was packed away. Immersed in the excitement, my eyes glued to the action and my ears straining to hear what was being said, I was brought back to earth with a jolt. I'd thought Tracy was in the bathroom – but there she was, out on the street.

Clad only in underpants and a tight-fitting singlet, she screamed at Dunkley while rushing over to assist Brayden. More and more people were watching. It was a command performance. The fight had fizzled out, everybody's attention turning to Brayden and the near-naked Tracy. Maybe Tracy was the weapon to end all wars.

'No point in me poking my head up,' said Dunkley's friend, clearly having no intention of hanging around in case the police turned up. Within seconds he was in his car and gone. But it's not that easy these days, disappearing from the scene. Somebody besides me was bound to have recorded at least some of it – *you're in it, mate!*

Stephen had taken off his shirt for the fight and, in a chivalrous act, draped it around Tracy. At least she was spared the stares of the onlookers. Gradually, Brayden began to regain consciousness.

Mrs Murray must have gone inside, because she appeared on the street with some water for Brayden and a nightgown for Tracy. The street did have some morals.

'What are you doing here, Tracy?' I heard a bemused Brayden ask.

It was impossible for me to tell what Tracy said in reply, but when Brayden's head turned abruptly in the direction of my house, I got the gist.

Tracy leant in close and embraced Brayden, who gave her a prolonged hug. It looked too much like a reunion to me, and I'd no intention of explaining to the chainsaw artist how Tracy happened to be near-naked in my house. That conversation must not happen. Particularly after having seen Brayden fight.

It crossed my mind that Tracy may have been using me to get her ex jealous. To rekindle the flame.

A BMW drove up. Fuck no. Bozanski's heavies were back.

I moved like a panther, rushing to get Cerberus and put the last of my belongings into the car.

Tiptoeing around to the front of the house like a cat on a hot tin roof, checking to see whether I'd forgotten something important in my haste, I heard an almighty bang from the back of the house.

The first thing I saw was Dunkley's head poking through my back door. If his skull stayed there forever as a trophy, that would have been perfect, but it was moving. Dunkley surprised me again, reaching his arm through and grabbing the key from where it was hanging above the door. The dumb bastard had turned into The Mentalist. His ferocious grin said he was coming and would soon be at my throat.

I scampered through the kitchen and into the garage, pulling the door closed behind me just seconds ahead of Dunkley. I estimated it would only take two or three swift kicks from his boot and he would be inside.

At least I'd made it to the car before the door gave way and Dunkley emerged from the rubble swinging a bicycle chain, like an enraged demon, looking bigger and more formidable than I remembered. The chain came crashing across the side window, sending shards of glass everywhere. As I ducked my head to avoid the missiles, I knew I had to do something else or Dunkley would get me before the garage door opened.

A siren sounded in the distance. I'd be kidding myself if I thought the police presence would be of any benefit.

I braced for another hit and it came just as I got the car started. Dunkley's chain hadn't smashed through the windscreen. If it had, I would've copped it in the face.

I accelerated forward then back, spinning the wheels, the car scraping the wall as I tried to keep Dunkley at bay. He was forced to retreat to the steps, where he gestured violently, showing no intention of backing off. He swung the chain again, but from the steps he could only pummel the passenger side of the vehicle. As the garage door opened further, I saw the BMW and Bozo's boys. From the corner of my eye I could see Tracy and Brayden walking towards my house.

An invidious choice: strangled by Dunkley, caught by Bozo's boys or apologising to a chainsaw artist. Or worse, coming to the attention of the police. If they searched my car, I would be in serious trouble – Cerberus, fake plates and an illegal firearm. God help me if any of them got hold of my computer files.

With the approaching siren's wail just streets away, the BMW sped off like a bullet. Dunkley eased off. He was exposed with the garage door open. The police car began slowing down and Dunkley stepped back into the house so he couldn't be sighted.

The siren stopped, and I was trapped.

After a lull of a second or two – maybe they saw the fight was over – the police unexpectedly accelerated away, burning rubber, siren raging. Perhaps they had decided to chase the BMW.

I drove out of the garage at speed. Tracy and Brayden jumped back onto the footpath. I waved goodbye to a perplexed Tracy. *Sorry, Trace, but did you really think I was going to hang around for introductions?*

I turned sharply onto the road with a frantic Dunkley on my tail. He had no vehicle and no chance of keeping pace. One side of my car had taken a hammering, but the front and back windscreens were still intact. There were splinters of glass embedded in my skull as a result of Dunkley's attack, but what the heck – I'd taken worse from that bastard.

At that moment, what I felt was lucky.

23

Metamorphosis

I'd learnt a lesson – get away from the hornets' nest before you stir up the hornets.

On the radio was a story that explained the behaviour of the police in the aftermath of the fight between Dunkley and the Murrays. They had been called to a domestic dispute nearby. A woman, Cynthia, had been killed by her partner, Darrell. I had heard their names mentioned at the Imperial but couldn't match faces. Tracy, Case and Bubba would have known them. If not for that tragedy, I'd have been toast.

What happened over the next couple of days would expose my folly, or otherwise. If more was to be achieved than just creating street drama, I had to up the ante, while Dunkley's threats to get even with Turner would still be fresh in people's minds. And I didn't want to give the bastard the chance to recoup and come looking for me.

Dunkley needed to be home. Preferably alone. Odds were in my favour on that one. I'd observed his behaviour often enough. On any given night he was likely to be home alone and inebriated. His licence was suspended and he didn't have a vehicle. He had few friends – none, at a guess. His mate took off like a shot after the fight with the Murrays. Even loyal friends desert the down-and-outer.

Away from the townhouse, I realised how imprisoned and claustrophobic the place had made me feel. I'd created my own sad cell of solitude. My car was a mess. It was undoubtedly illegal to drive but I'd just have to risk it. It had never failed me and what was required of it was one final assignment. I needed somewhere to clean up and change. I found a motel at Chullora, on the Hume Highway, which was perfect for my needs. After paying online, they'd given me a code for the room which meant I didn't have to enter the office.

If I wanted my disguise to be credible, it was imperative that I got Dunkley's distinguishing features right. The preparatory routine made me concentrate, keeping my mind away from useless thoughts. The powder I applied affected a reddened, raw-prawn in-the-sun complexion. I attached padding, taping it to my body to add bulk. The black wig was a cheap find on eBay. I'd been to Dunkley's favourite store and bought a chequered shirt and blue trousers. The Chicago Blues baseball cap and Nike sports shoes were crucial. And it wouldn't be old mate Dunkers without the cologne, gel and greasy hair. If it looked like a Dunk and quacked like a Dunk...

The Bersa Thunder 380 was loaded and hidden in my shoulder holster. I'd practised just once with the handgun – inside the house, firing two shots into bulletproof padding with the silencer on and a shootout scene from an old John Wayne movie blaring away in the background. I just hoped I could keep my hand steady in the heat of the moment. How convincing was my Dunkley lookalike? That depended on how closely my disguise was scrutinised. With any luck, not by that brilliant detective from the crack CSI team I'd seen on TV.

Confident I'd prepared as best I could, I set off for Turner's place, about twenty minutes away. I'd found his address in the phone book soon after I was released from prison and had driven past a couple of times to familiarise myself with the lay of the land. He lived just two streets back from a busy train line in a run-of-the-mill weatherboard structure.

When I got to Turner's house, I got a real surprise. His car wasn't in the driveway. I'd surmised the beating from Dunkley would have laid him up for a couple of days. At that moment I thought my plan was going to fail.

He arrived home half an hour later, though, and I could breathe easier. He struggled to get out of his car. Observing him in his weakened state gave me courage. Dunkley's bashing hadn't put him off his food, though. In his arms were two large pizzas – meatlovers, knowing his taste. It would be unlikely he'd be going far.

Leaving the condemned man to enjoy his last meal, I had Dunkley on my mind as I drove back towards my old neighbourhood. Nearing peak hour, the roads were busy. I coasted down my old street for one final pass. There was no sign of life at my place, but somebody had closed the garage door.

The lights were on at Dunkley's. Apart from Stephen's Evo 3, there were no other vehicles parked nearby. Dunkley was home alone, as I'd hoped. And even if some friend did happen to drop in on him and later swear Dunkley had been home all night, it didn't mean the friend would prove to be a credible witness in court. Not if there was overwhelming evidence the other way.

Driving smartly back to Turner's place, I parked around the corner behind a truck. Nearing his house, I passed a group of people ambling along the footpath on the other side of the road. I was more than happy to be seen by as many folks as possible – from a distance.

Turner had left his door open. Was the screen door locked? I checked the notes I'd scribbled on the back of my hand. My breathing was unusually shallow – not a good sign, considering the task at hand. I hadn't been this apprehensive when I attacked Chaffer. *Don't panic,* I said to myself. *Take deep breaths and stick to the plan.*

To find the courage, I reminded myself of what this man had done – the probing octopus hands, the smug curl of the lip. The time he pissed all over me.

I was snapped out of my reverie and had to dive for cover when Turner came waddling outside to get something from his car. Then came the unexpected – somebody was holding the screen door open for him. Bugger!

I experienced some relief after getting a glimpse of his companion – an old woman, in her eighties, at a guess. She moved even slower than Turner. I decided her presence could be useful. Hopefully her sight was good enough to be able to describe me.

My success depended on State Rail. That was not a good position to be in. There was still ten minutes until the train was due. After a nervous wait, I made my move.

In through the gate I went and up to the door of Turner's house. The screen door wasn't locked. I knocked twice. Looking to the sky, I pleaded to the railway gods – *let the train be on time.*

Again, the waiting, the anticipation, the look on Turner's face when he appeared a few seconds later.

At first he actually thought it was Dunkley and was hesitant, in no hurry to open the door. My nervous smile gave away my cover. Dunkley wouldn't smile.

'What the fuck?!'

He became comfortable, and a twisted smirk came over his face – it was a practical joke. He opened the screen door and stepped out.

'How much did Dunkley pay you? He's one funny bugger. Tell him it was a real hoot. You can piss off now.'

I said, 'You don't remember?!'

'What…? There's no fucking tip if that's what you're waiting for!'

My expression became stern. 'Have you forgotten who I am?'

His thoughts were clearly doing cartwheels. There was some sign of recognition, but he couldn't place me.

'Is this a fucking quiz or something? Who in the fuck are you?'

In the distance I could hear the distinctive rhythmic clunk of metal on metal, a train rolling along the tracks. Emotions came flooding to the surface. My hands were shaking. Tears were forming. My voice was wobbly.

'You and your old prison buddy, Dunkley – the two of you sodomised me.'

'Is everything right, love?' the old lady called from inside the house.

Turner hesitated. 'All's fine,' came the confident reply.

I began to cry. Tears and mumbling meant one thing to Turner – weakness. Chin held high, his body language said it all. *Who is this fucking loser?*

He started moving towards me with menace. 'Now you listen to me, you prick. I'll tell you this once…'

He was about to issue a threat, but his pumped-up aggression was curtailed and replaced by bewilderment when he saw the gun.

'Is it money you want?'

The atmosphere reeked, heavy with the pungent scent of gardening manure, piss and fear. The metallic din of the approaching train grew in intensity, as did my anger.

'Money! Not money. This isn't about fucking money. It's about what you and Dunkley did to me. You abused me.'

'You're that guy from prison – Tom or something.' Once he recognised me, he thought the dynamics had changed, that he held the upper hand. 'Is that gun even real?' he asked, with the hint of a smile, as though this moaning lump before him was incapable of possessing a real weapon.

My confidence was weakening. I could feel the energy draining from my body. The noise from the train had passed its zenith. It couldn't wait.

I reminded myself of what a disgusting man Cyril Turner was. I counted down in my head.

Three. Two. One.

With the pistol pointed at his head, Turner's expression became uncertain. As I fired, he ducked, moving with surprising agility, but he lost his footing, slipping and tumbling into the garden.

I stood there, dumbfounded, wondering how in the hell I'd missed from that distance. He seized the opportunity, reaching for a brick. The action exposed his torso, and I fired two bullets in rapid succession into his chest.

As I stood there, trembling and frightened, what struck me was how quiet the sound of the gun had been. Turner was motionless but not unconscious. Even in his dying moments, beady-eyed moron didn't seem to have anything but contempt for me. Just a lousy crim from the bin – probably just one of many prisoners he'd abused.

With sweat dripping from my face, I switched into survival mode. Was there a camera I hadn't noticed? Had anyone seen me? I tucked the gun under my jumper and checked my clothes. There wasn't any blood on me.

Inside the house, the old lady called out to Turner. As she came to the front door, I made my way down the pathway to the gate. Cyril let out a groan. When the old lady saw him lying in the garden, she let out a muffled scream. She looked up and saw me. *She'll be slow to ring the cops,* I thought, as I fled the scene.

I kept to my predetermined route, staying off the main road, not making myself visible until I reached the corner where, in the dim light of the streetlamp, the four or five people waiting at the bus stop could sight a Dunkley-like figure skulking through the night.

Back in my car, I put on a pullover and drove back to the motel. I showered and changed, killing the stench of spent gunpowder and fear. The inner fright would be harder to lose.

My concern was that Bozo's boys or the police would catch up with me while I was at this vulnerable stage. Bozo's boys knew the vehicle, as did my neighbours. Again, I imagined the consequences if someone got hold of my computer. Although I'd made all efforts with regard to security, who knew what some smart techno could find?

The next hour was crucial. If I came out at the other end, my odds would vastly improve.

Out went anything that wasn't essential, dumped into industrial bins. The blue-and-grey number used for the Chaffer stunt went, as did all the other clothing I'd used as part of a disguise in the past. The greedy ghost in me wanted to sell the surveillance equipment on eBay, but it wasn't worth the risk. It would be a lucky day for a scavenger at the tip, as the gear was top quality.

The traffic was heavy as I drove along the backstreets and wound my way through Ashfield. Arriving near to where my van was garaged, I moved my gear from the car to the van in three panicky trips. Before leaving the car, I did enough with the wiring to make it appear to have been hot-wired. I left behind a beanie, just like the one Dunkley wore, and reported the car stolen, last seen parked out the front of my old place.

Driving out of the garage, I felt enormous relief. The van was my sanctuary. Nobody knew I had it. As I drove along I listened to the radio. There was nothing regarding Chaffer, nor any breaking news on Cyril Turner.

My destination was the Royal National Park on the southern edge of the city. Despite the shower, the astringent smell of gunpowder hadn't left me. The smell would be evident to a cop poking their head in the cabin. *Do they make decent air freshener anymore?*

Flicking between radio stations, listening for news, I accidentally tuned in to a religious talkback show, where the topic of sexual abuse came up. When the host, whose religion escaped me, began to talk about remorse and the benefits of forgiving, I nearly lost it. Again, images of Dunkley and Turner swamped my head. Did this bloke have any idea?

I got so angry that I pulled off the road and rang the program. They allowed me on air and I went into a rage.

'Follow the scriptures, that's my advice. Embolden oneself with the principles of justice, Old Testament-style. *Lex talionis* – an eye for an eye. Be a crusader for your own cause. Get even with the bastards that have fucked you over.'

They shut me down before I'd finished, but all was not lost. It had given me an idea for a Benedict Sparkel upload.

My phone buzzed – an incoming message. I looked at the screen. It was quite bizarre, considering the situation I was in. The message was from Matilda, an invite to go to the movies the next day.

My head was a confused muddle. At that moment Matilda seemed like an alien from some other planet, light-years away. Imagining myself sitting in a theatre by her side was surreal, a momentary distraction from the replays, the images flashing and the sounds reverberating in my brain. Turner in his death throes. And that old lady, the look on her face, her initial fright.

'Would love to. Meet you at the ticket box, I replied.'

Feeling dirty and tired after the events of the last couple of days, I was looking forward to stopping. After turning off onto a fire trail, I drove a hundred metres or so into the bush before pulling over to the side and dimming the lights.

My first job was to bury the gun and ammunition. Next I filled my plastic sink with water and, using turps, made another attempt to get the lingering stench off my hands and face.

I wondered what would happen with regard to Turner's homicide. What would the police do? After an initial investigation, they should have enough to question Dunkley. He'd be suspect number one after they got a description of the culprit and linked it to his threats and aggressive behaviour.

Mulling over the day's work, I was emboldened with a sense of triumph, polishing off a Coopers Red before I opened a bottle of Glenfiddich that had been reserved for just such an occasion. After what I'd done, I had no appetite. Or perhaps the cancer was taking hold. Eating seemed crude, but tomorrow I would try to get in a solid breakfast. Soldiers can't fight when they're hungry. The Germans found that out in Russia. Besides, who wants to die in an undernourished state?

When doubt crept in, my mantra was – *Justice has been done. Adopt the mindset of a resistance fighter who carried out unspeakable acts in wartime. Learn to live with it.*

Lying on the mattress in the back of the van, I continued to drink. Flicking through my bag of movies, I discovered one of my old favourites,

'King David'. I thought about what I'd said on the radio. Compared to those Old Testament characters, my acts of violence didn't even rate. I wondered whether the soothsayers were conmen, or they really could see into the future.

A soothsayer would not be required to predict mine. According to what the callous prison doctor had told me, I had only weeks of decent health left. If the past few weeks were an indication, the short time I had left would seem longer if I stayed out there on the highwire and ensured the future was loaded with risk.

Camping out in the bush with Lydia had been a special time in my life. During the day we'd swim, read, and go for walks along the coast. When we ran out of food, we'd walk into Bundeena for supplies. At night we'd listen to music, talk and fuck into the early hours. Although we'd been on the run, we were madly in love and felt secure in each other's company.

The night after I'd shot Turner was the antithesis. I heard my own primal scream. I drifted in and out of sleep, my nightmares vivid and frightening.

I was sitting on a sofa alone in a strange house. An impending gloom hung in the air. There was a loud bang out the back. I felt it was my duty to investigate. The lock had been smashed off the door, but there was nobody there. Closing the door as best I could, I went back inside, aware of the inherent danger but with no impulse to flee the scene. No sooner had I sat back down on the sofa than I heard the back door creak. Again, although frightened, I felt the need to investigate.

Out to the back of the house I went again. This time the door was moving, as though someone had just pushed it. From nowhere a giant was lurching towards me. The giant had Dunkley's face and was impossible to keep at bay. There was an aura of inevitability about the situation, as though resistance were futile.

The giant began choking me; I felt sure I would die.

Waking from the dream, I was in a cold sweat and feeling completely powerless. If I'd swung an iron bar at the giant it would have simply flicked it aside as though it were a feather. The van felt like a coffin. My neck was sore. I realised I'd wet the bed. I became terrified that Dunkley was nearby and would find me.

I went outside and sat in the dark, well away from the van. After half an hour, when nothing happened, I went back inside. Eventually I dozed off.

Around four in the morning I awoke again, hyperventilating, my whole body one all-encompassing ache. In the dream, I had been swimming in a race. A coach was screaming encouragement from poolside. The finish line was just a metre away. Every muscle in my body stretched towards the finish line, but I couldn't move. When I turned to inhale, the coach had transformed into a priest. He was no longer encouraging me but shouting, warning of hell and brimstone and how the demons would surely be coming for me.

I lay there in the dark. The double hooting of an owl and the guttural mutterings of a possum in a nearby tree made sleep near impossible. Cerberus wasn't handling the bush well either. How do you convince a two-headed snake that it might not survive out in the wild?

24

Welcome to the New World

Later that morning I awoke with a jolt. The harsh sound of engines at full throttle lacerated the silence like razorblades. I got to my feet and quickly threw on some clothes. My greatest fear was that it was the police. Surely the authorities hadn't closed in on me already. If so, it had been wise to bury the gun. If it was Bozo's boys, that was another matter. I still had a knife and a baseball bat. Of course, Cerberus had scared them off before and might do so again. Could I outrun them? Unlikely.

The sound of the engines continued to increase – they were coming my way, and quickly. But it didn't sound like a car engine.

The first thing I saw was the red and blue of the helmet, then the rider. His face hidden behind a mask, he slowed as he approached the van. Two more were close behind him. The lead rider indicated to the others with his hand and then the three took a left and were soon thundering off along a small track. They were probably relieved I wasn't a National Park ranger. Motorbikes were not permitted in the park.

After I'd calmed down I had breakfast, washed myself using an outdoor shower, dressed, and left for my rendezvous with Matilda. On my way I dropped by an internet café and uploaded another Sparkel offering – 'The

Wild Boys of the West Starring Dunkers and Crew'.

Some of the action of my frantic escape from Dunkley was captured with my car camera. But once again, from the comments people were making, many doubted its authenticity. They thought it staged. A shortened version from Sabrina's birthday party titled 'Rrrrrrats' was also doing the rounds.

I parked near Ashfield Station. It was busy, a mix of high-spirited school students, serious suits and the casually attired. In my jeans, T-shirt and sports coat, I blended in, just one of many in the passing parade. After catching a train into the city I walked to the theatre, which was just twenty minutes away.

The theatre, a quaint brick building, was once a church. It was situated at the centre of a large square, where a small crowd had gathered. Two women standing at a table near the entrance were engaged in friendly chatter with a small group. There was a coffee shop with tables and seats in the courtyard.

As soon as I set eyes on Matilda I knew something wasn't right. When I asked her what was wrong, her pushback was immediate.

'Why didn't you tell me?'

I had no idea what she was on about. Had I slipped up? Did she have something on me? The way she looked at me was unnerving.

'Sorry?'

'I ran into Lydia.'

The name hit me like a punch. Had Lydia told her about my antics at Sabrina's birthday party?

'Dom, it's none of my business, but have you considered having chemo?'

Relief – Lydia had told her about the cancer. That's what it was all about.

'Too dangerous,' I replied. That wasn't the truth. The truth was that I was not big on doctors, not after what I'd experienced with that callous prison doctor.

'You can talk about it, you know, Dom.'

'I'm not going to burden you with my troubles.'

'Dom… it's okay.'

'If I think about it… it will just grind me down.' I wasn't going to fill her in on the details. Get all emotional.

'Geez, Dom, you've had a horrid run.'

Matilda displayed the same empathetic body language and sympathetic frown I'd witnessed on previous occasions when she'd been discussing the Great Barrier Reef and the plight of the blue whale in the Antarctic. At least I was in top company. My chances of survival were lower than the humpback and about as much as the reef.

Matilda had said nothing for a while, but in the end she couldn't help herself. 'What about herbal cures?'

'Bit late for that stuff,' I said.

By then I was feeling down in the dumps. Dunkley had gotten inside my head. But it got worse. I discovered it was not a movie but a documentary we were going to see. I'll watch a movie about some sick serial killer or a romantic comedy most days, but please, not some bloody bleak documentary. Putting it mildly, I was not at all thrilled about Matilda's selection.

Then came the unexpected. After having braced myself for an act of endurance, the doco soon had me transfixed. As can sometimes be the case, life throws up some interesting surprises. Though the protagonist was much further up the food chain, his treatment by the system mirrored mine.

That was why Matilda wanted me to see it.

The similarity was uncanny. It was sheer coincidence that 'No Justice for Justin' was playing at this time. Or was it a sign of the times? Justin Vandewyk was a renowned economist. He had been a university professor who was set upon by the powermongers of international finance. What was his crime? He possessed a moral compass and acted in an ethical manner, exposing the dishonesty of ruthless opportunists who manipulated international currency markets and robbed unsuspecting mum-and-dad investors in the process.

For his selfless actions, the man got sentenced to thirteen years. The use of the word 'selfless' did have me raising my eyebrows. Let's be honest – if you're mixing in a grubby corporate environment, you should expect what you get. But watching the protagonist suffer and fight the corrupt system did give me more understanding of what motivated Matilda and her friends. Of why people spend their lives exposing the lies.

After we left the theatre I thanked Matilda, telling her how much I enjoyed it. She said that she had hoped it would not be too overwhelming, after what I'd been through. I said I wasn't overwhelmed and, although it mightn't help me, there was some consolation in knowing that somebody had received justice.

Did Matilda believe I was innocent? She might think I was incapable of carrying out such devious swindles as had happened at FGI.

Matilda had mentioned she was meeting up with Wayne and Phil. I'd been meaning to see Wayne, to push him further on what he knew about FGI, so I asked if I could tag along. She said that it would be fine, and although she seemed to be enjoying my company, again I reminded myself – *don't blow it with this woman. There's no-one else. And don't let her know how desperate you are. Nobody likes a desperado.*

The streets were vibrant with activity, workers and a splattering of tourists wandering around the old parts of the city as we made our way to the bar. Matilda was five-ten, about my height, but she took long strides and I had to walk quickly to keep up.

We passed a container terminal loaded to the brink.

'More goods from China,' said Matilda, inferring this was not a good thing.

'Trade. The sign of a healthy economy,' I replied.

'Spoken like a true capitalist,' she said, not missing a beat.

A helicopter buzzed overhead. Matilda said it was delivering the harbourmaster back to shore after he'd steered a ship out of the harbour.

Matilda seemed to enjoy the stroll and took notice of what was happening. I walked with my head tilted to the side, hiding from the road, hoping to go unnoticed. What would Bozo be thinking about the Chaffer business? The text he received, and the fact that Chaffer was seemingly still doing the long-distance swim?

We arrived at our destination – a ubiquitous corner pub; a charming sandstone building with large wooden doors and a colourful interior. There was a large lounge area where, on a small stage in the corner, a young woman sat singing and strumming a guitar. She was playing an old Sinead O'Connor song, 'Nothing Compares' – a song I loved and associated with Lydia. I felt a pang of lust and loss, my body and mind burning for the unattainable. The singer's voice was soulful but didn't contain the emotional power of the original. Nothing compares to Sinead's version.

All around the place were posters urging action on a number of fronts – coal-seam gas, whaling, climate change, animal welfare, refugees.

The singer went on to do an original song with a political bent that people seemed to be familiar with.

'Wise man, disguised man
Hear the people's cry, man
Leave it in the ground.'

I didn't know whether she was singing about coal, uranium, underground rail, electricity cables or graves at a cemetery, but her song had a catchy chorus and her guitar-playing gave it gusto. Her foot pounded to an imaginary beat as though she were used to playing with a drummer. It was an impressive performance. Matilda said the woman had an album out.

'Doesn't everyone?' I said. Matilda didn't laugh.

For her next song, a ballad about sailing, the performer was joined on stage by a gangly-looking man. He came in on the chorus. Boy, did he come in – dominating the mic, out of tune and wrecking it. Yet the audience responded with generous applause. He made a dull announcement about an upcoming protest, letting it be known that those not attending would be letting the side down – naughty lefties. Then he asked for generosity, thanking everyone before sending around a glass jar labelled 'Save the Whales'.

Mr Gangly possessed a dreary, cleric-like persona. Why he managed to annoy me so much I'm not sure, but when the collection jar got around to me, I took the opportunity to lift a twenty.

'What a dick,' I said to Matilda, who gave me a reproachful scowl.

'Don't be cruel, Dom. Vic's put in the hard yards over the years.'

Surely she doesn't like the guy? Silly me – already I'd forgotten my place. Was Vic a victim, another of her strays?

What was noticeable was how much Matilda was revered. She was popular and well-respected by this crowd, just as Tracy was down the Imperial. Again, I was hiding in the shadow of a popular woman.

I sat where I could see a television, though there was no news on our swimming champ Chaffer. But then came a brief news report about a fatal shooting in Turner's suburb (details were sketchy). About time.

I'd been expecting to see Wayne, but it was Phil who arrived first. Matilda was called away by a young red-headed woman, leaving me alone with the American.

Phil had had a few and I was content to be the attentive audience. He sounded like the US ambassador, speaking proudly about our close security links and the history between the two great nations. According to him, it went back to World War II and the Battle of the Coral Sea. *Goes as far as Pine Gap,* I thought but didn't say, as he continued to give his assessment of the battles and wars we had fought together. 'Good soldiers, you Aussies,' he said, as if I were part of the cohort.

Not to be outdone on war stories, I told him about the heroic acts from the Dutch resistance during World War II, stories my father had told me. Phil became morose – drink can do that – talking about mates, ones who didn't come back, the damage, physical and PTSD, the lack of support for veterans unable to fit back into society.

'It's wrong. After risking your life, doing your patriotic duty. Ex-soldiers should be appreciated, not cast adrift. Does it make you angry?' I asked, in recruiting mode, wondering what this man was capable of.

'That the government will not look after returned soldiers? Yes, of course I'm angry about it. But… what the hell can I do about it?'

'We'll have computers going at each other soon. War will become like a reality TV show. We won't need soldiers in the future.'

Phil became irate. 'That is utter bullshit, my friend. There will always be a need for soldiers.'

He proceeded to lecture me about decisions and assessments made in the heat of battle that computers were not capable of. The politics of war.

I was about to say to Phil that a mechanical soldier wouldn't suffer post-traumatic stress, but I didn't want to infuriate him any further – he might prove to be a useful person to know.

He told me a story about bodies being shifted home in the dead of night and got really angry, the emotion palpable. Breathing heavy, he suddenly stood up, lifted his fist and slammed it down on the table.

'No regrets!' he said in a loud voice, as if trying to convince himself.

People looked across.

Phil went to the bathroom. He had a temper and harboured a grudge. The big American bear had a cross to bear. When he returned five minutes later, I wondered whether he had taken a sedative or something. He was more relaxed.

I thought about his relationship with Wayne. And where did Matilda fit in? I told Phil I'd seen Wayne in Newtown, dressed as a hobo. He laughed a little before replying in a matter-of-fact tone that Wayne worked undercover at times.

I said, 'I thought he was a security officer.'

'He's got his fingers in a few pies. He was a chopper pilot back in the war. Then he worked in Washington for some institute. These days he's mostly kicking back, taking time to smell the roses.'

When Wayne had done security work for FGI, he certainly had been doing more than shooting the breeze. He was part of a team that was trusted with the care of visiting US dignitaries and officials.

Phil began rapping on about his younger days. If it was meant to impress, it did. He sounded like a gangster as he recounted his deeds riding with a motorcycle gang and doing drug runs between Mexico and Canada before signing up. My younger self would have been impressed. I imagined what Phil would have been like in the heat of battle. I imagined having Phil and Wayne in cahoots with me – the Fuck It! List dream team. Plus, of course, Matilda. Even more so after what I was about to hear.

Matilda returned to the table, apologising for her absence. Phil picked up a newspaper lying on the table. It was a university publication, a month old. On the front page was a picture of a large whaling vessel with a smaller boat in the foreground. On board the smaller boat was a film crew and a band of protesters, with the iconic Antarctic iceshelves beckoning in the distance.

Phil said to me, 'Do you recognise this woman, the one in the photo?'

It took a moment before it clicked. There was Matilda, one of two women standing beside three men, out on the high seas.

'Matilda can't help getting up to her neck in things controversial,' said Phil, leaning forward. 'Just after that picture was taken, their vessel was rammed and she nearly went overboard,' he added with avuncular concern.

Matilda played it down. 'They were just trying to scare us.'

'Can you believe it?' said Phil. 'Chains herself to machines in the forest and fights with police.'

'Certainly gung-ho. But it takes people with guts to make a difference. Most people just talk about what should be done. Look at what people like Mandela and Gandhi did to change the shape of the world.'

'Hell yeah… Matilda as Mandela, I like it.'

Or Joan of Arc,' I said, the comment getting a chuckle from Phil.

'The Jesus complex, that's what I call it,' he said. 'Wanting to save the human race from itself.'

Wayne arrived, nodded hello and pulled up a chair next to us. Wayne gave Matilda a peck on the cheek and Matilda responded with a friendly hug.

'I'm talking about Matilda,' said Phil to Wayne. 'She's a brilliant woman… but she wastes her talents. That's all I'll say.'

Matilda passed me a look that said she had heard it all before. It didn't seem to bother her in the least. Whenever Phil spoke Matilda's name, his passionate feelings for her were on display. Was I like that with Lydia? Probably. Cursed with overwhelming infatuation. Impossible to hide.

Matilda's phone rang and she stepped away from the table. Despite her absence, Phil continued to talk about her and her dangerous behaviour. Wayne said he respected the Matildas of the world, but they were up against insurmountable odds – banging their heads against the wall.

I told them it was a worthwhile thing to do, trying to repair and prevent the damage we humans cause.

Phil turned his enquiring gaze on me. 'So, are you also a saviour my friend?' He winked his friendly American wink – *whatever you say is fine with me, buddy.*

'No, not me. Just an observer, watching from the sideline.'

Phil boasted that he had helped Matilda out with regard to security and operational matters. Wayne passed him a critical look, which I interpreted as meaning he'd said too much.

Phil changed the subject, telling Wayne that I'd seen him in Newtown, dressed as a hobo. They both laughed at this, Phil whacking Wayne on the shoulder.

'What you got to do to make a crust, eh man?'

I asked them what it was like being Americans in Australia, and we ended up talking about American television shows and movies, as well as the similarities between the two countries. I stirred them up by saying America's power was on the decline. Who could argue with that proposition?

Phil said they were too thinly spread and was soon giving us a State of the Nation Address – an analysis of cybercrime, as well as the danger posed to the USA by the emerging might of China. America had been diminished because of poor leadership, according to Phil, and he proceeded to list the failures of past American presidents.

I was eager to speak with Wayne. Alone. As Phil prattled on, I looked across to where he was sitting. He tilted his head and winked in sympathy. He knew his verbose fellow American was hard to take.

When Phil started on about the civilian casualties of war, Wayne got to his feet and announced he was going out for a smoke, stopping Phil mid-sentence.

'Can I come?' I said.

'Of course,' he replied.

Phil said, 'Man, I had you pegged as a non-smoker.' He informed us he had given up six months ago and brushed us away with a sweep of the hand. 'Coffin nails.'

As we walked together, Wayne told me he liked the idea of smoking zones because it made him smoke less. More talkative away from Phil, he said the non-smoking area was controversial. Patrons had complained about the money spent on the lavish renovations.

When we got there, it was easy to see what they meant. The large rectangular area had a fashionable glass roof that allowed in natural light. There was an aviary with a variety of colourful parrots, a garden down one end and pot plants hanging from the ceiling. I said that perhaps an inspired manager had done it to cancel out the smoke fumes.

'Carbon neutral,' Wayne joked.

We had the place to ourselves. Wayne began imitating a white parrot that had been putting on quite a performance. His imitation was striking in its accuracy. When another bird emitted a more intricate cadence, Wayne responded with what he said was the male response to the female mating call.

'What did you say? Were you available or not?'

'I said I wasn't available,' he replied, with a laugh.

'You learnt that in the Marines?' I asked.

He didn't answer directly but said the ability to mimic voices was a useful skill to have during close-combat operations.

'But you were a chopper pilot, weren't you?'

He was surprised I knew. 'Yep.'

'Did you fly missions in the Middle East?'

'Hell, man, I can't talk about that. That's classified,' he replied, curtly.

It was interesting to see he was still following orders. A hobo or a soldier – will the real Americano please stand up?

'I'll tell you this much, Dom. No-one comes back from war unaffected. Things you see, things you have to do.'

'But you did pick up some useful skills?'

'Hell yeah, learnt to fucking whistle like a bird,' he said, and we both laughed.

Observing the quieter of the two Americans, I decided that if Wayne wanted to be Matilda's lover, he would probably succeed. He was attractive and well-groomed, and possessed the charm to find his way to a woman's heart. Phil was forever pigeonholed as 'uncle', but Wayne would be hard to compete against with his looks and accomplishments.

Cadging a second cigarette, I brought things around to the subject of Bozanski and FGI, but Wayne wasn't as forthcoming or knowledgeable as I'd hoped. Had my behaviour made him wary? He would have a finely honed bullshit-detector.

I did, however, find out an interesting piece of information. FGI was being investigated by the Australian Taxation Office for using offshore tax havens. No surprise there. When Wayne mentioned the Federal Police were involved, I got excited, thinking it might have some bearing on my case, but that was not to be. And how long would the investigation take? It was pleasant to hear, but essentially of not much use to me. Unless Bozanski was directly involved and charged.

'What did they say at FGI when I got arrested, the big wigs?'

'Not much. They all ducked for cover. You were left high and dry. Bozanski and others had their office lights on late about a week before the shit hit the fan.'

'I know Bozanski's a crook. Who else could have been involved?'

He shrugged his shoulders, telling me he would keep his ear to the ground, but I didn't expect much. Despite the lack of anything concrete, it was a good feeling to talk to someone I felt was on my side.

I left the pub a short time later, making my way back to Ashfield Station to collect the van and prepare for another night sleeping out in the bush.

Mr Twinkel's latest upload had him dressed as a preacher, delivering a diatribe from a pulpit. Earlier in the week, I'd posted a piece on my Benedict Sparkel site, 'Power to the People'. Inspired by Matilda, it was about the need to hold the industrialists and politicians accountable for the damage they caused. Nothing new in that proposal – it had been in the leftist handbook for decades. Twinkel had latched on to it.

'If you, like Benedict Sparkel, are not long for this world, why not make your mark before you depart? You too might progress beyond a mere

personal vendetta and carry out an act for the benefit of humankind. With nothing to lose, there is no higher calling, no more enthralling and fulfilling exit strategy than to become a sociopath for the people!

'Target those dangerous, destructive men (they are mostly men) – the industrialists, politicians and loudmouths who are in it just for themselves. You know them. I know them. The ones who don't give an iota about the common good.'

The Fuck It! List song could be heard in the background. Twinkel was trying to pass Benedict Sparkel off as a 'sociopath for the people'. Really? Nobody would come at that, surely.

That was what I thought. But what did I know about trends and audiences? Benedict Sparkel's following tripled overnight. When Twinkel gave me a forty-grand bonus, I knew we were doing well.

25

The Good Doctor

The previous day I'd been caught off guard by the motorbikes. I didn't want to risk being seen again, so the next night I decided to go deeper into the bush. I found a secluded spot well off the road, but the setting was uninspiring – no water, no view. The vegetation was bland. Just clapped-out forest.

Cerberus became restless again. He seemed to be picking up on something, maybe another animal. It wasn't hunger, as I'd already fed him. I drank some bourbon and listened to Prince and Bowie, music that Lydia and I used to like.

In the early hours I finally drifted off. In my dream, Lydia was with me. It was dark and we were making love. Then, in a cruel switch, it was not Lydia but Dunkley on top of me. His smell and the pressure of his body felt real. Screaming, shaking and disorientated, I reached across the mattress, half expecting to touch the brute.

My next dream had a mild-mannered Turner in my face, pleading. 'But I must look after my mother,' he said. His ghostly self was humane, not at all like the sleazy Turner I'd known. Was it possible to feel spirits weep?

I tried to stay awake to avoid the nightmares. Awake, my past haunted me. Asleep, I was with the living dead.

The wildlife that once had me enthralled now annoyed me. Nature seemed to be scowling at me. Would the cicadas ever shut up! Music I once loved didn't sound right. Even my favourites sounded empty. I turned it off.

In the morning I had no appetite, but I forced myself to eat something small. The news on the radio was heartening. The police were holding a man for questioning regarding the death of Cyril Turner. Enjoying the sense of success, I should have known not to get too carried away with intangibles. What happened next reminded me I was skating on thin ice. It was a warning – a wink from the gods.

After packing up, I left the camping spot and drove off along the dirt track. Having just reached the main road, I encountered a National Park ranger coming from the opposite direction. How early did these rangers start work? Definitely earlier than I'd thought. It was only just after seven o'clock. I did have the appropriate camping sticker on my vehicle, but still, I didn't want to be seen.

The second incident was more serious. There was only a sprinkling of vehicles on the road at that time of the morning, most headed towards Sutherland. No sooner had I turned onto the main road and was accelerating away than the BMW containing Dunkley's thugs came around the bend from the opposite direction.

Reality hit with a classic thud. They didn't seem like camping folk to me. How were they tipped off? They didn't take my turnoff, but if I'd driven out a few seconds later I would have been staring them in the face – a kangaroo caught in the headlight.

At that moment, after my horrid night in the bush, I felt drained and unmotivated. It seemed that life itself was being sucked out of me. The doctor's appointment was coming up soon. Was the cancer affecting me?

The answer to that question would come in an unexpected manner.

I received a text – Lydia wanted to meet with me. It caught me by surprise and lifted my spirits. She suggested a café near Centennial Park. I drove the van through Randwick to Centennial Park and parked well away from the café.

Lydia was already there when I arrived, looking gorgeous as usual. She'd just flown back from Melbourne, where she'd been doing an advertisement for some energy drink. When she asked what I'd been up to, I was cagey. Lydia had all but accused me of harassing Sabrina. She probably wouldn't have thought I was capable of swindling the money from Sabrina's account, but I bet she suspected it was me who crashed Sabrina's birthday party and gave the birthday girl a rat for a present.

'Nothing much. I spend a lot of time sitting around, playing computer games.'

'How come your townhouse is up for rent? Don't you have to stay as part of your parole?'

'How did you know it was empty?'

'Bozanski told me.'

The thought of Lydia talking with Bozanski made my blood boil. 'Bozanski. What are you doing talking to him?'

'He rang me. Said you won't return his calls.'

'There haven't been any calls. Don't trust him. Not for a second.'

'Bozanski's worried about Chaffer. Nobody's seen him for days. Have you?'

An image of Chaffer flashed before my eyes – his arms held high, the perfect stroke, thrashing through the waves. I knew Lydia was fishing for information.

'Chaffer – no. Why would I want to see the guy? So that's why you wanted to meet! To get information for Bozanski.'

I was ropeable. Lydia left a short time later. Sitting there alone, I felt an immense disappointment. It was always a thrill to see Lydia, but to think she'd met with me at the request of Bozanski tore me apart.

I went online using the café's free Wi-Fi. My latest upload was really popular. I even managed a chuckle imagining Dunkley's fury at seeing his brutality exposed.

That day, the major news services ran the story about the young fund manager from FGI who had gone missing. Some online comments were derogatory. One said he was probably drunk and fell off the ferry. Another suggested he may have run off with another woman. Soon Chaffer's story would be providing material for comedians.

With Turner's murder and Chaffer, I had been responsible for over half of the news on one popular FM station. I decided it was time to post Chaffer's mobile phone to the police. The last message I'd sent from his phone to Bozanski and the FGI director should interest some young Sherlock. It should give them enough to bring in Bozanski for serious questioning, at least. But he was clever and able to dodge and dart. He would undoubtedly deny his culpability in Chaffer's disappearance and point the finger at me. If what Wayne had told me about FGI was correct, that Bozanski hadn't found me yet may have been because he had more pressing issues to deal with at work.

An item posted by the NSB Network caught my attention and had me smiling. An ex-warden had been arrested for the murder of Cyril Turner. Not a lot was said, just a brief profile mentioning how Turner and the accused had met working as prison officers. I hadn't expected Dunkley to be able to track me down, but still, it was a relief to have him behind bars.

Sitting at the table, thinking, I looked out of the window. There was a strange moment just before recognition and realisation. It was the cleft chin that got me first, and then that dour face with the judgemental eyes. Who else but the good doctor, the man who had treated me so atrociously in prison?

At first I figured he was waiting for someone, but then I noticed he was holding a lead – his dog was actually pissing on the café wall. It was peculiar, seeing the doctor standing less than two metres from me. Lydia would say it was fate and that our paths were meant to cross. Prison memories flashed before me. The heartless man delivering the harrowing news of my condition in his droll, monotone voice with his who-gives-a-fuck attitude. The doctor handing me a slip of paper on which two words were written – BRAIN TUMOUR. I had stood there like a stunned mullet, staring at the piece of paper as he spoke.

'Make sure you make an appointment to see me as soon as you get out.'

He'd raised his eyebrows and grinned. I grinned back, a stupid idiot-like gape, until gradually it dawned on Dumb Dom that he wanted me to leave. And then, the bizarre experience of having him speak as I was about to close the door on my way out. I'd thought he was talking to me, calling me back to talk about possible treatment options. But when I turned to face him, he was hunched over a device, talking about my condition into a dictaphone. A damned dictaphone!

He didn't look up. His accent was reminiscent of the hardened German doctors I'd seen in old war movies. But we would not be needing the Nuremberg War Crimes Tribunal to deliver the good doctor's verdict. The badge I would pin to the doctor's lapel would read – CALLOUS BASTARD. If I had any say in it, we would soon resume our non-conversation.

When I got outside the café, the doctor was still waiting at the lights on the corner. This gave me time to gather my thoughts. The man appeared frail – he could be easily overpowered. He'd developed a slight hunch, probably from stooping to talk into his dictaphone. His gait was more a shuffle than a step. Perhaps *his* doctor had advised him that owning a dog might be good for his health, because he didn't appear to be the dog-owning type.

After crossing the road, the doctor walked along the footpath adjacent to Centennial Park before entering a stately residence a few doors along. He was carrying a package from a bakery – afternoon tea, perhaps. Someone came to the door and let him in. The dog, a cute cocker spaniel, was left to play on the front lawn.

Walking across the road to the park, I waited in the shade of a large oak tree. Wayne was on my brain. He would know the best tactics. A story he had told me from the Indochina War was playing out in my head. The villagers worked the fields in the morning, then changed into military garb and fought the Americans in the afternoon. They lived underground and in the tunnels and had everything they required to function, including honeymoon suites.

Was Tran's family involved in that? Some of his relatives still lived in Vietnam. Others lived overseas. Did they flee the advancing force from the north?

Half an hour later, the not-so-good doctor came out of the house, put the leash on the dog, waved goodbye to whomever, and was off. My excitement grew when he crossed the road and dawdled off into the park.

What I did next felt simple and fresh. When I was fairly certain of the direction the doctor was going, I raced ahead, seeking out a quiet spot to lay in ambush. The man who valued my life so little may have had his last scones and tea.

About a hundred metres into the park, there was a path that led towards one of the larger ponds. The copse of plants and large trees was luxurious and abundant. Fifteen metres in and I'd found a relatively secluded spot. Searching for a weapon, I discarded a rock in favour of a solid piece of wood. It fitted my hand perfectly. Then I created a pretend body by gathering some branches and placing my coat on top before racing back up to the main path.

There was only ten or so seconds to wait before the doctor came trudging along with his dog. Approaching him, I did my best to appear flustered.

'Please, sir, can you help me? My wife has collapsed in the trees near the pond. I think it's a heart attack.'

'Have you called an ambulance?' he asked.

'Of course. They're on the way.'

There was nobody nearby. I hurried him along. From the way he behaved, there was no doubt he believed me.

'I'm a doctor, you know,' he said proudly, as we made our way to what was to be the scene of his demise.

'A doctor... it must be my lucky day.'

There was another dog-walker across the lake, strolling close to the water's edge. I just hoped they didn't have prying eyes.

We approached the coat and the doctor immediately became wary, looking from me to the coat and then back.

'What in the hell are you playing at?' he said, like a man used to wielding authority.

As sweat dripped from my body, I couldn't speak. I just stared at the old man, expecting some form of recognition. But, just like Turner, he had no idea who I was. At that moment I blamed him for all that was wrong with my life. His dog must have sensed something was wrong, because it pulled itself free from the lead and barked, before taking off like a bat out of hell. The doctor became alarmed, but not frightened.

'What is it you want?' he said firmly. His composure surprised me.

'You don't remember me, do you?'

He studied the lunatic standing before him. 'Your face is familiar. Who are you?'

I was shaking as I spoke. 'In prison. You were the doctor. If you had diagnosed my brain tumour earlier or got me treated inside, things might have turned out different. Now I'm a dead man walking.'

He was shaking his head. 'No, no. You've got it wrong, buddy. You've got the wrong end of the stick. You were supposed to see me when you got out. I tried to contact you on a number of occasions after your early release. You don't have cancer. I diagnosed you with cancer to get you out of prison because you were being abused.'

'What?!' Was he lying to save himself? 'I don't believe you. You were so fucking rude to me.'

'Rude? I was nervous. I could have been deregistered for what I did. Still could. The chaplain told me about your situation.'

For a moment I didn't know what to think. The doctor still sounded stuck-up, but my instincts told me he was telling the truth.

My Fuck It! List deeds flashed before me. I began thinking about the implications of what I'd done. My actions had been underwritten with a bitterness and understanding that I would not be around to suffer the consequences. It was entwined in my thinking and integral to the Benedict Sparkel spiel. Would I have found the courage to toss Chaffer overboard or shoot Turner without my own death looming? Would I have risked serving life in gaol?

I stood there, staring at the doctor. The doctor who had done me a massive favour. The doctor I'd detested all this time. A man who had taken an enormous risk, but in doing so pushed me in a direction I might not have otherwise gone. Then I wondered –had it made any difference to how I had acted?

My head couldn't get a handle on this startling information or the new situation I found myself in. The fear of being imprisoned again became overpowering. My energy was zapped. I could barely mumble an apology.

'Sorry… I thought you'd lost your moral compass.'

The doctor gazed at me with his doctor eyes – *schedule that lunatic.*

I thought it best to flee the scene of my stupidity before somebody noticed. With my tail between my legs, my head down and a knot in my stomach, I meekly walked away.

Back at my van I logged on to a public Wi-Fi network. Mr Twinkel had added another clip.

Depicted as a cartoon character, Mr Twinkel is a pilot in battle. He is dive-bombing a brigade of creatures – ants, rats, cockroaches and lizards, who are marching in rows, walking upright and carrying a variety of weapons. Heads down, they don't even change direction or attempt to fire back as Mr Twinkel dives and somersaults, spraying them with machine-gun fire from above.

A rap-style musical chant accompanies the visuals.

'To hell man, you persist

Life can be a real bitch

Ring that bell, you enlist

Put 'em on the Fuck It! List.'

Twinkel's facial features seemed to alter at times, taking on another persona. Was it a Dom lookalike or was I being paranoid? After viewing it numerous times, I was still uncertain.

26

The Yacht

I caught the train over to the north side of the harbour to meet up with Tran. My head was still spinning, grappling with this new reality – my life wasn't automatically ending. The goalposts had moved. Could I remain undetected? Should it be 'run rabbit run'? Was it time to toss in this Benedict Sparkel business?

I could hide and survive. Even still, there was always the possibility of being found. What I did have to do was come up with something that took the possibility of a life behind bars out of the equation. That was my greatest fear.

What should I say to Matilda and Lydia? I'd appear to be a real dill if I told them the truth – *Hey, guess what! I just happened to run into this doctor and I found out I never did have cancer.*

How would I explain it to Benedict Sparkel's growing band of followers? My profile had been built on it – *destined to die within twelve months*. I needed time to think. Meanwhile, I'd tell nobody.

I arrived at the arranged bar and saw Tran sitting in the corner. It was not until he began giving me strange looks as I approached that I remembered I was wearing a disguise.

When he realised who I was, he laughed at the old grey-headed man standing before him. 'Fuck, man, you look freaky.'

'It's not funny. I have good reason to be careful.'

Tran got me a Tiger beer and a Coke for himself.

'To success.'

We clinked bottles.

Tran had been in on the Bozanski journey from the beginning. He had listened to my Bozo diatribe and knew how much I detested the man. We never talked about the Fuck It! List outside prison, but he'd heard me rave on about it plenty of times inside. I sometimes wondered whether he knew of my success with the Benedict Sparkel alias. If he did, he didn't say anything. The less he knew of my deeds the better. But if he did come across the site, he would make the connection.

Tran was having difficulty hacking into Bozanski's accounts. 'Most times I can gain access using. WAN or LAN. Not with this Bozanski dude. He's definitely using more than the dime-a-dozen commercial routers.'

'Is there a way of finding out?'

'If we could get a look inside his house or office.'

'His house has cameras and a security guard. I wouldn't go near the FGI office. They're under investigation, and the people there would be being closely watched. Even in disguise I wouldn't risk it. But there is another possibility. He has a yacht moored at Rushcutters Bay. I know he sometimes works from there.'

'Funny place to do work!'

'Bozo's into multitasking. He likes to take women there as well. They think that fucking him will make a difference to their careers.'

I pulled up a clip of Bozo and his crew from Facebook. Bozo was praising the team for their wonderful effort in the Sydney to Hobart race.

'If you were one of the crew, you'd want to be pulling your weight,' I said. 'You'd be overboard like ballast in a second if it suited his purpose.'

After leaving Tran I drove to Rushcutters Bay, where Bozo's yacht sat moored at a private pier. The entrance was protected with barbed wire, CCTV and an alarm system. Scouting around the area, I spotted a small park with a ramp leading into the water less than a kilometre away. For what I had in mind, it would be necessary to do some shopping.

Later that day I waited for Bozo to appear outside his office, switching between the major news stations, hoping for news on Dunkley or Chaffer. Finally, something. Police had filed charges against Dunkley and were arguing against bail, as it was suspected that he might try to intimidate witnesses.

At four o'clock Bozo came out of his office and drove to Kings Cross. I followed him in my van, still dressed in my grey-headed old-man garb, the likes of which Bozo would brush past without even noticing.

At this time of day there was a real mix of people about – tourists, office workers, rich business types, bohemians, plus a few homeless. A young busker was playing soulful music on a saxophone and a ragged-looking fella banging two pieces of wood together.

Bozo went into a corner pub, stayed for an hour and left. He drove back to his Double Bay house and parked his car in the parking lot underneath. I waited outside for about twenty minutes and then returned to Rushcutters Bay.

Still coming to grips with my new situation, I didn't feel less motivated or more fearful, but I was more aware of the risks involved. My plan was to sneak onto the yacht via the water, thus avoiding the roving eyes of the

CCTV cameras. I parked across from the small park that reached down to the water's edge. I made my way to the water, carrying a large brown bag that contained an inflatable Intex kayak.

There were some dog-walkers about, but it was relatively quiet. To anyone passing by I was fairly innocuous, just a sporty type going for a twilight paddle. It took me less than ten minutes using a manual pump to inflate the seat and both sections of the kayak. The paddle came in three parts and was simple to assemble. As darkness approached, I put on a life jacket and pushed off into the water.

The kayak moved quickly and was easy to manoeuvre. My kayaking skills were something I could thank my old man for. When I was a kid, he'd take me fishing in a wooden kayak not much bigger than my inflatable. Hugging the shoreline and hiding in the shadows of the larger vessels, I paddled towards Bozanski's yacht. I imagined Chaffer cutting through the gloomy, dark water, caught in a time warp for evermore.

The ghouls were with me again. At one stage a jolt of fear raced through my body and I thought I'd lost my mind after I mistook two fishermen for Dunkley and Turner. Logic said that was impossible, but the misty grey light was playing tricks with my senses.

I approached Bozanski's yacht. Bright lights flooded the pier. The pearly white hull glistened like a gem, casting shadows across the water. From here, the impossibility of sneaking onto the yacht from land was obvious – the shoreline was well lit and there were two CCTV cameras. There was barbed wire to contend with, plus an unavoidable confrontation with the padlock.

The yacht swayed gently on the water as I tied up the kayak. I climbed up the ramp and onto the chocolate-coloured deck. I kept down low, staying on the starboard side, where I couldn't be sighted from the marina.

There was a small window that hadn't been properly secured. It was simple enough to force it open and slip my hand through, reach across and unlatch the door. There was no alarm system that I could see, so I stepped down into the cabin.

A TV was perched high on a metal bracket. There were green leather seats fixed in place around a table. But it wasn't going to be easy to access the main control area – it was protected by a laser security system, plus a padlocked door. I could glimpse the computer and electronic gear through the panel of glass at the top of the door. I began taking photos, hoping it would be enough for Tran.

As I was considering the practicalities of forcing the padlocked door open, the sound of a car coming to a stop nearby drew my attention. Peeking out through a gap in the blinds, I was soon in a panic.

It was Sabrina's car. Bozanski got out of the passenger side, closed the door and stood there, leaning on the bonnet, waiting for Sabrina.

That should have been my cue to run, but it would've been a running dive into the sea. It was too late to escape unnoticed. There wasn't even time to get to the kayak. Bozo was soon unlocking the gate, which was only metres from the yacht.

I closed the window and door and searched furiously for somewhere to hide. The best I could do was a broom cupboard on the starboard side. After pushing aside a vacuum cleaner and fishing rods, I scrambled inside.

Would they see the kayak? Not unless they walked around to the other side of the yacht. If they discovered it, I was gone.

Their conversation was breathtaking.

'You've been hard to pin down lately, Sabrina.'

'I feel like I've been put through the mincer. Someone hacked my school reports and I got blamed for having poor security. And I told you about the money stolen from my accounts.'

'But you're covered? The bank will pay you back?'

'Probably, but they haven't yet. They treat you as though you're the one who did it.'

'Have they got any leads?'

'No. That's the problem. I reckon it was fucking Bruno. Is he capable of doing it?'

'Probably. He could have someone helping him. I reckon he's the reason FGI's being investigated. I've got people searching for him. I think he's hiding somewhere in the Royal National Park near Bundeena.'

'Lydia won't talk about him,' Sabrina said.

'I bet she knows where he is, though. I'll get somebody to watch her, see where she goes.'

I heard the sound of liquid on ice cubes. It was becoming increasingly claustrophobic in the closet. From Sabrina's response, Bozo must have made a move, which Sabrina resisted.

'Come on, Adrian,' she exclaimed. 'Now's not the time. Is that all you think about?'

'I can't help it... I dream about ravishing your beautiful body. You're one hell of an attractive woman. What man could be alone with you and not want to make love to you?'

Sabrina made him work for it, but after a while she ceased to resist his advances. Why else would she have boarded the yacht? Certainly not to go sailing.

Waiting until they were making sufficient noise, I opened the closet and quietly crept towards the door. I turned the knob and the lovemaking abruptly stopped. I froze, not daring to make a sound.

'What was that noise?' asked Sabrina.

After a few seconds Bozo said, 'Just the wind.'

'Funny-sounding wind. Go check.'

'Oh, it's nothing.'

They were soon back at it.

I tiptoed onto the deck, slid down the side of the boat and untied the kayak. I pushed off into the water, and the yacht was soon a speck in the distance.

Afterwards I gave myself another Dumb Dom badge. Why hadn't I arranged for someone to watch Bozanski? Tran would have done so if I'd asked.

I reviewed the photos I'd taken and sent them to Tran. Fortunate to have escaped, I hoped it was worthwhile and that Tran had enough to hack Bozo's accounts. I really didn't fancy another excursion onto the yacht.

How did Bozo know I'd been hiding somewhere in the Royal National Park? Was there more to that encounter with the boys on their bikes than first met the eye? Unlikely. I'd used my phone near Sutherland, so it could have been traced. Had they made a guess about me being there after checking the local hotels and rentals?

That Sabrina would have it off with Bozo came as no surprise to me. But I bet Lydia didn't know. If I told her, she wouldn't believe me. She'd accuse me of being up to no good and ask why I had been near Bozanski's yacht. That Bozanski was going to have Lydia followed was a matter for concern though.

27

The Charade

With Bozanski alert to me hiding out in the Royal National Park near Sutherland, a change of habitat had been necessary. I'd spent the previous night at a free camp near Broke in the Hunter Valley. There were four tents and two caravans. I made a small fire and kept to myself.

I awoke in the morning to the sound of birds chirping. I had an apple and a banana for breakfast. Elongated clouds hung like mountains in the distance. Occasionally the sun burst through the trees, spotlighting the van.

Once on the move, I realised I was surrounded by open-cut coal mines. There were high fences and warning signs – *Keep Out*. Dead kangaroos littered the road. This desecrated landscape was not good for my mental health. This was supposed to be wine and horse country. Where were the gee-gees and vineyards? I began to imagine worst-case scenarios. Somebody might have worked out Dunkley was framed. There was no doubt he would be protesting his innocence. Had I been fingered for Chaffer's disappearance?

My text messages warning Lydia that Bozanski was having her followed had gone unanswered.

I did receive a text message from Matilda, inviting me to a Fred

Williams exhibition at the Art Gallery of New South Wales. Her text said I was welcome to join her at two o'clock in the foyer. She must have been feeling sorry for me.

Going into the city wasn't a smart move. I should have been lying low, but the urge to see Matilda again negated my fears. And if I did encounter Bozanski, at least I would be with someone.

I did take some precautions. After parking the van at Glebe I caught a taxi into the city. Wearing thick glasses, a grey hairpiece and a beard, I ditched the cab when I got close to the gallery, went into a toilet in Hyde Park and removed the disguise.

I arrived at the gallery early. Sitting there, sipping a glass of wine in the café, I wondered whether Matilda would be by herself. When she arrived alone five minutes later, it surprised and pleased me. She wore the ubiquitous blue jeans and T-shirt, but a smart-looking black hat and a colourful satin scarf made her stand out from the crowd.

She smiled and gave me a short hug. 'You smell of smoke. Have you been around a fire?'

'Slept out last night. I stayed in the car at a camping area.'

'I thought you had a place out in the Western Suburbs.'

'I did, but I lost it because the owner wanted to move back in.'

'That's ridiculous! Can they do that?'

'It's okay. I'll eventually find somewhere else. I don't mind sleeping in the car.' I'd told nobody about the van and I wanted to keep it that way.

'Sleeping in your car – that's crazy. Come back to my place. We've got a sunroom we often use for visitors. You can stay there until you get yourself sorted.'

'That's really generous, but I don't want to impose.'

'Nonsense. You'll have to look after yourself, though. I'm out a lot.'

It didn't take much coaxing for me to cave in. Undeserving of her generosity I may be, but I'd pull my weight. I didn't want Matilda to regret being generous. *Behave carbon neutral – do not suck oxygen from others. Do not drain Matilda as you drained Lydia.*

With Bozanski and who knew who else on my tail, having a bolthole for even a night or two would be a blessing. It made me feel better, and our conversation was upbeat. I got the impression Matilda actually enjoyed being in my company, but I was biased and didn't really know her that well. I couldn't fathom why Matilda, a successful, attractive woman, was bothering with Dom Bruno. Was she so dogmatic and forceful that other men avoided her? Not from what I'd seen down at the pub. Men seemed to like her. Perhaps she was one of those highly intelligent women who were so involved in their field that they didn't have the time or need for serious relationships.

The Fred Williams retrospective contained many brilliant depictions of the outback. I became more interested in Matilda than the art – the way she stood with a slight lean, her various facial expressions, her passion when she spoke. I had the sense not to reveal my ineptness, making just the occasional comment.

My appreciation of the artworks was based not on what I thought or the artist's genius, but on the prices the works fetched – their intrinsic value formulated on price and capital growth. We got into a discussion and I revealed my monetary bent, mentioning the dollar value of the artist's works once too often. Matilda chided me and I defended myself.

'But it's economics, Matilda. The more our country's artworks are worth in dollar terms, the more wealth we have as a nation.'

'That's warped, Dom,' she said. 'Really suss thinking.'

After the gallery we went for a stroll around the gardens, and as we approached the harbour we came to a Vietnamese street stall, where we bought spicy vegetable and chicken rolls. Matilda probably thought I'd gone inside my shell, as I didn't say much. The truth was that my roving eye was constantly on the lookout. Earlier it had felt brave going out in public without a disguise, but the truth was we were in Bozanski territory and I was nervous, fidgety, and feeling the pressure.

We returned to Matilda's place at Newtown with takeaways – vegetarian pizza and a pasta with a creamy mushroom sauce. I had a half-decent bottle of Hunter white. Once we'd polished that off, we got stuck into a cask she had in the fridge.

Matilda caught me looking at an old black-and-white photo hanging on the wall. The portrait showed two serious strong-looking women – Matilda's Polish great-grandmother and the great-grandmother's sister, as it turned out.

She told me a story about how they had been banished to Siberia by the Russian government during World War II. The sisters had four children between them and were expected to die, exposed to the below-freezing temperatures. But they struggled through the ice and snow to find a village. The villagers fed them and said they could stay the night, but they themselves were without food and couldn't accommodate more people.

Matilda's great-grandmother had been observing and making notes, studying a building site where some of the villagers were constructing a brick house. She then told a lie that may have saved their lives. She claimed to be a bricklayer and insisted on helping out, joining the team to repay the village for their lodging. Her bricklaying skills were based on observation, but she managed to pull it off and her help was appreciated by the other workers. She continued to work nonstop into the night and the head of the village relented, letting them stay.

When the war was over, they went to South Africa and eventually on to Australia. The family had felt the stigma of being foreigners in another land. They started what became a family tradition of giving their descendants an undeniably Australian name. Matilda's brother was called Bunny.

Matilda said she'd followed my case with interest, reading up on FGI since running into me in the city. She believed my story about being framed by Bozanski.

'Anyone who looked closely into FGI's offshore activities would discover they avoided millions of dollars in tax,' she said.

'That's probably legal.'

'FGI had financed mining investments in projects in Africa where toxins were dumped into rivers and people died as a consequence.'

'I haven't heard that before,' I said, 'but nothing about FGI would surprise me.'

'FGI also has interesting joint ventures in Eastern Europe.'

'That's Bozanski.'

'I don't know who does what, but that Stanley Dochmar seems to have his fingers in a lot of pies.'

Dochmar's name had come up again. As Chairman of the Board, Dochmar must have known I'd been set up. He was probably in on it, and my hope was that Tran could find a way to hit both Bozanski and Dochmar where it hurt – balls, wealth and reputation.

Since my encounter with the doctor, I'd become wary of posting potentially incriminating material. The safe distance I'd felt from my Benedict Sparkel persona was lessening. Yet I still had the urge to act. There were a number of factors at play. A desire to impress Matilda. Twinkel egging me on, and the notoriety. With the possibility of living a longer life than anticipated, I'd come to the realisation that more money was required. If I wasn't dying, I couldn't afford to retire. Furthermore, I didn't want Benedict Sparkel to just fizzle out. I still felt like taking risks. But what was required was something different. Something significant.

Matilda had been talking about the American entrepreneur, Robert Matherson Jr. He had worked on overseas joint ventures with FGI. He would soon be visiting our shores and Matilda was organising a protest at some charity golf day against his company, Depron Holdings.

Although Matilda would never agree to my modus operandi, her disdain for corporate vandals made me wonder just how far she was willing to take it. She had shown herself willing to break the law – for the right cause. I fantasised about the two of us working together like some modern-day Bonnie-and-Clyde team, as I had with Tracy.

It was time to test the waters.

'Forget about taking on corporations,' I told her. 'Focus on the people behind it. Make it personal. Go for Matherson, not his company. Imagine the publicity if Matherson was attacked while making his speech. That would be something.'

Matilda didn't reply, so I made a derogatory comment about Matherson based on what I'd heard her say. A beat later, she got to her feet, turned to me and said, 'I'll catch you later, Dom. I've got a call to make.'

Oh no, I thought, *I've bored her so badly she's turned to work. Or worse still, she didn't take me seriously.* It incensed me that Matilda thought I was all talk. I was determined to show her there were more effective ways of gaining publicity than a stupid banner-waving exercise that, in the end, would achieve nothing apart from stirring up the beehive and providing cops with overtime.

Pissed off about Matilda's dismissive attitude, I went to the sunroom and closed the door. I'd said nothing to her about Cerberus. I pulled out the canvas bag and untied it. Cerberus slithered out.

'Don't wander,' I said, but in the back of my mind I thought, *so what if he gives Matilda a fright?*

A short time later I discovered I might have been wrong about Matilda's reason for abruptly ending our conversation. There was a gentle tap at the front door. The hallway light went on. I heard the rapid patter-patter of feet on the floorboards, followed by the creaking of the door opening.

'Hey,' Matilda whispered in a sexy, welcoming voice.

There was a short interlude – prolonged kissing, I suspected – before the fridge opened. Soon there were two happy voices whispering as they made their way to Matilda's room and shut the door. They became rowdy for a few minutes. It sounded like a pillow fight. This was followed by laughter and then soft music – a classical quartet.

From then on there were few spoken words, just the crescendo of panting and quick breathing, sighs of pleasure and cries of fulfilled desire, which left me jealous and wanting. *Can you two please be conscious of the fact that there is a sex-deprived guest in the house?* I wanted to call out. With Ben Harper playing in the background, as I put Cerberus safely away for the night, it occurred to me that this was the second time lately I had had to listen to another couple making love.

Matilda's friend departed quietly in the early hours. I had no idea who it was. The next morning I was hungry. I roamed the streets, looking for a pastry shop and somewhere to purchase fresh coffee beans for Matilda's espresso machine. The neighbourhood was quiet, just a few shift workers on the move.

I came back with the coffee, a loaf of fresh bread and some eggs, tomatoes and mushrooms. Four croissants infused with almond cream had screamed at me from the window of a French patisserie, impossible to resist.

Matilda was reading when I returned – something to do with the Pacific Islands and climate change, if the magazine cover was any indication. I told her I would make breakfast.

She stuck her head out behind the magazine. 'Go for it,' she said.

Matilda was in good spirits after spending the night with her lover. I was jealous of them. Matilda had a meeting to attend that day. Before leaving, she gave me the spare key and thanked me for breakfast.

I did some digging into Depron Holdings and the American, Robert Matherson Jr. He was an ex-senator and his name was synonymous with right-wing think-tanks in the US. His major interests were in munitions and weapons manufacture, and his detractors claimed he'd made a massive profit from the Iraq and Afghanistan wars. He had links with Saudi Arabia.

He had connections with some investment banks, too, and that was where his activities tied in with FGI. Depron Holdings had instigated lending arrangements that sent poor countries in Africa and South America broke. Like vultures, they feasted on the ruins. That was legal.

Matherson's advice to people was to dream big and take opportunities when they arose, so I decided to do just that. Could his visit provide the means by which Benedict Sparkel cracked it big in the USA? An indulgent smile materialised as I reflected on the prospect.

I wondered how Tran was getting on with Bozanski's accounts. I rang him but wished I hadn't. It was disappointing to find he was still struggling to crack the Bozanski Code and was getting increasingly frustrated. He reproached me for contacting him by phone, becoming quite irate. That was a side to Tran I'd not seen. We agreed to meet the next day and talk more.

On another front, I found out that Dunkley was due to appear in court for a bail hearing. Since I'd fled the townhouse, Dunkley might not have been in close proximity, but the nightmares had continued – the foul stench, the weight of his body when he had me pinned. Again I wondered – what would it take? Would I ever get rid of him, or was he an infection without a cure?

I imagined seeing him sitting in the dock, cuffed, sedate and powerless. It made me feel like a kid anticipating something special, like a visit to Disneyland. How I'd love to be a fly on the wall in that courtroom. Priceless was the value I would put on that experience. Could I summon the nerve to turn up? It was unlikely he'd be released for twenty years or so.

Although Dunkley had been arrested, Chaffer might be like one of the aeroplanes that go missing and are never found. Certainly the story of how a man survived being tossed from the Manly ferry hadn't materialised in any of the major tabloids. The fear of being caught and incarcerated had been bothering me since the doctor had revealed I wasn't suffering from a life-ending illness. I'd worked out how to, if not eliminate, then at least to put a lid on this fear. I got the idea from something I'd seen happen in an old war movie. A German spy was captured, but – afraid of being tortured into revealing secrets – before the Americans had a chance to interrogate him, he tossed a pill into his mouth, taking his own life.

After some online research, I visited a couple of chemist shops and a hardware store. Chemistry was not my strong suit, but the instructions were not difficult to follow. I managed to concoct a poisonous mix.

The vial containing the poison stayed with me always, even in the shower. It would kill me reasonably quickly, albeit with a fair degree of pain. If I chose that road, then at least taxpayers' money would not be wasted on court cases and prison accommodation. Can you imagine the extensive list of charges and the immense court costs that would accrue if some modern-day Columbo got on my trail and Dom Bruno had to stand trial?

28

The Ghost

I'd called Wayne on the pretence of thanking him for giving me the lowdown on events at FGI, but I really wanted to make a time to see him again. He agreed to meet me at a bar in the city.

On my way to meet him, I'd just parked the van when a vehicle drove past slowly and my heart skipped a beat. I thought I'd encountered Bozo's thugs. The car was the same make and model, but luckily it turned out to be a false alarm. It might have been nothing but it really put me on edge.

As I approached the Piccadilly Bar and Grill, I saw Wayne pulling into a parking station in a four-wheel drive. His vehicle was caked in mud. He saw me and we waved to each other.

Wayne entered the bar five minutes later. I'd been to the bar and had a schooner of Coopers on the table waiting for him.

'Your car needs a wash,' I said, and he laughed before telling me he had just spent a couple of days away camping. He had stayed at a property near a river on the edge of the Blue Mountains, a spot he described as quiet and picture-perfect with a wonderful array of wildlife. It sounded like something from a storybook.

When I pressed him to be more specific about the location, he became vague. I found it hard to believe he didn't know. As if Wayne would just follow directions without having a clue where he was going. Maybe he just didn't want me to know – secret Americans' business. Was one of us paranoid?

Although there was a niggling sensation in the back of my mind telling me to be wary of both Wayne and Phil, I had to remind myself that Wayne had gone out of his way to help me after I'd been arrested. And he had disclosed information about FGI when he could've said he knew nothing. What puzzled me was his connection with Matilda. Why did he hang with that crowd?

If I were to deal with Matherson effectively, help would be required. There were not many possible candidates for that gig. Would Wayne accept such a job? Unlikely! How much could I disclose to somebody like Wayne? I thought about the time I'd seen him dressed as a hobo in Newtown. How much did he get paid for that type of work? Would he do any job for the right fee? I'd need to be careful of just how I framed the job description.

I started with a topic that an American, ex-military, working in security would love to talk about – or so I thought.

'Do you do much shooting when you're out in the bush?'

Wayne's face came alive. He beamed across at me, and I began to get excited too. But it wasn't guns that had him all fired up. He began raving on about the merits of the crossbow.

To say I was disappointed was an understatement. I told him the crossbow might be good for doing party tricks like splitting apples when you're drunk, but that it wasn't a real weapon.

He was adamant. 'It's the science of stealth, Dom.'

At that point I thought I was talking to the wrong man. Where was John

Wayne? I didn't want William Fucking Tell.

Wayne continued to highlight the merits of the crossbow and I remained indifferent. But just as I was beginning to get annoyed with the direction the conversation had taken, he said something that caught my attention and had me hanging on every word. The modern crossbow was *lethal* – as powerful as a handgun.

He showed me a YouTube clip of a crossbow doing serious damage to a range of materials, including a bulletproof vest. Wayne could be convincing, and a short time later I was hanging on his every word – not only was the crossbow silent and compact, but the simplicity of it sent my imagination into overdrive. The one he favoured was a metre wide. I'd need to be careful, because a licence was required.

I said, 'Wayne, will you give me a lesson on how to use one? I'll pay you, of course.'

'You honestly want me to teach you?'

'You bet I do,' I replied, forthright.

He was happy enough to be asked, but tried to fob me off, saying he had a lot of work. After I continued to push he capitulated, saying he'd work out a time and contact me.

Neither of us was drunk, but we'd both had a few schooners by that stage. I needed to know whether pursuing Wayne as a possible assistant was worthwhile or a waste of time.

'Do you ever feel the urge to get even with the people who have wronged you?' I asked him.

'Hell yeah. But where would I start?'

'You could start with those responsible for sending you away to war under false pretences.'

Wayne was offended, patriotic as an American. 'What do you mean, false pretences? I don't know about that, Dom.'

'Wayne, those weapons of mass destruction that were supposed to be in Iraq – they didn't exist.'

'You might impress Matilda with that line, Dom, but not me.' He smiled before adding, 'Not all political and military decisions are the right decisions, that's for sure. I do know where you're coming from.'

His last comment gave me some hope.

'Wasn't it your own countryman, Nobel Prize-winner Bob Dylan, who sang "Masters of War"?' I asked. 'The ones behind all the weapons – the politicians, the industrialists. The ones who fired the big guns?'

'Hell yeah! But he also said the answer was "Blowin' in the Wind".'

Touché! We both laughed, but a serious undercurrent remained. I continued, my tone sombre but with a touch of the whimsical.

'The industrialists who make a mess all over the globe. The corrupt bankers who make billions of dollars from the poor. We could do without some of those parasites. Without them the world would be a better place.'

'Ahh, Dom... you are one crazy fuck. Do you really think getting rid of a few tycoons will save the world?'

'Did you kill anyone when you were fighting for your country?'

'Wow... that's a bit out of left field.' His manner became solemn. 'Man... in some situations you don't know who killed who, with everyone firing at once. You do what you have to do, in the line of duty.'

'Does that justify it?'

He gazed at me and pointed his finger in a reprimanding fashion. 'Come on. That's unfair.'

I had overstepped the mark. Neither of us spoke for the next few seconds.

'Look man, nobody likes to see the death of men, women and children,'

Wayne continued. 'Not unless you're inhumane. But it happens. Has always happened.'

'A toast,' I said. 'To the Aussie-American alliance.'

I didn't push the point after that, not wanting to get him offside. We parted company a short time later with Wayne promising to contact me shortly to fix a time for the crossbow lesson.

I was eager to do some research on the subject of crossbows, so I logged on to the internet. There was an enormous amount of information to sift through. The weapon I decided on was the Barnett Ghost. Not a spiritual encounter, but impressive nevertheless. According to the spiel, the Ghost delivered over double the energy required to take down anything on the planet, and was accurate from sixty metres.

Legal requirements had me connecting to a site on the dark web that was used by some of the patrons I'd met at the Imperial. I nominated a post office in the city as the delivery point and paid extra for next-day delivery.

The delivery went off without a hitch. Included in the order were fifty quality carbon arrows and spare twine. For good measure, my contact, Joe, tossed in a pistol bow – a tiny contraption that could fit in one hand. A disc was with it, containing an amusing three-minute YouTube clip of a man using the tiny bow to punch holes into beer cans.

Once the crossbow was assembled, I drove to a quiet spot in the bush near Hornsby where I could try it out. I'd been to the same reserve years before and there had been an abundance of native birdlife: kookaburras, crows, pigeons and magpies. It was clear after walking deeper into the reserve that the number of native birds had greatly diminished.

I did however notice a group of smaller birds attacking a crow. It triggered a memory of something I'd seen on television about the Indian myna, a foreign species that hunted in packs. Although small, it was quick and effective and responsible for chasing native species from their habitats.

Would Matilda approve of my method – taking potshots at these invaders to save the natives? Probably not, but she would be happy with the outcome. I aimed at the target through a powered scope, and it didn't take long before I became proficient. There was a nifty adjustment mechanism to make the bow more balanced. I practised and soon could reload and fire the silky black Ghost efficiently. And apart from a swish and a thud when the arrow whacked into the target – nothing.

What I did next might have appeared strange to a man like Wayne, especially as I'd been so keen. I rang and told him I'd gone off the crossbow idea.

I didn't need the lessons, and the fewer who knew about my newfound archery skills, the better. Sounding like a person who didn't quite know how to apologise, I tried to make up for my change of heart with Wayne by declaring I'd buy him a drink next time we met up. Maybe he was busy or perhaps I'd offended him, but he didn't want to talk and the call ended a short time later.

The afternoon sun cast shadows across the dashboard as I drove back towards Matilda's. I'd been feeling like a boxer on the ropes lately, struggling to see out the end of the fight. It had probably been due to lack of sleep or maybe a simple case of the flu. I was still getting the occasional headache, but nothing like the painful throbbing I'd experienced while I was living near Dunkley. Maybe just being in the proximity of the malevolent arsehole had been enough to cause them. Of course, it was possible they'd been psychosomatic; simply knowing headaches were a symptom of brain cancer might have been enough to amplify their intensity.

I acted badly within minutes of arriving at Matilda's place. Being a trusting person, Matilda had left her phone on the kitchen table. Unable to resist, I availed myself of the opportunity to flick through her log of calls.

She came back into the room suddenly. For a moment I thought, *fuck, I've blown it.* My adrenaline pumped, and in rapid motion, I put it back in the correct position. I tried to look innocent. That was a close one!

I had discovered Matilda had been in correspondence with Lydia recently. There was nothing odd about the two being in contact – they had been good friends at school. The problem was in the timing. According to her phone records, Matilda had contacted Lydia two days prior to the day she'd told me she had accidentally run into her. The day she supposedly found out about my cancer.

Matilda and Lydia. I'd have to be wary. But neither would betray me to Bozanski. On that I'd have bet my life.

Matilda stayed in the kitchen, so I grabbed my backpack and took out a bottle of Taylors merlot, offering her a glass, which she accepted. We talked about the legal system and politics, topics she knew far more about than I. She told me about a politician she'd met who'd tried to convince her that the government should sell *Blue Poles*, an artwork by American artist Jackson Pollock that was owned by the National Gallery of Australia. When she went into a serious diatribe about the importance of integrity, I wanted to ask her why she'd lied to me about contacting Lydia, but I held my tongue.

A cockroach crawled out from under the fridge, and Matilda picked it up and took it outside. I told her about the time Lydia and I had a fight and Lydia told me I'd be reincarnated as a cockroach.

'No offence to Lydia, but to believe that bad humans come back as cockroaches for punishment – give me a break.'

Hearing Matilda being so scathing of Lydia's belief took me aback. She seemed to be a tad jealous. Was it even possible? That I could make an intelligent, desirable woman jealous?

'I don't mind the cockroach option,' I said. 'A quick death after being sprayed with poison.'

The cockroach was a life form and Matilda knew her life forms, contradicting my claim that cockroaches had an easy death. She told me of a wasp that stings and immobilises the cockroach, keeping it alive while eating its insides.

'Well, you've certainly turned me off the cockroach option,' I said. Then I began banging on about the benefits of Catholicism. 'Just admit the sin, do the penance and then move on.'

'There aren't no pearly gates, mate, that's my belief,' Matilda said. 'Our ancestors were apes who lived in the trees and eventually moved to the ground, then walked out of Africa, hundreds of thousands of years ago.'

'Yeah... we've all got a bit of the primitive in us. I'm with you on that one.'

As the sun set on the second bottle, we were both a bit pissed. I began doing ape impersonations. Matilda joined in. She knew some of the actual sounds that apes used to communicate.

Matilda was not one to suffer fools, and I was on the backfoot again a short time later. We'd gotten onto the topic of political activism. Matilda had been telling me about the exploits of the Baader-Meinhof Group and the IRA back in the sixties. I'd said it would have been exciting to be part of the IRA.

'Come on, Dom, are you serious? You reckon you could hack it, being hunted and on the run? Killing people and being shot at?'

Matilda liked to make a point. Matilda liked to argue and win. Again, I was incensed that she thought I was all talk. Still, I swallowed my pride and steered the conversation away from the subject, aware that I was drunk and might say something that I'd regret. I asked Matilda what motivated her to become a political activist.

She said, 'I'd feel like a betrayer if I just did nothing while the planet was being wiped out.'

No matter how I tried to put it out of my head, I couldn't accept that Matilda had me classified as a dreamer who didn't act. Perceptions were everything in the modern world. Directing the conversation towards the Matherson protest, I did what I'd been considering doing since reading up on the man. I offered her my services, asking if I could join the protest against Depron Holdings and the US dignitary.

Matilda appreciated the offer, saying they could always do with help. She told me the details of their upcoming meeting.

'I'll want to do more than just hand out the half-time oranges,' I said. 'I want to man the barricades.'

She laughed at my joke. She had no idea how far I was prepared to go.

Whether it was the wine or Matilda's influence, I wasn't sure, but my life didn't feel all gloom-and-doom at that moment. It led to a moment of regretful honesty.

'I'm not going to die,' I blurted out, immediately wishing I'd shut my stupid fucking mouth as I waited anxiously for Matilda's response.

'You're so stoic about it,' she said, a tear forming in her eye.

In a twist of fortune, I realised Matilda had misread what I'd meant. She thought I was bravely facing my demise. That or she thought I had religious beliefs and meant my soul was not going to die. God only knew, yet despite a moment of panic where my reddened complexion and stifled breathing made me feel distinctly uncomfortable, I made no attempt to correct her interpretation.

While we were having dinner, I told Matilda I wouldn't be staying in Sydney. The places were too expensive. I'd stay for the protest and then head up the North Coast.

She told me about a party she was hosting on Saturday night that I shouldn't miss. 'There'll be live music and great food. It'll be heaps of fun.'

'Sounds good!' I replied, but the idea of socialising at a party and having fun seemed ludicrous in the frame of mind I was in.

29

I Rest My Case

By arriving at the courthouse as soon as the doors opened, I was able to claim the exact seat I'd hoped for – one adjacent to an ornate cedar column, behind which it was possible to partially hide. Dunkley's bail application was listed to be heard first. In this labyrinth of legal wheeling, anything was possible, but bail was very unlikely – he was under arrest for murder.

According to reports, Dunkley had been belligerent and rude, showing no remorse. That man certainly knew how to make enemies. And there was nobody to stand by poor old Dunks when the chips were down. Well, that's what happens when people think you've done someone over. Even if it's only a worthless dodgy ex-warden.

Dunkley and Turner featured on the front page of the *Sydney Morning Herald*. Unable to say too much with a trial pending, the story related to the period the two had worked together as prison officers, and mentioned that Dunkley had been to gaol.

My contribution to Dunkley's case was not without risk. I had contacted a popular online crime investigation site and put forward a theory that explained how Dunkley could have disposed of the gun and clothing. When asked if I worked in law enforcement, I praised the person's sagacity, making a comment about how all citizens should be ever vigilant.

Dunkley's neighbours hadn't done him any favours, either, and I had added fuel to the fire by posting clips of his acts of aggression against them and Turner. Add to this his violent history plus the drugged-while-driving charges, and Dunkley was an easy target for community outrage – *keep the thug locked up, for God's sake.*

As the time drew near for Dunkley's appearance, the courtroom filled up fast. Reporters buzzed about like a coterie of summer flies, jockeying for the best position. There was an element of excitement, as though something substantial was about to happen.

Dunkley was brought up from the cells underneath the courthouse through a trapdoor adjacent to the dock. He appeared distraught and defeated. He'd probably worn himself out protesting his innocence to the authorities. I knew that feeling. There was a guard in front of him and one behind. Head low, Dunkley seemed indifferent to the attention. It wasn't until he was seated that he chanced a glance around.

What a snarly, mean-looking specimen! He was probably fifteen metres away, but his belligerence was palpable. I had to remind myself he was cuffed and heavily guarded.

As the magistrate was preparing to start proceedings, I moved forward, out from behind the cover of the pillar, affording Dunkley a side-on view. *Come on, Dunkers, notice me.* Dunkley's cruel eyes did a slow sweep to the right, to the left, and back to where I was sitting. It was my gleeful smile that caught his attention.

At first it was curiosity, the inquisitive tiger. Then I opened my blue jacket, keeping it open just long enough for Dunkley to read the print on the front of my T-shirt – *D for Done, O for Over, M for Mate.*

I moved my head from side to side, taunting Dunkley, goading him to act. The moment he saw through the old-man disguise I wore, his entire body began to shake. It was a wonder he didn't levitate. He attempted to indicate in my direction, but it wasn't easy with cuffs on.

Finally he found his voice. It came out loud and aggressive. 'That's Bruno! That's him! He's the one you want!'

People inside the courtroom gaped at Dunkley like they would a wild animal that had mysteriously managed to speak. They had no idea what had enraged the prisoner. Some – including a couple of reporters – cottoned on to where Dunkley was trying to indicate. As they turned towards where I was seated, I simply turned as well, giving the impression that the source of Dunkley's distress was to be found elsewhere.

The guards were slow to react. The prisoner had shown no signs of misbehaving up until that point. Attempts to subdue Dunkley were to no avail, and a struggle developed. Gradually the mood in the court changed and the crowd began to worry. Cameras clicked and police came racing in to help.

Dunkley then lost it totally, and even with the reinforcements, security was severely tested. *For God's sake, don't let him escape,* I thought. Imagine coming face to face with that malicious devil from hell – again.

'The man's a complete lunatic,' somebody said, and nobody argued with that assessment.

'Taser the arsehole,' said a woman sitting near me, and eventually they did, having no other option. Dunkley was stunned into submission, dragged from the dock, through the trapdoor and back to the cells beneath.

The legal system would not be kind to a prisoner who caused a ruckus in Her Majesty's court. Whether he had attempted to escape was a point of conjecture. It appeared so, in which case he would be facing very serious charges indeed. The magistrate had barely looked up – he had seen it all before. Dunkley had ruined any scant chance of bail before the hearing had begun.

For me, there was a magic moment that made the risk I'd taken worthwhile. When it was clear nobody was taking any notice of Dunkley's ranting, I cast one last triumphant sneer in his direction. Our eyes met, mine calm, his red and full of rage.

Dunkley's courtroom meltdown went viral on social media, even trumping Trump's latest tweet. Dunkley could get a book deal after that performance. The clip that led the ABC News featured a rampant Dunkley glowering like an ogre. There was no mention of why he exploded or his bizarre courtroom claims.

In the aftermath of my triumph, though, Dunkley still had a victory. Even as I mocked him, I knew I still wasn't free of the man's clutches.

On my way back to the van I saw two kookaburras fighting over scraps in a park. Then I observed a magpie diving at a bike rider and continuing to pester the distressed man as he dragged his bicycle along the street. It might have been the unseasonal balmy weather, but dive-bombing cyclists at this time of the year? *Come on, fellas, the season hasn't even started.*

I'd only just reached the van when I received a coded message from Tran. He wanted to meet at a café in the city as soon as possible. When we arrived he was in a jubilant mood. The information I'd provided about brands and numbers from Bozo's yacht had enabled him to crack Bozo's accounts. He had located an offshore account linked to Bozanski – with a forty-million-dollar balance. The FGI auditor was either hopeless or in on the swindle. Dochmar was most likely privy.

Tran then surprised me by saying he had nabbed all the dosh that morning in one transaction, moving the money using an elaborate system of piggybacking, targeting susceptible sites.

'Soon you can live the high life,' Tran said.

I replied, 'I'm already living the high life.'

What we did next had been discussed endless times within the confines of our prison cell. I'd fallen asleep dreaming about the possibility. But I'd no idea we would have anything like forty million dollars to play with. We agreed to risk half of the swindled money. If our endeavour was successful, we would not only take the heat off ourselves, but destroy Bozanski, Dochmar and FGI's credibility.

The attraction for Tran was the possibility of increasing our riches. Sure, I was more than happy to have more money, but for me it was about revenge.

We had to move with haste, before Bozanski discovered that it was not only his offshore bank accounts that had been hacked, but his FGI executive email account as well. After picking up a hire-car Tran had organised, I parked the vehicle and went to a café located on the ground floor of a skyscraper in Kent Street, found a table and waited. Tran had set up the rendezvous and given me a description of Lucy, the stockbroker I was to meet.

Casting an eye over the tables nearby, I saw groups of young men in trendy attire and women talking and sipping drinks. Some had folders, others briefcases. Just what they were discussing, one could only guess. Perhaps a business proposition, or maybe the gossip from the latest reality TV show. From what I'd caught of the conversation at the table behind me, there was a job interview in progress there.

I ordered a coffee and logged onto the local network. The case of Dunkley and Turner was trending, having captured the public's imagination. Maybe not up there with the dingo and the baby, but up there nevertheless. The name Dom Bruno was most likely being shrieked with reckless abandon by a boisterous Dunkley. But would anybody listen to the accused? Of course Dunkley would deny and try to deflect blame. If the interview with the police prosecutor was any indication, there would be more immediate matters to contend with due to Dunkley's recent outlandish courtroom antics.

A woman matching Lucy's description came into view. She was young, thin and of Asian appearance, and had the required red rose pinned to the lapel of her black two-piece suit. I introduced myself and she greeted me with an easy smile. There was no indication that she found my appearance in the least strange. Tran had probably joked about my old-man disguise and told her to humour me. But I'd have been a fool not to take precautions. Someone could recognise me from my previous life at FGI.

We caught the lift to the sixth floor and walked into a small office Tran had hired, with a desk, small fridge and an assortment of power points. The space featured two massive glass windows, the vista showing off the Sydney Harbour Bridge, Opera House and stunning harbour.

Lucy opened her bag, taking out her computer and an apparatus containing a silver microphone and a set of headphones. Once she was set up, she logged in online to the Australian Stock Exchange and perused the share prices. She then took a small notebook out of her pocket, opened it, waited half a minute and rang Tran.

I'd learnt some everyday Mandarin phrases as a courtesy to the Chinese businessmen I had to deal with at FGI, but I couldn't follow the gist of the conversation. Knowing Tran, he and Lucy probably had their own coded language. Over the next couple of hours Lucy purchased thousands of FGI shares. Then Tran sent out a press release – authorised, supposedly, by Adrian Bozanski – announcing a takeover of FGI by a Chinese investment company. In the statement, Stanley Dochmar was named as the chief negotiator for FGI.

Lucy and I watched the screen patiently. She nudged me as the FGI share price began to climb sharply. About fifteen minutes later, still conversing with Tran, she stopped buying and began selling off the FGI shares, getting more than double the price we'd paid. Lucy was still unloading the last of the stock when FGI shares hit a hiatus (Bozanski's press release would have been retracted), then crashed to an all-time low.

Job done, Lucy packed up and I paid her the agreed amount. We left the office and walked to the hire-car. Forty minutes later I bade Lucy farewell at Kingsford Smith Airport.

FGI was left floundering in full damage control, and trading in FGI shares was suspended while authorities investigated. News of the FGI share market disaster was all over the radio and social media. From the accusations being made, just like the FGI share price, Dochmar and Bozanski's reputations were at rock bottom.

According to Tran, once the experts were brought in, they'd find a trail. Bozanski would have to explain not just the sixty grand he received during the FGI share fiasco – my idea, and money well worth sacrificing – but the offshore millions that had been stashed away and somehow mysteriously disappeared.

Tran said it would take at least three days to sanitise Bozanski's money. I walked through the city in a buoyant mood, pleased with my impending riches and Bozanski's predicament. I tossed fifty dollars into a busker's tin. I gave three fifties to a trio of homeless people – wow, did they get a surprise (which was fine until one of them followed me back to the van, asking for more). I had a fleeting thought about sending Lydia money, but decided she had plenty. *Besides, it might offend her Buddhist sensibilities,* said my sarcastic self.

Finally there was something on Chaffer. A missing person's alert had been issued. But why hadn't he surfaced? There were online postings hinting at Bozo's involvement and a few nautical jokes regarding the swimming champ. My contribution was to make public what the police already knew – Adrian Bozanski had sent a threatening text to Rodney Chaffer around the time of Chaffer's disappearance. The evidence was building, or so I hoped.

There was a story in the *Herald* about Robert Matherson Jr and his upcoming visit. It referred to his appearance at the charity golf event. His love of golf (he played regularly with the US president) was well-known. He would be presenting the prize at the Pro-Am tournament. There was a photo of the golf course where the event was to take place. It was situated on a massive expanse of coastal land at La Perouse near the entrance to Botany Bay.

I pondered the idea of long-term survival. If I did survive the Matherson stunt, would it be possible to simply disappear or fake my own death? If the police didn't nab him for Chaffer, I could even set up Bozanski for the crime.

Part of me wanted to forget about Matherson – to wait for the money from Tran and then run. But I couldn't. I might have been given a reprieve from the doctor, but I'd become addicted to freewheeling – living life on a roller-coaster. And while there was danger and risk, Dunkley was not inside my head. Maybe his fingertips still brushed the skull, but on the roller-coaster my mind was occupied, and other emotions came to the fore – excitement, fear, then joy and satisfaction – the afterglow, the triumphant thrill of having pulled it off.

Back at Matilda's house, I logged on to the Mr Twinkel site.

Mr Twinkel strolls onstage and up to the microphone.

'Benedict Sparkel, before Sparkelisation, was a man who let selfish personal vendettas dominate his life. Eventually he found inspiration and the right path – Benedict Sparkel became a crusader for the common good. You too can become like Benedict Sparkel – brave enough to stick up for the common man.

'And remember, you don't have to match it with the likes of Mandela, Gandhi or Matilda – just leave a legacy of which you can be proud. Do a deadly deed that will benefit mankind. If you are not long for this world, what do you have to lose? Leave the world the way you came into it – with one big bloody commotion.'

At first I thought Twinkel was just reinforcing a theme that had proved popular – *be a sociopath for the people.* But he was laughing in my face. How in the hell did he know about Matilda? Sure, she was in the public domain, but that line about her, mentioning her with Gandhi and Mandela... it was similar to something one of the Americans had said while we were drinking at the hotel.

Surely Mr Twinkel was not one of the Americans... but how else would Twinkel have come by that information? Was somebody listening in on the conversation?

30

Assistance Required

It was imperative that I speak with Wayne again soon. Working in security, he would be able to shed some light on the methods used to eavesdrop on our conversation at the pub. I also wanted to try to secure his services – to make him an offer that he might find hard to refuse.

I didn't really see how Wayne or his mate Phil could be behind Mr Twinkel. If I hadn't accidentally crossed paths with Matilda when I was spying on Chaffer, I'd never have been at the pub with Matilda to meet Phil or bump into Wayne.

When I contacted Wayne, he was standoffish. He claimed to be busy and I had to almost beg for some of his precious time. He told me to meet him at Corretto Dee Why, across the road from the beach. Apparently he was working somewhere nearby.

Being out in public without a disguise made me aware of the threat of not just Bozo's boys, but the police, who might want to question me about Cyril Turner's murder or Chaffer's long-distance swim. There was less chance of being recognised over this side of the harbour, but still, there was reason to be watchful.

I drove along the beachfront looking for a parking spot. There were joggers, dog walkers and beach-goers, out enjoying the day. At the north end of the beach was Dee Why lagoon, and in the distance Long Reef. The natural beauty of the area and laid-back atmosphere lifted my spirits. I had only been here once before, and that was with Lydia. Dee Why wasn't as densely populated as some of the beachside suburbs nearer to the city, but it had its share of high-rise apartments. Some were close to the beach and for a moment I imagined myself sitting on a balcony, sipping a beer, enjoying the stunning ocean views. I eventually parked a block back from the beach.

I arrived early at Corretto, bought a bottle of wine from the bar and found a spot in the corner. Wayne arrived twenty minutes later. He didn't want alcohol, just a glass of water.

I wasted no time in telling him our last conversation at the pub hadn't been as private as we'd thought – that it had been recorded and posted online anonymously. I didn't mention Sparkel or Twinkel.

I'd thought he'd be intrigued, but he didn't ask a single question. Maybe Wayne knew he'd said nothing of importance at the pub that day, because he was surprisingly nonchalant about the matter. He didn't even ask about the part of our conversation that had been made public.

He didn't have the slightest doubt that what I told him was possible. He went on to say that with the number of electronic devices available, hackers were able to get access to a phone or device and to activate the microphone. He shrugged. His advice – change phones and get a new email address.

The assumption that I was the source of the breach annoyed me. I said I'd had my phone turned off on that particular occasion. Wayne told me what I already knew. Even if I'd logged off, my location could be tracked from my credit card, tolls, parking fees and previous behaviours. The hacker only had to be in the vicinity. He then proposed another possibility – my phone could have been hacked before I went to the pub.

'It wouldn't surprise me if it was somebody from FGI who recorded our conversation,' I said. 'Wouldn't put it past them. You've seen enough to know how corrupt they are at the top. People like Dochmar and Bozanski – they should be held to account for their crimes.'

'They'll eventually get their just desserts.'

'Will they? I don't know, Wayne. The Dochmars and Bozanskis of the world... They can afford topnotch legal teams. Even when they are in the wrong, people like them manage to have matters tied up in the courts for years. The wave of destruction continues unabated, with only a ripple of effective opposition. A man like yourself would surely see my point. Look at Matilda, putting her life at risk and achieving what?'

Wayne looked at his watch. 'Come on, Dom. I haven't got time for this.'

'Just hear me out.'

'Five minutes,' he said, putting me on notice.

It was then or never. I'd learnt from a previous chat with Phil, after he'd had a few, that both he and Wayne had been involved in dodgy activities in Mexico before signing up for the military. When I spoke I tried to sound businesslike. I wanted to offer him enough money so it would be hard to refuse.

'I want to hire your services for a few hours. I'm willing to pay you well – eight thousand in cash. I'll give you four grand upfront.'

He gave me the oddest look. 'To do exactly what, Dom?'

'All you will have to do is cause a diversion.'

'A diversion?' said Wayne, his questioning squint telling me that he wanted to hear more. Was he desensitised like me? Did he have the thirst for adventure? If the price was right, would Wayne still be up for something dodgy?

'What I want you to do is not illegal. It will provide the opportunity for me to sneak in under the radar and get access to somebody.'

'It's a lot of money to pay to get access to somebody,' said Wayne.

'It's a publicity stunt. It will get worldwide attention.'

'Who is this person?'

'It's better that you don't know.'

Wayne dismissed my reply with a flick of the hand and gave me a poignant, prolonged stare. Perhaps I was a public art piece.

Pulling an envelope from my pocket, I placed it on the table. 'Four grand. Well? What do you say?'

I'd seen that look before. I'd lost him.

'Are you for real, man?' Shaking his head in disbelief, he patted me on the shoulder as he eyed my near-empty bottle of wine. 'Dom… Go home and sleep it off.'

He'd insulted my intelligence and I his. I needed to lighten up the mood. 'Come on, mate – you're from a country with grand ideas… "I had a dream… I had a dream".'

'Martin Luther King,' replied Wayne, playing along with me, more than happy to change the subject. He put his phone into his top pocket and got to his feet. It had been worth a try.

'Thanks for listening, mate. It was just an idea,' I said. 'I might see you at Matilda's party!'

'Oh, are you going to that too?'

I'd assumed Wayne would know I was staying at Matilda's. We parted company amiably, but what was going on in Wayne's world was anybody's guess.

Maybe I would drop by the party to say goodbye to Matilda and Wayne. If I did, I wouldn't stay for long. I'd be safe with Wayne there, but Bozo and other unknown predators were after me, so I had to be careful. For my safety, it was best to be like the proverbial old coin – out of circulation.

A short time later I made my way to the address in Newtown where the protest meeting was to be held. It was not that far from Lydia's place. Without a disguise I was exposed, but once again there was no option. If I turned up in disguise Matilda would think I was a real oddball. She might reclassify me. At least at the meeting I would be inside.

Once I arrived, I found Matilda. Those in attendance seemed to know each other well. Some were shabbily dressed, as befitted their role as saviours. Matilda introduced me as an old friend and I was acknowledged with either a brief nod or a curt hello. One or two of the men regarded me with a degree of suspicion. I'm sure it was jealousy because I was friends with Matilda, the darling of the ball.

There was a couple, stern patrician types – too taciturn to cry at a funeral – who ignored me completely. I made sure I was standing near them when I took off my denim jacket. I'd decided to make an impact.

Do in a Dickhead or Two, the logo on my T-shirt read.

I'd gotten the shirt for free as part of a two-for-one deal at the time I purchased the one for Dunkley's court appearance. A little crass, sure, but it got their attention. Hopefully it would signal to them that I was out-there enough to carry out what I'd be proposing. Disbelief from Matilda, frowns, the odd chuckle, cold stares from some of the intellectuals – *the blow-in's an ass*.

There were fourteen of us in the kitchen. After twenty minutes of listening to them express adamant opinions but settle on doing little, I became impatient. I got to my feet and announced in a loud voice, 'We need to make a ruckus near the clubhouse. That's where Matherson will be speaking. That's where the press will be. Not out on the road.'

'But we can't get access.'

'Buy a ticket to the golf.'

'The police know us. They'd never let us in.'

'They don't know me. If you lot cause a diversion, I'll do the deed.'

'What do you mean, do the deed?'

'This waving-the-placard business is so old school. Lucky if it even makes it into the twenty-four-hour news cycle. If you want to be noticed, you need to make an incursion beyond the barriers. Sneak in behind enemy lines.'

People looked at Matilda. *What species have you introduced?*

'What the fuck do you mean, an incursion?'

'I'll throw a boot at Matherson – maybe full of wine. It'll get extensive media coverage in the States.'

There were a few laughs. A group of three joked openly to each other about me – a bald man with an earring laughed in my face. But in the end they were willing to discuss my proposal, so at least I gave them credit for that.

One argument against it was that it would prove to be a bad strategic move long-term if anyone got arrested. One in favour agreed media coverage was a real problem these days. Matilda argued against it because it would be breaking the law.

'A bit rich, Matilda,' I said, 'knowing your past deeds.'

Matilda didn't react. Maybe she didn't want to see me in trouble. Or was she more respectful of the law these days? A career move, perhaps.

Points of order were called. An old hippy-looking character claimed it was worth a try, even if the silly fucker – me – got carted off by the police. The meeting became quite heated, but the outcome of the vote was eleven to four against supporting my plan. I'd been one of the four.

There wasn't any official help, but afterwards two who had voted for my plan – a seriously large bearded man and his waif-thin girlfriend – came over and asked if I was fair dinkum. They introduced themselves as Chris and Sam.

I whipped out a map of La Perouse and surrounds from my backpack pronto, and began. Over the next twenty minutes, the nascent plan developed as the logistics were mooted and scrutinised.

Chris and Sam agreed to crash the barricades at the required time. Praising them for having the guts of their convictions, I told them it was imperative that they cause the diversion at precisely five o'clock, no sooner, no later. Before parting, I added that it was better if we didn't contact each other again – they were fine with that.

I'd disclosed nothing of my real plan. The plan we'd just agreed to was insane – I'd be arrested in two seconds flat. Silly nongs, the pair of them, but still, I was grateful for their help.

After the meeting I went to my van, which was parked in a shopping centre near Matilda's place. From there I logged on to a public Wi-Fi network and the Mr Twinkel site.

My pulse was soon racing and I began to sweat. There before me was footage of Dom Bruno fleeing the scene of Turner's murder.

Was Twinkel trying to incriminate me? From the angle of the shot, it had been taken from across the road. Could it be used by Dunkley's defence team to create doubt? Would the police start looking for another possible suspect?

Zooming in on the image, I realised I'd dodged a bullet. The definition was poor and the face became fuzzy once you homed in. Our height difference was not noticeable, and difficult to judge given I was hunched slightly. And what a relief that my too-thin-for-Dunkley legs were not visible.

The more I thought about the situation, the more my earlier fears were alleviated. From across the road it looked like Dunkley. Although I'd first thought the photo would be useful for Dunkley's defence, I wondered whether the Crown might use it to help prove his guilt.

Also in my favour – he had been arrested for Turner's murder. From the crime shows I'd watched, once the police had an arrest, the last thing they wanted to do was create more work for themselves by having to investigate another suspect. And they didn't enjoy having to admit to arresting the wrong person.

In any case, I wanted the footage removed. When I attempted to erase the file – using every available method – I experienced a gut-wrenching feeling of dread, followed by anger as it became apparent that I'd lost control of the Benedict Sparkel site.

I sent an irate enquiry to Twinkel, asking for an explanation. Minutes later he was vilifying me on my own site.

'Shame on you, Benedict Sparkel. To claim to be suffering from cancer when it is not actually true. You have been lying, not dying. How can Mr Twinkel or the public trust you? You have betrayed all of us who loved and believed in you.'

I sent an email back – *Who are you, Twinkel, a fucking priest?*

I attempted to apply a few tricks I'd picked up but nothing worked.

Eventually I decided to contact Tran.

Tran. This is a matter of urgency. Please contact Dom immediately.

He would know how to handle the situation.

31

Party Time

When I stepped into Matilda's house, the party was in full swing. There was still no reply from Tran. Inside were over thirty guests, many of them colourfully dressed. Reds, yellows and greens woven in intricate patterns.

In the lounge room there was a band playing. Lights were flashing and people were dancing to the music, which had a South American flavour – Brazilian, perhaps. They were a joyful crew, not a frown of doubt or a funless face amongst them.

Matilda was wearing blue jeans, as she often did, and an eye-catching rainbow-coloured crop top. Dom the Dag stood out in mundane grey and black. Perfect for anonymity usually, but in that setting, as obvious as a hippo on a tropical reef.

I recognised some of the faces from the meeting earlier. A woman came up and spoke to me in an accent I couldn't place. It was hard to understand what she said with all the noise. What a fool I felt like afterwards – I'd thought she'd asked whether I liked *fuck music*. I had laughed, thinking she was making a joke, replying the music was a bit slow for sex. Then it dawned on me that she had actually asked me whether I liked *folk music*. The woman was soon conversing with another guest.

Two dancers came out of a bedroom and started performing before the band, their hands moving slowly and sensually, provocative in contrast to the rapid movement of their feet. A dance of desire. They kissed occasionally, much to the crowd's delight.

There was a performance of a traditional Spanish love song and a short break before a trio began to play more upbeat tunes. The music featured an unusual time signature, and wow – for acoustic music, it kicked up quite a storm.

Phil the American arrived, but there was as yet no sign of Wayne. Matilda introduced Phil to the people she was with. Soon I'd slip away into the night. I became a bit agitated at the thought of sleeping out again, but I would have to bear it.

I was about to get my bag from the sunroom and approach Matilda to say farewell when I noticed there was somebody in the adjoining room drawing the attention of a group of men. At first I couldn't see clearly because someone was obscuring my view. Seconds later I was in panic mode.

What in the hell was Lydia doing here? Was that why Matilda and Lydia had been communicating, because of the party?

My senses came alive, my eyes like two high-voltage torches scanning the room. Did Bozanski and his boys follow her? Probably and, if so, would they come inside or wait out on the street? Bozo would have no hesitation walking in on this.

I raced over to where Lydia was dancing. My hands formed tight fists and my eyes were firmly fixed on the door. My voice was frantic, accusing.

'What in the hell are you doing here? You were probably followed by Bozanski or his stooges!'

Her tone was terse, tired of such idiocy. 'No-one's following me, Dom. Aren't you getting tired of all that?'

'Lydia, for God's sake. It's important that you listen to me.'

She brushed me off and returned to her dancing.

Bozo or his baboons were bound to know Lydia was here tonight. Bozo might be caught up with issues at FGI – that thought did make me feel pleased – but that wouldn't stop his thugs doing his dirty work. Lydia didn't seem to give a damn that she might lead them to me. She was in denial. Sabrina was probably in her ear, telling her I was full of it.

People were still arriving and, as I'd feared, amongst the new arrivals were Bozo's boys, the same ones I'd previously met through the screen door of my townhouse. In amongst the bohemian crowd, they stood out in their Hawaiian shirts like an anachronism from another era. The trouble was that I stood out as well.

Moving swiftly through the kitchen, I ducked into the sunroom. I gathered my bags from under the bed. Taking deep breaths and wiping away the sweat, I regained some composure and applied theatrical make-up to transform my appearance by creating an aged face. I attached a beard and wig. I'd had to rush and just hope it worked. Pulse throbbing, I looked in the mirror. Would Bozo's thugs see through the disguise?

Leaving the safety of the sunroom, I made my way with some trepidation through the kitchen and out to the lounge room. As I passed through the party crowd I was greeted by happy faces and the occasional second look. Most ignored the old bugger.

I saw Phil chatting to an attractive brunette. Still no sign of Wayne. I cautiously made my way to where Phil was standing.

'Phil, please do me a big favour and walk with me out to the street.'

Phil raised his eyebrows and began laughing. 'Dom... it's you! Man, you look ridiculous.' He whispered in my ear, 'Can't you see I'm occupied?'

I was insistent. 'Please. Just help me get out of the house. There are people here who are after me. She'll still be here when you get back.'

Apologising to the woman, he begrudgingly did as I asked. 'Come on then,' he said, his tone gruff.

Lydia seemed oblivious to the danger she was in. Either that or she was on their side. I didn't believe that. Lydia might have tired of me and been heavily influenced by Sabrina, but she would never betray me. Bozo's boys were watching her like hawks but showed no interest in Phil or me as we made our way to the exit.

I raced out of the house and down the steps, my progress slowing considerably when I saw, less than fifteen metres in front of me, Adrian Bozanski.

He had just stepped out of a Mercedes sedan. He had a mate with him. If I raced back into the party I would be trapped. I just hoped my disguise held up.

Phil had stayed with me as I'd asked, and stopped when I did. 'What's going on, man?' he said.

I nodded in the direction of Bozanski and his mate. 'These two – can you help me avoid them?'

But the two were upon us before we'd reached the street.

'This Matilda's place?' asked Bozo.

In a split second he saw through the disguise. Grabbing me by the throat, he pushed me to the ground.

When Phil protested, Bozo shouted at him, 'This is not your business! You'd be wise to stay out of it if you know what's fucking good for you.'

While he'd been talking I'd tried to slither away, but he'd trapped me with his foot. After threatening Phil, he grabbed me by the ankle, reeling me in.

I prayed for a car to drive up. I screamed out to Phil to go and get some help. But what happened next came as a shock to both Bozanski and me.

Bozo was used to his threats being heeded. But Phil did nothing of the sort. He waited for the opportunity to catch Bozanski on his blind side. Then, in what seemed like a surreal few seconds, he advanced quickly and hit Bozo with two quick left jabs – then, to seal the deal, clobbered him with a solid right to the nose.

Bozo went down in a screaming heap. I lay on the ground, mesmerised, watching on in admiration.

Phil turned and faced Bozo's friend as I was getting to my feet. Bozo's friend stepped back out of Phil's range. He'd seen how easily the American had disposed of Bozanski.

Phil told me to follow him to his car. We walked away at a steady pace but didn't run.

By the time we got to the car a small crowd had gathered outside. Bozo was gingerly getting to his feet, brushing himself down.

In the car, I rang Matilda to warn her about the two men who had followed Lydia into the party. I told her Bozanski was downstairs. Knowing Bozanski, he'd be too embarrassed to bother Lydia or anyone else in his present state.

Matilda said the two men I'd described had just left the party. I told her to ring the police if they came back. She told me she'd make sure Lydia didn't leave her place alone.

We watched from Phil's car as Bozo and his thugs drove off. They didn't search for us, probably assuming we'd already left. Phil said he would take me to a safe place on the city's outskirts. He said it was about an hour's drive. *Why so far?* I wondered, but he seemed to be genuinely trying to help. Without him I'd have been finished. The way he destroyed Bozo was impressive. Really impressive. I'd underestimated Phil.

Phil turned on the ignition and the radio and airconditioner sprang to life. As we drove away, the nine o'clock news came on. It felt surreal sitting in the car with Phil, hearing Chaffer's name mentioned by the announcer. He was still missing. Cyril Turner's murder was mentioned, but with the court case pending, discussion was not permitted. Hearing their names on the radio made me feel like a musician who had two songs in the top ten.

When Phil spoke, I thought he was asking about Bozanski and crew. 'You knew that man?'

'Bozanski, sure.'

'No. Not him. That dude who was murdered. Cyril Turner.'

It was peculiar, hearing Phil say The Warden's name.

'Yeah, I did.'

'They got the bloke. An ex-crim called Dunkley killed him.'

'I can tell you without doubt that both men are trash.'

'That guy Turner had a wife and kid. See the picture there?' He pointed to the newspaper that was folded on the back seat.

I reached over and picked it up, looking at the picture. The caption said that Cyril Turner was separated from his family.

'He does too. They don't look too healthy – a bit pale and wispy if you ask me.'

'Fuck, Dom… their father has just been killed. And you joke about it.'

'I tell you, he was a real prick. Those kids will cry a few tears, but in the end they'll all be much better off without him in their lives. Anyway, why are you so concerned?'

'You told me at the pub that Turner was shot with a Bersa Thunder, remember?'

'Can't recall, but yeah, so what?'

'See what it says. That information was only released today.'

My reply was quick as a flash and I felt pleased with myself for coming up with an answer when put on the spot. 'I know a cop who's working on the case.'

'You also said witnesses at the bus stop would have seen the killer escape. Why did you say that?'

'Everyone knows they've been interviewing people. And Turner's place is not far from the bus stop.'

Phil didn't say anything, and I began to wonder how convincing my explanation had been. It also bothered me that I couldn't remember telling Phil about Turner being shot with a Bersa Thunder. I could remember saying something about the bus stop when I was showing off after a few too many.

What I did next was risky, but it was worth a try. I'd seen it work in some old movie from the fifties.

'I'll be honest, Phil,' I said. 'I was responsible for the Turner shooting. And for that bloke Chaffer's disappearance.'

'What?'

'I did both'

I laughed.

He laughed.

'And I've got all these bodies buried in my backyard.'

I laughed again. Phil laughed. Phew! What a joker!

Phil had been direct when asking me about Turner's murder and, although the conversation had finished on a light note, I still couldn't be sure whether he really did suspect me. Although he'd saved me from Bozo, I felt it wise to tread warily. I insisted we backtrack to where my van was parked, and he declared such a course of action too risky. But I was adamant.

'I will follow you, but it's important I have my own vehicle.'

It started to get nasty, him arguing that it was a stupid idea and me threatening to jump from the vehicle. Desperate to get to my van, I decided on a tactic that had worked before. I took Cerberus out of the bag and put him on my lap.

Phil put on the brakes. 'What the fuck!'

He was terrified. After watching him confidently flatten Bozanski, I'd thought he would be more resilient, especially being an ex-soldier. I think it was Cerberus's twin heads up near his face that did the trick.

'Take me to my van. Now.'

'Okay, okay … just put that snake away.'

Phil followed my directions and drove to where my van was parked. At that stage, judging from his curious gaze, he must have thought I was strange. What a bizarre sight I must have been with my fake wig and beard, brandishing a two-headed snake.

'Where in the hell did you get it?'

'I found him in the bush.' To keep him on task I let Cerberus's heads protrude from the bag.

'Is it venomous?'

'Only if it bites.'

Phil looked at me twice, but I managed to keep a straight face.

We arrived at the van and Phil was more than happy to have both Cerberus and me out of his car. After a quick wash and change of clothes, I signalled to Phil that I was ready, and we drove off. The traffic was reasonably sparse for this part of the city on a Saturday night. We headed north-west towards Dural, Windsor, then up the Putty Road. Phil turned off to the right and onto a dirt road that eventually led to a large clearing situated on the banks of a river, which must have been the Hawkesbury.

There was a large log fire burning and a couple of smaller ones. Five tents were pitched along the riverbank, the scene reminiscent of a bucolic postcard. Phil said most of the campers had nowhere to live and the farm owner let them camp there for a small fee.

At first I thought it might provide a perfect hideaway to rest and prepare for tomorrow. But after meeting a couple of the inhabitants, I wasn't so sure.

Raffer, the first man Phil introduced, was about forty, bald and with dark, tormented eyes. Sando was a wiry man who spoke with a stutter and had a foreign accent. He asked too many questions and was wary of my presence.

Raffer had a pot of stew brewing and he invited us to have supper with him. Phil readily agreed, which suited me fine, as I was hungry. The stew was tasty, with a Mediterranean flavour. Being the paranoid type, I ate only what Phil ate, fearing the food might be drugged.

Sitting on a log where it was possible to sight my van, I caught a glimpse of someone trying to open the front door. The van was locked, but this hadn't deterred the man. If successful, he'd get the fright of his life – Cerberus was loose in the front section.

I got to my feet and shouted, 'What are you doing? Leave the van alone.'

The culprit slinked away towards one of the tents. I looked across at Phil, seeking an explanation.

Phil said, 'He's harmless.'

Harmless to whom? I wondered.

When it became apparent there was no radio or internet coverage, I made the decision to leave the camp. But how could I slip away from Phil and his freaky friends?

While Raffer and Phil were making coffee, I went to my van on the pretence of getting a jacket. I put Cerberus away, and just moments later I was racing through the night like a bat out of hell. My acceleration and braking techniques weren't perfect, but if Phil or one of his weird friends wanted to chase the van, they would have to move fast to match me for aggression and pace.

After driving around aimlessly for nearly an hour, I pulled over near Hornsby and studied the map. I then headed north, spending the night beside the Hawkesbury River at a popular free camping spot just off the expressway.

I didn't get out of my vehicle. The less people saw of me the better. A shower was what I needed, but that would have to wait. The presence of the other vehicles meant it was more likely I'd be noticed, but it was comforting to know other people were nearby. With my thoughts focused firmly on tomorrow's endeavour, after a couple of nips of whisky I slept relatively soundly. For once, the demons stayed away.

32

The Lone Wolf

I awoke to a dreamlike scene. Across the river, distant mountain tops of green eucalypts soared above the smoky grey mist like a mythical land, creating an atmosphere of tranquillity and mystique. A car zoomed by, a reminder that the expressway was only fifty metres away. Snippets of a conversation wafted across the water. A boat engine sprung to life.

After a quick breakfast, I changed the plates on the van. Not even Phil could find me now. Again I tried to contact Tran. He still wasn't responding. Even though he might have been in the air or caught up at Customs, as time passed I started to wonder. He'd never before been unavailable.

Mr Twinkel was out of control, claiming to have created the world's first virtual psychopath through his alias Benedict Sparkel. People were flocking in droves to the site. The posts and real-life material all pointed to Dom Bruno – if somebody wanted to make the connection. The Fuck It! List concept was attracting mainstream attention. Many people still thought it was all a stunt.

Could Twinkel have had someone film the footage for him? Maybe it was taken by a press photographer. One shot showed Dunkers in court causing a disturbance, and then me turning away from his rage. Another of me from behind, leaving the chamber. Nothing incriminating – maybe I had been lucky.

I was constantly checking my old phone for messages and missed calls. My body went cold, and I began to sweat after reading a text from Case.

Sorry to be the one to deliver the bad news. Have had trouble contacting you. Terrible tragedy – Tracy has been killed. Will advise when know details of funeral.

Reading it again, I felt ill. Tears flowed, slowly at first, and then uncontrollable cries and sobs. I rang Case, but my call was sent to voicemail. In my panicked state, although he could not have possibly done it, images of Dunkley came flooding in. Maybe it was seeing the upload of his out-of-control court appearance once too often, but once again, like a virus that senses weakness and lies dormant in the body, waiting for its moment to pounce, the decrepit Dunkley stench was upon me.

In my reduced state, my achievements and plans seemed worthless. Had Bozo's men killed Tracy trying to get to me? That would make me responsible – a load that was too much to bear. Hungry for information, I madly scanned the media as I rang her number; something inside me wouldn't believe Tracy was dead. Infuriatingly, her phone rang out. Tracy's name did not appear online, nor was there a victim fitting her description. There was nothing about a murder in her suburb. But did that mean anything? Sometimes the media withheld information if the police wanted it so. Courts could also make rulings that prevented the media reporting.

Using a burner, I again tried to contact Case, but still nothing.

Although I'd questioned Lydia's loyalty when Bozanski turned up at Matilda's party, now I was more concerned about her safety. I sent her a text using a code we'd made up as teenagers to avoid our parents' scrutiny, asking her to meet me at an internet café in Chatswood, finishing off the text with – *IT IS IMPERATIVE YOU ARE NOT FOLLOWED*.

Whether or not Lydia would turn up was uncertain. If she really was on Bozanski's side, I was in trouble.

As soon as I got to the café I was on alert, surveying the surrounds. There was no way of knowing who was lurking behind a newspaper or listening on a headphone, or even in disguise in a queue. Again, call me paranoid, but Bozanski's thugs were dangerous and real. There might be plenty of witnesses around, but would that give me protection? After the smack in the head from Phil, Bozo would be furious.

I watched Lydia approach. Her distinctive sway was recognisable from afar. Wearing a green-and-white outfit, she had deliberately dressed conservatively for our rendezvous. She could try all she liked, but she could never look ordinary. Just seeing her sent my heart racing. It gave me a thrill to be in her presence.

I watched and waited out of sight for five minutes to ensure Lydia was alone, occasionally glancing downward to ring Tracy and Case's numbers. Nothing.

When I walked across to join Lydia, she didn't recognise me immediately. It pleased me that the effort had been worth it. Once it dawned on her that it was me, she shook her head, inferring I'd lost it. There were no pleasantries – if Lydia was unimpressed with Dom, she was even less impressed with Dominica. When I tried to explain the reasons for the disguise she was dismissive, speaking over me.

'The police want to talk to you, Dom.'

'What about?'

'How do I know? I can imagine you'd have a fair idea.'

'It's probably about a parking fine or something. Tell them I'm on the road. Up north. Everyone goes up north.'

'I'll tell them fucking nothing, and just so you know, Sabrina and Bozanski are both taking legal action against you.'

My deadpan face peered back at Lydia as I tried to think of a response.

'So Bozo and the prancing Pilates queen are suing me. It'll get thrown out of court. Bozo never forgave me after I pushed him into the fountain. The YouTube clip is still doing the rounds.' I forced a laugh. 'And as for Sabrina... '

Lydia interrupted me. 'No, Dom... don't! I won't have you dismissing everything I say as if it's a fucking joke.'

I'd been worried about Lydia's safety, particularly after receiving the text about Tracy. Now she was annoying me.

Her phone rang and she stepped away from the table. I tried to eavesdrop but she was too smart.

When she came back over, she gave me a long, cold stare. 'That was Sabrina. Chaffer's body has washed up on the rocks near Manly.'

'Rodney Chaffer, eh? Ol' mate Chaffer.'

As I'd said his Christian name, there'd been a pang of remorse. Lydia saw it, read the emotion.

'You know something, don't you?'

My tone turned spiteful. 'About Chaffer? Only that I thought he was a good swimmer.'

'I wouldn't be a smart-arse if I were you. The police know that Chaffer got on the Manly ferry that Friday night. But he didn't get off.'

'Meaning what?'

Lydia opened her iPhone and pulled up the latest news. She placed it in front of me and moved away so I could read it. 'The Man Overboard Incident', it headlined.

'Well, who would have thought, eh? Chaffer… "The Man Overboard". That's quite an achievement. To have an incident named after yourself. Who would have thought?'

'Sabrina and Bozanski believe you killed him.'

Lydia, like Tran, had known of my Fuck It! List back in my prison days. She knew of my disdain for Chaffer. At least she seemed to believe my boasts were not just idle threats!

I became deadly serious. 'Don't trust those two lying villains. Chaffer told me he was terrified of Bozo.'

'You spoke to Chaffer.' Lydia took a newspaper from her bag and flung it at me. 'Page three.'

On page three there was a picture. It was taken from above while I was disembarking from the ferry. I felt a flicker of recognition at seeing myself. There were others around me. Studying it closer, my fears subsided. Facial recognition was always possible with modern techniques. But this was a distant shot, taken from the side. Half the face was concealed.

Would the police or a jury believe that was me? No way. Besides, the cotton dress sat nicely on my hips and the cleavage screamed *female*. The hours of preparation had paid off. The dress was always going to be recognisable to Lydia, though. Maybe she still had photos of the one I'd worn to that party all those years ago.

I read the highlighted text – *Police have been following a number of leads in regard to the Chaffer disappearance. They would like to speak to a woman who was on the ferry the night Chaffer disappeared. If anyone can remember seeing this woman…*

I threw her a guilty smile. 'You caught me out. Just our little secret. Like the old days.'

Her eyes, full of ire, bored into me. 'You wore that dress on purpose. To involve me. Are you trying to implicate me?'

'What? I'm trying to save you. I'm worried sick about you and these people you're mixing with. Your life is in danger. Tracy, a barmaid I knew – she was killed just for knowing me. Probably by Bozanski.'

Meeting over.

After Lydia left, I found out all I could about what was being said about Chaffer. Despite some police and talkback hosts alluding to the fact that it might have been suicide, friends and family were adamant that it was completely out of character. They probably knew Chaffer was too selfish and too much of a coward to jump off a ferry. I couldn't plant Bozo on the Manly ferry, but the message sent from Chaffer's phone surely must make Bozo the prime suspect. Particularly since the unravelling of FGI.

I checked the Benedict Sparkel site, but still couldn't regain control. On top of that and Tracy's apparent murder, there was something else to worry about. Tran still hadn't responded to my call for help. The longer he didn't respond, the more my emerging suspicion grew – Tran may not be the solution but, rather, the actual problem. If this were true, it would be a real blow.

I was becoming increasingly frustrated. Something had to be done. After much deliberating I decided to take on Twinkel at his own game. There would be no point in carrying out what I'd planned for Matherson if I couldn't upload my actions.

I managed to create a new site on the dark web after doing some research and drawing on my experiences watching Tran. My next posting was under the alias 'The Real Sparkel'.

Under the banner of 'The Real Sparkel', I reinstalled my previous uploads, including recent footage and some unpublished material. This included Turner's final gasp with the real Dunkley edited into the picture in a Twinkel-inspired creation. Plus more of Turner groping Suzi. There wasn't much on Bozo, just the footage of him falling into the fountain playing in slow motion, with the message sent to Bozanski from Chaffer's phone about Bozanski threatening to harm Chaffer playing over and over in the background.

That the Real Sparkel site was still operating half an hour later was promising. It gave my spirits a lift.

The police had set up a hotline for the Chaffer case. Time to put the boot in – another of Bozo's favourite euphemisms.

I played the role of a terrified FGI employee. 'Sorry, sir, but my life wouldn't be worth living if Bozanski found out I was a whistleblower, so I can't give my real name – but I did witness Adrian Bozanski threatening Chaffer on a number of occasions.'

There was a popular online forum where FGI's troubles and Chaffer's disappearance were openly discussed.

These cops have been slow, so slow, I whined, claiming to be an FGI insider, name withheld.

In response to a question – *Yes, I mean no, sorry. I can't verify whether that is true or not. To say many FGI employees suspected Bozanski and Dochmar of being involved in the death of Chaffer... It comes down to what you define as 'many'.*

Somebody else chimed in – *FGI board members are being investigated by the Federal Police.*

Before leaving the group discussion, I let them know the police had possession of Chaffer's phone and that it contained material implicating

Adrian Bozanski, claiming the info was from a cop. The Real-Life Crime Solvers swarmed over that bit of news like European bees.

There was still no response from Tracy or Case. I tried to push my culpability in Tracy's death to the back of my mind. I needed to think clearly. If Tracy had been murdered, the police would have access to her phone and now to my new number. They could track the location, but there was no link to Dom Bruno. Still… I ditched the phones.

The pleasure of revenge might have been sweet, but it had been ephemeral. I realised that my appetite was not yet sated. Except for Chaffer, for whom I now felt indifference, the hate I felt for my Fuck It! List targets had not diminished. For Bozanski, the loathing had increased. I'd need to kill him a dozen times over to level the scores with that arse for what he did to Tracy. Who else could it be but Bozanski or his thugs who killed her?

Tracy's pleading face appeared like an apparition. I might try to put her to the back of my mind, but it was an impossible task. I really needed to concentrate on Matherson, but I had to try to find out what had happened to Tracy first.

The best place to start would be the Imperial. Changing my appearance was mandatory, then I'd have to be careful. If Bozanski had linked Tracy to me, he'd know about the Imperial. He might even have an informer stationed there.

Disguised as a woman, I drove the van past the pub and pulled over nearby. It was eerily quiet as I strolled over to the back door and peered in through the glass. I couldn't see Case or Bubba. The boss wasn't in and the place was nearly empty. There were recognisable faces, but none I knew well enough to trust. I didn't risk going inside.

Next on the list was Tracy's place. I'd never been inside but I knew where it was. Crawling past her flat, I did a U-turn and parked. After observing the place for five minutes, I walked up to the front of the building and paused to furtively check the mail. Nobody had cleared Tracy's box for days.

I was returning to the safety of my van when a suspicious-looking car appeared. The blue Toyota panel van crept ominously along the street, passed me and turned into the laneway at the back of the block of flats. I felt vulnerable; caught in no man's land, like a lone swimmer far from shore with a large shark fin on the horizon.

That blue Toyota wasn't a vehicle that had worried me before, but so what? Changing cars was probably par for the course in the surveillance game. Hadn't I done the same myself? What a relief it was when the vehicle darted off towards the main drag. My disguise had probably saved me. That and the change of vehicle. But something wasn't adding up.

I had been unable to contact anyone for over twenty-four hours. Tracy hadn't been murdered at home or the police would have her place cordoned off. And when I thought about it, why wasn't Tracy's mailbox empty? Surely the police would have done that. Again I searched for news online, but still there was nothing.

I returned my attention to Matherson. His name came up everywhere. He was a publicity machine. There was an upload of a speech he'd recently made. Listening to it, you'd think he was vying for sainthood. As usual, Matherson finished with his mantra, asserting that the world was a safer place with America armed and strong. Matherson had met with the Australian Prime Minister and they had issued a joint statement, praising the cooperation between two great nations who had been allies for over a hundred years.

'A great American patriot and a great friend,' some politician was quoted as saying. It was much too mawkish for my liking and made me dislike Matherson even more.

In the corporate world, this man's stature was godlike. His PR shots were interesting. One was shot in a pristine forest with Matherson decked out in his khaki greens. He was pointing to a map, and if you didn't know otherwise, you might mistake him for a park ranger. The same theme again in a US press release, where he was photographed with the Rocky Mountains as his backdrop. I'd watch that one closely – knowing his record, he was probably sussing out sites to mine or buying up land for a munitions dump.

Matherson was described in his bio as a brilliant businessman, an intelligent and astute God-fearing man. Surely at the pearly gate Saint Peter wouldn't be tricked. Some sagacity would be applied when he encountered this conman.

Just like so many others who seek power, Matherson was, by his very nature, the narcissistic type who should never have it.

The number and positioning of security personnel at the charity golf day was crucial to the success of my plan. It had been impossible to find out all the details. It could well come down to whether Matilda's friends created the distraction at the right time. Or would they chicken out? Just in case, I'd planned a distraction or two myself.

I logged on to the Real Sparkel site. Due to the footage I'd uploaded, viewers had made the link between Benedict Sparkel and The Real Sparkel. Still operating, still not being taken seriously by authorities – yet.

Again I wondered – was some smart detective just watching, seeing what else would appear before closing in to make an arrest?

The idea that Tran was behind Mr Twinkel was again on my mind. I still hadn't heard from him. Mr Twinkel would have to possess considerable skills – as Tran did.

I felt a growing anxiety about what to do post-Matherson. Of course, that was if – and it was a big if – I managed to stay alive and free. Flee, sure – but where and how? Although I might not have had a burning zest for life, at least I could envisage existing beyond the short-term.

In one fleeting moment of survival fantasy, I imagined living as a woman, never being sighted as Dom Bruno again. Tran would find that amusing. I retrieved my head from the clouds. The more I thought about the situation, the more I had to face the real possibility that Tran had deserted me. Left me to take the fall while he made off with the loot.

Was I really so gullible that I'd been conned by Bozanski and then by Tran? The Warden used to say to never trust a crim. The thought of not being able to trust Tran was a depressing one. That and the Tracy business had me thinking of the poison vial in my pocket.

My next message was intended to be my last. It was short and to the point.

It is true that up to this point Benedict Sparkel's actions have been selfish and motivated by revenge. But my next act will be for the common good. The latest addition to the Fuck It! List is a man whose crimes against humanity have been substantial. His elimination will leave the world in better shape. This man's careless and malicious actions, motivated by power and greed, have caused pain and death to millions throughout the world.

You are wondering, who could this man be? There are so many candidates. Watch this space for a live podcast of the dramatic event from The Real Sparkel later today. Follow #LeaveTheWorldInBetterShape.

With what I'd proposed and the growing interest in the uploaded material relating to Dunkley and Turner's murder, Mr Twinkel, The Real Sparkel and Benedict Sparkel became the biggest show in town. The authorities could do what they liked, but the material was reaching the market. All efforts to find those behind the façade were to no avail. I lay low, resting and preparing, planning.

There were all sorts of speculation. Some claimed Mr Twinkel was a spy, working for the Russian government. Another theory was that Mr Twinkel was run by members of a Chinese triad. One cartoonist in a popular daily depicted Benedict Sparkel as a broad-shouldered, swarthy guy with an ISIS-style beard, dubbing him Jihad Sparkel.

The greedy ghost in me cursed the fact that Twinkel had not only sabotaged my site but was taking revenue that was mine. Not a cent had gone into my account since Twinkel dumped me.

33

Fight Them on the Beaches

I drove along Anzac Parade and through Maroubra Junction. Before reaching the Malabar shops, I made a left turn and wound my way down to the bay, past Malabar Beach and around to the boat ramp, driving down the steep incline and parking the van near the water. This was a part of the coast I was familiar with. To my left were the golden sands of the small, secluded Malabar Beach. It was invariably calm. The long narrow bay and high headlands provided protection from the wind; perfect for launching and landing a small craft. There was a small wave near the beach at times, but it was only during Christmas tides, or when a southerly hit, that the swell got serious enough to worry the watercraft. Across the bay to the north was the rifle range, set in bushland that stretched all the way to South Maroubra.

I'd disguised myself as an older woman. The brief for this assignment was to appear feminine – fake breasts and make-up – but not to attract attention.

After unloading, I moved the van up to the road above, put on a knee-length raincoat, grabbed my Brasilia bag and hurried back to the gear I'd left by the water. Nobody paid much attention to me. A car towing a boat was leaving. There were kids fishing from the rocks. The serious fishermen would have been on the water at sunrise.

I used a portable battery to inflate the Saturn SD290. After that I attached and primed the motor so it was ready to go. Once it was on the water I jumped in, lowered the motor and pulled the cord. The three-and-a-half horsepower outboard engine sprung to life.

The sky was a pale shade of blue and the sea looked calm out beyond the bay. It was as the Bureau of Meteorology had forecasted and was expected to stay that way for most of the afternoon. It was the word *most* that worried me.

The overseas contingent had praised the condition of the golf course, though the locals said conditions would be difficult for the leaders if the wind came up later in the day. Although the wind might aid one of the diversions I'd planned, it could also make the return trip hazardous. Just how the inflatable craft would hold up in a swell was a concern, and I wasn't keen to do a Chaffer and test my swimming ability. I'd considered launching the craft from close range at Little Bay. It would have meant spending less time on the water. However, escaping the scene might have been tricky, particularly if the police barricaded Anzac Parade.

Up until that point, thinking about my treatment at the hands of Dunkley, Turner, Bozanski and Chaffer had been motivation enough. But with Matherson, I couldn't quite convince myself. I didn't feel the rancour towards him that I did for those other men. The damage he'd caused throughout the world was substantial, and the possibility of gaining international media coverage was a powerful incentive. But the killer instinct was not there.

And something else unusual had occurred. Sabrina had spied on me for Bozanski. She had set Lydia against me. The idea of Lydia and Sabrina being together still drove me mental, but I no longer felt the intense hate towards Sabrina that I once had.

Approaching the end of the long bay with caution, I continued straight out to sea to avoid the possibility of being seen at close range by the rock fishermen.

It was impossible to eliminate risk. As I thought about the possibility of being caught, I felt for the poison vial in my pocket. The cowardly way out, maybe, but was my fear of imprisonment less valid than the fear of the English sailors who'd once sailed these waters around Botany Bay back in the eighteenth century? Some were more than happy not to be able to swim. They preferred to drown if the ship went down rather be left to the mercy of the sharks.

After a while I turned the boat south. Early days, sure, but the sea was reasonably calm and all was going to plan.

When I'd visited the golf club two days earlier, I'd given some cock-and-bull story about being part of the catering team. They had been helpful, confirming the timing of events leading up to the presentation. Silly me had attempted to hire a golf cart but was told in a blunt manner by the woman in the Pro Shop that the course was only open to members and tournament players. Everyone apparently knew that. Still, I made the most of the opportunity. The golfers were not the only ones who needed to be acquainted with the course layout. A tent and small stage had been under construction in the car park. That was where Matherson was to appear.

I'd tested a new camera, which was supposedly of a higher definition than the one I'd been using. My satellite feed had worked, although I couldn't tell the difference in the quality of the images. I'd considered setting up the transmission on a half-hour delay to give myself time to flee the scene. But in the end I decided it would be far more powerful to broadcast live. It was worth the risk.

There were a few options for entering the course. On the trial run I'd taken the craft south as far as Little Congwong Beach, close to the entrance to Botany Bay. The landing place I'd eventually chosen was just up from Cruwee Cove Beach.

As had occurred during the trial run, the couples, tourists and families picnicking barely noticed me as I dragged the craft up onto the rocks. If the gear was not there when I returned it would be a long hike back to the car. Most people were trustworthy. My biggest worry was that kids might see the craft and be tempted to take it for a joyride.

Stage one complete, I made my way around the rocks to a secluded cave. I touched up the lipstick and eye shadow. The reddish-brown wig and fake breasts had held up well. I'd chosen a conservative cream blouse with a three-quarter-length sleeve, a long pair of brown cotton pants and flat sports shoes. Neat and tidy, but too plain to attract the eyes of the young bucks who'd be at the presentation.

Burying the items I didn't need, I left the cave carrying the Brasilia bag, which contained Cerberus, the crossbow and arrows, plus a T-shirt, shorts and a pair of sports shoes. Making my way along the beach and onto the path that led up the incline, I was soon strolling along the Henry Head walking track, my mind on task; watching, assessing, ready to make a snap decision, the one that saves you or brings you down in one crumbling heap – all over red rover.

I wound my way around the sandstone headland. The vegetation was thick and traversing the track was a risky proposition, as I had no way of knowing just who might be coming from the opposite direction. At worst, I decided, I'd be sent packing, but I didn't want to fail. When I reached

Henry Head I attached a fake press pass to my blouse and took the fire trail, setting forth towards the clubhouse.

As the track straightened out, I came across a cordoned-off section where two security guards were stationed. It gave me a real fright and I backtracked quickly, hoping neither had noticed my late change of mind. I had no intention of having my disguise or pass scrutinised at close range.

I'd been expecting security where the two trails converged, not at that point. It meant I had to leave the track earlier than intended. As I trudged slowly through the thick, dry bush, Cerberus stirred inside the bag. This was snake country, not all that far from Cerberus's original home. Later I planned to return him to the wild. But that could wait. His services might yet be required.

Through to the edge of the fairway, I took off the coat, placed it at bottom of the bag and checked Cerberus. I was still over a hundred metres from the clubhouse. It was prudent to wait, just a minute or two, to ensure nobody was around. I didn't want to be seen entering the golf course and I was ahead of schedule. If I were sighted emerging from the bush, my story was that a professional golfer had lost a ball in the trees earlier and I was souvenir-hunting.

After the required time had passed I carried out a quick reconnaissance, then stepped warily out onto the edge of the fairway, setting off at a steady pace towards the clubhouse. Barely metres into my stride, my stomach dropped when two members of the green staff came out from a shed just up ahead, driving towards me in a golf cart. But there was nothing to fear. They showed no interest in my presence, driving past me as though I were invisible. If I had been a man they might have uttered a guttural 'Gidday mate', or at least waved in acknowledgement. It might not be good for the ego, but the plain Jane look had worked. Still, I'd have been in trouble if the disguise hadn't worked from that distance.

Ambling around the hedge and into the far end of the car park, I saw the last of the golfers putting out on the eighteenth green. I looked at the leader board. One golfer was three strokes clear of the others. That was a relief to see. If there was a tie, I would be presented with a real headache. A playoff would be required, meaning the presentation would be delayed.

Nestling in behind a group of fans, I could see five police officers and four security men. Just how many more there were was anyone's guess. Matherson would have his own security if he was true to form. For the duration of his recent public appearances, the human dynamo was accompanied by two thickset bodyguards.

People were beginning to come in from the golf course and gather around the stage. The media presence was noticeable. Two television crews and a number of reporters were visible. If I was caught on camera it might help or hinder, depending on whether someone saw through the disguise. So far nobody had looked twice. This lot were a cut above me. And there were enough cute young women strutting about in their revealing outfits to render someone like myself invisible. These golfers sure were magnets for glamorous women. Some were probably wives and girlfriends of the competitors. They were eye candy for the security men, which helped my cause by providing a distraction.

Just when I was feeling quietly confident, my composure was suddenly given a real jolt. *What the hell?* I cursed, wondering just what it meant. I hadn't considered the possibility of seeing Wayne. Certainly not acting in an official capacity. Despite being in disguise, I felt bare and the longer I stood there, the more exposed I felt. What a crazy position I would be in if he saw through it all.

Having nearly pissed my pants and with my pulse in overdrive, I went racing towards the portaloos, which were twenty metres or so away. Did Matilda know Wayne was doing security for the Matherson gig? Wayne certainly knew Matilda was organising the protest.

Recounting all I'd said to him in the worst of our drunken raves, I couldn't remember revealing too much about my intentions regarding Matherson. I'd purposely not mentioned his name. If Wayne was suspicious of me, he would have been on the lookout, searching for a face in the crowd. Wayne was astute and I'd be a fool to forget it. But I had my diversions and the disguise was first-rate. As long as I kept a safe distance from him, things should be fine. But I needed to be confident, else I'd be made to pay. Despite the increased risk, to turn back at that stage, after all the work I'd put in, was not something I would do easily.

Act like you belong. That was what I needed to do, and that was my mantra as I set my mind to the task that lay ahead. There was still ten minutes until the presentation ceremony was scheduled to begin. Each second ticked away for what seemed like an eternity.

I wondered whether The Real Sparkel was still operating. It had been well over an hour since I'd checked. I put in the code and logged on to the golf club Wi-Fi. A few seconds later I was staring at the screen in disbelief. Before me was the interior of the Imperial. Tracy was pouring beers behind the bar. And in the distance, sitting at the table with Bubba and Case, was me.

I'd never mentioned the Imperial in any of my correspondence with Twinkel. I was sure of that.

There was another ominous upload – Twinkel onstage, talking to a group of policemen.

'If we don't stop this devilish woman today, we'll have hell to pay. If the dammed press gets a whiff of it, no doubt there will be some myth

circulating about a red-headed creature that came out of the sea.'

Twinkel must have hacked into my satellite feed when I was testing during the trial run. Which meant he was probably tracking me still. Feeling confused and panicky, I immediately disconnected from the club Wi-Fi.

Twinkel could no doubt cut my satellite link at any time, or even expose me. But the more I thought about it, the more convinced I was that he wouldn't take that course of action. If he was going to do it, he would have exposed me already. My guess was that he would wait and see, knowing that whatever I was up to, it would probably make him money.

But there were other repercussions of this new development that had me concerned. What else did this Mr Twinkel have that I didn't know about? How far would he take it? Showing that footage from the Imperial was a low, treacherous act, considering what had happened to Tracy. It was also a display of real arrogance, a demonstration of power. It was so unlike Tran. But if it wasn't Tran, who was behind it?

I was shaken from my reverie by someone testing the microphone. Proceedings were about to begin. There was a lot to do. After composing myself, I left the safety of the cubicle and joined the crowd.

The scene was an innocuous mix of golfers and dignitaries, minglers and malingerers – all talking and drinking, mulling round, waiting for the presentation to start. Some glowed with the radiance of the very important. Some had hangers-on – their very own pilot fish. I could hear the faint chant of the protesters who had assembled where Cape Banks Road met Henry Head Lane.

The man at the microphone welcomed the dignitaries and golfers to the club and made a joke about the protesters, which I missed. A representative from some golfing magazine said she was chuffed and honoured to be in the presence of such distinguished guests. Weren't we all!

Right on cue, Robert Matherson Jr, with the expected two bodyguards, came striding out from the official tent. In performance mode, Matherson clearly enjoyed the attention. He smiled and waved to the crowd, acknowledging the applause as he clowned about with those lucky enough to be in his orbit.

Cameras clicked. People he passed strained to hear Matherson's off-the-cuff remarks. There were looks of admiration from the outer galaxies. No wonder the guy had such a big head.

As I studied the man from a distance, there was no doubting his commanding presence. His deep, resonant voice oozed confidence, poise and charisma. He referred to his own appearance in the popular television series, 'The Men and Women Who Rule the World'. He then got a laugh making a joke at the expense of his golfing buddy – the US Vice President.

By this stage I'd heard enough. This bloke was the American version of Bozanski. It was time to shut him up.

My plans for a diversion were inspired by a story my pop had told me many years ago. When he was young, the most eagerly awaited day, apart from Christmas and birthdays, was Empire Day. The primal attraction of smoke and fire, that irresistible, intoxicating smell of bonfires, Tom Thumbs, bungers and skyrockets. Grandpa and his mate were villains. The night before the big occasion they'd sneak around the neighbourhood, lighting other people's bonfires. It was their methodology that made them hard to catch. Simple but effective – just a box of matches and a cigarette – there was no need to carry serious fire-igniting gear.

With all eyes on the stage, I made my way out the back of the parking area in the direction from which I'd come. My destination was the bush between the fairway and Henry Head Lane, about thirty metres from where the crowd had gathered.

Stepping in amongst the acacias and banksias so I was hidden from view, I took the filter off the cigarette, lit it and jammed the unlit end into a partly opened box of matches, up against the red tips. The saltpetre in the tobacco would keep the cigarette burning, and when it reached the red tips, ignition should occur. I placed the package in amongst the dry debris. There was a slight breeze, strong enough to fan the fire so it would spread quickly. It would be easy enough to extinguish. As long as they didn't muck about. I wasn't expecting a horticultural award, but the fire would be doing the trees a favour by killing off some of the weedy undergrowth.

Back near the crowd, I noticed a policeman talking anxiously into his walkie-talkie. After he'd conversed with the other police and security guards, two of the police officers and three security guards headed up the road towards the protest. Gazing over a reporter's shoulder, I could see on her screen that there had been a confrontation at the entrance between the police and protesters. I hadn't been sure they had it in them, but Matilda's two comrades had done as requested, increasing my odds of success. It gave my spirits a boost.

Ambling away from the crowd and the clubhouse, I ducked behind a car where there was protection from the breeze, took a packet of Tom Thumbs and two bungers from my bag and lit the wicks. After dropping the bundle into a nearby garden, I walked quickly back towards the gathering.

The crackers had extended wicks and the bungers were set to go off first, but even so I'd only just made it to the edge of the gathering when the first cracker went off. After the second bang people were looking at each other nervously, uncertain what to do as police and security moved warily towards the source of the noise.

'Someone's got a gun,' a man yelled.

Then the bunch of Tom Thumbs went off.

'That's a machine gun,' called another.

The word *terrorist* was uttered as Matherson was dragged away from the microphone. He wasn't too bothered. Probably knew it wasn't a gun. Or maybe for Matherson – knowing his line of work and home state – crazy gunmen were the norm.

I'd thought he might head for the car park, but he stayed put. At a nod from the man himself, one of his security guards moved off towards the commotion. Just one guard left with Matherson. That was as good as it was going to get. I had planned to attack Matherson while he was in the car park, from the edge of the crowd while he was on his way to his car.

From the accent, it was an English golfer who spotted the flames first. Less than a minute later it was possible to see them from where I was standing. The fire was beginning to take hold. Security, police and helpers began running towards the shed and were soon reeling out hoses and attaching them to the water outlets.

The cracker incident was still being investigated. The crowd was confused, pointing and yelling, on the move, criss-crossing with no idea which direction was safe.

I moved in closer, towards where Matherson and his bodyguard were standing. Reaching into my bag, I checked to ensure the arrow was set and the crossbow was ready to go.

Suddenly there was screaming nearby. People were bumping into each other, scrambling, trying to distance themselves from something on the ground. Without even having to check I knew instantly what had happened. Cerberus had escaped. The number of people encountering him was measurable in shrieks. This gathering had taken the word *mayhem* to another level.

I tried to put all the chaos occurring around me to the back of my mind and concentrate on the task at hand. *Control the breathing. Be efficient, but don't rush.*

Many times I'd practised this procedure. Out in the bush and inside my head. Down on one knee I went. Breathing slowly, I took out the bow, hiding it near the bag as best I could while eyeing the target and positioning my hands. Breathing slowly, I raised the bow, turned, steadied and fired.

The shot just missed Matherson's hip, smacking into the clubhouse wall. The bodyguard hurled himself in front of Matherson.

Part of me wanted to run, flee the scene immediately – as I would have, had the shot been successful. But I couldn't leave without trying again. In my favour was the fact that there was only one person guarding Matherson. The bodyguard's ferocious gaze searched the crowd like a weapon as he attempted to locate the shooter. The broad-shouldered man continued to shelter most of Matherson's body, making my next shot difficult.

Quickly reloading, I aimed for Matherson's right knee and fired. The arrow whacked into his right thigh. Not a bullseye, but close to the mark. I could barely contain my satisfaction as I watched him falter, then slip to the ground.

The security guard spotted me.

'There she is,' he shouted. 'Up there.'

He pulled out a handgun and pointed it straight at me.

The nearest policeman was over twenty metres away. He was watching the flames and trying to control the crowd. He had no idea what had occurred near the stage. There was too much confusion and noise to hear what the person next to you was saying, let alone someone that far away.

All the other security guards and the police were well and truly occupied. Even before the disturbance they had steered clear of Matherson. They had probably left him alone because he had his own men. Maybe Matherson wanted it that way.

I stayed low to the ground as I put the bow in the bag, making it impossible for the bodyguard to fire a shot without risking hitting innocent bystanders. An older couple had seen me shoot the second arrow but had turned away as though the event didn't happen – blind monkeys. Already I could imagine the headline – 'Terrorist Attack: Red-headed Woman Attacks Matherson With Crossbow'.

Matherson's bodyguard continued to point and shout as I strode towards Cerberus. I'd thought the bodyguard was duty-bound to stand by his man. But he began moving away from Matherson and towards me.

I'd expected to have to shake off one bodyguard. What I hadn't expected was to have one on my tail this far away from the bush. I took off like the wind.

Chancing a glance over my shoulder, I saw the bodyguard's progress had slowed. He'd frightened the already panicked crowd, who were pointing at him, worried at the sight of a man wielding a gun. At the same time he was on the phone, looking at me, then over his shoulder at Matherson, not wanting to let his boss out of his sight.

The press was having a field day, as excited as kids at a theme park; phones and cameras clicking away, words being spoken into dictaphones, a myriad of front-page possibilities as they struggled to make sense of it all. What a front page Cerberus would make!

The activity around the snake was still frantic. Even though people were trying to warn others, in the pandemonium it was impossible. Some inadvertently stumbled upon Cerberus. When I saw some guy walking towards him, wielding a golf club, I increased my pace. It was to be his homecoming, but not there, not like that. I couldn't leave him to the mercy of this lot. I gave the golf club guy a heave then picked up Cerberus, holding the reptile up close to the guy's face. He slid away on his back like a crab scurrying for a rock – great footage, that.

Many spectators were leaving the scene, walking back out to Anzac Parade. I joined them, striding, on edge and in a hurry. There was no sign of the bodyguard – *still in with a chance*, I thought. Then I realised someone was following me with a camera. Probably a reporter. I accelerated away, keeping my back to the pursuer, as though I was going towards Anzac Parade. Everyone around me was preoccupied, worrying about their own situation. At the first turn in the road I darted off into the trees.

Moving with all the stealth I could muster, I crawled through the bush. This area was perfect – thick enough for me to remain unseen, but easy enough to penetrate. Now and then I'd stop and listen. I was in a state, dripping perspiration, alert to every murmur. Nobody was following – yet.

After crossing the southern section of Henry Head Lane unseen, I began backtracking towards the Henry Head walking track.

The siren from a fire-engine sounded faintly in the distance as I came to the path that would lead me back to my boat. After scrambling through the bush had left me with cuts and scratches, I was looking a little worse for wear. I took off the clothes, bra and wig, washed off the make-up as best I could, and changed into a T-shirt, shorts and shoes, ditching the disguise and the crossbow in a thick clump of spiky weeds.

With the acrid smell of make-up remover strong in my nostrils, I moved off swiftly along the track. *Me, I'm just your regular guy, sweating copiously from the effort I put into my exercise, an unfit suburbanite, trudging along the track carrying a bag.*

Cerberus was meant to have been discarded by now, but after that close call back at the clubhouse, I couldn't return the snake to the wild. Not yet anyway. And Cerberus might yet be needed.

My ears pricked up. Somebody up ahead was talking. It sounded like the crackle of a walkie-talkie. And it was coming in my direction. I dived into the bushes.

What a close call! It turned out to be a policeman, and a serious-sounding one at that. I listened as he stopped and quizzed a young couple, telling them to go back up to the main road. *Get back up there and help your mates, copper!* My plan was in disarray. If this was his new posting, I was in trouble. But after he had another brief conversation on the walkie-talkie, him mostly listening, I heaved a sigh of relief. Off he walked, back along the track towards the golf club.

Matherson's security man would identify me. The woman with the camera would be saying I had escaped in the direction of Anzac Parade. That's what I hoped. As long as nobody discovered my discarded clothes and crossbow too soon.

After passing a group of Sunday walkers, I was soon nearing the path that would take me to the spot where I'd left the boat. The most dangerous part done – or so I thought. I'd only just begun to relax a little when I heard the dreaded clipped static of another walkie-talkie. Hitting the ground, crouched on all fours like a lizard, I crawled away and attempted to hide. To remain unseen in the low-lying coastal heath near the cliff face was near impossible.

Then I heard the sound of shoes on stone. Looking sideways, I saw a security guard in a brown uniform standing less than five metres away, surveying the scenery while puffing on a cigarette. Horrified, I didn't dare move or breathe. I could only wait and hope. A chopper passed overhead, further south.

Should I make a dash for it? If he turned and looked I was finished. While I was contemplating, I heard that dreaded canine sound. Was that a police dog? Already? *Here come the hounds. They'll discover my clothes for sure.*

The thought of having to confront that lot had me rolling away ever so slowly, the stones and spiky plants paining me. There was a drop of about a metre, and I had to refrain from groaning after I lost my grip and began slip-sliding down the rocky escarpment. What a sight I made, scrambling down the rocks. Pumped-up and covered in cuts and bruises, my dishevelled appearance screamed *trouble*. Rocks and pebbles hit the rock platform below. Luckily, the fishermen and picnickers who had been there earlier were gone. I chanced a glance above and couldn't see anyone glaring down.

It was getting late – not yet sunset, but increasingly gloomy. The wind was getting up. The inflatable craft was where I'd left it. Who said you couldn't trust people? Drained as I was, in pain and looking a mess, returning to the van via the rocks would have been risky, slow and arduous.

I scanned the area and checked that nothing had been left behind before pushing off into the choppy sea. Seconds later I was confronting myself again, catching a glimpse of my reflection in the water. My own horror movie. A man under pressure. And not all the make-up had come off, which made me look hideous.

The taste of the salty ocean on my lips summoned me to task. I started the engine as soon as I was far enough away from the shoreline. Ahead was a rough ride in diminishing light. If all went to plan, I would arrive at Malabar as darkness fell.

I could see a large vessel further out to sea. Apart from myself, there was one other small boat, and it was heading towards Botany Bay. The further north I went, the safer I felt. My description would have been distributed by now – that was a certainty. Hopefully authorities would be looking for a woman. Until the police dogs found my bag. *Good doggie, good doggie, find that person. Can doggie swim?*

All ahead the coast looked clear. The outboard motor was running at near full capacity and the craft did bounce at times, but I was going mostly with the breeze, and it handled the increasingly difficult conditions well.

Then, from above, that distinctive aerodynamic slap – the unmistakable sound of a rotor engine. The chopper was upon me in a flash. My stomach tightened in fear as I waited for the inevitable orders over the megaphone. I considered heading out to sea or making a run to the coast, where the chopper might struggle to find a place to land, but I was shaking with fear. A paralysis had overcome me. In the end I slowed the craft to a crawl.

The chopper hovered above for what seemed like an eternity and then dropped lower, churning up the already choppy water. Were they trying to capsize the craft? It became increasingly difficult to manage the boat.

I chanced a glance above. There were two people in the chopper. Neither was in uniform. The pilot seemed young and he was concentrating, his gaze fixed straight ahead. The co-pilot had me looking twice. Hunched in the passenger seat, talking profusely and seemingly giving the orders, was a larger man who I knew well. It was Phil, the American.

Of course, vision isn't perfect, and you often question your perceptions in retrospect. But in those few seconds the two Americans made sense to me. Phil and Wayne had endeared themselves to Matilda and her friends. They had infiltrated her organisation. Watching Phil take out Bozo should have been warning enough. And the fact that he had questioned me about

Turner's murder. Ostensibly friendly and talkative as he was, there had always been another agenda. At that moment I felt foolish for being so trusting.

My dread of what lay ahead was at its zenith. I put a hand into my pocket and held the vial of poison. Was it time?

Crazy thoughts they seemed just a few seconds later, as the chopper unexpectedly dipped to the left and accelerated off south towards Botany Bay. It was soon just a speck in the sky.

There were so many unanswered questions. Did Phil recognise me in my dishevelled state? Why had I been allowed to escape? And who did Wayne and Phil work for? Was one or both of the Americans happy to see my plan unfold? Perhaps having to admit to knowing me was an embarrassment. Maybe my discarded clothes – surely the dogs weren't that slow – hadn't been found, and they had been looking for a woman?

I continued northwards at a steady pace. The sea was becoming increasingly rough, forcing me to slow down. In the fading light, despite the fact that they'd found Chaffer's body, I still imagined the man crawling through the murky water, stroke after stroke, trying to match it with the boat.

As the sun sank lower the weather turned cold, and I began to shiver uncontrollably. The velocity of the wind increased and the fear of capsizing became a reality. Whether it was that or the smell of the sea that brought it on was uncertain, but Dunkley's frightening presence was inside my head again. Would I ever cleanse my soul of his stench? Would I ever see a day when I forgot what that bastard looked like, or was the filth ingrained for eternity?

Crawling along the coastline that afternoon, I imagined sharks and all sorts of mythical sea creatures. It was with relief that I finally made it to the entrance and turned into the long narrow bay. One moment I was being churned up in a washing machine – the next the swell eased and I found myself in calm water.

Lights were on in some of the houses facing the bay, but it wasn't yet completely dark. I slowed the craft down further, not wanting to arrive on the beach when I could be easily seen.

The area around the boat ramp was lit up and alive with people. It seemed as though there was a function on. What a ragged sight I'd look walking from Malabar Beach to the van, scratched and bruised, smeared with make-up. That it was busy around the boat ramp was a problem, but as I got closer I saw something that gave me reason for further concern – there was a police vehicle parked not far from where I'd left the van.

During my trial run I'd been able to get phone service from inside the bay, so I slowed the motor to almost a standstill. First I checked for news on Matherson – nothing.

I sent a text message to Lydia – *Please pick me up. Malabar Beach in twenty minutes. You are my only hope, Dom.*

Whether she would come or not was uncertain, but it was worth a try. I reduced speed to a standstill, waiting just in case Lydia did decide to come. When she hadn't responded to my text after five minutes, I decided to move. For all I knew she could be working in Melbourne. Or perhaps she had cut me off for good.

I had no idea whether Tran had deserted me, but I did know that if I was to survive long-term, his help would be crucial. I reminded myself that my old phone was turned off and in the van. That number had been our emergency contact. Still, there were other ways. But he wouldn't know my present number.

Then I was taken aback, given a real jolt. After ringing Tran's number so many times, I was so conditioned to not getting a response that my heart jumped on hearing his cool, welcoming voice. Too stunned to respond, when I did I sounded so joyful that he must have thought I was high on something.

After recovering from the initial shock I told him my accounts had been hijacked. His had as well. I joked that I'd thought he'd made off with the money we'd swindled from FGI. He laughed at the absurd idea, and I felt relief as well as guilt for having doubted him. Sitting on the water after what I'd just done, it felt strange to be talking so calmly to Tran. I told him nothing about my latest escapade or my present predicament. We made a time to meet the next day. *With a bit of luck,* I should have added.

Communication restored, I got another welcome surprise. I was successful in making contact with Case. I was slightly hysterical when I asked about poor Tracy, but Case had no idea what I was talking about – he thought I'd lost my marbles. News of Tracy's death had been a hoax. Case told me that Tracy had moved out of her flat and in with a girlfriend at Marrickville. She had a new job and only worked the odd shift at the Imperial. The place was on the nose. Case, Bubba and many other patrons had changed pubs after the Imperial's reputation had been tarnished with the leaking of material from its own security camera.

We agreed to have a drink together one day soon. I'd just said it to be friendly. Case had probably done the same.

Scanning the news services, I saw that the Matherson attack was the leading story. The Real Sparkel feed was being played and replayed by the major networks in Australia and the United States. It had gone viral on the internet, attracting millions.

The police said that they were looking for a Caucasian male around thirty in relation to the Matherson assassination attempt. The press who had been at the scene disagreed, claiming the assailant was female and at least forty. Some said it had to be an inside job. Others blamed the Russians, aliens and fake news.

The attack caused diplomatic tension between the United States and Australia. Knowing Matherson's track record, I felt sure he would see that as a business opportunity and start a war over the matter, selling weapons to both sides.

I learnt that certain politicians and businessmen had become worried as the Fuck It! List concept gained a cult following. Mr Twinkel, Benedict Sparkel and The Real Sparkel were deemed by the authorities to be a serious security threat and were put on the terrorist register. *Public enemies – find them now.* According to the mainstream press, they were a blight on our wonderful way of life. *Stop glorifying them,* said some commentators, but the public couldn't get enough of Sparkel and Twinkel. The press wouldn't leave the story alone.

A group of over-sixty-year-olds in Louisiana, USA had formed a splinter organisation, calling itself NFY (Not Finished Yet). Their motto was MAA (Motivated, Anonymous and Armed). They'd shot a local politician.

The Real Sparkel site had been dubbed 'The Bouncing Kangaroo' in the USA due to the authorities' inability to shut it down. The postings kept reappearing, adding to their notoriety.

My attempts to log on to the Mr Twinkel site were unsuccessful. Sparkel's image was frozen, a picture on a screen filled with a still shot of the universe.

At the bottom of the screen the caption read, *Twinkel little star, Twink... Twi... Mr Twinkel Now in Hibernation Mode.*

As Mr Twinkel slept, his notoriety exploded throughout the globe. The inability of government cyber security units to contain the Twinkel/Sparkel outbreak was an embarrassment for politicians and governments worldwide. One systems expert claimed that Mr Twinkel's tentacles were so ingrained in the World Wide Web that getting rid of him would be akin to filtering the sands of the Sahara Desert grain by grain.

I still had no idea who Mr Twinkel was, but one story caught my eye. It was by an investigative reporter for *The Guardian*. She claimed that Mr Twinkel was the brainchild of multi-millionaire Christian Zeus, who died five years before. He was wealthy and had business interests in Silicon Valley.

After he was diagnosed with a terminal illness, Zeus purportedly created Mr Twinkel for the purpose of growing his money and having influence long after his death. There was a rumour he'd had his body cryogenically frozen while still alive, with instructions that he be brought back to life when a cure was found for his particular cancer.

Approaching Malabar Beach, I could make out an amorphous shape in the dim light. It wasn't Lydia, but still I waved. The person didn't wave back. Perhaps it was an unfriendly local out for a walk.

Jumping into the shallow water, I detached the motor, putting it inside the craft with the oars and bag before dragging the lot up the beach. It wasn't as cold off the water. All looked quiet up ahead. The person I'd waved to was gone. Maybe I'd scared them away.

Looking up towards the car park, I was met with disappointment. Something inside me had expected to see Lydia or the lights of her car.

I left the craft near another boat, where it was concealed from above. The quickest way to get to my van would have been to use the steps, but it was impossible to see what was going on at the top – somebody could be on me quickly. If I walked to the north end of the beach and approached the street from the park, I'd have a clearer view of what lay ahead. All good in theory.

It was eerily quiet as I caught my breath and set off along the sand. I was thinking about the police vehicle I'd seen near the boat ramp when I was hit from behind.

The metal object nearly rendered me unconscious, and somebody began whacking me with a baton. That was followed by a volley of severe kicks that ripped into my body and were impossible to defend against. I was left shaken and disorientated, writhing in pain. I had no idea what had happened to my bag. It had been flung somewhere. Where was Cerberus?

Searching for courage and something solid, I eventually settled for the soft option, in one motion grabbing a handful of sand and flinging it into the eyes of the man standing over me. My attacker pulled back and strained to regain his vision. I recognised him as the taller of Bozo's two thugs who had visited me at the townhouse.

My attempt to defend myself only made Bozanski's mate more irate, and he laid into me with renewed vigour. When he was finished he dragged me to my feet, tied my hands together and strung me up to a council signpost.

Then Bozanski was in my face, waving a handgun. He jammed something into my mouth. Any attempt to call out would be muffled. Hands restricted, I couldn't even reach the poison vial in my bottom pocket. Torchlight stung my eyes.

'Finally, Fuck-knuckle.'

Whack! Thump! The pain and fright I felt was made worse by Bozo's triumphant smirk – he was enjoying himself.

'Think you can steal from me and set me up for Chaffer?'

More whacks, this time aimed at my groin. Spittle sprayed from Bozo's mouth as he exhaled. The pain was severe as I took a few more smacks to the head. My thought at that moment was that he would have been a dirty rugby player, putting in the boot whenever he could get away with it.

'This is what you're going to do,' he said. 'First you sign this document admitting to hacking my accounts. Next you tell me where you have the money stashed, account numbers, everything. Then a confession regarding Chaffer. Got it?'

Thump went the butt of the gun into my ribs to ram home the point. I nodded my agreeance.

'I'm going to take the gag off so we can talk. Yell and I'll shoot,' he said, ripping off the gag.

Yelping like a mistreated puppy, I pleaded, my voice barely audible, 'Give us a break, Bozo. I don't know what you're talking about.'

For a moment I thought he'd missed it. I'd finally found the courage to call him Bozo. But I paid for it. He was into me again and I thought I'd pass out.

Bozanski's mate stepped forward. 'Calm down, Adrian, you'll kill him before he talks.'

I knew that once I'd signed or admitted anything, I'd be finished. The best I could do was play along, try to stall.

'Okay, okay, I'll sign. But I can't do it while I'm tied to the post.'

It was nearing complete darkness. This spot was secluded and far away from the nearest houses. Even if there was somebody out walking, they were unlikely to see what was happening down on the beach.

Bozo's mate untied me and I slipped to the ground. He stood over me, amusing himself by swinging his baton, missing my head by inches and making me flinch as Bozanski prepared the paperwork. Frightened and in intense pain, I could barely move my body, let alone find a way to escape this dire situation.

When all seemed hopeless, a figure holding a torch appeared at the end of the beach and began walking towards us.

When Bozo's mate realised it was a woman, a leer materialised on his face. He nudged Bozo – *now for some real fun!* When I recognised the woman, my only thought was of my own stupidity in sending the text asking for help. At least Bozo and his clown had suspended trading.

'Let him go now,' Lydia demanded.

She spoke forcefully and without apparent fear, but she was no match for these two. They were merely amused by her demand. But I had to admire Lydia – she had guts and wasn't in the least deterred, despite Bozanski having a gun.

'I'm not stupid, Adrian. The police have been notified. They'll be here any moment.'

Bozanski laughed. He didn't believe her. 'Yeah, right, Lydia. That suits me fine. The cops will arrest this arse and lock him up for good. Either way, Bruno's finished.'

'Just leave, Lydia,' I called. 'Get out of here.'

Bozanski's mate gave me a kick to shut me up and turned to Bozanski. 'She's full of shit. I say we get what we need then feed both of them to the fishes.'

The brief wailing scream of a siren nearby had Bozo and his mate looking at each other and wondering. The reflection of flashing lights from above was followed by the sound of two doors being slammed shut. The vehicle must have pulled over near the top of the stairs. Only seconds later, the sporadic flickering of torchlight indicated that people were coming down the steps.

Bozo turned off his torch and tossed the gun into the nearby bush. His mate dilly-dallied for a few seconds before he followed suit, tossing the bloodied baton in the bush just as the glow of torchlight illuminated the four of us.

Two police officers approached with their weapons drawn. I lay there on the sand, bloodied and in pain.

Lydia came to my side to see how badly I'd been hurt while Bozanski stepped towards the police officers and began explaining his side of the story. The female officer ordered Bozo to get back and stand with his mate, making it clear they would be the ones asking the questions. She looked over at me and called for an ambulance and backup.

While the male officer watched over us, the policewoman pointed her torch to where Bozo and his mate had tossed their weapons. From the look of dread that suddenly appeared on Bozanski's mate's face, he must have thought he'd gotten away with it.

The policewoman put on a pair of gloves. She was away for less than a minute before returning with the gun and the baton in separate plastic bags.

We're all in big trouble, I thought. *Should I take the poison vial?* My hands were free. The irony of the situation had me almost laughing. I was on my own Fuck It! List.

The male officer made it clear to Bozanski that he and his mate were under arrest and would be going with them to the police station for questioning. Neither Bozo nor his mate took it well.

Bozo pointed at me. 'He's the one you want. That's Dom Bruno, the one who killed Chaffer.'

The female officer seemed to take an interest in what he was saying.

Bozanski sounded convincing, and my grip on the poison vial tightened. All of this talk about Chaffer did have a plus side. It meant that neither the police nor Bozanski knew of my involvement in the Matherson attack.

The male officer soon began to tire of Bozanski's diatribe. 'We'll deal with that later,' he said, his manner peremptory, making it clear they wouldn't be deterred from the task at hand.

Bozanski claimed to know their superior at Maroubra Police Station. He probably did. When this tactic didn't work, he became aggressive again.

Lydia shook her head in sympathy with the police. 'What you police have to put up with!' she said.

I was not out of the woods, not by a long shot. The male officer was stern. He pointed at me.

'Don't go far. We'll deal with you in a minute.'

It was the harshness of his tone that had me worried. And the implication of the phrase *deal with*.

Bozo continued to rant. It was getting repetitive by that stage; he was still blaming Dom Bruno, while his mate insisted he had only just arrived before the police. A ridiculous claim.

From what I overheard of the conversation between the police officers, it seemed they'd found the chief suspect with regard to the Man Overboard Incident. The male officer tried to cuff Bozanski and he upped the ante, spitting and kicking. It took both officers to corral the frisky colt.

The paramedics appeared on the beach. Could they be my saviours? My mind went into overdrive as I tried to conjure up an escape plan.

On the way to the police vehicle, Bozanski and his mate's misbehaviour continued. Bozo was someone who enjoyed the spotlight. By that stage he had perpetrated a litany of crimes. As well as the Chaffer business, he had resisted arrest and committed assault, and was in possession of an unlicensed handgun. The cops had their hands tied for the moment, but Bozo would soon be in the wagon. It wouldn't be long until backup arrived.

The paramedics – another male-female team – came over to where I lay. They checked for breaks and cleared most of the blood from my body and face. What an odd sight I must have been: sweat, blood and salt, plus the remnants of the cosmetics. If I was to find a way out, it had to be soon. I began to formulate a plan.

It caught both of the paramedics by surprise when I raised my hands and quietly refused further treatment. As I gingerly dragged myself to my feet, the medics were not impressed. They shook their heads with annoyance and disbelief. *Is this guy for real? Fucking timewaster,* their demeanour implied.

Lydia had already begun the trek back up to the car park. Turning on my torch, I gained my bearings and went across to my bag. I couldn't find Cerberus. After checking the bush nearby, there was still no sign of him. I wondered how he'd fare in that environment. There was plenty of bush stretching from here to the rifle range, and all the way to Maroubra Beach for that matter – but there were also houses across the road from the park, which meant dogs.

The ambulance officers packed up their gear and began walking back to their vehicle. I was being tugged from both directions. I combed the surrounds again, desperately searching every crevice for Cerberus as the clock ticked away and my chances of escape diminished.

Nearby was a signpost. I could just make out the outline of an animal. My hopes began to fade – I thought the sign indicated that this was a park where dogs were allowed to run off the lead. Cerberus would be doomed.

But when I went up closer to inspect the signpost, my fears subsided. The picture indicated that the area was a wildlife reserve. Cerberus was in with a chance.

Hearing a distant whirling, I looked out to the headland and saw a chopper ducking low as it searched the southern coastline. If I stayed around any longer I'd be finished.

Bozanski and his mate were in the wagon. The police were still getting details from the two. Some people had come out of their houses to see what the commotion was about. Lydia was up ahead near her car, talking on the phone. I had no doubt that she'd wait and talk to the police. She'd been the one to call them.

The helicopter was fast approaching. With a strange mixture of fear and exhilaration, I limped away, making my way to where the paramedics were at the back of the ambulance, packing their gear away.

I approached the two, thanking them for coming to my aid and apologising for my behaviour, all the time watching the police and waiting. The moment both the cops had their backs turned, I took off.

I stuck close to the hedge lining the pathway, using it as cover, edging myself along like a maimed rat on the run. A group was having a barbeque on the boat ramp. I saw no sign of the police vehicle I'd observed from the boat earlier, but there was a worrying moment when the police backup vehicle passed.

Exposed to the inquisitive eyes of the locals, when I could not be seen from the park, I crossed the road. As I got closer to where my van was parked, I realised that the point of interest was the police presence, not the drab-looking, lopsided loser struggling along the footpath.

With the helicopter's powerful light doing a sweep of the beach, I approached my van.

A young couple asked me what the hullabaloo was about.

'The police have just arrested some maniac down on the beach.'

A short time later, I was one of many motorists driving along Anzac Parade towards the city that Sunday night.

THE END

Thank you for reading Benedict Sparkel and the Bucket List. What started out as a short story turned into a novel, as the plot continued to develop. I had imagined the protagonist as a person who would react to adversity in a manner entirely different to myself. When a friend, after reading the manuscript, jokingly asked if it was an autobiography, I realised that perhaps there was more of myself in Dom Bruno's character than I was willing to admit.

Thank you Janet, for reading the initial drafts, providing invaluable feedback and giving me the confidence to write. Thank you Vicki, for providing much needed advice and encouraging me to publish. Thank you Gaye, Steve, Colin, Pete and Ginny, for your astute insights.

I hope you enjoyed the story. If so, please stay in touch for the release of my second novel, Hunting the Wolf, a mystery set in Newcastle and Sydney's Eastern Suburbs, which is due to be released in 2021.

If you have the time, please review the book on Amazon. You can contact Denis at dbrightbooks or denisbbright@gmail.com

Extract from Hunting the Wolf

The neighborhood is empty and in the dim grey light the occasional street lamp barely reveals the creature

It is running along the street, staying close to the gutter, the stride is even paced, constant

The wolf's disposition is unnerving

There is no vicious snarl, no growl, the face is straight-faced, expressionless

In the solitude and darkness the boy awakes, immersed in soul sinking dread

He knows it is coming

The wolf will not be deterred

One night it will arrive

www.ingramcontent.com/pod-product-compliance
Lightning Source LLC
Chambersburg PA
CBHW020359260626
47156CB00007B/2183